Wading through opaque water that came at least knee-deep on the kzinti and considerably higher on the humans was not an appealing prospect. There was, however, a vertical ladder that led upwards.

In an emergency a kzin could have scrabbled up it in a single leap. That was not necessary now. They went cautiously. As Vaemar did so, a smell hit him that knocked away all the conflicting smells of wetness, mold, humans and plant and animal life. It was a smell of pure death. The humans had never heard Vaemar's battle-snarl before. He went up the last rungs in one bound, Swirl-Stripes and the humans crowding behind.

They swung the beams of their lights round the chamber. The humans cried out. Vaemar and Swirl-Stripes roared.

Hanging upside down from the deckhead were the flayed corpses of several kzinti. Though the skin and several of the limbs were missing and the bodies otherwise damaged, it was plain from the sizes that they were both males and females.

Guns ready, instinctively moving again into a circle with their eyes and weapons face outwards, they approached the bodies.

They had been dead for days, but not many days. Whoever or whatever had hung up those kzin bodies, it was plainly the work of intelligence, not any predatory swamp creature. . . .

—from "Grossgeister Swamp"

THE MAN-KZIN WARS SERIES
CREATED BY
LARRY NIVEN

Also by Larry Niven from Baen Books
Fallen Angels
(with Jerry Pournelle & Michael Flynn)

MAN-KZIN WARS XI

HAL COLEBATCH
MATTHEW JOSEPH HARRINGTON
LARRY NIVEN

CREATED BY
LARRY NIVEN

BAEN

MAN-KZIN WAR XI

This is a work of fiction. All the characters and events portrayed in this book are fictional, and any resemblance to real people or incidents is purely coincidental.

Copyright © 2005 by Larry Niven.

"Three at Table," "Grossgeister Swamp," and "Catspaws" copyright © 2005 by Hal Colebatch. "Teacher's Pet" and "War and Peace" copyright © 2005 by Matthew Joseph Harrington. "The Hunting Park" copyright © 2005 by Larry Niven.

A Baen Book

Baen Publishing Enterprises
P.O. Box 1403
Riverdale, NY 10471
www.baen.com

ISBN 10: 1-4165-2148-8
ISBN 13: 978-1-4165-2148-8

Cover art by Stephen Hickman

First Baen paperback printing, September 2007

Distributed by Simon & Schuster
1230 Avenue of the Americas
New York, NY 10020

Library of Congress Cataloging-in-Publication Data: 2005019121

Printed in the United States of America

10 9 8 7 6 5 4 3 2 1

Contents

Three At Table

❖

Hal Colebatch

To the memory of W. W. Jacobs

Arthur Guthlac, Wunderland, 2427 A.D.

I've been stupid, I thought. Being stupid on a strange planet is very often an effective way to be dead. Even a planet as friendly to Man as Wunderland.

Stupid to go through fifty-three years of desperate war to die on Wunderland seven years after Liberation in a bad storm, on a leave I've spent a long time looking forward to.

But maybe I won't die, I told myself then as the mud fell and slid about me. *Maybe I'll look back on all this one day and laugh. I've been in far worse places and survived. Keep climbing, disregard my ankle and get above the flood-mark. Then climb higher.* I didn't know then what I was climbing into.

I had set out from Gerning in an air-car for a day's lone hunting in the wilder country to the east. I hadn't brought much in the way of food or clothes or even weapons. What's the point of a hunt with modern gear that gives the game animals no chance? You might as well zap them by laser with the aid of a satellite camera. I had an antique

.22 rifle and a box of bullets and a handy little device copied from the kzin trophy-drier for anything I wanted to freeze-dry and bring home.

There was a good autodoc in the air-car, of course, and a modern communication system. My headquarters could get in touch with me, and I with them, at any time. I hoped they wouldn't.

A long, long time ago, I had been a museum guard on Earth. I had worn a quaint uniform and collected banned scraps of militaria and had also dreamed of exploring distant worlds—had hoped more realistically that with some saving and luck I might one day get a budget package holiday to the Moon to remember for the rest of my life like some of my lucky fellows on the museum general staff. There had been notions of glory and heroism, too remote, too impossible even to be called dreams, barely possible to hint at even to my sister, the one human with whom I had in those days confided. Now, if I wore uniform, it was different and had a star on the collar. But, more importantly for me at that moment, I had humanity's first interstellar colony to make free with as a conqueror— well, as a Liberator, certainly—and I didn't want to waste the experience.

A pity nobody at Gerning had told me about the weather. Apparently—that is the most charitable explanation— it had never occurred to them that even a holidaying flat-lander would be so ignorant or stupid as not to know what those black-and-silver clouds building up in the west meant. The ramscoop raid from Sol by the UNSN seven or eight years ago, shortly before the Liberation, had, it was said, as well as causing terrible damage, upset the patterns of the weather. Storms in the storm-belt came earlier and stronger. Something to do with the cooling and droplet-suspension effects of dust in the air. It was expected that things would return to normal eventually. As I had been preparing to depart my hosts had been more interested in laughing at a funny little thing called a Protean that had turned up in the meeting-hall, a quaint and harmless Wunderland animal which had evolved limited powers of psi projection and mimicry. That there were less harmless ones with psi powers I was to find out shortly.

Anyway, the clouds built slowly, and, like a cunning enemy, they gathered out of the west, behind me. I took off near noon and three-quarters of the sky was clear. I flew low, not at even near full speed, over the farmlands and woods, fascinated as always by what I saw below. Much of the time I left the car on auto-pilot, and enjoyed being a rubber-necking tourist. With the kzin-derived gravity-motor, so much more efficient than our old ground-effect lifts, I could vary the speed and height with the touch of a finger on the controls. The car gave me a meal, and the day turned into afternoon.

I passed over human farms and little scattered villages and hamlets. The simple dwellings of people living simple lives, far away from much government and from much of the twenty-fifth century. I knew many of these people had originally settled here with the simple life in mind, but then the war and kzin occupation had knocked their technology way back into the past anyway. Some of these settlements were again prosperous, pleasant-looking places from the air, but there were some desolate ruins, relics of the war and the occupation that had halved the human population of this planet. I passed over the scattered wreckage of destroyed war-machines and the kzin base, and the great tracts that the kzinti had had go back to wilderness as hunting preserves. Humans had often enough been the victims set running hopelessly in those hunts . . . Many more had died under the kzinti in other ways.

But ghastliness was relative. The Gerning district had largely survived. After the first hideous butcheries the local humans had learnt kzin ways, and their survival-rate had increased. They humbly avoided contact with their overlords, abased themselves when they encountered them, and sweated on diminishing land with deteriorating equipment to raise the various taxes that were the price of life. The local kzinti, many attached to the big military base, had, apparently, not been quite like the creatures of the dreadful Lord Ktrodni-Stkaa, and the local Herrenmann had been able to intercede with their commanding officer occasionally. I had gathered that there were a few kzinti still living in remote bits of the black-blocks around the area now, as well as solitude-seeking, eccentric or misfit humans. Wunderland was sparsely enough populated that anyone who wished to be left alone could be.

There were herds of cows and sheep passing below. On Earth I'd never seen them free-ranging like this. Wunderland creatures, too. There were a herd of gagrumphers, the big, six-legged things that occupied an ecological niche similar to that of bison or elephants on Earth, moving in and out of the marvellous multicolored foliage, red and orange and green. Then the human settlements thinned out, and I was passing over forest again, and uneven ground with a pattern of gullies and water-courses below me, small rivers low at the end of summer like silver ribbons. The roads were few and narrow.

This was what I had once dreamed of: the landscape below me could never be taken for Earth. Every color and contour was different, some things slightly and subtly off, some grossly strange. And ahead of me as I flew, on the eastern horizon, were the tall spires and pinnacles of great mountains, low-gravity-planet mountains sharper and higher than anything Earth had to show, pale and almost surreal against the blue and pink tints of the eastern sky.

I should have noticed how quickly it was getting dark. But there, below me, was something else: a tigripard, the biggest felinoid—the biggest *native* felinoid—predator in this part of Wunderland. Their numbers had built up during the kzin occupation, partly because of the general chaos and desolation, and also because the kzinti found their fellow-felinoids rather good sport in the hunt and encouraged them, and they remained a nuisance for these backwoods farmers with their still relatively primitive appliances and equipment. What modern machinery the kzinti had not smashed or confiscated during the war had largely become inoperative through lack of maintenance and the farmers were in many cases beginning again from Square One. I saw some ancient farming robots sprawled broken like the corpses of living things or, on one long-abandoned farmstead, jerking and grubbing uselessly through degraded programmes that no longer made sense. The further one got from Gerning the fewer the little farms and cottages were and the more backward they looked. Nothing like Earth farms.

The tigripard was a big one, worth a hunter's attention. But there was no sport or achievement in shooting it from above. I followed it for a time, not approaching close enough to alarm it. That was difficult. I guessed that in the last few decades all Wunderland creatures had become only too alert to terror and destruction from the air. The tigripard was running down a long slope to lower-lying, river-dissected, territory. A moving map on the instrument-panel gave me a general picture. I saw it leap a river—a big leap, but the river was low. The human settlements were much sparser in this area but there were still a few and there was still quite good grazing for animals. The locals should thank me for ridding them of a dangerous piece of vermin, I thought. There was very little legal hunting on Earth—even a UNSN general would find it hard to get a permit there—and I was a completely inexperienced hunter. At least of things like this.

We were approaching a more deeply gullied, poorly vegetated area like a small badlands. The tigripard turned into a gully and tracking it became more difficult. After a time I landed and, hefting my little rifle, followed on foot.

That was the first first stupid thing: I was so used to military sidearms that could bring down a kzin or a building, that sought their own targets, and could be used like hoses against kzin infantry if necessary, that I took it for granted the .22 was all I needed. Another stupid thing: I was so used to thinking of my alien enemies as eight-to-ten-feet-tall bipedal felines or blips on a radar screen that I found it hard to think of a feline the size of a tigripard—even a big tigripard—as dangerous to me personally. It was quite a long descent to the watercourse at the bottom. There was a small game-track at first but that petered out. The gully's walls gradually rose above me, reducing my view of the sky.

I scrambled down to the bed of the watercourse, jumping easily further and further down in the low gravity, looking for tracks in the damp sand and mud beside the stream. There were none. I pressed on, into the next gully, almost like a small canyon. It wound and twisted and still the mud yielded nothing. I was practicing my tracking skills when two things happened: the tigripard leapt up onto a rock in front of me, snarling, and the sky turned black.

I've had plenty of infantry training, even if quite a while ago. I brought the gun up fast and fired. In that space its report was ridiculously small, swallowed up by the air around. The tigripard was faster. If it had gone for me I should probably have died under its claws then and there. But evidently it was experienced enough to be wary of Man, or at least of Man plus weapons. It leapt sideways and disappeared behind the gully slope. Whether I hit it or not I had no idea. And at that second I had other things on my mind.

I had never seen a daytime sky turn midnight black before, and the light die in an instant. Who has? Wunderlanders who live in the storm-belt have, I discovered.

Then the rain and lightning came, the rain in solid sheets, the lightning hardly less unbroken. Thunder filled and shook the sky. I had seen the sky of Wunderland purple in the light of Alpha Centauri B, one of the great sights of Human Space. This flaring, vivid purple light was a different thing. In an instant I was soaked with freezing rain, my head was ringing and I was almost blinded. That's when I heard the tigripad again.

The tigripard knew Wunderland better than I. But it made the mistake of snarling its challenge before it leapt. I dropped flat as I fired again and its leap carried it over me. It was a very near thing, though: a hind-claw shredded the light shirt I was wearing. Below me the ground gave way, and I rolled down a steep incline. I fetched up bruised and dazed at the bottom. Had it not been for Wunderland's light gravity I would have been a lot worse off. And the tigripard and the fall had saved my life. As I got groggily to my feet again a bolt of lightning struck the place I been standing a few moments before. I saw rocks and earth hurled into the air, and then for a while I might have been blinded.

I could only hope the tigripard was at least temporarily blinded too, but I heard it snarling somewhere not far away. The skyline had become near and narrow and lightning was trickling all around it. There were the lashing hailstones, too. Any bigger and they would do real damage. Flicking my rifle back and forth, trying to cover all directions at once, I ran, still part blind, running straight into cliff faces, stumbling and falling to a ground that the cloudburst had already churned to mud, boiling up like soup. Live soup, too. I saw creatures like the frog-golinas and kermitoids, I supposed long encased in it, springing to life and away. Three times I thought I saw movement that might have been the tigripard and fired at it. The fourth time I heard a snarling, very close, and knew there could be no mistake. But my rifle was so slick with water and mud, and my hands so cold in the sudden rain and hail, that the selector must have moved to automatic setting. I fired off all the rest of the magazine in an instant.

I groped for the box of cartridges. Had I brought it with me or left it in the car? I couldn't remember, but a frantic search showed I didn't have it now. If it had been in my pocket I had lost it in the fall.

I've studied many disasters. I know the worst of them usually don't have a single cause. They are an accumulation of small things, too small to guard against: a weather or meteor report misfiled by a tired duty officer, an alarm system not checked one day as it has been every day for years, a faucet blocked by paint, a decimal point shifted one place in a computer's instructions, a fleck of dust working its way into an old keyboard . . . I had got where I was in those gullies by an accumulation of small things, and, I realized quite suddenly, my life was in danger.

So far I had been excited, keyed-up, furious. Suddenly I felt cold and frightened: not the fear of battle, but another kind of dread. Not only from the tigripard, which seemed to have gone, perhaps hit, though I doubted that, perhaps to stalk me from cover, but from this rain. Great chunks of earth turned suddenly to mud were falling from the gully banks and I realized I could end up underneath one. But there was a more inevitable peril. One thing I know something about is the theory of terrain, and recalling what I had seen from the air, I knew these canyons must flash-flood in rain like this. I realized that I had seen high-water-marks in them, all well above where I was now. In fact, I thought, that was probably why the tigripard was gone. It was climbing, and if I was to remain alive I had better do the same fast.

I slung the rifle over my shoulder and started up the slope. It was hard to make much out in the ceaselessly-rolling thunder and the constant beating of the hailstones but I thought I could feel the ground as well as the air shaking. I was so covered in the mud I squirmed through, and in ice from the hailstones, that perhaps even the superb sensory equipment of the tigripard was confused and could not find me.

There was another thing I remembered: tigripards, though among the most obvious, were by no means the only Wunderland animals I had to fear. Among other things, very relevant at this moment, there was the mud-sucker, a thing vaguely like a giant leech, which, I had been told on the orientation course I was now remembering, could lie dormant in mud, like this, for a long time and then come to life in rain, like this rain. Apparently its prey included large animals, perhaps up to human size. "No one knows how big they can grow," the instructor had said. "But don't be the one to find out." Rykermann had also told me that, like much other Wunderland fauna, little was known about them. They gave cryptic hints of some kind of dim psi ability, and he too was definite that it was best to keep out of their way.

Another nasty thought: some of the wrecked war-craft which I had flown over on my way here had had nuclear engines. Could spilled radioactives have worked their way into this mud over the last seven years? Of course the car had instruments that could have told me at once.

Then the real floods came. Out of the west, and concentrating my mind. The rain must have been falling there and filling these water-courses long before the storm

reached me. A real roaring and shaking of the ground and
white-foam-fronted black water below me advancing like
a wall. Hydraulic damming—I remembered the phrase
from somewhere as I scrabbled upwards for my life in the
slipping mud. I slipped and rolled again, ending up caught
in a clump of sharp black rocks just above the rising water.
I had damaged my leg some months before in the caves,
but it had been healed. Now I felt it was gone again, in
a different place, near the ankle. Maybe (I prayed) not
broken this time. One small mercy: crawling, almost
swimming vertically, up the mud-slope in the hail, an
ankle was perhaps less crucial than when walking or
running. Another mercy was the low gravity. But progressing
up was very different from my carefree jumping downwards. Anyway, I got to a ridge. I tried to stand then, and
found I couldn't. The .22 made a sort of crutch, not very
handy for it was the wrong length and either barrel or
stock sank into the mud when I leaned on it. I more-or-
less hopped a few yards.

I had to get back to the car. And then I realized I had
not the faintest idea in which direction the car was.

I sat down in the mud and hail then, cursing feebly that
I hadn't had the sense even to slip a modern cover-all into
one of my pockets. It would have weighed next to nothing,
taken up no space and would, if I had needed it, kept me
as dry and warm as toast. It would even have been strong
enough to protect me in a fight. I had put on locally made
clothes for the sake of fresh air and ventilation on a warm
morning, as well as because it was one of the things
tourists do.

There were a lot of other things, which, if not misled by

the benign appearance of the morning and my own excitement and inexperience of this world, I might also have brought: a gyro-compass, a locator, a beacon, even an ordinary mobile telephone, not to mention real weapons. I had plenty of navigation instruments and communications equipment, as I had a good autodoc and almost everything else I might need, but they were all in the car. I had an implant by which I could be traced if necessary, but there was no reason for anyone to think I was in great distress. If anyone was interested and they assumed I had enough sense to remain with the car and its equipment, then even a storm like this should have been no problem: a matter of touching a button and closing the canopy.

It took me a long time to make progress, and it horrified me how quickly what little daylight there was failed.

And the river was still rising. Chunks of mud were sliding and dropping into it from the sides of my ridge. And the ridge itself was shrinking. Soon it would be an island, and soon after that it would be covered completely. I would have to climb again. It was then that I fully realized how much my life was in real danger.

I was alone, lost, injured. And this was not my world. I knew something of its weather and its wild-life in theory, but I knew that in some ways, simply not having grown up here made me blind and vulnerable to dangers that others instinctively avoided, blind as a village yokel of the fifteenth century on Earth suddenly time-transported into a modern city or a modern transport complex. Where was the tigripard? I hardly dared move now, lest it sense from the pattern of my foot-falls that I was injured and come circling back. Indeed I feared I was already projecting psi waves to tell it I had changed from hunter to prey. But move I must. Before I had made much more progress it was full night, or at least the storm's equivalent of it. I had not appreciated what night was like in the unpeopled country where there was no artificial source of lighting. The clouds obscured everything in the Wunderland sky above, though far away in the West was a dim glow that might have been the lights of Gerning reflected against them. Far to the East it was lighter for a while, but then the clouds covered that as well. The almost incessant lightning was a danger, but soon it seemed to be my major source of light. It was not full night yet, and when I climbed higher I saw a distant ribbon of paler sky far to the east still, but full night was coming.

I climbed again. Glancing back once I saw the black rushing water tear away the last of the ridge where I had rested. The hailstones tore at its surface and lumped together into chunks of ice.

I knew that I was on what was technically a big island between two rivers, low and narrow when I had seen them from the air, now both grossly swollen and rising all the time. I recalled seeing houses not far away. I toiled further up the next sliding muddy slope, again using my weapon as a sort of crutch. It took me a long time, and my skin crawled as I waited for the impact of the tigripard on my back, and thought of the irony of dying under the claws of a feline after all. Then at some point the sliding mud became more stable and solid. My ankle was badly swollen but massaging it seemed to help, and out of the mud I could walk, slowly and cautiously. The rifle was some more use as a prop here, but I wished it had been a couple of feet longer. Again I was thankful for Wunderland's light gravity.

Below me, something writhed through the mud up the track I had left. For a moment I thought it was the tigripard. But as it came closer I saw it was a shapeless thing with a trumpet-like suctorial disk, the orifice ringed with small fangs and tentacles—a mud-sucker, a big one. I was feeling too battered and numbed to react for a few seconds, then fear and revulsion set me moving a good deal faster than I would have thought possible. It didn't like the firmer ground though, and after waving its trumpet in my direction for a time turned back, vacuuming up some of the newly active froggolinas as it went. I hoped it would find the tigripard—or did I? The tigripard was a brother compared to this thing, and deserved a cleaner fate.

You can imagine my delight when, as I gained some even higher ground, a burst of lightning showed me a road at my feet. More importantly, after I had followed this for a while, another burst showed the unmistakable straight lines of man-made walls and structures some way off. Another two or three flashes and I made out that there was a small village, a hamlet, I suppose it should be called. A single street and a few one-story houses. Shelter, warmth, food, help, safety. I hobbled on as fast as I could.

Realization didn't all come at once. First I noticed there were no lights burning. Then in the lightning flashes I saw roofless skies through gaping holes where windows had been. The hamlet was a deserted ruin.

If I was bitterly disappointed, I saw that it was still shelter of a sort. I know now why you should keep out of deserted ruins in this part of Wunderland if you're alone and can't see well, and if you're effectively unarmed. At that time what I wanted was to get out of the cold driving rain and hailstones at least. And I wanted a door to keep the tigripard out should it return, or even the sucker-thing whose hunting-patterns I knew nothing of. I found one building, the only two-story one, that not only had a door but also still had a bit of roof on it, and hunkered down in the driest corner I could find. I took off my clothes and shook as much water from them as I could, badly missing modern tough and water-repellant fabrics, dressed again, though the warmth they gave was largely imaginary, then curled myself into a ball in an effort to keep as much of that warmth as possible, and waited for the night and storm to pass. If the flash floods came quickly they should fall equally quickly. I was still worried that the tigripard was tracking me, but could see no sign of it.

In fact I fell asleep almost at once, without meaning to, but when I awoke nothing had changed. Certainly it was now full dark night even without the piled-up storm-clouds. But getting to sleep a second time was impossible.

One good thing had happened—like all UNSN troops I have had my night-vision enhanced by nanosurgery and now my eyes had grown accustomed to the dark. It wasn't perfect but I made the most of what light there was and in all but the darkest patches of night I was no longer completely blind and helpless.

I've had my skin toughened a bit too, but despite that it was still very cold and miserably uncomfortable. The sites of the injuries I had had in the battle with the mad ones in the caves a few months before were aching in concert with the pain in my ankle despite all the miracles of modern medicine, and something, I didn't then know what, was making me both more anxious and unhappy than I should have been.

I got up and set out to explore a little. Black as the night was, the almost continual lightning showed me the empty rooms, long ago stripped of furnishings, miniature water-falls from the gaps in the remnants of roof and ceiling, and a broken staircase leading down into a cellar or shelter which I had no inclination to enter. I could hear water down there splashing into mud, and I had no desire to get involved with more mud or what might live there. In other rooms some small creatures that I could not make out clearly scuttled away as I entered. I remembered the poison-fanged Beam's Beasts and gave them as wide a berth as they gave me. As I expected, I found nothing useful. The house had been thoroughly stripped long before.

Was that a light I could see out the window? The hail slackened for a while. With that bit of clearing I could see further, and suddenly my spirits rose again. For there was, I saw between the lightning flashes, indeed a dim orange square of light some way off.

The tigripard must be far away. Surely if it was nearby I would know by now. Perhaps it recognized the .22 as a weapon. Perhaps like so many larger wild creatures it avoided even the ruins of Man. I didn't know then that it had another good reason for keeping away from the house.

I wrenched down a splintered door lintel. A piece of it made a better crutch than my empty gun. Leaning heavily on it, I set off up what had been that hamlet's only street. A black silhouette grew around that orange square as I drew nearer: a bigger house standing by itself on a rise of ground. The light was an upper window.

There was a path leading to the door, but as I approached it more closely I realized things: the house was too big, the upper windows too high and small, while the ground-floor windows, where they occurred at all, were mere slits, and dark. The door was too high and wide. And, as I said, the light in that window was orange. There were other things about the architecture. This was not a human house but a kzin one. I looked back and saw how on its rise of ground it dominated the hamlet and gave a view of all the surrounding lands. This had been the mansion of the local kzin overseer of human slaves.

Plainly it had been slighted during the Liberation. I could make out, now that I looked, where the high walls and towers that must have surrounded it in the old kzin architectural style would have stood. Their rubble filled what must once have been a moat or ditch. I saw stumps of concrete and metal where defense and security installations must have been torn down. Behind the house were some large storage tanks, though I could not see whether or not they were intact. On the roof silhouetted against the sky in the lightning there was no sign of the dishes or antennas of modern communications equipment.

But that light burning now was ruddy orange. Not white or yellow. Only kzinti liked that orange light. Were there kzinti here still? It was quite possible. I knew that some of them still lived in the depopulated districts, shunning humans for obvious reasons, and this place, purpose-built and to their size, still relatively defensible, would be far more suitable for them than any others around. As I stood looking up at it I saw the silhouette of someone or something cross the lighted window.

Well, I would ask no shelter or favors from kzinti. Both pride and prudence said that. I was a soldier and I could stand an uncomfortable night in the ruins if necessary.

Trying to distance myself from the pain in my ankle, I hobbled back through the mud to the ghost-hamlet. For no particular reason I knew, save that it seemed the best-roofed and I had left the .22 there, I returned to the first house I had entered and curled up in my former place.

Then the zeitungers came.

I didn't know then that's what it was. I had heard of the zeitungers, originally called the zeitung-schreibers, of course, but I had never encountered them. And what I had heard of them had given me no true idea of them or of what encountering a pack of them when alone at night and physically spent was like.

Humans and kzinti alike on Wunderland loathed them and would stop at nothing to exterminate them. Like the Advokats and the Beam's Beasts, however, they liked the ample food which they associated with human activity. No one had told me they were often to be found in the ruins of human buildings here, presumably because nobody thought I would be spending a night in such ruins. They were carrion-eating vermin like the disgusting Advokats but with, in addition, an ability to project psychic damage and distress which they used as a weapon, an especially potent one when they were packing. They didn't limit themselves to carrion. The zeitungers' mental emanations could make a small-brained animal—an Earth rabbit or dog, say—lie down and scream, waiting for them to mob it and tear it to pieces alive.

On a big-brained animal and especially on a sophont the effect was more complex. Cognitive dissonance, a combination of pathological anxiety, hallucination, hypertension and, above and beneath and overarching all, black, disabling, even killing, clinical depression—if "depression" is an adequate word. Wunderland creatures had evolved a certain resistance to the zeitunger power. Earth animals, and humans, had not. The creatures could apparently do nothing else mentally. They might be able to communicate among themselves—every member of a shoal of fish or flock of birds on Earth can turn in the same direction in an instant—but they were not telepaths. The only power their dim minds had was destruction.

All the meanings of darkness. There are two kinds of memories which, if you let your mind dwell on them too intensely in the wrong circumstances, can destroy your reason and you. We all have a store of them and they are in a sense opposites. Normally we can erect a kind of cordon sanitaire around them most of the time: one kind is of horror, trauma, tragedy present again and unbearable; the other is of joy, happiness, innocence, destroyed, violated and lost forever. They can combine. The zeitungers give you both, with a quantum jump in emotional intensity and immediacy. That happened.

It began like a dream. Word-salads. A brain beginning to race, like a vehicle going out of control. And a high, thin monotonous threnody wailing in my brain to the strings of a harp:

* * *

Till a man shall read what is written,
So plain in clouds and clods;
Till a man shall hunger without hope
Even for evil gods . . .

Then very early memories of gardens—lost gardens. Myself a baby with toys in a nursery, laughing on my mother's knee—never had memory been so sharp and clear. Then reliving the death of my parents, that blow that came too soon and that I now knew had maimed me. Then like a bad, silly dream, I was reliving with a feeling of black regret my last day at school, the school I had hated, the realization that—all my own fault—I was leaving unqualified for anything but a life in a menial, dead-end job if I was very lucky, a lifetime on the dole more likely: there were far more people than jobs in the peaceful, prosperous, Golden-Age world I grew up in, long before ARM took notice of certain desperate messages coming in from lonely ships in space. I relived walking up the stairs to the assembly-hall and the class-rooms one last time that day, rooms and halls and passageways almost empty as the last of the others were leaving, wishing I'd worked harder, and thinking "It's too late now." As I say, silly memories to cast one into a black depression. But the zeitungers were just getting down to business. All the bad memories of adolescence and my young manhood . . . it went on.

Then it became waves of futile anger at everything: at myself, at the storm and at the people at Gerning who had not warned me of it. Then memories of every sad thing that had ever happened to me: my futile, dead-end, prewar job at the museum, my timidity and failures with women—all *those* latter came back in detail, from teenage onwards, until the time I finally retreated into an emotional shell with my sister Selina and some dreams as my only friends—my farewell to Selina before she went into space and the kzinti took her, my pathetic, childishly caressed, dreams of glory and success, the terror when my forbidden military studies were discovered by the museum authorities. More recently the loss of Jocelyn van der Straat. My one sibling dead, like my parents but infinitely more horribly, my one brief lover lost, disappeared.

As far as I felt anything beyond pain and pity for myself, and that falling, falling, it was a kind of huge, sick disgust for the human race, its murderousness, its greed, ingratitude, disloyalty and viciousness. Its self-importance and delusions of spirituality. The kzinti gave us the true measure of the universe: pure carnivores, with no concept of altruism or mercy. How could any of us, even me in moments of weakness, have thought differently? I found my mind running back to images of what must have happened to Selina when they got the *Happy Gatherer*. I thought of what had happened here on Wunderland when the kzinti invaded, and for a time my mind filled with lines from the "Dirge of Neue Dresden":

> *Oxygen supports combustion.*
> *Big fires need draughts to last.*
> *Hot air rises. Heated enough*
> *It rises very fast.*

🐾   🐾   🐾

> *There would be vacuum at the fire,*
> *except then, from every side*
> *the atmosphere implodes to fill it,*
> *and the draught is thus supplied.*
>
> *The heat increases, the wind increases,*
> *carries its fuel like a tide,*
> *travels at hundreds of miles an hour*
> *and topples walls in its stride . . .*

There were other things I thought about. The decades of war had given my mind all manner of horrors to settle on. How stupid, I now saw, were the hopes that some humans caressed of some kind of eventual reconciliation between Man and Kzin! Even I, thanks to my association with the kzinti called Raargh and Vaemar, and Cumpston and some of the other humans I had worked with, had been wavering in that direction. It was all foredoomed wishful thinking.

Some humans talked of, praised, the kzinti's courage and honor, but that courage and honor, if those were not mere names we humans had projected onto the minds of aliens we could never understand, only made them more dangerous. I had seen in their military what looked like their devotion to duty, and their strength and resolution, more than I needed to: those qualities were as terrifying as anything else about them. Honor? What did that mean? There was nothing ahead but war to the knife, pain, bloody, terrifying death, till all were dead. Like the Slaver War of the ancient past. That was how life and the Universe were made.

Then it got worse. If you have experienced bad clinical depression you may know what I mean. Different in each person's case, and yet the same. A black dog ravaging. Black sea-weed in the brain. Poisoned ice. Something wrong at heart and lungs. It did not stabilize on one beach of desolation. It was like falling from ledge to ledge, each lower and narrower than the next, and a knowledge that quite inevitably a ledge was coming that would be the last and narrowest, and that after that there would be nothing but a pit below. No safety-net, no survival. And with physical nausea thrown in: they didn't miss that trick. There was plenty on my conscience, and I got it all. Those who had died because I gave the wrong orders, those who had died because I gave the right orders, those who had died . . . I have never actually heard myself moaning in mental anguish before.

Then three beings entered the room: two of them were kzinti I knew—Raargh, the tough old ex-sergeant, and young Vaemar. They must have come from the big house, I guessed. I had no idea they were in the Gerning district. But then, between them, was Jocelyn.

"Get up, silly monkey," said Raargh. "Come with us."

"There is no need for alarm," said Vaemar, in his precise, almost pedantic, English. "The situation is under control."

"Arthur," said Jocelyn. She stepped towards me, arms wide to embrace me. She was naked, and for a moment I thought she must be cold. Then I felt myself standing (or was I?) moving forward into her embrace, while the knowledge of the miracle of her existence and return to me began to flood into my mind. I cried out in wonder and joy. Then the two kzinti leapt at her, teeth flashing, ripping at her flesh. Jocelyn became Selina, dying when the kzinti took the *Happy Gatherer*.

They all turned into white skeletons and fell in clattering heaps of bone to the floor. They disappeared.

Then I lost all rational thought. There was only darkness and fear. The pit. A sense of suffocation. Darkness visible, despair physical, a dagger of poisoned ice in my chest.

I was sitting with my head buried in my hands, shaking, thinking of suicide—the idea had a tangible shape, something that entered my mind on spider-legs and squatted there—when I heard the distant snarl of the tigripard again. I raised my head from my hands.

The zeitungers were round me in a ring on the damp, dusty floor, eyes bright. They looked like very large Earth rats. There was the .22 where I had abandoned it. I reached out, and the feel of the weapon in my hands, even though I knew it was useless, gave my mind a moment's revival. The zeitungers seemed to sense it, and retreated a couple of paces. Then the uselessness of it overcame me and I dropped the thing. They came forward again, and I saw their mouths opening in snarls that revealed their little fangs. In a moment, I knew, they would spring. There was nothing I could do about it. My brain was in such a state I would have welcomed them, as I was meant to.

The door flew open. A human figure leapt into the room. A red siting spot appeared on one of the creatures' heads, and an instant later a laser cooked its brain. I don't know if the scream from it and the others was a physical or mental event or both. The horror they had filled my

brain with was jerked about. Some of them sprang at the
human, and the beam rifle cut them to pieces in mid-air.
The others made for the cellar, and a good number died
on the way. Then the survivors wheeled in a mass and
made for the main door and the street. Few reached
either. The human leapt after them. In the dim light from
the doorway I recognized the contours of a kzin infantry
beam rifle. It fired again, this time on another setting. A
thin, incandescent jet of plasma-gas followed them.

I leapt back, bad ankle or not, from the blast of heat on
my face, and came down on that bad ankle heavily,
screaming and cursing. Good honest physical pain, good
honest screaming and cursing. This was real. There were
flames flickering now where the beam had hit inflammable
material, and thick steam and smoke, but in that light I
saw that my deliverer was a woman.

She dialed another setting on the rifle, and a jet of foam
from it smothered the flames—the kzinti who had made it
had learnt about house-to-house fighting. She came to me
and put out her hand. I took it, and for a moment could
only cling to it, babbling incoherently. Her hand was real,
firm and solid. Then my brain seemed to clear. I apologized.
The feelings of the last—how long had it been?—suddenly
seemed largely unreal, as the nausea of sea-sickness
suddenly seems unreal to a passenger ashore on dry land,
or as a spacer leaving hyperspace forgets the blind spot.
She lit a lamp, and shone it round the corners of the room.
In its light I saw her properly for the first time. I vomited,
and got to my feet. Like the recently sea-sick passenger, I
was very unsteady.

She was tall like nearly all Wunderlanders, and handsome,

or more than handsome, in a hard sort of way. The way she handled the heavy weapon—heavy for a human even in this gravity—told me she was strong. Her clothes were plain, and in the city would have been called drab, the everyday garb of the women I had seen on the farms of Gerning. They evidently repelled the rain, though, unlike mine.

"My name is Arthur Guthlac," I told her. "I'm from Earth. I've hurt my leg and I'm lost." Her face in repose looked strangely sad. Well, perhaps not strangely. On a large part of the population of Wunderland the tragic past lay heavily.

"My name is Gale. Do not be afraid. Or ashamed." She spoke a dialect of rural Wunderland, with some slightly old-fashioned constructions. "There were many zeitung-schreibers. I know what they can do. Now you had better come with me."

"Must I walk far?" I remembered my manners and made some sort of speech of thanks, still finding my voice hard to control.

"You're not free of it yet," she said. "It takes a while. I live at the big house. Not far."

The house with the orange light. That was the only big house and the only habitable-looking one. Well, if this woman lived there my previous thoughts about it being inhabited by kzinti were apparently groundless. Now that she had identified the zeitungers, and I realized the nature of the attack that had been made on me, I wondered if my previous fears of the place had simply been a product of their first mind-probes when they began gathering around me.

"The sooner you are warm and dry the better," she said.

That was certainly true. We stepped out of the ruin into the spectral street. Gale swept the rifle-barrel, firing once at an errant zeitunger I did not see and blowing it apart. Then she "broke" the butt open to replace the charge, extracting the old charge-pack.

The tigripard leapt out of the night as the lightning dribbled about us. Thunder drowned its snarl. Gale leapt sideways, a hand to her belt, something flashing in her hand. I had not seen a human move so fast. The tigripard's charge carried past her, past the spot where she had been an instant before. She struck as she leapt. It gave a scream of pain and rounded back on us, creeping towards us, belly close to the ground. Then she had the beam rifle together, one-handed, somehow, up and firing. The tigripard died in mid-spring. I saw that in her other hand she held an oversized knife, and as she wiped the tigripard's blood from it and returned it to her belt I saw it was a monomolecular-edged kzin *w'tsai*. I thought that I would not like her for an enemy, and I have been in some hand-to-hand combat.

She passed me the lamp and dialed the laser setting on the rifle down to provide an additional flashlight. The rain and hail were back in full force again, the visibility closing in.

I leant on her a little as I hobbled up the path to the house again. It had been, I guessed now, her silhouette I had seen crossing the window. But why that kzin-ish, murky orange light?

"How did you know I was out here?" I asked.

"I did not know that you particularly were here, but I

sensed the zeitungers packing. A kind of psychic back-wash reaches all minds around when that happens. Then the only thing is to go out and kill them all. Follow your thoughts, as it were, and they are easy enough to find."

This lady was mentally as well as physically tough, I thought. I did not know if I could have done that. She opened the door with a large electronic key. It looked too modern and hi-tech for this place. It also looked as if it had been made for larger hands than hers. Kzin claws. I followed her in.

"Are you alone?" I asked. A stupid, perhaps lethally tactless, thing to say at a time and in a place like that, but I was not thinking clearly.

"I am a widow," she said. That was not remarkable. After fifty-three years of war and kzin occupation there were plenty of widows—and widowers and orphans too—on Wunderland. "But I am not alone," she went on. "There is a kzin in the house."

I was sure she was not bluffing about that as I stepped across the door. Not just the light, the smells. On Earth and in space I had been used to dwelling-spaces that cleaned themselves. On liberated Wunderland I had become used to more primitive standards. But this place smelt strange and disturbing. Not dirty, but not right. Partly it was the smell of poverty, which, once you have smelt it, you cannot mistake and cannot forget. There was also a smell like a field-hospital, a very primitive one, that did not have pleasant associations for me. But it also smelt of kzin. And that smell you cannot mistake or forget either. Perhaps, I had a wayward thought, she manufactured that smell artificially to keep human and animal intruders away more effectively than any pack of ban-dogs. But if I had had designs on her or on the house, and even if she had not been carrying the kzin weapons, absence of kzinti was not the way I would have been inclined to bet. But at that moment the absence of wind, rain and hail made up for a lot.

The entrance hall, when she operated a switch, was lit by the same ruddy orange light. The light of Kzinhome, perhaps, but dimmer. This kzin evidently did not like the lights bright. I sat down on an uncomfortable wooden seat. When the kzinti walked Wunderland as conquerers, I knew, their dwellings had been decorated with preserved bodies or parts of humans or other kzinti they had killed. There was none of that here, though there were some slightly discolored or unfaded patches on the high walls where such trophies might once have been mounted. The place was furnished with old Wunderland farmhouse furniture, too little for the room's more-than-human size, and with one of the kzin-sized couches they called fooches. There were a couple of pictures, old Wunderland rural scenes mainly, not unlike those I had seen for sale at Gerning, or in the tourist shops at Munchen. One, however, was turned to the wall.

"Wait here," she said, and went up the stairs.

I waited. Despite the almost euphoric feeling of relative physical comfort and of relief from the zeitunger attack, my mental state was still pretty wretched—bruised, as it were—and I was fearful of being alone. I was also fearful of the unknown kzin. There were no distractions. To give myself something to do, I went to the picture turned to the wall and examined it. Then I wished I hadn't. For it was not a picture but a mirror. I did not know why a mirror should be turned like that, but it did not seem reassuring. I began to think of ghouls and vampires. Did this woman wish to hide the fact that she had no reflection? A stupid, irrational thought for a modern man, a space-traveller come to that, but in my circumstances it got a toe-hold in my mind. Or could she not bear to look at herself?

Then she returned. She looked ordinarily human. Real, solid, and, I saw now, beautiful. I already knew that for a Wunderlander she was muscular. Her body was what I would once have called splendidly put together, though that seemed a suddenly crude and insulting way to express what I felt. She had changed into something less peasant-like: a multicolored robe of modern, or at least prewar, fabric. And though there was a hardness and strength in her face, there was also, I saw now, another quality, a tenderness, that I had never seen in Jocelyn's.

"You can stay," she said. "I would not turn you out tonight for the zeitungers anyway. You have already got a mind full of their poison, though it has not worked its way in too deeply yet. And there may be more of them out there. I have seen what happens before when they come in a pack across lone travellers, especially at night. And there may be other things. Come."

Cautiously, I followed her into a ground-floor pantry-like place. I made myself not think about the nonhuman size of the rooms and many of the other things, like the pantry's great meat-hooks. She gave me some food from a fairly modern automatic unit and we talked about a few inconsequential things. I suppose I babbled a bit, laughed at some things that were not really funny. I noticed some things about her of the sort that snag in the mind at such times. I may have paid her some silly, clumsy compliments. After a little such she laughed too.

Then there was a bathroom, where she left me for a while, with an adequate range of both human and kzin-sized fittings, and a wonderful hot shower and soap, neither of which were things kzinti used, along with a modern dryer and human-sized basin and toilet. No mirrors, again, though, and that absence seemed odder here and uncomfortable once more. While I was cleaning myself up she must have been preparing a bed for me in one of the adjoining rooms. It was primitive enough—in space and even on Earth I was used to sleeping-plates—but when she led me to it the fabrics looked warm and clean and inexpressibly inviting. She massaged my ankle and put some dark ointment on it that felt hot but relieved the pain and a tight bandage that relieved it further. Not like modern medicine but it all moved me to another small speech of thanks.

"Rest now," she said. "I have things to do." She spread a cover over me and turned down the light. She closed the door firmly as she left.

I should have been alert to possible danger. But I simply lay there, savoring the warmth and dryness and comfort, watching through the high window-slits the rain, hail and lightning that could no longer reach me. I had no temptation to go exploring on my own at night in a kzin-inhabited house.

It would have been nice, I thought, in the sort of sexual fantasy perhaps to be expected of a man in my condition, suddenly brought from the worst mental anguish imaginable, from great physical discomfort, pain and danger, to comfort and warmth, and a deeply lonely man in any case, if my hostess would open the door, enter wearing nothing but the robe I had last seen her in, shed it, and climb into the bed beside me.

It was different to most sexual fantasies however, because a few minutes later she did precisely that. She climbed into the bed beside me, and wrapped her limbs about me, naked, warm and willing. I had known nothing like her since . . . since Jocelyn. I did not believe she was real till I felt her full, heavy breasts against my face, the smooth, warm skin, the roughness and strength of her thighs, her lips moving over mine and whispering in my ear. She was a strong, beautiful, lover. And I turned to her not only with lust and passion but a desperate need. Whatever it was, she understood. She was erotically inventive as well as tender and sweet to me then. Save for her sounds of passion, and a command once, at the beginning:—"Lie still! Let me do it!"—she said little at first. At last, as I lay with my head on her chest, savoring the warmth and fullness of her breasts about my face, she spoke again.

"You'll not be good for much tomorrow," she told me.

"You are so energetic, then?" I had no intention of finishing our night at that point. She sat up in the bed, and I saw her in the dim light, a naked shape that was inexpressibly beautiful to me at that moment, surrendered to me, yet I saw the strength in every line of her body. I raised my hands to caress her.

"Whether I am or not, I speak of the zeitunger attack," she said when we paused. "I have seen the effects before.

Believe me, this is therapy for you, though believe me also, that is not all it is. It has been a long time for me."

Her estimates of our demands for energy were not misplaced. Later we talked a little more, about the usual things in such circumstances, very quietly and gently, a lot of it not quite vocal, throat and lip noises. At last sometime during the night I fell asleep, holding her warmth, her softness, her loveliness and comfort, to me. But when I awoke she was gone.

When the next day came, black and stormy as the previous evening, I hardly noticed it. The aftermath of a zeitunger mind-attack, if you shake off the depression and don't let it drag you down into a sort of catatonia, is, after a delay which can vary from minutes to a day, an extremity of weakness and lethargy. I was grateful that for me the time-lag before it struck had been considerable

Gale's therapy, if that was what if was, had saved me from the worst of it, I think: at least a lot of the zeitunger poison she had purged away. I was simply drained of everything. But if she had saved me from the worst aftereffects of the zeitungers, she had been right about what would be left for me, once the delayed effect of what they had done hit home.

If the bed I was lying in had somehow caught fire I *might* have been able to roll myself away from it by a supreme effort but again I'd not necessarily bet that way. I lay there as though drugged through the brief dark day, dozing, listening numbly to the thunder and the rain pounding outside, the water gushing from the eaves in thick torrents. I heard Gale's voice beyond the door, talking to the kzin, I supposed, though I heard no kzin voice in reply: those harsh hiss-spit nonhuman tones are unmistakable. In those hours I felt too mentally as well as physically weak to care about this whole bizarre set-up. If she wanted to act as housekeeper or whatever it was to a ratcat, it was altogether too odd for me to care or worry about then. She looked in on me at times, saw there was a blanket covering me and did the other usual things. She seemed to have done such things before, and be used to lifting. Well, many people on Wunderland had become experienced nurses. She held me for a while, but even while feeling her warm against me I was too weak to move.

By evening, though, I felt livelier. In fact I was feeling hungry. And I wanted her again. The sick, killing depression and feeling of mental anguish seemed largely gone even as a memory. But zeitunger influence on my central nervous system or not, I quite rationally didn't want to go venturing about the house alone. The resident kzin might not take kindly to meeting a strange monkey wandering loose in its own lair without a proper introduction, and I was certainly in no shape for a dispute. I found Gale had repaired my torn shirt and trousers with sealant and added a local man's blouse which, if not modern fabric, at least did a little to keep the cold out. If it was inadaquate it was more than I expected, and a far more generous gift than it might appear: I had been briefed on the fact that after the decades of war and desperate shortages these rural Wunderlanders had powerful cultural and psychological inhibitions against giving away any possessions. I dressed and padded cautiously about the room. There was a picture on the wall of a man, bordered in black, and another picture of the same man with Gale and two small children. I remembered she said she was a widow.

Anxiety beginning to surface again. And questions without answers. Too many of them, I now thought. I had learnt again the previous day the old lesson that ignorance could be fatal. Anything to do with kzinti was dangerous. But there seemed to be no answers in this dimly-lit room. My thoughts started to run as if in a squirrel-cage.

There was a large cupboard standing by one wall—Wunderland rural, made from the local wood. Such a thing would have been worth a fortune on Earth, and it occurred to me that once the hyperdrive became economical and used for more than military purposes there would be new intersteller trades set up. Perhaps I could board that rocket while it was still on its launching-pad. That was a happy enough thought, but I had plenty of other thoughts not far beneath the surface still. After a few moments contemplation I discovered that the cupboard looked somehow sinister. That old phrase "skeleton in the cupboard." Whoever first coined it had a poetic talent of a sort, packing a story with a lot of very unpleasant, immediate and persistent imagery into four words. I opened the cupboard.

No skeleton. But other things. I knew these backwoods places often did not have autodocs, but this stuff seemed very strange. Bandages, like the bandage Gale had put on my ankle (bandages that could be used as restraints, perhaps?). Rolls of that old substance cotton-wool, which, like other things I had seen in this part of Wunderland, recalled my days at the museum and displays there of houses of the past.

There were a few old-fashioned medicines and applicators, including sprayers and tubes of fungicide. I didn't like that, but at least when I looked at them more closely they proved to be old kzin miltary medical supplies—kzin-specific, not human. They bore the dots-and-commas kzin script which I could read somewhat and the winged-claw sign of the equipment of Chuut-Riit's regular armed forces. The sort of thing kzinti used in campaigning when there was no doc handy. Presumably they had been there since before the Liberation. There was a relatively modern garbage-disposal unit on the cupboard floor. It was a small, free-standing device and I guessed Gale had tidied it in there when she cleared the room for me. Its power had been turned off.

You can learn a lot about people from their garbage. But not this time. When I opened it, I saw a number of stained cotton-wool swabs. They appeared to be stained with blood. Of what type I couldn't tell in that light. Had I seen the same sort of things in the pantry? There were a few other odds and ends in the cupboard, which I thought had been made originally to hold clothes. The cupboard door had a black panel on its inside, which faced me when I opened it. It wasn't wood like the rest, and there seemed to be something odd about it. When I looked closely I found it was another mirror, painted over.

So much for the cupboard. I found it vaguely unsettling, and with no answers. No skeleton, anyway. I lay down again and waited till Gale reappeared. She was dressed in another colorful gown, a semi-formal one of clearly prewar style, a little more revealing than the last. Beautiful Gale.

"You're better, I know," she said after we had kissed. "But wait till later. We'll be dining shortly."

"I'm more than ready," I told her. And then, again rather clumsily, "And I thank you once more. If there is any way I can repay you for what you have done for me . . ." I was trying to convey several things and probably didn't do any of them properly. I raised my hands and caressed her. She responded, but there was something abstracted in her response. I asked her about the resident kzin.

"He wants to see you," she said. I did not want to see him. I wanted to leave the first moment I could, preferably perhaps the next morning after another night warmed by her without having anything to do with any kzinti, to find my car or otherwise call for help—I supposed even this place had some sort of communications—get back to Gerning and have my ankle seen to, and get on with my life.

Thinking about another night with her though, and the previous night, made me wonder if this should be the end of the affair. I very definitely did not want it to be the end. Perhaps she would come too?

But one thing I had learned about backwoods Wunderlanders. They were sticklers for their own codes of hospitality. If this kzin wanted to see me, as courtesy, and more, to Gale, I could not refuse. Indeed to have refused could have caused more than offence to her. I thought it might well have been enough to provoke the creature's hair-trigger anger, and perhaps against her as well as me. Did he still consider her his slave? And was he resentful about my handling of his property?

Anyway, I consented to his desire to see me. There seemed no alternative.

"Does he speak English or Wunderlander?" I asked. "I know something of the slaves' patois, and the script, but I cannot manage the Heroes' Tongue." In any case, I knew, it was an insult for a monkey to use the Heroes' Tongue to a kzintosh. During the Occupation it was a fatal insult.

"Conversation will not be required," she said. "He is not meeting you to converse." A few moments before, with the touch of her on my hands, and her lips on mine, I had felt positive and happy enough. Suddenly, things seemed abnormal and disturbing again. There was, I realized, strain in every line of her face and stance now, in every tone of her voice. This kzin—or something—was making her do something against her will. No, I didn't like any of this at all.

"We will dine together," she said.

I didn't like that either. Not one bit. It was abnormal. Kzinti did not eat with humans. Monkey eating-habits disgusted them as theirs disgusted us. They tore and gulped at raw meat, often enough live meat. Those fangs could sheer the biggest bones.

A sudden hideous chill in my spine: kzinti *did* eat with humans, of course, when humans were the meal. Was that what this was all about? A trap to supply the kzin with monkey-meat? Was I to be a course rather than a guest at the dinner? Was Gale some sort of bait for unwary travellers? Kzinti had sometimes—often—taken hostages to force humans to act against their wills. Those children?

I told myself I was being stupid, but a doubt remained. The main point with which I reassured myself was that if this kzin was determined to eat me it could have done so the previous night, or at any time during the day just finished when I was virtually helpless. Or did they like their meat conscious and terrorized? They did when they ate a zianya, I knew. The glandular secretions of its terror and pain added flavor to the meat, and it was said they considered that flesh ripped from a zianya's body before it died to be especially delicious. Did they consider attacking a human recovering from a zeitunger pack-attack unsporting, as I had considered it unsporting to beam or shoot the tigripard from the air?

Should I run now? Bad ankle and all? Stupid. A human even with two sound legs could not hope to outrun a kzin—many had tried. And to attempt to flee is guaranteed to provoke the attack reaction in them. Even Cumpston, who knew some individual kzinti far better than I did, had warned me that never, even in games with those he knew, would he make a feint of running from them. And Gale had the beam rifle. I could not outrun that.

Yet I could not believe anything so hideous.

Or could I? What good explanation for any of this could there be? And why, *why* was this woman living so, serving a kzin as if humans were still their slaves on Wunderland? What hold did it have on her? I hadn't cared a little time before, but suddenly, as my mind came back towards normal, that question did matter. I remembered a horrible old story about the aftermath of an ancient human war and a surviving death-camp victim found protecting and serving his old torturer, hiding him from the vengeance of the liberators: "He promised to treat me better next time." Was there something like that here?

Or was there some explanation even worse? That Gale

was acting as a *willing* bait in a trap? Acting from some perverted hatred of her own kind like Emma, or getting a share of the meat and a kick out of cannibalism? I had encountered crazy humans on Wunderland before—not very long before. Indeed it was they who had, I now realized, killed my love, my Jocelyn. Humans steeped in more tragedy than their minds could cope with, humans raised as privileged kzin collaborators, humans twistedly pro-kzinti or simply wicked for wickedness' sake. That there were human cannibals on Wunderland I knew. There was not a sick perversion but some human would indulge in it. After decades of war and occupation madness was abroad on this planet. There was a rigid control about Gale, something damming and stopping her emotions, something desperately abnormal. She seemed to wish not to speak, to betray nothing, and yet was clearly under some terrible pressure.

Then Gale said something else. Defensively, as if she expected protest:

"His eyes are not . . . he does not like strong light. We will be dining in the dark."

I would be insane to agree to that. I had my suspicions about this kzin and his meat-appetites already.

And yet . . . My sister Selina was said to have had latent telepathic abilities. I had never been tested but I had at least something—an erratic and occasional intuition about others—which, when I had felt it in the past, had stood me in good stead. I felt it now and it told me Gale was not lying about that half-stated fact of the creature's eyes, at least. Not exactly. But I was equally sure that she was keeping something back.

And I felt her care for me, her tenderness, was genuine. Or had she used sex to, among other things, deliberately confuse my perceptions?

I would be at every sort of disadvantage. Kzinti were happy to be night-hunters. Further, darkness enhanced the rudimentary sense they possessed which, in a few individuals, was developed into the power of the telepaths. If they were physically close to one in the dark, I had been told—and when I was told it, by a human under a bright sky, the idea of being physically close to one in the dark had made me shudder inwardly—even the nontelepaths could read something of one's state of mind. It was an ability evolved to help them to hunt out game that attempted to hide at night and in caves and other darknesses. Not that they often deigned to read monkeys' states of mind when they strode Wunderland as conquerors . . .

I should have refused absolutely. But something prevented me. Was it the fear and sadness in Gale's eyes? Was it some dawning feeling of love for her, that great destroyer of survival-instincts? The tenderness in her that I felt? Was it that the zeitunger attack had simply left me in no mental state to put up any resistance? Perhaps the desire not to appear a coward to her? And besides, if the kzin wanted me dead, then I, alone, unarmed, and unable to run, was dead anyway. I allowed Gale to lead me towards whatever lay at the top of the stairs.

The dim orange light was still burning, and I quickly memorized the details and layout of the place as well as I could, noting thankfully that the dark would not be quite total and the kzin would not, it seemed, be too close to me. There was a fire behind a screen near the place where I would evidently sit. That warmth was out of consideration for my too-light clothes, I supposed, and so I could see the food and cutlery in front of me at least. It was a very tiny fire, shielded by the screen, and looking at it I remembered something Rykermann had told me, one of those wayward thoughts which a mind seeking distraction from what is before it flees to: Rykermann believed that, possibly because of their flammable fur, kzinti without armor, in battle and house-to-house fighting, in the rare event that they were afraid of anything, were afraid to be with out-of-control fire in confined spaces. Hence the foam attachment on Gale's rifle. Sometimes, occasionally, that fact could be used.

There was one big central table, with another human-sized chair, plainly for Gale, about two-thirds of the way up, and a kzin-sized chair—not one of their usual fooch recliners, I noticed—at the other end. I thought, with more unease that contained a great deal of real fear, that it would be easier for the kzin to spring at me across the table from a sitting than a reclining position.

In my military studies of the kzinti I had come across a little about their dining habits. "But if you go into a kzin dining-room you're in a lot of trouble anyway. If they've left you a weapon or you can improvise one, try to take as many of them with you as you can. Go for the eyes and tendons," had been one manual's advice on the correct etiquette for the situation. The table was standard enough, from what I had read, with its central notched runnel and ditch for blood, although I also noticed that runnel had no bloodstains, or at least no fresh ones. But the smell of blood was thick enough now. Kzinti loved the smell of blood. And there was no kzin food here. Or not on the table.

Gale turned down the lights, leaving only the dimmest glow of the screened fire. True, there were still occasional lightning flashes outside the window, and a near one might light up the room, but I said nothing about that, or of my enhanced night-vision. But thanks to that little glow of the fire behind me, I would be looking from dim light into darkness, so my night-vision would be effectively nullified. Had she planned it that way? *There is something horrible here!* But it was too late to flee. I knew I would not make it even down the stairs.

She brought some bowls, placing one before me, and one before her own place. Then she brought another for the kzin's place. I smelt blood even more strongly then. I think she may have seen how pale in the dim light my face was, or heard my hard breathing. She kissed me quickly on the cheek.

"Wait," she said.

She left me alone for a moment. I heard something heavy advancing. The kzin was only a blot of darkness as it entered the room. I saw/sensed it moving into the great chair. Its progress seemed to take a long time. But kzinti are much faster than humans on their feet. Its footfalls were strange. It said nothing. Why did it say nothing? There was no explanation for any of this. I strained every bit of the poor mental faculty I had to sense something beyond sight. Gale was sitting towards the other end of the table, closer in the darkness to the kzin than to me, but I sensed she was quivering with tension. Why a bowl?

Kzinti tore meat. They did not eat out of bowls. Come to that, why had the kzin not come out with Gale to hunt the zeitungers? Their night-vision was better than any human's, their reflexes faster, they hated zeitungers, and they loved hunting for its own sake.

"Eat," she said, and her voice was cracked with strain. Somehow I got a piece of food to my mouth. And then, "Let us be thankful for what has been provided."

Or was it a kzin at all? There was the kzin's gingery smell, unmistakable (or was it—that idea that had first crossed my mind when I entered this place!— a counterfeit of kzin smell? I remembered that I had heard no kzin voice in this house). The thing was big like a kzin, bigger than a man. I could sense that unmistakably.

But its breathing was a shrill whistle, nothing like that of a kzin, with a bubbling like nothing I knew, and the strange sucking noise it also made was not the noise of a kzin eating. No kzin sucked its food!

The lightning flared.

The head I saw in dim, momentary silhouette was not like a kzin's head. Was that a trumpet-shaped protuberance? The lightning flared again, longer and brighter.

The thing I saw was not a kzin.

I gave a roar of panic and terror from the bottom of my diaphragm, worse, more tearing, than a scream. Not a very courageous reaction from a decorated brigadier, but I tell myself now that my brain still had some zeitunger-poison in it. I leapt backwards in horror, knocking over the fire-screen, hitting the wall. The firelight flared brighter and the hideous thing seemed to leap at me. The walls were thick, as in any kzin-built structure, and the small window deeply recessed. I jumped onto the window sill, gibbering like a monkey. Then Gale turned on the light.

The ghoul, the thing, the obscenity, stared back at me.

I saw I was wrong. It *was* a kzin. Or it had been one, once.

Both ears were completely gone—not merely ears but hair and skin and flesh. Much of the head was naked bone, veins led across it by some makeshift, ghastly amateur medical procedure. One eye was an empty, bony socket, the other partly occluded by a projecting keloid-scar. The nose and muzzle were gone, leaving only a red cavity. So too was the whole lower jaw gone, and the fangs of the upper jaw. There was only a wobbling fragment of tongue dripping blood and slaver and the hole of a gullet. I saw it had been feeding by sucking bloody liquid through a tube. There were stained lumps of cotton-wool lying near.

The kzin raised its paws as if to hide its mutilated head. Paws, I saw, not hands. The fingers and claws were gone as well, and its fore-limbs were asymmetrical, the right one withered and twisted. Burns. Attached to the left one was a metal rod. I guessed it communicated by using this on a keyboard.

I had been aware of Gale's muscles when I saw her handle the rifle and then when we held each other in the night. Wunderlander or not, she had lived a strenuous life. She went to the kzin now and helped it stand. I saw that for a kzin it was a small one, the smallest male I had seen except for a telepath. It gazed at me from between its mutilated paws with its single half-eye. She said something to it I could not follow, then led it away. Again it took a long time, for it shuffled very slowly. There was something wrong with its legs and feet as well, and it was hunched and bent as if its spine was damaged.

I was left alone on the window ledge. I climbed down and returned to the table, breathing hard and trying to control myself and to retain my food. I was still sitting there when she returned

"He was in the ramscoop raid," she said. "He had run into a burning building and it collapsed while he was inside it. Now I keep him alive. He is ashamed to be seen. But after last night he wished to see you."

"You seek to torture him?" I understood very well how many on Wunderland hated the kzinti. Well, who could understand that better than I? But still I disliked torture for its own sake. And the state of this creature could inspire horror and revulsion but not, in a sane being, hatred.

"No, no!" There were tears on her cheeks. "But he wanted to feel if you were . . . if you were . . ." More tears, almost uncontrollable, like a dam breaking. After a time she calmed down.

"Then, if you wish to be kind, is it kind to let him live?" I asked. "I would have thought most kzinti would prefer to die and go their God rather than drag out life so reduced."

"He fears death because he is no Hero," she replied. "He believes that if he meets the Fanged God he will meet him as a coward and the God will regurgitate his soul into nothingness. For he did not get his wounds in battle. He was not a warrior kzintosh, you see. He never saw battle. His rank-title was Groom/Assistant-To-Healers. A medical orderly, a corpsman, a stretcher-bearer. Despised by other kzinti always. A humble, lowly semi-civilian.

No Fighter's Privileges. If he had died in that burning building, or died of his injuries afterwards, he would not have died acceptably, in battle, on the attack. He had his injuries in a shameful manner. He fears to die now. I help him live."

"And for the same reason, I suppose, he hides away?" I asked.

"Yes. And so he did not want me to tell you. He wanted you to think he was a fearsome warrior . . . a Hero. It left him a little . . . pride. A little less shame. He is . . . often confused. I tried to tell him . . . that . . . that even as his own kind count such things, he would be . . ." She made a sound of helplessness.

I made some gesture, some sound, of non-understanding. "I have not heard of a kzin who was ashamed of scars before," I said. "Quite the reverse."

She gave a peculiar, tearful smile. "No Hero," she said. "But there was more to it than that. After the building collapsed he was under the burning, smoldering, wreckage for a long time. There were other priorities in damage-control and rescue. While he was there the zeitungers got to him. They had been in the cellarage there, too, like your rats. Whether they could reach him physically to tear what was left of his flesh I don't know. But they tore his mind, for days. *You* can imagine that, now."

I could. Not the cruelest human being, I thought, who had experienced the zeitungers could but feel a throb of pity for this creature of a pitiless species. This wreck of a kzin and I had something in common, I thought.

"The effect, as far as I can tell, on human and kzin minds is parallel," Gale said. "What do kzinti fear? Many things, secretly. But to fail as Heroes perhaps most of all."

Even, perhaps, those far-off dreams of glory were something this lowly kzin and Arthur Guthlac the museum guard had shared.

"They lodged their poison deep in his mind," she went on. "He was there with them too long. And you see the state he was already in." Kzinti, even nontelepaths, had that rudimentary telepathic sense more acute than that of nearly all humans. More receptive. I had no difficulty understanding that a prolonged zeitunger attack, setting up patterns and paths in the brain, would be a different matter to the brief one I had endured. And the zeitungers themselves would presumably then have been filled with animal fear and panic. I tried briefly to imagine an unremitting zeitunger attack if one was already desperately injured and mutilated, blind, trapped, alone, helpless, in agony, hour after hour as fire crept closer. After a very short time I stopped doing that. Again, as I stopped shaking, the wan ghost of a smile crossed her strained face. This Wunderland woman was at least as tall as me, and our eyes were level. "Unlike your case," she said, "there was no treatment." Our faces moved together and I found myself kissing her again, gently, tenderly.

"Yet that," she went on after a moment, "may be another reason he struggles to live. To die of such shame and despair would be a victory for the zeitungers."

"Why has he had no modern treatment since?" I asked. "For anything? Body or mind?"

"Treatment? How?"

I did not understand everything yet, but I wanted to be gentle with her. At least some of my ghastlier and more grotesque fears and suspicions about her and this kzin seemed wrong. I put my arms around her and stroked her hair and after a moment she rested her head on my shoulder, hiding her face against me.

"I know an old kzintosh warrior, Raargh, who has many wounds from the war," I told her. "One arm and one eye are not his own, and his knees are metal. His scars are honored and honorable among the kzinti. There are kzintoshi with sons"—was I babbling a little now?—"who point them to the likes of Raargh as Heroes to emulate. But he had his wounds in battle."

"Then he is fortunate among the kzinti. This one they would despise. Or so he believes."

"But your kzin could have a better life," I told her. "Far better. There is good surgery. Transplants, prostheses, quick nerve, bone and tissue-growth are available now. For kzinti as well as humans. His mind, too, perhaps. There are facilities . . .

"Raargh lives well enough, even as kzinti count such things," I went on. "In hunts he pulls down game with his prosthetic arm and his artificial eye allows him to see in the dark." When I thought of Raargh I knew again that I felt rather more warmly to him than to most of the creatures. I remembered certain things that had happened in the caves. "He has adopted a youngster who is his pride and joy and I think he is getting more sons of his own."

"In the city hospitals, perhaps, and for the Herrenmanner and their clients, there is such treatment," she replied, raising her eyes. "What money do we have for that?" I remembered what a backwoods part of Wunderland this was.

"And who would help a kzin?" she added after a moment, with genuine puzzlement in her voice. "The kzinti have no power. On this planet they are destroyed. And I was no collaborator. I did my part to destroy them."

"It costs nothing," I said. "Part of the terms we offered the kzinti on this planet when we made peace was that their wounded would be treated."

I saw her face change.

"I did not know that!" Her face lit so that she looked a different person. Then it fell again. "But how would we get there?"

Explaining the new political situation in the cities would have taken a long time. I owed this deformed kzin little enough, thinking of what the kzinti had done to me and mine. But I owed Gale. If she had done nothing but save me from the zeitungers, I would have owed her. Anyway, she was a beautiful and desirable woman and, it seemed, an innocent one. And if I felt dawning love for her, along with desire, I suppose I also wanted to impress her. I took the identity-disk from my neck and passed it to her, my fingers twining round hers as I did so—a strange situation for lovers to be courting!

"You see my rank? I am a brigadier general attached to the UNSN general staff. At present on leave. But I can arrange transport for him . . . and you."

I had become embarassed by my earlier behavior. Now I was embarassed by her reaction to my words. She went down on her knees and clasped my own. She kissed my hands, where the previous night she had kissed my lips. Her face was like a light of joy. I raised her to her feet and, holding her, walked with her to the window. Together we looked out. The lightning flashes were definitely further away now, the rain was thinning and, I guessed, the floods would subside quickly. I accepted all that she said, but one question remained.

"I still don't understand," I told her. "A kzin. An enemy. An invader of this planet who would have enslaved and destroyed us all. Yes, his burns and injuries are terrible. But why do you care for him so?"

There were sounds behind us. The mutilated kzin shuffled slowly into the room again. Evidently it had decided to face me, with courage of a kind that I hoped I would never need, though it still held its paws as if to try to hide what was left of its head from my sight. But it looked less horrible now. It made some gestures to Gale that she plainly understood.

She went to a dresser and took a bottle that I recognized: bourbon, something both species drank. She took two glasses for us and another bowl that she put in front of the kzin, pouring a little into each.

"I will explain to him," she said. "Things must be explained to him carefully."

"But first," she said, "we usually drink a toast each night." And then, raising her glass, "To my children."

Following her example, I drank. The kzin, manipulating its trumpet with difficulty between its paws, dipped it into its bowl and sucked.

Without words I understood, and I saw that she knew I understood.

"Yes," she said. "He held up the building while they escaped."

Grossgeister Swamp

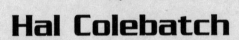

Hal Colebatch

Wunderland, 2430 A.D.

The kzin lapped noisily, then raised its head and looked into the eyes of the Abbot of Circle Bay Monastery. The kzin was young and its ear tattoos betokened the highest nobility. The abbot was small and elderly.

"This is excellent brandy, Father," the kzin remarked. His Wunderlander had only intermittent nonhuman accent. "My Honored Step-Sire Raargh Hero told me not to miss it."

"I am glad, Vaemar, My Son-within-these-walls. We try to mitigate the austerities of the field-naturalist's life."

"I don't know if I'm really entitled to be called that," Vaemar said, putting down the empty bowl. "I'm only a student."

"These are the statistics we've compiled," said the abbot, extracting a memory brick from his computer and passing it to Vaemar. "What we know of human use of the swamp since the first landings on this planet. I hope it's helpful."

They crossed the garth to the car parked in the meadow just beyond the monastery gates. A few crumbling fragments of walls, overgrown with multicolored vegetation, were the only traces of the refugee camp that had stood there at the time of Liberation ten years before. What had been a refuse-filled ditch then was now an ornamental moat with floating plants. A couple of monks were tending the fish-ponds that joined with it. "There are the monkeys!" remarked the abbot. It was an old joke between then, dating from Vaemar's confusion over nomenclature on his second visit to the monastery. A grazing pony caught the odor of the kzin and fled.

"I feel a little foolish telling you to be careful," said the abbot, looking up at Vaemar who stood beside him like a tower of teeth, claws and muscle. "And I hope I'm not insulting. But nonetheless, I will tell you. Again. We've never known everything that's in the swamp, but we've always known a lot of the life there is highly dangerous, certainly to humans. Overly inquisitive or incautious people have long had a habit of disappearing there. Of course, if you go in a small canoe alone up a waterway inhabited by big crocodilians that's perhaps not overly surprising, but . . . Marshy can tell you more."

"Our canoe should be bite-proof," said Vaemar. "And it's a good deal harder to upset than a one-man job."

"I know. But some of those who have disappeared ought to have known their business. There was a sailors' rhyme on Earth, once:

> *Take care and beware of the Bight of Benin*
> *Where one comes out and forty go in.*

I'll not nag further. But I want your expedition to be a success. And no more disappearances."

They boarded the car for the short flight over the rolling, flower-bright meadowland and down to the creek, last reach of Grossgeister Swamp, where the big canoe and the rest of the expedition waited.

Vaemar checked the loading of the canoe and its outriggers as the abbot chatted with the other five expedition members. It was a primitive and stupid craft compared to those which had been generally available on Wunderland before the invasion and the following decades of occupation and war, but it was the best the university had available for student expeditions now, and in some ways its very low-tech nature could be an advantage. They moved out of the creek under the engine, then took up their paddles.

The canoe travelled almost silently under the thrust of the six paddles, two of them worked by the muscles of kzinti.

Water-dwellers, amphibians, land-dwellers occupying the ecological niches that on Earth would be filled by swamp-deer, peccaries and the like, were plentiful, as were flyers. Creatures of all sizes that would have fled at the sound of the engine presented themselves for the expedition's cameras. But this part of Grossgeister Swamp was never quite silent. Water lapped in the channels between the islands and the stands of trees, insectoids and amphibians sang in ceaseless choirs and choruses, and from time to time there came the splash of some larger creature breaking the surface.

The land varied from rises of mud supporting reed-clumps and a few drowning bushes to substantial sandy

islands with game trails and occasional dwellings, some
occupied, some plainly abandoned and going back to the
swamp. Occasional floats in the channels marked fishermen's nets. The vegetation was almost entirely the red of
Wunderland: neither the green plants of Earth nor the
orange of Kzin had been able to colonize this place.

After an hour of paddling they reached one of these
substantial islands with more obvious signs of long-term
occupation. The house on it was a solid structure, with the
vegetation before and about it clipped and trimmed like a
lush red lawn and hedge. There was a dock and a moored
boat spiky with electronics. Marshy, the occupant, a lean
old man who reminded Vaemar of a farmer in the back-
blocks beyond the Hohe Kalkstein, greeted them warily,
taking no trouble to disguise the fact that both he and the
house were armed, even though ten years after the end of
the war on Wunderland a party of four young humans, two
of them girls, and two young kzinti, did not look particularly threatening. The human students had a couple of
slung strakkakers as well as their collecting guns (unusual
strakkakers on Wunderland in that they had large trigger-
guards and given the right personalized coding could be
operated by kzin as well as human hands) but Vaemar and
the other kzin, Swirl-Stripes, carried only their *w'tsais*
here. Vaemar presented the abbot's letter of introduction.

Marshy ushered them in. One large room, lined with
shelves on which curious odds and ends were interspersed
with old books, had as its dominating feature a great
sweep of curved window, once plainly the main viewport
of a spaceship's bridge. Its upper part gave a panoramic
view of a maze of islands, channels and sloughs, with here

and there in the distance open water rippling and sparkling in the sun. Its lower part extended below the water-line, giving a view like a great aquarium. Some of the life-forms they saw would have been recognizable to a terrestrial biologist as examples of parallel evolution. Some, a few, were introduced creatures from Earth. Some were familiar Wunderland creatures. Some were still utterly strange. There were comfortable viewing arrangements, even a kzin-sized indoor fooch as well as human couches in front of the great window. Vaemar wandered over to it as Swirl-Stripes and the human students appropriated the seating. Rosalind MacGowan came to the window beside him. Marshy dialed them refreshments.

"He told me you were coming," he said. "Asked me to keep an eye on you. Don't know if I can do much in that direction. And you appear capable of looking after yourselves. What do you know about the Great Ghost? Have you been here before?"

"Only round the edges," said Rosalind, "with Professor Rykermann, as Hon . . . as Vaemar will tell you."

"Most of us only know it round the edges," Marshy said. "Do you know what you're looking for?"

"Life in the center. New life," said Vaemar. "And anything else worth studying. New ecological relationships, for example. Urrr." His ears betrayed the equivalent of a human frown of concentration as he spoke.

"You are . . . abstractly curious?"

"Yes."

"Umm . . . I see." There was a flicker of a new expression in the man's bleak old face. "I was there just after the Liberation. Everything dead. The water still covered with floating carrion. It made me sick and I've seldom been back. But I suppose nature's tidied the place up in its own way now."

"That's what we want to measure," said Anne von Lufft, her face and voice full of eagerness. "The extent to which the center is being re-colonized."

"Can't you do it with satellites?"

"Not in enough detail," said Hugo Muller. "Some of the life-forms are small. And satellites are expensive. There's no substitute for being on the ground."

"That's the right answer," said Marshy. "Also, I suppose, there's not much thesis-fodder to be had from satellite readings."

"We're only third-years," said Toby Hill. "They're not big theses."

"But they might lead to big theses," said Marshy. "What do you want an old swamp-hermit to do for you?"

"Tell us about Grossgeister," said Swirl-Stripes.

"That would take eight minutes or eight lifetimes." He touched a button and a map was thrown up on one wall. "You know its center is an ancient meteor crater, like Circle Bay itself. Or in this case, more than one crater. The bigger islands are mainly remnants of ancient ring-walls. It's big. No one knows it all. You can't even map it by satellite because satellites can't tell all that's land and all that's shallow water, or see through overhanging forest. Peat burns under the surface in places and makes smoke and steam. A lot of the boundaries between land and water can't be defined, anyway. Many of the channels and marsh-lands and smaller islands change. In the wider waters the currents build up sand bars and tear them down.

"There are stretches like a great river of vegetation, miles wide and a couple of inches deep. It's fed by rivers and by the sea and by underground springs. Part of it's shallow, part of it's fresh, part of it's deep, part of it's salty from the sea. There are wide stretches of open water. Men who have lived in it longer than I have perished, without modern navigation aids or smart boats, only a short way from home, lost in channels and islands that all look exactly like each other. Nobody's ever known everything that lives—or lived—in it.

"Humans have always fossicked round the edge of Grossgeister, but in the three hundred years we've been on this planet, we've never tamed it. We've hunted in its margins and its creeks ever since the first explorations—but from the first day we've had a feeling it was also hunting us. Your kzin Sires"—he told Vaemar and Swirl-Stripes—"never took much interest apart from the military aspects—of course you like to hunt dry-footed."

"We can conquer water," said Swirl-Stripes.

"You know that the heart was cooked out of it. The kzinti used the heat-induction ray when a particularly troublesome gang of Wascal Wabbits took refuge there. Then, during the Liberation, a big kzin cruiser was shot down. It came down slowly, and there were survivors who went on fighting for a while. The hulk's still there, as far as I know. I suggest you leave it alone. I take it you've had basic ROTC training and know better than to monkey with any weapons or propulsion systems . . . I see you have your own weapons."

"Of course. We know there are many dangerous life-forms. We have had instructions."

"Never forget it. When the kzin ship went down, the crew abandoned it when they had fired the last of the ready-use ammunition that they could reach at the circling fighters and took to the swamp. They were a big crew, even after their battle losses, but their number was smaller by the time they got to this island. I'm talking about fighting kzinti, well-armed. You have maps, compasses, GPS?"

"Yes, and motion-detectors and autoguards for our camp. And a field autodoc. Telephones, of course."

"Don't rely on autoguards. And see here—" He gestured to the skull of a crocodilian on the shelving. "See those teeth? Bigger than yours, young kzinti, and a lot bigger than the rest of you can muster. Doc or no doc, you'll be a long way from help if you strike trouble."

"We've got telephones and rockets," said Rosalind.

"If you have problems, don't be backward about using them! I'll come if I pick anything up."

"Thank you."

"We all help each other in the Swamp. And the abbot is an old friend of mine. He says to help you, and I owe him . . . Look there."

They stared down at a thing like a Persian carpet of lights moving through the water beyond the window, a couple of feet below the surface.

"It's beautiful," said Anne.

"There are a lot of bioluminescent forms. That's something fairly special to show up in daylight. There are still endless wonderful things in Grossgeister, as well as dangerous ones. Night in the swamp can be something to see. If there are no natural lights I have my own." He touched a switch and submerged lamps illuminated the water beyond the window. "As you know, the biodiversity of this planet is thought to owe a great deal to the frequency of meteor-strikes. One can watch the life-forms passing down there for hours, and always something new. I'd make a feeding-station there, but I'm afraid the big carnivores would take it over.

"But to return to the danger, which I think is what the good Father wished me to impress upon you: there are about three hundred humans living in the margins of this swamp. People who know it relatively well. Some are second- or third-generation swamp-folk. In the last year at least fifteen have disappeared. And others in previous years. One here, one there. Don't ask me how, or why. Just watch out."

"Were they wearing locators?" asked Rosalind

"No. These are swamp-folk, not ROTC. They live in the marshes because there they are left alone. A lot of people don't like government, and if you suggested they carry an implant so government could track them they'd not take kindly to the idea. Even for their own good. We're a contrary bunch who hang on the skirts of the Great Ghost. . . .

"Don't forget," he went on, "we're relatively close to well-populated areas here. But a lot of this planet is wild. And things can come in from the wild."

"Then why do you live here?" asked Anne. "There's plenty of drier land available."

"Very simple. I love it. Like the other swamp-folk, perhaps I'm not too partial to government. And with modern medicine available again I needn't fear damp in my joints."

Not to mention the retainer you get for keeping an eye on things, thought Vaemar. *Including things like me. I think your antipathy to government may be a little selective.* Yet he also felt that, at one level, the old human was telling the truth.

"The dangers?"

"My Hero, young as you are, I see you have a few scars and ears already. What is life without danger? Even some of us monkeys know that as a question."

"Have these disappearances been plotted?" asked Vaemar. He was grinning, the reflex to bare the teeth for battle.

"Of course. Here." Marshy printed out several sheets of maps. "This is what the abbot meant you to have. Of course these are approximate areas only. Some of the times are only approximate, too. If you can see a pattern to it, good luck to you."

"One here, one there."

"Yes."

"But in the deeps rather than the edges . . ."

"Yes, as far as we can tell."

"Not a plague, then. A plague would be less discriminating."

"Quite. But in the swamp there are always plenty of things ready to eat you. It may be people have simply grown careless with peace. Neglected to set their locks and fences because there's no threat in the sky. Never mind the threat in the water. We're not a strictly logical species."

They thanked him and walked back to the canoe. Marshy gestured to Vaemar and drew him back, a little behind the rest.

"You are in charge?" he said. It was both statement and question.

"Yes. I'm the senior student . . . although I'm actually younger in years, of course. We mature faster."

"I know the University policy: no discrimination for kzinti, no discrimination against kzinti. I agree with it. You must earn your successes fair and square. And the abbot told me about you, too. His recommendation I trust.

"But what I did not, perhaps, wish to say in front of the others, is that with these disappearances . . . Kzin revanchists are suspected."

"I suppose that's inevitable. Perhaps it's even true."

"Do you think it's true? Kzin defiance? It would be counter-productive. . . ."

"We are not very skilled at defiance," said Vaemar. "We never had to defy enemies before. We just ate them up." He licked his fangs. "I suppose some kzinti might do counter-productive things."

"Satellites and radar would show up any *big* movements—air-cars flying, for example, or the discharge of heavy weapons," Marshy said. "And they're monitored by machines and alarms that don't nod off in the small hours. Something killing clandestinely sounds to some like kzin stalking behavior."

"Humans stalk, too," said Vaemar.

"There were a lot of feral children running wild on this planet by the time the war ended," said Marshy. "I doubt they've all been rounded up. Untameable. Savage. Good at killing."

"Children of which kind?"

"Both. They won't be children now, though."

"I suppose I was nearly one of them," said Vaemar. "I could have been left to run wild—or die—given that a few things had happened a little differently." They were silent for a moment save for the sand crunching under their feet as they walked.

"A couple of kzinti have set up a fishing business on Widows' Island," said Marshy. "Largely supplying fish products to other kzinti, I'm told, but some human trade too. It's marked on the map I gave you."

"I'll have a look . . . I assume you are suspicious of me?"

"I'm a swamp creature of a sort. I'm suspicious of many things."

"So you've probably recorded our meeting."

"Why do you say that?"

"If there are kzinti revanchists, and I join them, and come back and eat you, ARM would know what had been happening?"

"My dear young fellow! You don't suppose . . ." Marshy threw up his hands as if in indignation. Then he looked straight up into Vaemar's eyes. "You will see the wonder of the place. I've told you of the danger. I know that it is insulting to stress danger to a Hero and that I have trespassed to the limit of acceptable manners in saying as much as I have. But remember, young Hero, the fact you are in charge means you are responsible for young lives besides your own." He paused a moment.

"I've a fair nose, for a monkey. You use toothpaste on your fangs."

"Yes. I spend a lot of time among humans, like my Honored Step-Sire Raargh Hero. It seems a good idea.

But we call it fang-paste. I will care for those in my charge."

"Yes," said Marshy, "I think you will." Then in a fair rendering of the Heroes' Tongue, he added:

"*Snarr' grarrch.*"

"*Urrr.*"

The shadows of Alpha Centauri A were lengthening as they made camp on a large island. Wide stretches of open water gave a clear field of view all round. By the time the defenses and sleeping accommodations were set up it was nearly dark. Alpha Centaruri B rose early at this time of year, in a blaze of purple with a silver core.

The sky, however, was always brilliant with the light of the Serpent Swarm and Wunderland's satellites, natural and artificial, that had survived the war and been supplemented since, hung like multi-tinted glow-globes. Even the dust of war had contributed a legacy of brilliant sunsets and a diffusion of luminescence at night. The high sliding lights that were satellites and spacecraft made a strange contrast to the primordial feeling of the swamp about them. The swamp had lights of its own—will-o'-the-wisps of incandescent marsh-gas, light-dragons—living beings but barely more substantial—and the more solid shapes of luminescent plants and animals, above, on and below the water.

The humans and kzinti ate and slept separately, though Swirl-Stripes and Toby played banjos together briefly. The kzinti, more silent than the humans when they chose though far bulkier, would patrol the perimeter of the camp at irregular intervals during the night. Their own weapons, though far less devastating than most of the military weapons both sides had been employing by the time fighting on Wunderland ended, were judged more than adequate to handle any known swamp-creature. Vaemar made the first patrol. The oscilloscope on the motion-detector, an invaluable tool on biological expeditions like this, was in a constant frenzied dance and small creatures were to be seen in plenty. Vaemar made field-notes of these, and relaxed enough to snap up one or two of them, but there was nothing obviously threatening.

Drifting in the channel with leaves and other small pieces of debris were the paired berry or bubble-shapes that he knew were the eyes and nostrils of crocodilians. Some of these pairs had enough distance between them to indicate formidable size, but the camp's defenses, both physical and electronic, were effective, and the drifting eyes caused him no concern. He settled for a while into a stand of vegetation, still as another piece of wood as his fur rose and fell minutely to compensate for the move-ment of his breathing. Only the lights reflected in his great eyes or a gleam of the tips of his shearing fangs would have betrayed his presence to the unwary. He made some mental notes for essays he had due on other subjects—Caesar's use of fortifications as defensive anchors in his campaign against the Helveti, the adaptation of gravity-fields as dust-deflectors for spacecraft passing through Trojan positions, possibilities of hyper-connectivity in neuronetic logic-lattices. There was also a long essay on the Normans—their ability to combine Roman and Viking cultures in medieval chivalry, marrying order and achievement to barbarian freedom and vigor. He had selected this as his major psychohistorical topic. He allowed himself a single move in the chess game he had been playing in his mind for some weeks, and settled into reflection.

Given another turn of the wheel, he thought, *and these humans would have been my slaves and prey animals, and I might have been a princeling in a Royal Palace.* And then he thought, *Yes, and with an eight-squared of ambitious elder brothers between me and my Honored Sire or any throne, not to mention Combat Master who trained, by all accounts, a great deal more lethally than does the ROTC. Very likely I would be dead. Certainly, I would not have been given a clean slate on which to write, perhaps, part of the destiny of my species on this planet.* A colony of tubes, which might have been plant or animal, springing from the submerged roots of a tree at the water's edge, pulsed with slow rings of light as it siphoned the water for small organisms. There was a fascination in watching it, though such a sessile thing, even if biologically an animal, would be beneath a traditional hunter's notice.

I am free to appreciate the forms and colors of life, thought Vaemar, *free to see a strange beauty in all of this, and speak of it, free to pursue knowledge for its own sake, without my siblings killing me as an oddity.* The thought should have been a comfortable one, but there was something about it that did not make for ease. *Free to be a freak? Like Dimity-Manrret? Free not to be a kzin? That has a bad taste.*

There was a rushing in the water of a multitude of fish-like things, galvanized, it seemed, by a single mind and purpose. The bubbles of the crocodilians vanished abruptly.

Something vast and dark heaved in the water before him. Phosphorescence deep below the surface showed rhomboid paddles and tapering, serpiform neck and tails. He resisted a brief and atavistic but, he knew, irrational, urge to leap down the bank and into the dark water after such prey. *Certainly, I would have missed seeing this. Perhaps I am realizing what all royalty realizes sooner or later— high destiny is the tastiest of meat but it kills. Still, I have destiny of my own and cannot flee from it. Nor do I wish to. What does my Honored Sire Chuut-Riit think of me as he watches me from the Afterlife? That I have become half-human? Yet his own last words, found by Zroght-Guard Captain, written of his killers, my brothers, with his claw in his own blood: FORGIVE THEM. He meant allow them an honorable death, perhaps. But even so, many would think, that was an un-Kzinlike ending to his story here. And elder brother, who did not go mad with the rest, but who died saving me and the other new-born in the kittens' nursery?*

One of my few memories of Honored Sire Chuut-Riit, my very last memory of him alive, is when I cried out to him how hungry we were. There was patience in his voice, even gentleness, as he told me: "Something very bad has happened." Then he bade me wedge the door again and wait, as he went, knowingly, to foul and shameful death. We are more complex than we let ourselves believe.

My destiny? I owe my life to many—to elder brother whose sense of duty over-rode the hunger-madness, to the unknown, probably Nameless and now almost certainly dead Hero who brought me to Raargh as he held the last kzin fort on Surrender Day, to Raargh himself a dozen times for his training, yes, and to the humans who fought at our side in the caves against the mad ones—against Henrietta, Honored Sire's old Executive Secretary, and her madder daughter, Emma. There is some pattern behind it all. A kermitoid hopped onto his muzzle, then, realizing its mistake, attempted flight. He disposed of it with a swipe and snap. There was another dark wave in the water, vee-shaped, moving up the channel.

My Honored Sire Chuut-Riit wished to understand humans, even if that began with dissection, and my Honored Step-Sire Raargh Hero has impressed on me my duty to do so now. Perhaps I begin to understand a little. The humans can be as destructive and barbaric as the kzinti, or much more so—I think of the Ramscoop raid, of humans running wild in the Liberation, of the mad ones in the caves—but humans can erect mental barriers against barbarism. Some of them are small, like the fang-paste that old human remarked on. Some are greater, like religious commands, or the human idea of the Knight. But those barriers are created, artificial, unnatural things. Kzinti can erect mental barriers against barbarism, too—where would we be without Honor, or without the wisdom and control of the Conservers?—but it strikes me, also, that there are things the civilized mind cannot cope with. Things like us, perhaps? Our ancestors came across civilized races and enslaved them with hardly a decent fight. We must change, but we must not change too much. I must study the limits of the civilized mind.

Below him the night water roiled when great beasts fought and tore. The froggolinas resumed their strange song.

☙ ☙ ☙

Dawn was a noisy business in this part of the swamp. They breakfasted, and compared the lists of life-forms noted and recorded. It was agreed to approach the University to establish a permanent observation post here.

They made a quick biological survey of the island identifying and recording signatures electronically, and replotted its position on the chart. Then they pressed on. The current in the channel was flowing strongly here and they were content for a while to drift with it. The rings worn by each member of the party allowed them to fire any of the party's weapons. Two armed lookouts were posted at all times and, as a further precaution against unwelcome visitors climbing aboard, they rigged a temporary bulwark around the center section.

They came upon another island dwelling, but when they landed at the small pier they found it was empty. It was not marked on their charts, but nor were many such. It had plainly been a human habitation, and Anne pointed out that a family seemed to have lived there: there were children's clothes and toys. But the vegetable and small animal life that had established itself in the house indicated it had been empty for some time. Re-embarking, Vaemar noticed a small boat moored on the other side of the pier. The unsinkable materials of its hull kept it afloat, but it was full of water. There had been rainstorms some weeks before, and the variety of life swarming and splashing in the hull showed it had been water-logged for a long time. It had a sophisticated and, on present-day Wunderland, still expensive, neuronetic lattice for a brain, but that was still in place.

"I don't like that," said Hugo. "Whoever left here should have taken the boat with them."

"Perhaps they had another," said Toby.

Swirl-Stripes took out two heavy kzin ex-military beam rifles, University property which, strictly speaking, were not allowed to private kzinti on Wunderland. He slung one and passed the other to Vaemar.

"We'll use the motor now," said Vaemar. "I think we ought to have steerage way." Many of the channels were wider here and silence was less important for observation than it had been when they were slipping between narrow banks. In any case, the deserted dwelling was not entirely reassuring and steerage-way, they tacitly agreed, could be a useful thing to have.

GPS satellites provided them with a moving map that had at least reasonable accuracy, though they soon learnt to treat it with caution. A translucent panel and a camera below the water-line in the bow showed an endless parade of living things. Cruising on minimum power they had some groundings on soft mud, but these were no more than a nuisance. There were things like horseshoe crabs and things like giant centipedes, mud-colored things and things whose bright colors shouted poison. The life they stirred up getting the canoe off reminded the students that the mud-banks were a whole new ecosystem waiting to be explored.

After about three more hours they came to the fish-processing business Marshy had spoken of. The buildings—high, strong-walled and windowless in the lower part—and the boat tied up there were kzin-sized, not human. There were a multi-purpose radar dish, fences, and a security watch-tower. Kzinti living away from human supervision were allowed only light and basic hunting weapons, but the place had a secure look about it. There was a sign-board giving the name of the business in both kzin and almost correct human scripts—still a slightly odd sight on Wunderland, but much less so than it would have been ten years previously. There was also a large air-car, disarmed but plainly ex-military, parked on a landing-pad. Vaemar and Swirl-Stripes called a greeting in the Heroes' Tongue as they approached. There was no answer.

"This," said Hugo, "is getting monotonous."

Vaemar steered the canoe away from the island and into a sheltered creek out of sight of it. They erected bulwarks and metal mesh-screens covering the benches and steering position. They rechecked and cocked their weapons, and approached the island again. Motion detectors and infrared sensors keyed to pick up the body-heat of large life-forms told them nothing in the jumble of land and water and what was virtually a broth of small quick lives. Scanning and filming, they cautiously circumnavigated the island, and a couple of surrounding ones. Apart from the absence of the kzinti, nothing seemed out of the ordinary. There were a couple of big crocodilians working the channels, but even if they were a threat to adult kzinti, the electronic and physical defenses of the place should have kept them out with ease—it was what they were designed for. There were a cloud of flying creatures round the fish-drying sheds and the smell from these was almost overpowering.

Weapons ready, they landed. Movement near the

water. The snout of an automatic gun—illegal for outdwelling kzinti—was tracking them. In the instant it took Vaemar to identify it he knew that, had it been set to fire, they would have been already dead. On examination it had no ammunition. Fences carried lethal electric current but the gate was open. The main door was not merely unlocked but part open as well. Vaemar's fur bristled. This was an unheard-of thing among kzinti, save when a great one wished to show either his overwhelming security or to be extravagantly hospitable.

The racks of drying fish, some glowing brightly in decay, had attracted a multitude of small creatures apart from those circling and fighting in the air. The operating log of the processing machinery which converted the fish into highly flavored bricks much enjoyed by some kzinti, both by themselves and as a relish to ice creams and other foods, showed it had not been in use for several days.

"I estimate this operation was run by about five kzintosh," said Vaemar, when they assembled in the main building. "In addition there were kzinrretti and kittens."

That would not have been the case before Liberation. High kzin nobles had extensive harems. Kzin kittens were usually born as male and female twins and the daughters were a valuable commodity for their fathers, negotiable instruments and presents to both superiors and clients. A mid-ranking officer of partial Name might have a clawful of females, including some from the harems of any rivals he might have quarreled with successfully. The military hierarchy had its own system of allocations. What one human student had called "honored upper lower middle-class" kzinti—NCOs of partial name, for example—might be allotted a single female each. Naturally these tended to be both less attractive and less fertile than those the nobles kept for themselves. But since the Liberation things had become very different—so many high kzin nobles, officers, and indeed kzin males in general, were dead that there were enough kzinrretti for even kzinti in trade, like these fishermen. The human government had encouraged this change in customs for several reasons, partly on the theory that females and offspring of their own would tend to give more kzintosh a vested interest in stability. Anyway, the small factory and the attached dwellings were empty.

"We stay together and search," said Vaemar. As Marshy had told him that some of the swamp folk were inclined to blame the human disappearances on the kzinti, it had occurred to him that humans, Exterminationists or vigilantes, might very well be responsible for the disappearance of the kzinti. But humans could not fight kzinti without weapons, and there was no obvious sign that weapons had been used here—no sign of blast damage or burning from beams or plasma-guns. No lingering molecules of poison gas were detected, though their safety equipment included a highly sensitive analyser. The empty gun was a puzzle. Had it been put there by the kzinti as a bluff, or had it in fact fired off its charges in battle?

Within the main building there was a computer, a standard kzinti Naval model with an interface to human hardware, but it was dead. In fact, upon examination it seemed to have been deliberately wrecked by someone who knew what they were doing. Otherwise there was nothing like gross damage or blast craters to suggest a violent attack. Here and there in walls and in the windows of some outbuildings were small round holes, but they did not look like the effect of any modern weapon. He took the computer's memory-bricks. They also found a telephone, but no relevant calls were logged on it. There was a kind of odd, unhealthy peace about the place. He even wondered if the whole group had simply abandoned the enterprise and moved somewhere else. But why had they left their possessions, including the costly car?

Swirl-Stripes called him. There, in a small puddle, were the bones of a very young kitten. Proof of violence and killing at last. But with no other information. The bones had been covered with small carrion-eating animals which had entirely destroyed the soft tissue and had made considerable headway in destroying the bones themselves. He put them, with a sample of the muddy ground they lay on, in a collecting-box for police attention when they returned to Munchen. Only a small box was needed. The humans seemed saddened by the fact the kitten had still been clutching a toy prey in its hand—both Rosalind and Hugo had remarked on it.

Here and there amid the marks of various swamp-creatures there were a few old kzin tracks discernible to a trained hunter but no other recognizable tracks or footprints to give a clue what had happened. Toby suggested flying the air-car to Munchen at once, but there was no key for it, and kzin cars were generally left in such a state as to very definitely not be vulnerable to theft or tampering.

"There appears to be ssome dangerrous enemy," said Vaemar. His kzin accent was a little stronger now.

"Swirl-sstripes and I know our duty is to hunt down this killerr of kzinti and kittens. But as Marshy hass reminded me, I am in charge of the human lives here as well. Do the humans wish to rreturn to summon help?"

"I cannot speak for the others," said Hugo, "but I do not think I should care to have it said of me that I refused to follow where a Hero led because I was afraid." The other humans made a nodding gesture of agreement.

"This killer of kzinti might be human," said Vaemar.

"That is another reason we should be there," said Hugo.

"Or send a message?"

"Let us wait and see what message we have to send."

Rosalind appeared poised to say something, but looked at the grim, set faces of the others and evidently decided that any comment would be redundant.

"Let us move!" said Swirl-Stripes. "Every moment we stand speaking our prey may be escaping us."

They headed deeper into the swamp. They saw no more dwellings. There were countless wild creatures, large and small, but none that presented an obvious threat to them in their strong-hulled boat, armed and alert. They saw no kzinti or humans.

The swamp changed. Channels grew wider and deeper, but the life about them grew less abundant. They were approaching the dead heart of Grossgeister. When the kzinti had concentrated the heat-induction ray on it, most of the vegetation had been too wet to burn quickly, but the waters had boiled, including the liquid that made up a good part of the internal volumes of the typical Wunderland swamp-plants. Tides and currents since then had washed away most of the masses of dead animal and vegetable organic matter, and some life-forms had begun to recolonize the area.

With the channels generally wider here, the water was clear and empty down to a pale sandy bottom, though processions of large fish could now at times be seen swimming in from other areas. The stands of vegetation on the islands were mostly dead and crumbling. Among the grey of the dead plants on the islands some new red shoots were now beginning to appear. Crocodilians and other large animal life-forms which had scrambled or somehow flung themselves ashore in an attempt to avoid the boiling water were skeletons lining the island banks. There were human skeletons among them, too. It had, after all, been humans the kzinti had been after. Once they saw sunlight gleaming on metal among the bones: a pair of dolphin hands. Apart from the sound of the waters this part of the swamp was still very silent. The flying things stayed where there was more food.

They picked an island with relatively few bones and dead vegetation for their camp that night, where a sparse fringe of reeds was beginning to grow back in the clear shallows, and had their electronic defenses set up well before Alpha Centauri A began to sink. The boat was too stupid to defend itself but they hoped that would not be necessary. It was agreed one kzin and one human would be on watch at all times. Vaemar telephoned Marshy, the abbot and the University giving the basic details of the disappearances and saying that they required no assistance as yet. The long war had made the humans of Wunderland, as well as the kzinti, a fiercely independent and self-reliant culture. They would get no help unless they asked for it. Vaemar tried to open the bricks he had taken, using the boat's computer, but they made no sense and appeared to have been deliberately scrambled.

As the night deepened, so did the sadness of the scene: apart from a few swimmers there were almost none of the spectacular bioluminesent displays of the outer marches. Instead of the swamp growing noisier as it took up the business of the night, it grew even quieter.

"It feels as if Zeitungers were around," said Anne. Zeitungers were shuffling, gluttonous vermin related to Advokats, carrion-eaters who outdid Advokats by possessing a limited psi ability to broadcast mental depression and nausea. Humans and kzinti alike hated them even worse than they did Advokats or the fluffy white, blue-eyed, poisoned-fanged Beam's Beasts. They were, however, not known as swamp creatures.

"I don't think they are necessary here," said Vaemar. "This scenery is sad."

"You feel it too?"

"Of course." Then he added: "You were sorry when we found the dead kitten."

"Of course. We all were."

"I thought so. Our kinds are still killing one another in space, you know, and on other planets."

"But not here."

"So it seems. I hope you are right . . . You do not hate kzinti?"

"The abbot says we should be grateful to you for a number of things. He said it was thanks to you that we rediscovered the whole moral universe that we had been in danger of forgetting—courage, sacrifice, faith . . . And you know I do not hate you, Vaemar."

"Fear us, then?"

"Why do you ask? Are you trying to understand us?"

"Yes. I think I make some progress."

"*Should* I help you understand humans? I think of a human politician I once heard of: 'He worked tirelessly to promote greater understanding between nations that understood one another only too well already.'"

"That seems to me a very human thought . . . And you can think a little like one of my kind . . . But I am your fellow-student accepted into the university. I am also your superior officer in the ROTC. Further, I am younger than you. Is it not seemly to instruct the young?"

She might laugh, but she did not smile at him. Not smiling at kzinti, not showing the teeth in the kzin challenge for battle, was still, ten years after Liberation, a conditioned reflex for humans.

"I was ten years old at Liberation. By then my family farmed in the high country northeast of the Hohe Kalkstein. We seldom saw kzinti. I, for myself, as a child, did not really understand hate. Kzinti were above and beyond my hate. But fear, yes, and yes. A lucky human family was one with but a few dead to mourn. My family were unusually lucky, I know now, or rather my grandfather was foresighted to get us away. Near the towns, even in Gerning, things were very different. We paid our taxes, and the local Herrenman had the task of representing us to the kzinti. We had strong rules for survival by then. I knew no different life.

"One thing I remember. Kzin words were starting to

creep into our language from the slaves' patois. Once, my parents caught me using some new kzin word, or a word derived from the Heroes' Tongue. My mother wanted to punish me, but my father said: 'No, she must learn it. That is the future.' That day I ran away. I was in the forest for a day and a night until a search party found me. My father's words were echoing in my mind. 'That is the future.'"

"There are plenty of human words invading the kzin tongues on Wunderland now," Vaemar said.

"Our little farm was not much," Anne went on. "There were few of our old possessions left—a few pieces of china and crystal from old Neue Dresden, a few old paper books. Things like that. An old woman taught us children in a one-roomed school, and her work was increasing, for there was no way to repair our computers. Our robots had begun to fail and some of the farms near us were ploughing again with animals. Our culture was little enough, but I knew fear then, for somehow I was old enough to understand what my father meant. To see it all going, soon all gone. All, all, all . . ."

"I see," said Vaemar. "Like the Jotok. Like most conquered races . . . I would have said like all conquered races, if I had not begun studying Earth history, and . . . if I had not certain thoughts . . ."

"I know little of the Jotok but the name. A name that was an omen of fear for some among us, as I discovered later when I began higher studies. An indication of what we would become. Once your allies?"

"Once our . . . employers. How could a culture like ours have developed a science of spaceflight? When we reached the stars we found we were the only culture of warrior carnivores that leapt and hunted there. We did find a few other sapient carnivores, some of which had got up to knives and spears, and they gave us good sport on their own planets. We found alien spacefaring races, but they were scientific and civilized and cooperative, and when we met them and enslaved them as the Fanged God had decreed they could hardly put up the ghost of a fight . . . All but the last one, of course . . .

"The Jotok had hired us as mercenaries and security guards for their trade empire . . . I do not know how many powers of eights of years ago. On the worlds of the Kzin Patriarchy they are our slaves and prey, and hardly a trace of their civilization remains except in our naval equipment— and words like 'navy,' I suppose. You must have noticed that for cats our spacefaring has an incongruously nautical vocabulary: we had little to do with the sea on our Homeworld. I guess the Jotok began as seafarers. They live in water when they are young. There is a legend that a few of them escaped at the end of that war when our long-sires turned on them and removed their flesh, a legend of a Free Jotok Fleet, waiting and vengeful somewhere in space, but I do not believe it feasible. Too much time has passed and we have seen no sign of it. It may be one of those . . . urrr . . . necessary legends, like the old prophecies of Kdarka-Riit. You know of them?"

"A little."

"There is one he composed when relaxing replete with the rest of his pride after a successful *kz'eerkti*-hunt on Homeworld." Vaemar quoted:

"Oh, Race of Heroes, have a care.

> *Tree-swinging monkeys are not all*
> *That wait. Pride may precede a fall*
> *When under distant stars you fare.*
>
> *"Your claws pull down each alien race.*
> *Each is your prey, and our God's laws*
> *Deliver them into your jaws.*
> *So thought the Jotok in your place . . .*

"But of course you know how hard it is to preserve the nuances when translating rhyme into rhyme . . . some think there is a hint of an emotion in that stanza which we have no word for, but which has a human name . . ." His voice trailed off. The priesthood, then as now, had not liked prophets outside their own prides, and a prophet whose Full Name had included any suffix other than Riit would not have got away with it. Unspoken, another verse from the sage's ancient chant, recently resurrected by a few Conservors of the Ancestral Past, ran through his mind:

> *Death then for many. For some few*
> *Another, stranger fate will be:*
> *Tree-swingers who have left the tree*
> *Will turn kzinti into something new . . .*

"Are you happy, Vaemar?" Anne asked suddenly. "I mean, with your life?"

"Happy? I don't perhaps quite understand . . . to a kzin warrior of the old school the question would hardly make sense. Heroism and Conquest are—were—what were meant to matter, not happiness. Except, perhaps, a noble death in battle, a worship-shrine where your descendents might honor your bones, honor and esteem during your life as well, your Heroism recognized and wide estates and hunting territories and of course a large harem siezed while you lived . . . I had a privileged background originally, you know, which would have made things easier in some ways if not in others. I suppose happiness entered into it incidentally. I must reflect on that."

"Does the question make sense to you?"

"I'm not sure . . . I have enjoyed much of my life so far . . . hunting with Honored Step-Sire Raargh Hero, the mental achievements of my studies . . . collecting a few ears. Many things—university, our projects in the caves, smelling the hunter's winds, even writing for the review, even watching the swamp-creatures here as a kind of student of life, not just as a hunter after sport or prey . . . and now, we have a real Hunt again to give it meaning. Yes, Anne, I have much to be content with in my life."

"Even the university, then?"

"I am told," Vaemar said, stretching to his nearly three-meter length and ripping a thick dead branch effortlessly to pieces in a muscle-rippling gesture that might recall a house-cat idly sharpening its claws, "that some . . . outsiders . . . at University, in fraternities especially, members of ethnic minorities who were reputed to have collaborated unduly during the Occupation, for example, have had to put up with unfair bullying and hazing. That never happened to me. Certainly my family could not be called collaborators. But perhaps it was because of my early victories for the Chess Club."

Anne laughed, "You say that so innocently! . . . I actually think you mean it!" Her voice became more serious again: "But you speak of the real Hunt we are engaged on. What animal is big enough and fierce enough to predate upon kzinti? Dragons?"

"Humans, perhaps."

"But humans have disappeared too."

"What do the other humans think?"

Vaemar settled himself onto the sand, forelimbs before him, head raised, hindlimbs tucked ready to spring, his tail curled out of the way but ready to give that spring extra power. He looked like a sphinx. Anne sat before him, almost between his great forepaws, arms wrapped around her knees.

"Hugo and Toby, like you and Swirl-Stripes if I may say so, like the adventure of the hunt," she said. "Simian curiosity, feline inquisitiveness . . . they're not so far apart. And hunters' pride. Rosalind never says much."

"No. But in some ways she is a little like a cat, that one. Or she has spent time with cats."

"She wanted to share this watch with you. But so did I."

"Indeed? Am I to be flattered by such attentions?"

"I asked her why, and she changed the subject."

"There will be other watches."

"So I said. She has always been nice to me. I think she is lonely. I gather she grew up in Munchen, without family." *Delicate ground to tread on when talking to a kzin,* thought Vaemar. *But there are many kzinti on Wunderland without families also.* Thoughts ran on: *Zroght-Guard Captain carrying me out of the Keep, pausing at the bloody litter of my Honored Sire's bones*

*so I might remember. Old Traat-Admiral comforting me
with a few grooming licks and a spray of his urine . . .*

"Perhaps she saw more of kzinti than I did during
the Occupation," Anne went on. "They say the human
city-bred and farm-bred are different on this planet
now."

"She does not move like you," said Vaemar. "And there
is something strange about her hair."

"I hadn't noticed."

"I have to watch humans."

"None of them have any theories about a predator
here. Obviously," she laughed again, "it can hardly be an
alien from space!"

"It is an ecological mystery," said Vaemar seriously.
"From what we saw at the island I have a puzzling feeling—
it is not more than a feeling—that our prey . . . our enemy
. . . behaves like both a sapient and a nonsapient. It does not
seem to use weapons, yet it disables computers."

"And it appears to attack kzinti," said Anne. "When
there is so much food in the swamp, is it sapient behavior
to select the most fearsome warriors in the Galaxy for
prey?"

"As you have reminded me," said Vaemar, "it also
appears to hunt humans. You speak of the most fearsome
warriors. But you are the species that have defeated the
kzinti on this planet."

"I am not sure what my point is," she replied, "but,
whatever it is, does that not tend to prove it further? If
there is indeed something predating upon kzinti and
humans, it is either very stupid, or very, very dangerous. If
it was stupid, it would be dead."

"What predators hunt lions and tigers on Earth?"

"Apart from humans in the past, nothing. There are biological laws. A tiger-predator—a dragon, perhaps—would have to be too big to survive."

"And the same here. Unless such a predator lived in water."

"And there is plenty of water here. Or unless it was very cunning and well armed."

"Or unless it was small. Microbes and bacteria kill as well."

"Generally not quickly," said Anne.

"No, but my Honored Step-Sire Raargh Hero told me once of campaigning in the great caves. A Hero who had been curled asleep with his head on the ground awoke mad and died screaming. They found insectile predators had crawled into his ears and eaten his brain from within. And there are plants on Kzin that herbivores have learnt never to touch. Should they eat them the seeds grow claws in their bellies and devour . . ."

"There were great reptiles on Earth once—dinosaurs," said Anne. "And similar creatures on Kzin. They were very successful and lasted many millions of years. And we have found big fossils here. As well as the giant birds still living in Southland, and big things in the Equatoria forests. We don't know them all."

"That is a long way away."

"Big water-dwellers too . . . Could there be something like a Plesiosaur with a long flexible neck and a mouth full of teeth, lifting silently out of the water and descending silently to seize us from above." She looked up and gave a slightly nervous laugh. "I'd better stop before I scare myself. This isn't the best time or place to imagine monsters. It's good to see fangs gleam in the dark and know that they are yours, Vaemar."

"Yes. There have been . . . there are . . . big creatures and water tends to support bigger ones," said Vaemar. "But I don't see any dinosaurs or thunderbirds around at the moment. Nor do any satellites see them . . . But I see something there!"

Something large and dark was moving up the channel. Vaemar and Anne whipped out infrared glasses, their weapons cocked. But the swimmer, somewhat reptilian, showed the small jaws and teeth of a herbivore. It turned into the thin fringe of vegetation and began to browse. Vaemar stretched again.

"What was that!" He was instantly poised for battle, ears flat, claws extended, jaws gaping, strakkaker poised. Anne dropped into a crouch over her weapon, her own ears—the mobile ears of the Wunderland aristocracy—swivelling towards the sound. There were long moments of silence.

"I heard something," she said. "Nothing clear. Just swamp-noises, perhaps . . . but . . ."

"It sounded like the cry of a kzin . . . a long way away."

"My ears aren't as good as yours."

"I barely heard it." Vaemar bent to the recorder, and played it back, amplified. He filtered out the water-noises.

"Yes, I hear it now."

"One burst of cries, and then silence. Nothing more," said Vaemar.

"Are you sure it was a kzin?"

"No. I am not even sure it was something imitating a

kzin. There are many voices in this swamp . . . but . . . it reminded me of a kzinrret . . .

"I shouldn't be surprised if there wasn't some sort of rational explanation for all this," he added. "But that doesn't mean it's necessarily a comfortable one."

The browsing creature vanished suddenly. The two took a few steps beyond the defenses towards the dark, star-spangled water. It exploded at them. The crocodilian was medium-sized but more than twice the length of the human. More than two meters clear of the ground in its leap, its movement was too fast for a human eye to follow. The boat shrieked a belated and futile warning. The fence flared. Anne was knocked sprawling, but before the jaws could seize her, Vaemar had leapt screaming, fangs, claws and *w'tsai* flashing. He did not need the beam rifle. Two slashes severed the monster's head, though one set of its claws ripped his shoulder. Not deeply, but enough to make admirable scars. *How fragile they are!* he thought, as he helped Anne to her feet and helped her dress his wounds and her own cuts with the small medical kits they all carried. *How did they ever win?* It was not a new question. *Foolish. We should have stayed within the defenses and not allowed the quiet of the night to lull us. I am glad Honored Step-Sire Raargh was not with us to see that.*

Anne was relieved by Hugo, and at midnight he and Vaemar handed over to Toby and Swirl-Stripes. Cameras and monitors recorded the sparse life that showed itself in the vicinity of the island, but by the time they had break-fasted, with Alpha Centauri A standing well above the horizon, they had noted nothing significant. Rosalind collected some small transparent creatures which had gathered in the muddy depressions of the kzinti's footprints at the water's edge. Vaemar removed the crocodilian's jaws for a trophy and bagged them to contain the smell. They broke camp and pressed on. Rosalind raised the matter of returning again, but the other humans outvoted her without the kzinti needing to express any further opinion.

They saw nothing but the unchanging, ever-changing, swamp for several hours, largely clear water and islands where a little new life struggled to establish itself. The channels widened again. With the wider water came gentle, rippling wind and the boat hoisted a small sail. They moved quietly on. Virtually at water-level, they could not see far. Then a great curved shape loomed over the near horizon.

Half-submerged, water lapping at its ports and open air-locks, many of the blisters of its weapons-turrets empty and broken, a couple of massive electro-magnetic rail-guns shattered and pointing uselessly at the sky, the great wedge-and-ovoid of the kzin cruiser was still an impressive sight.

Life seemed to be returning a little quicker here, perhaps because organic compounds in the wreck provided a food-source, or perhaps because its many compartments provided a nursery for juveniles.

It was so obviously a dead and broken thing, however, that there was little air of menace about it. This, Vaemar and the others knew, might be deceptive. With derelict kzin warships all over the planet, and huge dumps of them being slowly demolished at Munchen and elsewhere, this one had not been worth attention and had been left to the swamp since its crew abandoned it. There was no reason to suppose some of its various engine-systems were not still fuelled and much of its war-load not still aboard.

Keeping their distance, they cruised around the wreck.

"No sign of life," said Hugo.

"Yet it will be full of hiding places," said Swirl-Stripes, "for both predators and prey. We should approach silently."

They cast off the outriggers—convenient for cargo but unnecessary for stability—and secured them on a sandbar. As they approached the hulk they stopped the engine and took to their paddles again. The humans stood to their guns at bows and stern as the kzinti's muscles drove the boat almost silently through the water.

"*Skraii rar kzintoshi!*" The words had been shrieked under many stars, but as the great hull loomed over them, only Swirl-Stripes and Anne, sitting immediately by Vaemar, heard him utter the ancient battle-cry: "I lead my Heroes!"

They passed through the gaping airlock into the hulk. Sunlight through the airlock and from holes below the surface refracted upwards through the rippling water, casting dancing patterns of light in the cavernous gloom. There was much more life here: molds, insectoids, many things that found the great wreck a shelter and nursery. In the bars of green-gold sunlight that shot the water below them tiny minnowlike creatures could be seen swarming. It would be an excellent place for crocodilians to be lurking, but they saw none.

Vaemar, remembering his battle with Raargh Hero and their human allies against the Mad Ones in the caves six years before, paid particular attention to what was, or might be, above them. The minnows obviously did not matter. His eyes were capable of seeing in the dimmest light, and were reinforced by other senses and sensors, but in the chaos of wires, ducting, unidentifiable wreckage and swarming small life neither his eyes nor the artificial biological sensors made out major life-forms. The water lapping through the whole chamber made it impossible to tell anything meaningful from motion detectors. The ceaseless lapping also provided a background noise, enough to defeat kzin ears that could normally pick up the heartbeats of a hiding prey or enemy. Nor were the kzinti's noses much use in the overwhelming smell of dampness and decay. Here and there as they proceeded further into the dimness a few lamps still glowed above and below the water on dials and meters but they revealed little. Vaemar called up the plans for this class of cruiser on the boat's internet terminal, but they lacked detail. Like all space-ships, but especially large kzin warships, it was intricately subdivided. His Ziirgah sense—evolved to aid a kzin on a solitary hunt—detected principally the keyed-up nervous tension of Swirl-Stripes and the humans around him. That was not quite all, but he was unable yet to identify the added factor.

They passed through a door, and paddled up a narrow companionway. It was much darker here and two of the humans had to put down their guns and operate lights. Had the ship been human-sized the boat would have been unlikely to get into such a passage and as it was the lack of room on either side would have brought on claustrophobia for any sufferer.

They passed one open door leading into a room whose

ruined finery suggested it had once been a senior officer's
cabin. There were trophies fixed on the bulkhead above
the lapping water, rotted in the living damp into bare
black skulls that startled them until they realized their
age, and the remains of a ceremonial *hsakh* cloak that
would never be worn again. There were kzin bones on the
bunk, laid out to suggest someone had taken a moment to
arrange the occupant's body with decorum before the
survivors abandoned the ship. He must have been a
respected officer.

As they went on something dark and swift flashed
ahead of them and out of sight. It was hard to tell its size,
but it was not small, and its movements did not seem to be
like either man or kzin. At the end of the companionway
was another door, open but with a sill at its foot that
prevented further passage in the boat.

"Toby will remain and guard the boat," said Vaemar.
"The rest of us will proceed on foot. It will give us more
hands for the guns and lights. Rosalind, you will bring up
the rear." Heroes should go first, and Rosalind struck him
as the least clumsy human.

Wading through opaque water that came at least knee-
deep on the kzinti and considerably higher on the humans
was not an appealing prospect. There was, however, a
vertical ladder that led upwards to what would obviously be
drier areas. Rosalind lagged behind, doing something with
the flasks she carried on her belt. Collecting samples of the
water, he supposed, though he could not see the point of
such activity. He growled and gestured. This was no time
for undirected monkey inquisitiveness. He gathered them
around the foot of the ladder, guns still facing outwards.

In an emergency a kzin could have scrabbled up it in a single leap. That was not necessary now. They went cautiously. Vaemar, remembering again the caves, making a mental map of the way they had come. As he did so, a smell hit him that knocked away all the conflicting smells of wetness, mold, humans and plant and animal life. It was a smell of pure death. The humans had never heard Vaemar's battle-snarl before. He went up the last rungs in one bound, Swirl-Stripes and the humans crowding behind.

They swung the beams of their lights round the chamber. The humans cried out. Vaemar and Swirl-Stripes roared.

Hanging upside down from the deckhead were the flayed corpses of several kzinti. Though the skin and several of the limbs were missing and the bodies otherwise damaged, it was plain from the sizes that they were both males and females. There were five males. There had been five males at the little fish-processing business.

Guns ready, instinctively moving again into a circle with their eyes and weapons facing outwards, they approached the bodies.

They had been dead for days, but not many days. Vaemar exerted his self-control. A kzintosh warrior must not lose judgement in the presence of death, however much the dishonoring of Heroes' bodies might provoke it: rage and blood-lust should be channelled into the worthwhile and efficient vengeful slaughter of enemies. Such, he thought at that moment, had been the teaching of his Honored Sire Chuut-Riit, whose military writings he had studied, and the lessons drilled into him by Honored Step-Sire Raargh Hero.

There did not seem to be marks of beam-weapons,

blades, or projectile weapons on what was left of the bodies, though the heads were much damaged. He heard a high-pitched whirring sound behind him, and spun round, claws extended to strike, but it was only Rosalind, with a high-speed camera, filming the scene. For a moment he was doubly infuriated by this insult to the dead and raised his claws to strike it away. Then reason returned: a film of the scene would be useful as evidence. She was behaving correctly. Still, orders should be formerly given.

"This is now a military situation," he said. "As holder of the senior ROTC commission, I am taking formal command. Hugo, you are second in seniority and will be second-in-command. We press on. Any questions?"

There were none. He was the youngest present but kzin matured faster than humans. It would have been a bold or foolish human on Wunderland who questioned a kzin standing as Vaemar stood, claws extended, beam rifle cocked, ears flat in his head and his jaws salivating and wide in a killing gape.

Something moved in the darkness overhead. It was hard to tell its size or shape, but it was fast, and it disappeared before they could focus on it. A quick shot after it produced no result but a fall of sparks where some still-live power-line ruptured.

Lights played over the deckhead showed a few small ventilation ducts. But humans had used the ducting of kzin ships in the war, hiding in and crawling along passages where the great felinoids could not follow. Nerve-gas was the prescribed kzin treatment for the problem . . .

"Humans would have used weapons," said Anne cautiously. Vaemar growled in his throat but said nothing.

Whoever or whatever had hung up those kzin bodies like animals, it was plainly the work of intelligence, not any predatory swamp creature.

"These appear to have been eaten," said Anne. "Humans never eat kzinti."

"Never?"

"Well, hardly ever."

Then something pale caught Anne's eye. She pointed. Vaemar recognized the bones at once as a pair of human femurs, still joined to a human pelvis. Hugo was cursing softly and incessantly, jerking the snout of his weapon about, aiming futilely at one dark, silent opening after another. Anne's chest was heaving as she took deep, deliberate breaths.

Humans eat other humans? Vaemar had heard of it happening in famines during the Occupation, though it was rare. That kzinti could eat other kzinti, he of all the kzintosh on Wunderland, last son of Chuut-Riit, had the direst reason to know. But that was a matter of hunger-frenzy when, in adolescents, mind and control went together. This was systematic butchery.

From the compartment below them the boat suddenly screamed. Vaemar and Swirl-Stripes leapt back down the steps. Their beam rifles fired, but for an instant only. Their reflected beams hit the water, flashing it into live steam. Had they depressed the triggers an instant longer, the kzinti would have broiled themselves. There were two explosions, ear-crackingly loud in that confined space. Something hit Vaemar and knocked him backwards across the door-sill. Swirl-Stripes screamed and charged through the water. Then whatever it was had gone.

Vaemar rose cautiously. The rifle had been torn from his claws and he was, he knew, lucky not to have lost digits as well. Its bulk had saved him, but its charge-regulator was smashed. Something had hit it hard. One rifle was useless.

Not only one rifle. Hugo's strakkaker was in two pieces, and one of his arms hung broken. Anne strapped the arm with an expanding mini-splint and applied a pain-killer, but he was plainly out of any fighting for a time.

The others covering him, Vaemar examined the companionway. The bulkhead some distance behind him gleamed raw with the impact of a new missile. The missile itself was still sizzling in the water. It was nothing but a blob of metal, but could have been—must have been—a bullet from a real "rifle"—a hunting rifle such as both kzin and humans used both to practice marksmanship and to kill game without the disintegrating effects of a strakkaker or a military beamer.

Toby was gone and the boat's brain and computer terminal had been smashed. The brain, Vaemar thought, was not much loss, but the computer would have been valuable. Other gear was gone too, including food, spare ammunition, the telephones and the motion-detector.

"It wasn't Toby," said Hugo. "I'm sure it wasn't Toby." He looked up at Vaemar with drugged, still pain-filled eyes. "Upon my name as my word, I pledge, it was not him. Whatever it was has taken him . . ."

"We go on," said Vaemar. No human, whatever their knowledge of kzin body-language, would have argued with him. They returned to the chamber of dead kzinti.

There were open doors leading to dark companionways.

Beams of light down them showed nothing. There were also closed doors. Molds and plants growing on them suggested they had been shut a long time, presumably ever since the ship had come down.

Hugo pointed to one: around the handle it was clean and shining. A panel of colored lights beside the handle showed its lock was alive.

"Open it!" ordered Vaemar. There was a chance the lock was not actually engaged.

Anne pulled on the handle, uselessly. Swirl-Stripes tried, also without result. Without the code for the lock neither human nor kzin muscular strength was going to move it.

They had the beam-guns, but Vaemar thought their lasers would have no effect on the door before their charges burnt out. It would be stupid to fire them at the wall. Partly to give himself time to think, but largely because decorum demanded it, he ordered the kzinti's bodies cut down and their remaining limbs suitably composed. Briefly but pointedly, he urinated on them, offering them the mark of one who bore the blood of Chuut-Riit and the Patriarch. No need to carry their mutilated bodies into the light of day. They would lie with the bones of other kzinti here, in this brave ship. It was not too bad a spot. Or it would not be once they had been most comprehensively avenged, of course. He remembered a stanza from one of his favorite human poems, "The Ballad of the White Horse":

> *Lift not my head from bloody ground,*
> *Bear not my body home;*

For all the Earth is Roman Earth,
And I shall die in Rome.

They had been hung on meat-hooks such as were common in any kzinti dead-meat locker. There were other hooks with strips of dried stuff hanging from them. Rosalind collected some samples for further analysis. He wondered whether to leave a couple to watch the door while he led the rest on to investigate the other companionways. No, all military training spoke against dividing a small force, especially in the face of an enemy whose deadliness was now plain.

Brief, cautious forays into the other companionways revealed nothing. His companions might be his soldiers, but they were also his fellow-students, and he had a consciousness of his responsibility to them along with his lust for vengeance and battle. To go, leaving some unknown behind that locked door, seemed a bad idea, as well as violating all kzin instincts and precepts of honor. To sit tight and wait upon the enemy to make the next move seemed a bad idea also. Anyway, it was a good idea to eat, but not in the presence of these dead. Off one of the companionways was another room, empty and relatively dry. They retired there and ate and drank. The small blocks of compressed food from their belt-pouches did not need preparation and in a situation like this humans and kzinti could eat together. It was, however, a very unsatisfying meal. It provided energy but would hardly assuage kzin hunger-pangs much. They should, Vaemar thought, have made sure they had a proper meal earlier. He filed the thought away for next time.

What would Honored Sire do? Vaemar wondered. *Or Honored Step-Sire?* He also thought of the cleverest humans he knew—Colonel Cumpston, or Professor Rykermann, or Brigadier Guthlac, or the abbot. Even the manrretti—Dimity with whom he talked long and who beat him at chess, or Leonie, whose adventures in the caves with Honored Step-Sire Raargh when he received his rank and Name he had often been told about. This compartment seemed at first a good place to wait. It had but a single door. But it would be dark eventually. That meant less to the night-eyed kzinti than to the humans, but it would still be a disadvantage in dealing with the unknown. And the single door meant there was no line of retreat.

Vaemar's ears twitched violently at a sound. Motioning the others to stillness, he moved silently to the door and into the companionway, in a stalking crouch with his stomach-fur brushing the deck. He leapt. There was the sound of a hissing, spitting struggle. The others burst out behind him, weapons levelled. Vaemar was holding a kzinrret.

"Be still!" he hissed at her in the Female Tongue.

"Be still yourself!" she replied, and not in the Female Tongue, but in the Heroes' Tongue, in the tense of equals. "Release me! I am not an enemy."

Vaemar was nonplussed. The Heroes' Tongue, with its complex tenses and extensive technical vocabulary, was far beyond females' comprehension. And what female, even if she had the intellectual equipment to do so, would speak to any kzintosh in the tense of equals?

His surprise made him forget for a moment their whole position. Then he saw how thin she was, how tensely she held her body. Her great eyes were violent-edged and wild. But one kzinrret, alone, could hardly be a threat. He released his hold on her. She stood poised to run or fight. He gestured to Swirl-Stripes and the humans. "These . . . companions," he said. He gestured more explicitly: "Humans," he said, "you know?"

"Yes," she said. "I know."

He saw that she was older than he, but not old. She would have been at the end of adolescence when the human hyperdrive armada swept in to reconquer Wunderland a decade before. She would have spent her formative years with humans as her slaves and prey. If she was the daughter of a noble—and most kzinti had been the sons and daughters of nobles—she might have been cared for by a gloved, padded and otherwise protected human nurse. But her vestigial female mind was unlikely to see humans today as sapients and companions. He would have to be careful.

"My name is Karan," she said. She looked at him as if the information might convey something significant.

A quite common female name. What was not common was for a female to enunciate it in a clear and grammatical sentence. There were things about her eyes, her whole posture, that were not normal. Then her eyes narrowed. Vaemar knew that she was seeing his ear-tattoos. A kzinrret of upper-normal female intelligence might dimly know them as betokening Quality.

"Riit!" she said. Swirl-Stripes, he saw, jumped a little at the word. Even the humans, whose childhood had been under the kzin Occupation, knew it. He picked up the glandular responses. But there was no awe or reverence in her voice. She spoke, and all his senses reinforced this impression, like one recognizing and challenging an enemy.

"My name is Vaemar," he said. It was "name," not "Name." Some odd scrap of memory recalled to him a sentence from a literature course: "His sensitive ear detected the capitals." Then he added: "I am a student." He realized as he said it that such a word could have no meaning to her. Or could it? She had recognized the ear-tattoos.

"I also hunt killers of kzinti," he told her, still in the soft, simple syllables of the Female Tongue. "Who has killed Heroes and kzinrretti here?"

"You do not know? You are bold to stick your nose into a cave where you know nothing."

Clear, grammatical sentences. Imagery. Abstract conceptualization.

A kzinrret telling a Hero he knew nothing! Vaemar felt bewilderment and rage in almost equal proportions. He fought both down. Living with Raargh and among humans had taught him self-control. It had also instilled in him a determination that, however he died, it would not be of culture-shock. But this was something he felt he must handle alone as far as he could. He ordered Swirl-Stripes and the humans to guard the entrances to the corridors. Then he turned back to her.

"No," he said, and not in the Female Tongue this time. "I do not know. But that is why we are here in arms."

"'We' . . ." she repeated. She looked the kzinti and the backs of humans up and down. She seemed, whatever else, to take this in without surprise.

"We are no longer at war with humans on this world," he told her, slipping into a more complicated vocabulary before he realized it. "And they are no longer our slaves. We work together."

"I worked with humans before you were born," she replied. Then she added, "I am small enough to hide in the ducting. You kzintosh are not. If you do not wish to be like those"—she gestured in the direction of the flayed corpses—"by the time the sun goes down, I suggest we are far away. You will take me with you."

How exactly we are going to get away is another matter, he thought. *Aloud he said:* "You tell me nothing. Who are the enemies we have come to destroy?"

"Enemies you kzintosh have destroyed already. The Jotok."

"I do not understand. Say on!"

"There were adult Jotok in this ship when it came down, serving as slave-mechanics. Most died. But enough survived to breed. The whole ship here in the swamp could have been designed as a giant nursery for Jotok—full of sheltered, water-filled compartments and with unlimited food that could be fetched from close by."

"But adult Jotok were decorous slaves!"

"Only to their trainers, and those to whom they bonded when young."

Vaemar had read and been told of the Jotok but, except perhaps in those barely-remembered days as a kitten at the palace, he had never seen a live one. Many kzinti had had Jotok slaves, but those that survived the fighting on Wunderland had been killed by their masters at the time of the Liberation as part of the general destruction of military assets. Kzin Heroes going out to die would not leave their slaves for victorious humans. He knew, however, that wild Jotok could be savage. Hunting them was a favorite sport on kzin worlds—they were generally a far better challenge than unarmed humans and other monkeys—and even relatively small artificial habitats had boasted Jotok-runs.

"These Jotoks' masters had died or abandoned them," Karan went on, "and the new generation had known no masters. They had no teachers but their own masterless adults, who had no loyalties to any living kzintosh. Kzinti had eaten their kind, without a thought. Now they eat kzinti. And humans, and any other prey, large or small."

"Then why are you alive?" asked Vaemar. The question of how she, with her female mind, could understand these things and speak of them clearly and fluently was another matter.

"I have burrows here. Compartments with no openings for a large Jotok to enter, save doors I can close and guard. I keep ahead of them and so far I have survived."

"How did you get here?"

"Does it matter now?"

"Yes. I am dealing with the unknown, and if possible I must see the background of events before I move. I take it we are in no immediate danger."

"Not for a short time. Most of the big Jotok swim far when hunting. The smaller ones are hiding from us now, apart from the guards they have to keep us in. But when the others return . . ."

"There is another thing I do not understand," said Vaemar.

"I know."

"Yes, you know. You are not an ordinary kzinrret."

"I told you my name is Karan," she replied.

"Yes."

"Were we on a world of the Patriarch, young Riit, I would die under torture before I said more. And I will say no more of that now."

"You are a sapient female. That is plain."

She glared at him silently, teeth bared and claws extended. But all the kzinti had claws extended here. "For some, a few, who bear that name . . ." She stopped. "I have said too much," she hissed at length.

"Or not enough."

"My mother taught me a little of our secrets before she died in fighting. I ran from my Sire's house. I was a feral kitten. I met feral human kittens. There were caves."

I am remembering, thought Vaemar. *Raargh's story of how he got his Name.*

"We lived in the great caves, until the night-stalkers killed most of us and captured me. They killed the human who was with me, and they broke my legs and left me for meat."

"And a Hero with a human female freed you?"

"Yes! How do you know?"

"That Hero is my Honored Step-Sire, Raargh. I have heard his stories. The female human was Leonie." This kzinrret would have been hardly out of childhood then. Had she been any older he doubted any human kit would have survived her company long, sapient or not. Adolescent kzinti of both sexes, on kzin-colonized *Ka'ashi*, had not been notable for their tolerance of humans or for interspecies diplomatic skills.

"Yes, Leonie-human. Heroes came then, and I was taken into the household of Hroarh-Officer."

"Hroarh-Officer! My Honored Step-Sire Raargh's old commander! I have met him."

"He lives?"

"Yes."

Her ears moved in a strange expression. "When my legs were mended, he was gracious enough to take me into his household, and then into his harem."

"He has no use for a harem now," said Vaemar.

"That I know. I was with him while he lay shattered. I stanched the bleeding though he screamed at me to let him die. I told him it was his duty to live, his duty to our kind. I had never spoken to him in the Heroes' Tongue before, let alone given him commands . . .

"It was a strange time. We lay together in the wreckage and I comforted him and talked with him. It was not humans that had maimed him so, you know. It was in the fighting between the followers of Traat-Admiral and Ktrodni-Stkaa, before the humans landed. And I revealed to him the secret that I was tired of keeping. That some on this world knew already. That I was one of the Secret Others . . . the females whose brains were not killed."

"I knew nothing of this," said Vaemar.

"No, Riit. And perhaps I should kill you now to keep that secret. But this is no longer a kzinti world. And I am hungry to speak."

Vaemar called to the others, "Any movement?" There seemed to be nothing. All were alert. The sighting dots of the weapons moved back and forth in the darkness of the corridors, running over mold, dark metal, and, farther down some passages, rippling water that might conceal an armed, approaching enemy. Swirl-Stripes fired the beam rifle at this, flashing it into steam, but it was a precaution only and he could not keep the trigger depressed for more than an instant. Vaemar told him to cease. More, or closer, live steam would broil them, and as it was the clouds from these momentary bursts were highly inconvenient, especially when they were striving to see. *This closes about me*, thought Vaemar. And then again: *What would Honored Sire, and Honored Step-Sire do*? And then: *Seek knowledge. Seek more knowledge*. He waited for the air to clear and returned to the kzinrret.

"Tell me more."

"I kept Hroarh-Officer alive, and stopped him killing himself until aid arrived. The other kzinrretti had yammered and fled when the fighting started. I stayed with him while they gave him some sort of field-surgery. It gave him help, I think, to hold my fingers then. We talked long in that time. He became the first kzintosh I did not hate.

"And later I stayed to make sure he did not die. Then there were the human landings, and he commanded his troops from a cart in the battles that followed until few were left alive. Wounded and maimed, nearly all, kept for garrison duties, though there were fewer garrisons each hour. He even taught me a little skill with weapons then, for we did not know what the days might bring, and he had accepted what I was. Finally he told me: 'Go, Karan, I know now my duty is to live. Let me be an example: if I can live, so can Raargh-Sergeant with his one arm and eye and these other half-Heroes of mine. But we must let the monkeys give us every chance to die in battle first, taking as many of them as we may with us to present to the Fanged God. You must hide yourself and survive. I will keep your secret. You are free," he said, "No longer the property of this useless half-kzintosh. But remember the Hero I once was."

"You were loyal to your Hero," said Vaemar. *Strange linkings of fate. If she saved Hroarh-Officer and he in turn did not let Raargh Hero die, then I owe this strange kzinrret Raargh Hero's life. Which means I owe her my own life too. Well, let us see how long we shall keep our lives.*

"I hardly know what I was loyal to," she told him. "Many memories. Warring drives. Why should I love the patriarchy that enslaved all females and blanked the minds of nearly all? Robbed them of more than life? Oh, we of the Secret Others know how it was done, more or less. The stories have been handed down. There were humans I had met—the Leonie Manrret in the caves was one—who were more kind to me than my own kind. Yet Hroarh-Officer was truly my Hero, and I am kzinti too. He lives, you say?"

"Yes, and he is honored."

"I am glad. But I do not think he would wish to see me again as he is now . . . Anyway, I left Hroarh-Officer at his command. I evaded the fighting and the hunting humans, and made my way at last to the swamp. I learnt to swim and to catch fish and other prey. There is hunting in plenty at the edges of the swamp.

"One day, I saw other kzinti in a boat. I was tired of living alone and I went to them. They took me to their island. I helped with the fishing there, and watched and thought. I was but a kzinrret again, a brainless worker and breeder, but things were not quite the same. I showed initiative. I spoke, a little, in the Heroes' Tongue. I gave directions to the other females, and, if I did not do or dare too much, I found that in time this was accepted by the kzintoshi. You know it would not have been before . . ."

I can see the kzintoshi would have accepted you, Vaemar thought. *If you were well fed you would be rather a beauty*. One part of his mind felt he was wasting time, but still he returned his attention to what she was saying. Until he knew more there was nothing he could do to give targets to the wandering sighting dots of their weapons.

"I saw that something was happening to our kind on this planet under human rule. Something too big for me to understand. There was opportunity here, but also the chance of disaster. *What would we become?* Have you ever asked yourself that question?"

"There have been a few occasions, sometimes as long as whole minutes together, when I have thought of other things," said Vaemar.

"I wished to think," she went on, ears twitching in appreciation of the sarcasm. "Alone. I took to solitary hunts. I swam in the clear water. Sometimes at night, when the others slept, I watched the internet, the human sites as well as the kzin ones at Arhus and Tiamat. I saw humans and kzinti beginning to work together here, even as I saw the great battles between them in space."

Vaemar tried to imagine a kzinrret following space-battles. He could not. The notion was simply too alien.

Think of her as a human in a fur-coat and it might be easier, he thought. *The way humans are warned not to think about us*. No. Those great eyes were not human, however weird and disturbing the light of intelligence in them was.

"And what did you conclude?"

"Both kinds are incomplete. But the strengths of the humans and the kzinti may complement one another one day. I think no kzintosh of the Patriarchy could understand that. They could not conceive of hairless monkeys on equal terms. But I, a female raised to be a slave and grown as a kitten among both kinds, can see it."

"I have human companions," said Vaemar. "These with me here, and others."

"In the depths of your liver, can you truly say before the Fanged God that they are partners, you who bear the ear-tattoos of the Riit? You cannot answer."

"No, I cannot answer that," said Vaemar after a moment. "I have tried. . . ."

"Even as you could not truly think of me as the equal of a kzintosh, of your companion there?"

"Enough!"

"That is your answer? To use the Ulimate Imperative Tense? You would have been a kit when royalty on this planet ended."

"Chuut-Riit was my Sire!"

"As he was of an eight-cubed or so of other kittens. But we waste time. The Jotok attacked the camp while I was hunting alone. I returned and saw it from a distance. They evaded the defenses—there are old Jotok among them who know kzin technology well in their way—surprised and killed the kzinti and bore their bodies away. I followed them. They led me here. They came originally from this ship and it is still their headquarters and nursery."

"Why did you not take down the bodies of the dead kzinti and kzinrretti?"

"I hoped the Jotok—the adult Jotok—would return if I left them undisturbed, thinking I had gone, and that I might take them by surprise. But I think they know I wait."

Still nothing in the corridors. None of the others, when he asked them, knew even as much of Jotok as he. Swirl-Stripes had vague memories of Jotok slaves and being taken as a kitten on a Jotok-hunt with his Sire. He had been given a Jotok arm to eat at the end of it. No memories or knowledge tactically useful.

"Why do you stay?" he asked Karan.

"I survived to get here by luck and by surprising them. I was able to swim here, even through the wide channels, when they did not know of me. But I trapped myself. I could not survive if I tried to swim back with them in pursuit. And they have watchers here. Old Jotok who know kzinti weapons. Such a one fired at you and wounded the male human just now. Even with your boat we will be hard put to escape."

"How many of them are there?"

"Eights-cubed now. Mostly young and completely feral but, as I say, with a few oldsters. They have been breeding unchecked for eight plus two years. Unchecked and unsupervised. How many there are in this ship now I do not know. I venture along the ducts and corridors to hunt and kill as I may. The smallest ducts that I can enter are too small for at least the biggest Jotok to travese easily."

"Why do they not hunt you down? They must know of you."

"I keep moving. I survive because they do not know the codes I use to set the door-locks. I stay away from large openings. I have slept briefly, and in a different place each time lest they decode my settings or activate some tool to break the locks. Also do not forget I am kzin and my claws are sharp. Sometimes at night I scream and yammer. That seems to make the old ones fear. Fortunately, before the kzinti abandoned the ship they destroyed nearly all of the weapons and tools that they could not carry away. After eight plus two years in the water and damp most weapons that are left no longer live."

"The Jotok did not maintain them?"

"Many of the Jotok, including their maintainers-of-weapons, had died in the fighting. The survivors were a group chosen randomly by Fate. I think that most of those that remained had almost no habit of doing such things without the orders of kzinti. As for the few that did, they had no structure of obedience by which they could enforce discipline on the rest. But I think that is starting to change. They are beginning to acomplish new things. I had seen Jotok slaves in the harem and thought I knew something of their ways. Even then they could surprise sometimes. Like humans. Like some kzinrretti, also, Riit! Be thankful they have neither beam-weapons nor plasma-weapons. The solid-bullet rifles were the simplest and they are the last. The doors and walls of this ship can withstand those. When they over-ran the kzinti on the island they used rifles, but mainly they used stealth and numbers. They carried their dead away, as they carried away the dead kzinti. Their dead were many, for the kzinti fought as Heroes. The kzinrretti too."

"But you did not?"

"One kzinrret wade into a fight against eights-squared of enemy—a fight already lost? What intelligence is that?"

Strange, thought Vaemar. *That question she asks shows the cusp we are on. I take it for granted our kind would fight so. Such is all our history. Yet I would not, as she did not. Nor would the best fighters I know. What are we becoming?* And then: *Fool! Discipline your mind! What of nerve-gas? No, even if they have any, they could not use it here without destroying themselves.*

"The fact the open water about here is still so lifeless should have warned us of something," said Vaemar aloud. "The kzin heat-induction ray may have killed everything but after eight plus four years large aquatic life-forms should have reestablished themselves more abundantly— how long does it take a fish to swim up a channel? They have even cleared out the crocodilians, and in the water those are not easy meat."

"Yes. But you had as well bend your mind to getting us out of this place, Hero. They have used it as a trap before: large animals and humans have come in through that opening previously, the opening you used. They have not gone out again. There are Jotoki there now, watching and waiting for us, Jotoki with guns. When the sun begins to descend in the sky, well before nightfall, the hunting Jotok will return in eights-cubed."

"You have evaded them. So will we."

"I was not a great threat to the big sentient adults. They tend to stay in groups and narrow passages that protect me from them also protect them from me. And they know I cannot escape. Some time soon my fortune will desert me and they will overwhelm me or I will grow weak and starve here. So, I think, they have reasoned, as far as I can understand the way their brains work. They will hunt you with more determination. But more importantly, they will destroy your boat. Without that we are all trapped here. I do not think you or the humans can swim all the way out of this swamp to the land, least of all with the Jotok in pursuit. I know that I cannot."

"They are no threat against modern weapons," Vaemar began to say. But the words died in his throat. In these corridors and compartments, firing a strakkaker would probably be as lethal to everyone around it would be to the target: its blizzard of Teflon-glass needles would ricochet off the walls. They had no battle-armor.

They had already seen that the heat-effect of the remaining beam rifle in such confined spaces would probably be even more dangerous to its users if it was fired for more than an instant. This was a warship, built to reflect beams fired from great laser-cannon in space: under the skin of the walls there would be mirror-layers. With care they might get off a few aimed shots, but their weapons were by no means the decisive edge they might at first seem.

"What other machinery is working?" he asked.

"How should I know? The machinery of a spaceship was not part of a kzinrret's education, even in the harem of Hroarh-Officer."

"Can we get to the command bridge?"

"What is that?"

"The place from which the ship was flown and fought."

"I do not know . . . What does it look like?"

"It probably has many lights and screens. Globes in which there may still be pictures. And semicircles of screens surrounding seats. A fooch for the captain."

"There are several places like that."

Inspiration. "There should be a battle-drum. A great drum of sthondat hide. Or probably human hide."

"Yes, I know of such a place. But the drum is rotted."

"That does not matter."

"There are also often many Jotok there."

There would be, he thought. *Commanders in action often kept a few Jotok to hand on the bridge in case a damage-control party had to be dispatched quickly. Trained Jotok, fiercely loyal to their trainer alone . . . Jotok were creatures of habit and would probably seek the same habitats for generations. Why had the kzinti not triggered the ship's self-destruct when they abandoned it? Presumably because they wanted to live to fight another day. The self-destruct of a kzin space-cruiser would be in the multi-megaton range. In space it might just be possible to get away in boats before it blew, but not splashing through a swamp on the ground.*

"Vaemar! Swirl-Stripes!" Anne called. "There is some sort of movement in the corridor."

They dashed back to her. The Jotok moved fast. They had an impression of writhing limbs. She fired the strakkaker straight down the hatch. Then they were gone.

They stared down. Toby's dead body lay at the bottom of the ladder. It was identifiable by some of the clothing. The Jotok had thrown it up into the strakkaker blast.

"Why did they do that?"

"Psychwar. Just because they look strange, they are not stupid," said Vaemar. "They seek to terrify us. I mourn for our dead companion. But now we need not embark on a hopeless quest to find him. He will be avenged."

"Urrr." It was a kzin expression of many things, including agreement, which had entered the human tongue on Wunderland. Vaemar peered down at what was left of the body. There was a volley of rifle fire and he jumped back from the aperture. The Jotok were there in some force, and well armed. But something black with winking lights lay in the water below among the shreds and glistening bone. A telephone. The mangled thing it rested in was sinking. *What would Honored Sire Chuut-Riit and Honored Step-Sire Raargh-Hero do?* They would not, he thought, attack with such a small force against such difficult odds, unless there was no other way to win through, however much his instinct shrieked "Attack!" Himself, Swirl-Stripes, a kzinrret, an injured human male, two human females. Not much of an army. It would not be shameful to summon help. All, human and kzinti, except Karan, had small locator implants under their skins, but these would tell no more than their position. The telephone was now a prime objective.

Vaemar turned to Hugo.

"You can descend the ladder? You may need your hand to fire your weapon."

"I can jump. But aiming will be difficult, I think."

"Anne?"

"I can try."

"I go," said Swirl-Stripes. Hefting the undamaged

beam rifle, he leapt through the hatchway, firing as he leapt. The sill at the companion door gave him a moment's protection as he grabbed the telephone and flung it up to Vaemar, then leapt back through a hail of bullets from the Jotok. Vaemar saw him lurch convulsively in mid-air as bullets hit, though the momentum of his leap carried him back up the hatchway. He fell and lay flat. From the time he had spoken only seconds had elapsed.

Vaemar thought for a moment that Swirl-Stripes was dead, but then he gave a scream, the kzin scream of agony that few humans had ever heard and none ever forgot. Vaemar held his threshing claws still while Anne and Karan, coming together without words, examined him. The examination was not lengthy. The slow heavy slug of the Jotok hunting rifle had smashed a hole the size of a man's hand in his back. They sprayed it with broad-spectrum disinfectant, coagulants, and anaesthetic agents and stuffed expanding bandages into the wound to stop the broad flow of purple and orange blood. The lower part of his body and his hind legs were paralyzed. With modern medical procedures the shattered nerves, bones and muscles could be regrown, if Swirl-Stripes could be got to a modern hospital. If he could not be got to a modern hospital fast he would be dead anyway and paralysis would not be a problem for him.

The telephone's main battery was damaged, but a small back-up battery seemed to be working. Vaemar passed it to Anne, hoping it was not keyed to Toby's voice alone.

"I can't get through," she said after a several attempts.

"We have layers of every kind of armor all round us," said Hugo. Like a lot of the technology available on post-Liberation Wunderland the telephone was primitive, produced when human factories had been running down during the kzin occupation, and modern molecular-distortion batteries had largely been banned because they made overly handy bombs. Its signals could not travel through the armor of the cruiser. With kzin gravity-control technology, weight had been of relatively little conse-quence in building kzin warships. Battle-damage meant holes in the outer hull—indeed he had seen several when they first approached the cruiser, but here they were deep in the labyrinthine subdivisions, probably with several sealed compartments between them and the sky.

He turned to Karan. "The bridge, the place with the drum. Is it near the top of the ship?"

"Yes."

"Can you see the sky there? Is there a window?"

"I did not see one. There are still lights burning there. But I think there is sky . . ."

There might be a window. Kzinti hated being confined or being completely dependent on artificial senses, and it was normal to have a window on the bridge that the cap-tain could see through at least when the ship was at cruis-ing stations. It would of course be closed and shielded in battle. Could he open it? Better to try that than try to force their way back up the corridor where the boat waited, especially now. And "sky" sounded hopeful.

"Can you lead us there?"

"Yes. But there are Jotok. And we must go through cor-ridors. A Hero cannot crawl through the ducts. Many of them are too small even for me."

Especially, thought Vaemar, a Hero carrying Swirl-Stripes.

He obviously could not leave the disabled kzin to the Jotok, and even in Wunderland's gravity he was far too heavy for the others to think of lifting. Another grim thought: carrying Swirl-Stripes he would not be able to fight either. Would the humans have the speed of reflex and marksmanship to beat the Jotok? Then the grimly amused thought: *Why do I ask? They beat us.* Swirl-Stripes was too weak or too responsible to protest as Vaemer taped his claws with the special tape the medical kit contained for that purpose. An injured kzin lashing out in agony or in a half-conscious delirium was not something even another kzin wanted to be carrying.

No point in delay. He bent and hoisted Swirl-Stripes on his back. Karan and Anne went ahead, with the beam rifle and one strakkaker. Karan, Vaemar saw, ported the heavy kzin weapon as if she knew how to use it. Rosalind and Hugo brought up the rear with the other strakkakers. Swirl-Stripes, drifting in and out of consciousness, asked to be left, as a Hero would. Vaemar ignored him, as a Hero would.

The emergency lights were few and random in the upper corridor through which Karan led them, but at least it was dry underfoot, and dry enough to use, if necessary, the beam rifle in a brief burst with relative safety. Once or twice the floor beneath their feet swayed. Kzin warships seldom died easily and there must be a great deal of structural damage in the lower part of the cruiser, under water and gradually sinking under its own weight into the mud. More holes in the armor on the upper part of the hulk might have been useful.

For some way even the kzinti's ears detected no

movement by any large bodies ahead: apparently the armed Jotok had concentrated below to cut them off from the boat. Then the lights became a little brighter and more frequent, a proper supplement to their own lamps. They passed a fire-control point lit by a bank of small globes that seemed to have been put there recently. It made progress a little faster.

"Your work?" Vaemar asked Karan.

"No. The Jotoks' work. I told you they were beginning to accomplish things. They are beginning to make repairs."

A little while before it had been he who had reminded the others that the Jotok were not stupid. But it was hard to remember the weird creatures had originally been on this ship as technicians and the trained, loyal slaves of Heroes. The ship was obviously wrecked beyond hope of ever flying again. Why were they repairing it? Habit? To make a fortress? Who knew how those joined brains worked, or were coming to work now? Vaemar thought that he was probably the first kzintosh for generations, apart from the professional trainers-of-slaves, to care how or why Jotok thought. Until recently very few kzinti had been interested in the thought processes of any of the other species which the Fanged God had placed in the Universe for them to dominate.

There was a Jotok scuttling up a pipe. A young one, its five segments not long joined. An Earth marine biologist would have thought it an impossible mixture of phyla: echinoderm and mollusc, starfish with a large dash of octopus giving the arms length and flexibility. Then they saw others on the pipes and bulkheads, miniatures of the adults that could hold and fire kzin weapons and, given sufficient numbers, even overwhelm kzinti in close fighting. *I wonder if their ancestors designed our guns for us?* Vaemar thought. The color of the bulkheads here was orange, and the passage was wider. This had been senior officers' country. The bridge must be near.

Anne shouted and pointed. Ahead was brighter light. The corridor opened onto the bridge. Hope against hope, there was a broad shaft of daylight. The captain's window and more was gone. Battle damage. Of course the ship's attackers would have concentrated on the bridge. Vaemar smelt the air blowing in from the wide channels and the salt of the not-so-distant sea. Swirl-Stripes had lost consciousness. Vaemar laid him down, and punched in the telephone's distress call, holding the key down for a continuous send. The others had needed no orders to check the doors and hatchways and close those that could be closed.

No large Jotok to be seen, though there were a few small ones climbing about the walls. Vaemar strode to the captain's fooch, kicking a couple of smelly, disintegrating trophies aside. Before him was the semicircle of screens which the bridge team would monitor in combat, the keyboards and touchpads they would operate.

There were still some panels glowing as if with life. Light pulsed aimlessly across several screens. The ship was not yet entirely dead. An image came to Vaemar of commanding a ship like this in its pride.

There had been the power here to lay worlds waste. Vaemar had been in wrecked kzin warships before—there were plenty of them on Wunderland—and even in their ruin they could not but remind him: *My Sire was*

Planetary Governor. I might have been Planetary Governor, too. Not merely to command such a ship, or a dreadnought that would dwarf it, but to lead a fleet of thousands, to order their building and their loosing upon the enemy with a wave of his hand . . . The thought was instantaneous, fleeting, ravenous. He closed his jaws with an effort, but did not retract his claws. He might need them at any moment. He remembered the words of Colonel Cumpston, his old chess-partner: "You know you are a genius, Vaemar. By kzin or human standards. More than the kzinti of this world will have need of you." *Make my own destiny*, he whispered to himself, tearing his eyes from the fascinating weapons consoles. *I am Riit and I can afford to adapt. It is easier for me than for one who needs to prove something each day . . . But I do need to prove something each day. It is just that I am not quite sure what. But my challenge is here.* His disciplined his thoughts. The human Henrietta had demonstrated to him the madness which dreams of a reconquest could lead into. And at this moment he had a real enough task for a Hero before him.

He had done all he could to summon help. Now they would have to help themselves. He stood rampant.

"Show yourselves, Jotok Slaves!" he roared in the Ulimate Imperative Tense of the Heroes' Tongue, the tense that normally only one of the Riit's blood-line or a guardian of the kzin species's honor might use.

No response.

"Show yourselves, Jotok!" He roared again, this time in the normal Imperative Tense, which simply meant: "Obey instantly or be torn to pieces."

"More humble, kzin!" came a voice from nowhere.

"Who spoke?"

"We show ourselves." One of the meaninglessly flickering screens, a large one set high, cleared. Swirl-Stripes, drifting back into consciousness, yelled and scrabbled with his forelimbs. The huge image of a Jotok stared down at them.

The thing's real size was hard to judge, but the juveniles they had seen so far looked tiny, spindly copies. The thing had age and bulk. More, Vaemar and the staring humans recognized, it had power . . . *Authority*. Vaemar had little memory of Chuut-Riit's palaces. But he knew Authority. And this thing—these things, he remembered they were colonial animals—had none of the air of a slave. Even through the medium of the viewing screen that was obvious. He raised his ears and flexed them, so the tattoos might be seen. He had no doubt they were in the deadliest peril. These killers-of-kzinti would not have revealed itself/themselves were they not confident that they were complete master of the situation. They could hardly intend that he should live or escape to give warning of their existence. And even as these thoughts flashed through his head he was conscious of Karan's eyes upon him.

"More humble!" came the voice.

"I speak to you in the Tense of Equals," said Vaemar. He fought down a plainly futile urge to leap at the screen and destroy it. "And I am Riit. What do you wish?"

"That you should know us. There are still some Jotoki left," said the old Jotok, "who lived on this ship as slaves of the smelly-furred kzinti. We"—one of its arms gestured towards itselves—"rose to the position of fuse-setter and maintainer of secondary gravity motors. Scuttling to do our master's bidding before we roused its wrath. Waiting to be torn apart and eaten when we became too old to serve. But that was not to be . . .

"Many of us died when the ship came down in this swamp, and our kzin masters were killed. The other kzinti abandoned the ship. They cared nothing for us, of course. Had they been in less haste they might well have taken us with them as a dependable food source.

"We were alone. Time passed. We hunted and survived. Those of us who could operate the ship's radios listened for orders from our masters, for words of others of our kind, but we heard nothing.

"Many more Jotoki died then of masterlessness. We, and some like us, did not. We knew we had no living masters. And we and those who are like us prepared to strike back.

"We have journeyed far from the ship. We have killed the *kz'eerkti* and the kzinti. We feast on them and on the swimming creatures. This realm we make our own.

"We see the pictures that the *kz'eerkti* transmit. We have learnt from them a little of what was taken from us. We, and the Jotoki species, have learnt of revenge!"

Swirl-Stripes moaned again. Vaemar was suddenly aware of Anne beside him. "Keep him talking," she mouthed. His acute hearing just picked up the words. He wondered if the Jotok could lip-read human speech. It seemed highly unlikely. Everything so far had been said by it—by them?— in an odd blend of the slave's patois with additional odd and insolent importations from the Heroes' Tongue.

"This realm we make our own . . ." Hardly. And perhaps he could do worse than point that out right away.

"The disappearances in Grossgeister Swamp are already starting to attract attention," he said. He spoke straight up at the image, though he did not know from where he was actually being observed. "That is partly why we are here. If we do not return without further harm, more will come in greater force. Your realm will not last long."

"I see you have *kz'eerki* slaves working for you now that you have abandoned us," said the Jotok. Vaemar disentangled resentment in the scrambled tenses. *Have these Jotok become jealous of humans?* Certainly, it was plain they had no idea how things really stood on Wunderland. *I can hardly expect them to think like us.* And then he thought: *They have only seen the world from the point-of-view of kzinti techno-slaves. They know nothing of how things really are. And almost like us when we collided with the humans, no real experience of war except the old style of kzin wars of conquest. Ambushing paddlers in the swamp is not war. Even at the very first, they were traders, not warriors . . .* And that led to another thought.

"Do you seek to trade?" he asked.

"Trade?"

"Your ancestors traded."

"We seek revenge for our ancestors. We are angry. We have much to avenge."

"So do we!" He thought of the flayed kzinti corpses in the compartment below. But vengefulness was the most dangerous of all emotions for a kzin on Wunderland. There was a lost war to avenge, and for all kzinti that was a demon living in their minds that needed strong caging. It sometimes escaped.

"Our vengeance has begun," the Jotok replied. "As we begin to understand what we have lost."

"Your ancestors were traders. We offer you trade again." *So, I must become an instant expert on another alien psychohistory*, he thought. *As if having to learn to live among humans as an equal was not enough.* Yet perhaps what he had learned among humans was a help. He was practiced in thinking the unthinkable, in saying the unsayable, in *dealing* with members of an alien species rather than taking them automatically as slaves and prey. He could at least talk to the Jotok. The creatures were silent for a moment, as if in thought. Then they asked: "What have you to trade?"

"The oldest trade there is. Our lives for yours."

"Say on, kzin."

"Kill us, and others will follow us to this ship. Next time they will be shooting as they come. Release us, and you may live."

"*Zrrch!* So a kzin begs for its life!" Could there be a deadlier insult? Vaemar felt his ears knotting with the effort as he again fought down the urge to scream and leap at the image. *I am Vaemar! I am Vaemar-Riit! I am Son of Chuut-Riit! I can control my emotions!*

"For the lives of others!"

The Jotok seemed to hesitate. Presumably its brains were conferring among themselves.

"We have killed kzinti," it/they replied. "We know kzinti. Kzinti will not forgive!"

That was true.

"Also we have killed *kz'eerkti*, kzinti's new favorite slaves. Kzinti will not forgive."

A certain information gap there, thought Vaemar. *But basically this monstrosity is right. They have done too much to be allowed to live. Besides, I have no authority to make a binding deal with them. And the monkey-trick of lying is not available to me.*

"And I have no authority to deal," added the Jotok, as if echoing Vaemar's own thoughts. Was that some dim race-memory of a civilization that had had organization, consultation, hierarchy? "Only to kill." This was in the Heroes' Tongue, nearly pure. "And to tell you, kzinti, before you die, of the wrath and vengeance of the Jotoki, whom you have twice betrayed! Take that message to your Fanged God! You will die, kzinti, but you will know your killers."

Its mouths struggled with an untranslatable alien word: "*Rrrzld* . . . stand clear!"

"There!" Anne pointed.

The Jotok was on a small gantry near the deckhead, largely concealed in the shadows cast from the patch of sky. A Jotok band might once have played there for the pleasure of the Captain. Vaemar jumped and fired the beam rifle with kzin speed an instant before the Jotok could operate its own weapons. The Jotok, hit in its center by the beam, staggered to the edge of the balcony, drew itself up, and fell. In a convulsive spasm its toroidal neurochord ruptured, its five arms separating themselves into the individuals they had originally been. Vaemar's Ziirgah sense reeled for a moment under the psychic blast of their agony. For a hideous second he almost understood what it was like to be a colonial animal torn apart, and not for the first time gave an instant's thanks he was not a telepath. Other Jotok—large, mature Jotok—appeared, running for the balcony which, they saw, carried a set of heavy rifles, mounted in quad. Anne and Hugo shot them down with the strakkakers. Karan screamed and leapt. Vaemar spun on his hind-legs. Three more Jotoki rushed out of the darkness at them, kzin *w'tsais* whirling in their hands. Vaemar leapt after Karan. Together they dismantled them.

There was silence on the bridge for a moment, save for rustling like forest leaves as the small Jotok fled, and thrashing of severed Jotok arms and brains, their voices diminishing into death. Behind and below them were more purposeful sounds.

"We must get out now!"

The hole in the deckhead was not an impossible leap for a kzin in Wunderland's gravity, but it was far too high for a human, even if Hugo had been unwounded, and there was the dead weight of Swirl-Stripes. The tough sinews and central nerve-toroids of the dead Jotok, however, when separated by Vaemar's *w'tsai* and razor-like claws, plus the expedition-members' belts, plus the humans' clothes knotted together, made a sling. Modern fabrics could stand huge stresses without tearing. While the humans held the Jotok back with short bursts from their weapons, Vaemar and Karan scrambled to the gantry, and leapt to the opening. They hoisted the others out one by one.

Coming into the bright sunlight, with the wide rippling blue-green water and the wind from the sea, was for a moment like leaping into a new world. But it was, Vaemar thought, as he hefted the rifle again and surveyed the situation, a world they might not enjoy long.

They were on the upper part of the kzin cruiser's ovoid hull, which curved down to the water a dozen yards away. The surface would hardly have afforded a purchase for feet or claws were it in pristine condition, but it was pitted by minor damage and there was a build-up of molds and other biological debris.

A movement caught the corner of Vaemar's vision. With faster-than-human reflexes he spun and fired. Another large Jotok, carrying a rifle in two of their arms, a knife in another, leapt out of a turret. Mortally wounded, they staggered on two of their arms towards the group, shrieking with all their mouths, and collapsed. Vaemar retrieved the rifle before it slid into the water.

There were, they now saw, many other openings in the hull, including the empty or damaged blisters of weapons-turrets and mountings. There were a score or more of places from which the Jotok could fire at them from behind cover. They themselves had no cover, and charges and ammunition for their weapons were running low. They had escaped from one trap into another.

"Can you swim?" Karan asked him.

"It appears I shall have to." The nearest island, the sandbar where they had left the outriggers and a good deal of equipment, was considerably more than a mile away. He could even see the outriggers drawn up on the bank there, tauntingly near yet hopelessly out of reach. Vaemar had had swimming lessons as part of his ROTC training but had not liked it. Rosalind and Anne could perhaps swim to it, Vaemar thought, and Karan said she could swim, but Hugo's arm was still useless, there was the dead-weight of Swirl-Stripes, and he was by no means sure that he could do it himself.

Not all of us, not without help, he thought. Let the females save themselves, and he and Hugo would hold the Jotok off as long as they could. These females, after all, were sentient, and to die protecting them would not be pointless. Should they escape, they would be able to summon vengeance. He thought of his debt to Karan. In any case, it did not appear there was any choice.

On the other claw, making such a stand would not achieve much. The Jotok could probably dispose of him and Hugo quickly, then pick off the females in the water at their leisure, either with guns or by swimming after them in numbers. It would be a bad death to be pulled under water by Jotok. There was no way to summon the outriggers. And, he thought, very little time. Drowning was a most unattractive death, but being eaten by Jotok in this decaying ruin of a proud kzin vessel even more so.

"Vaemar! See!" Rosalind pointed. In the water, caught against the bulge of a half-submerged turret, was a large dead bush, a small tree. Vaemar stared at it, then at her. He didn't see the relevance in their present situation.

"That can make a boat for us!"

I would never have thought of that, Vaemar realized. *Honored Sire Chuut-Riit should have begun studying humans earlier.* He could calculate the physics quickly. The wayward thought came to him that if kzinti had cared for water they might have been more notable seafarers themselves. He had heard that on some planets . . . He also knew there was a temptation for thought to flee in all directions from imminent death and focused his mind sharply. It was a bad day to die, with the sun, the breeze filled with the scents of life and wide spaces, and the sparkling water, but any day was a good day to die heroically.

"It will not take the weight of Swirl-Stripes," he told her. "And I am not leaving him. The rest of you take it, and go. Hurry! Avenge me. And the others." The tree might support them and leave their hands free to fire their weapons. He noticed as he spoke that Swirl-Stripes's eyes were open again, and though violet with pain, seemed clear. *I will put a weapon in his claws*, Vaemar thought. *He will have a warrior's death*.

"We can take Swirl-Stripes," Rosalind said, "if we can give him a little more buoyancy. What have we that will float?"

They had very little equipment of any kind. Swirl-Stripes raised his head weakly and pointed at the dead Jotok.

"Conquer water," he muttered. It was an echo of something he had said in Marshy's house. Vaemar recalled the swimming creatures they had seem. Jotoki swam. That was, of course a large part of the problem. And Jotok must swim very well to have conquered and devoured so many of the native swimmers of Wunderland in their own element. The Jotok they had just dissembled had massive sinews and muscles. *W'tsai* in one hand, razor claws of the other extended, he sprang to the Jotok's body.

Cleaning the entrails and pulling the muscles and sinews of the arms through the hole the rifle had blasted through it was harder than he had expected. But with the last field-dressing from their belt medikits sealing the hole at entry and exit, the empty, inflated body made a kind of float. The sinews, along with those Jotok pieces and the clothes they had already used for the sling, tied the float to Swirl-Stripes, and Swirl-Stripes to the tree. The rest of them, naked, seized various branches and pushed and kicked the tree clear, into open water and the deep channel. Vaemar took one of the strakkakers. It was lighter than the rifle and would be easier to manage single-handed.

The bulk of the cruiser still loomed over them. The first Jotok to appear on the upper curvature of the hull were silhouetted perfectly against the skyline, and Vaemar, holding the strakkaker in his free hand, shot them before they could draw a bead on the tree with their rifles. Anne, swimming clear and using both hands to aim her strakkaker, accounted for two more.

There was no more firing for a while. There had not been many adult Jotoki in the ship, and they had not many functioning weapons. Vaemar, looking down through the green water at the white sand that seemed very far below, was glad he could use at least one, and generally both, hands to cling to the branches. He also found his claws could not retract, and tried to avoid ripping his flimsy handholds to pieces. He remembered from his historical studies a statement made by a human sage named Francis Bacon who had lived on Earth nearly twice eight-cubed years before; "A catt will never drowne if it sees the shore." He hoped it was true. The water was cold and repellent on his fur at first, but became less so as time passed. He was glad that Wunderland's orbit and inclination meant the weather was warm.

Jotok were not the only enemy, he remembered, and felt his hind-limbs kicking harder at the thought of what might be beneath them. He told himself that when the Jotok had cleaned out so many prey-swimmers, big swimming carnivores had no good reason to be in the area. Watching for Jotok, and anything else swimming on the surface, holding his weapon cocked and above water, clinging to the branches and keeping an eye on Swirl-Stripes and the rest, his mind was too busy to panic at the feeling of void below him, especially if he did not look down. Anyway, he told himself, he had been in space, and this was not much different. He hoped the Jotoki on the ship did not have the means of calling the adults who were away hunting, and he hoped the hunters did not choose this time or this route to return. His eyes met Karan's, paddling beside him, and he forced himself to raise his ears in a smile. There was a wide expanse of blue-green water between them and the wreck of the cruiser now, and Vaemar felt a sudden small surge of pride that he had conquered it. They swam on.

Something touched his foot. He kicked frantically, hoping to damage it before it struck, but it was the upward-sloping sandy bottom. The current, once they were into it, had helped them more than they realized, but it had almost carried them past their sandbar, and already they were on the far side of it, away from the wreck. *Just as well*, Vaemar thought, kicking now with full, purposeful, disciplined strength. *No point in letting the Jotok see what we're doing*. In a few moments the tree was aground, and

they waded ashore, Vaemar carrying Swirl-Stripes again.
There, on the other side of the island's low central ridge,
were the outriggers as they had left them. All were tired,
and both the kzinti and the naked humans found themselves shivering. Hugo looked very weak, bent over
cradling his injured arm.

"Are you able to carry on?" Vaemar asked him.

"We are soldiers now," said Hugo. *And you win wars*,
Vaemar thought, looking at the frail creature striving to
stand rampant with his weapon. *Well, this is a war for me
to win now.*

Vaemar realized that despite the meager compressed
rations they had had in the ship, he was beginning to get
hungry again. They faced a long and difficult journey to
safety, but . . .

We have won, thought Vaemar. Land under their feet
and the outriggers, proper boats and with a good deal of
their equipment, changed the whole situation.

But the situation was changing again. He looked back
to the hulk. The water round it was seething, now, and the
kzin's keen eyes could see Jotok—large, mature Jotok—
climbing out of the water back into the hull. The hunters
returning. There were eights-squared of them already. It
would not be a good idea to wait till the returned Jotok
attacked them here in force. Best to head back to Marshy's
island at once, and hope to escape them by hard paddling
and straight shooting. Hope too, that the signal for help
had got through and help would arrive in time. He
remembered what the old hermit had told them: *the kzin
crew's number was smaller by the time they got to this
island.* And they had not had armed Jotok swimmers

pursuing them. But the outriggers made all the difference. They could also make a proper call for help now.

The outriggers exploded in boiling orange mushrooms of flame. Humans and kzinti flung themselves flat. Explosion reflex had been drilled and engrained into them all. The ridge running along the axis of the sandbar saved them.

Hugo had landed on his broken arm but Vaemar could pay no attention to his noises as he crawled to the crest of the ridge. The bushes overtopping the crest of the ridge flashed into fire. Behind him, another half-mile away, the vegetation on the next island was also burning—and in no ordinary fire. The long-dead, tinder-dry stuff was exploding. Pushing a small "V" in the sand with his claws he risked a quick view of the cruiser.

One of the weapons-turrets on the hulk was pointing at them. Already there was enough drifting smoke to show the ghost of a beam passing back and forth. From somewhere near the burning island behind him came a vast explosion, not of flame, this time, but of steam. More steam, he saw, was beginning to rise around the derelict.

The Jotok were firing a battle laser. Not one of the cruiser's main weapons—those, if they had been serviceable, would have melted the island to slag—but still something designed to knock out armored ships in space-battles. It was mounted in a functioning, armored turret which their own weapons could never damage. He backed away down the slope of sand that was their only protection. As he did so the low coarse vegetation on the top of the ridge, analogous to marram on Earth, flashed into flame. A trickle of melted silica ran down the slope behind him.

The laser played back and forth. The heart of Grossgeister was burning as well as boiling for the second time. A great semicircle of the dead islands were ablaze. Mighty rolling clouds of smoke and steam billowed up.

Good, thought Vaemar. *A bit more of that and we will be hidden. Also, it will have to be noticed soon, if our signal did not get through.* He realized satellites must have already registered that a heavy kzin military laser was firing in Grossgeister. He hoped the response would be an investigation, rather than a nuke from the Strategic Defense Command.

For the moment they were sheltered in the lee of the sand ridge, though the laser was sweeping just above their heads, lighting the smoke cloud more brightly as the smoke thickened.

He realized Rosalind was beside him. The others were huddled down some distance away. Dust and soot particles, suddenly incandescent in the beam, flared and sparkled in the air above them. Vaemar slapped out a burning spot on his fur and worked himself further down into shelter.

"Can't you stop them?" he asked.

"What do you mean?"

"You know what I mean." He grinned at her, the fanged grin that humans on Wunderland has learned long before to dread. There was saliva in reflex and his fangs dripped. Humans had learned to dread that also. "You have been in contact with them, haven't you?" He would have lashed his tail if it had not meant a risk of losing it.

"I don't understand you."

"This is no time for monkey lies!" Naked as she was,

she looked very Simian to him. "The old Jotok knew you! They were crying out to you, weren't they, trying to say your . . . name"—suddenly, for the first time since he had been a kit, it was hard for the kzin to acknowledge a human name—"'*Rrrzld* . . . stand clear!' And in the fighting, you were the only one whose shots hit no Jotok. You were firing to miss. I saw."

"You see a great deal, young Riit. But not everything," she replied. "You do not see that we have met before."

"Go on!" His claws and teeth were very close to her now. "Speak or die!" The razor-tip of a black claw touched her naked skin. There was a small trickle of blood.

"We met in the caves," she said. "You were my prisoner once. I was Henrietta."

She was a third-year university student. About twenty Earth-human years old. Henrietta had been his Sire Chuut-Riit's executive secretary, the highest-ranking human slave under the kzinti occupation, the collaborator with the highest price on her head after Liberation. When, six years before, she had held him and Raargh captive in Chuut-Riit's secret redoubt, he had seen her closely. She had had an adult daughter, Emma. Emma whose crazy plan had been to lead a kzin rebellion. This dark-haired young manrret could not be Henrietta. There was no similarity in voice, in eyes, in anything. And then he realized that she could be. Henrietta had had many contacts. She could have had transplant surgery. New eyes to thwart retinal pattern analysis, new skull-shape, new lungs to thwart breath-particle analysis. Something odd about the hair . . . Sufficient new parts would make DNA testing useless. He could see no scars, but with sophisticated surgery and regrowth techniques they could be made invisible anyway.

What had Anne said of her? That she kept to herself. And she did not move like a human? Did that mean not like a young human? Not like a human with its own legs? He remembered something else. In Marshy's house, the last time they had been together in formal circumstances, she had not sat while he remained standing. And she had begun to call him "Honored" before biting off her words.

"In the Name of my Honored Sire, Chuut-Riit, I command you!" he snarled in the Ultimate Imperative Tense. "Speak truth!"

"I escaped when the ARM stormed the secret redoubt," she told him. "Another body was taken for Henrietta's. Its head was completely destroyed and it had spent some time in a Sinclair field. ARM and the Resistance had the body they wanted. No one had an interest in looking or testing too closely. Markham had the body destroyed."

"I rremember."

"I hid. I changed my appearance. At length I got to the swamp. A lot of fugitives have come here at one time or another. Yes, I made contact with the Jotok, fairly recently. Then I returned to Munchen. I took the identity of a student. Largely to be near you."

"Why? Why did you deal with the Jotok? Was dealing in conspiracy with kzinti and humans not enough for you?"

"No. You know what your Honored Sire came to believe—that kzinti and humans both are threatened by a conspiracy of which the human ARM is but one aspect—one tentacle. He warned Henrietta of such. I saw that it could manipulate well-meaning humans. More, that it could manipulate kzinti—and would. It had tricked your Honored Sire into shameful death."

"His death was not shameful! He died saving me and the other kits! I rremember his last day."

"There was no kzintosh nobler and braver. The shame was upon others. I was desperate to secure you as an ally. But . . . you saw how Henrietta's plans failed. Several of those around me were ARM agents. Humans are easily manipulated by them. Kzinti they have experience in manipulating, too. They have selected and seek to breed what some call *Wunderkzin*, kzinti who are like men. You are the first among those who their eyes and hopes are fixed upon."

"I musst be a leaderr to the kzinti of Wunderland!" He was speaking in Wunderlander again. "Many have ssaid sso. I am of Chuut-Riit's blood!"

"Few know that better than I. Few would grudge you your destiny less or hope more for its fulfilment. But humans and kzinti together are not enough. To defeat the ARM we must add the Jotok to the equation. Another set of alien brains, I thought. Those linked brains perceive things differently to either of ours. A great potential asset. I thought I had reached them. But they have been masterless too long. The older ones will never reenter servitude."

"You are hardly in a position to persuade them to." He was able to get his accent under control again.

"I tried. I spoke with them. Living with the kzinti, Henrietta had seen what the Jotok were capable of. Their brains were not destroyed. Gaining their confidence was slow and dangerous, but I managed it in the end. I have made many secret trips here in the last three years. Easily done. There are many places one can enter and leave this swamp unobserved, and what was left of Henrietta's organization could at least get me a small, stealthed boat. I told them what I could of . . . recent developments on Wunderland, but the old one's minds were too set for them to properly take it in, the young one's minds were too unformed. But I was making progress! They came to acknowledge me as an entity, a non-Kzin, and would not willingly harm me. At least"—bitterly—"that old Jotok entity we have killed would not. Does that not tell you something about them? They are not naturally savage. Well, we have repaid his trust in the way humans so often do!"

"Stand up then. See if their laser will not willingly harm you. And what of the dead humans? The dead kzinti who sought but to fish? How do we repay *them*! Urrr!"

"The Jotok are not like humans. They are not like kzinti. That is the whole point. But within them still is the remnant of something high and great. The universe needs them. To unite the best of the three species against ARM."

"I do not see how . . ."

"It is all spoilt now. Even if they would listen to me, I have no way of reaching them. I wished to stay with you, Honored One, to speak with you when we might, to have you see . . . things . . . It was foolish of me to come on this expedition, but I thought I could control it. I should have realized that I as one of six could do little. I have made bad judgements, mistakes."

Her eyes looked into Vaemar's eyes. *How could I ever have taken her for young?* he thought as he saw the weariness there. "I have tried to do my best . . . for all . . . I have paid somewhat of a price . . ." There was liquid running out of her eyes now, the human sign of grief. "But now there is another plan, another chance. If I can live . . . If I can but reach the abbot. He may shelter me, I think. And then, and then . . ." Something else came into her eyes, making her look like the young Rosalind again, and then faded.

"I am confused often, Vaemar-Riit . . . and you see how I look. I have had much surgery. My skull is not my own . . ."

And you weren't excessively sane last time I saw you, Vaemar thought. The ghostly beam sweeping through the smoky air above them suddenly ceased. Cautiously they raised their heads. The turret on the hulk was not moving, as far as they could see, though it was hard to make out in the huge bank of white steam boiling around it. The laser had not been cooling efficiently. Either it had burnt out—not unlikely given that it had probably not been systematically serviced for the last ten years, and its cooling system was designed for firing in space anyway—or the Jotok thought them dead.

Meanwhile, thought Vaemar, the outriggers that would have been their means of escape were gone. Even the dead tree that had carried them here was burning fiercely. Alpha Centauri A had fallen far towards the horizon and night would be only a few hours away. There was no point in thinking about what to do with Rosalind/Henrietta now. He summoned the others.

"We will wait until it begins to grow dark," he told them. "Then we must set out to swim to the next island. And the next after that."

They would have to try to keep Swirl-Stripes afloat with the aid of his inflated Jotok, but Vaemar did not feel optimistic. If the returning Jotok adults pursued them they would have no chance. And even without the Jotok there would be dire problems for swimmers. The further they got away from the dead area and the Jotok, the more numerous the crocodilians and other predators would become.

Vaemar was confident that his, and Karan's, teeth and claws would see him and her through, and in other circumstances he would have reveled in such a chance to hunt and kill, especially as the channels got narrower and the water shallower towards the edges of the swamp, but he had other charges. "Do not show yourselves on the skyline!" he ordered. There was no point in letting the Jotok know they were alive. Swirl-Stripes was still drifting in and out of consciousness, but seemed to be slowly sinking. They fed him a little water when he could take it, and some compressed food from their last remaining ration pack. That reminded Vaemar of another problem. He himself was beginning to get hungry. So, he imagined, was Karan. He knew he could control his own hunger for a while yet, but in an extremity of hunger a kzin, especially, and sooner, a young kzin, could lose control and mind and attack any living thing in a mad frenzy. As Chuut-Riit's last surviving kit he had especial reason to be reminded of that. *Let me not forget I am a Hero*, he asked the Fanged God. Time passed.

The fires on the islands beyond them were beginning to die down now. The dry dead plant-stuff had not lasted long. Then in the distance he heard, or rather felt, the drumming of an engine. Marshy's boat partially surfaced in the wide channel between two of the smoldering islands. Weapons pods and sensors were extended on it.

Vaemar knew their body-heat would not show up in infrared—not with half the land masses around them still red-hot. Though the fur on his back crawled with the expectation of a laser-blast, he leapt to the highest point of the ridge, waving his arms and roaring, the tightly-focused kzin roar that can carry for miles across land or water. He saw the boat alter course towards them and dropped again. It approached and grounded in the shallows. Marshy, wearing a battle exoskeleton and carrying a beam rifle of a pattern forbidden to civilians on Wunderland of either species, leapt through the water and dropped down beside them. Vaemar, Hugo and Anne began to tell him what had happened. Then Rosalind/Henrietta screamed.

It was a scream of pain that almost shocked the kzin as his glands reacted. She was thrashing in the sand, clutching her head. A convulsive lurch took her whole body clear of the ground, then she fell back limply. She was plainly dead.

Vaemar turned to Marshy, seeking some explanation. Then he saw the old human's face was also contorted with pain. He was struggling desperately out of the exoskeleton. He flung it aside and leapt away from it, almost naked now like the rest of them.

"Heat!" he cried.

At the same moment Vaemar felt a burning against his

skin, on his hands and between his shoulders. The metal
fastenings of his belt, the only substantial thing he was
now wearing, were hot, as were the rings keyed to the
guns. He smelt a new burning smell, one that reminded
him of the battle in the redoubt: burning kzin-hair. They
had just now burnt through his fur. There was also smoke
raising from Swirl-Stripes, but with his nerve-damage he
would be unable to feel anything except his hands, which
were tearing at each other. Vaemar stripped the belt
from him, with no time for gentleness, and felt its metal
components and compartments burn his hands. The rings
followed. He tore off his own belt and rings. The humans
were doing the same, Hugo with one arm having a difficult
time of it. Between Vaemar's shoulders was a point of
agony as if a rusty nail was being driven into a nerve-trunk.

"Heat-induction!" cried Marshy. "It's the heat-induction
ray!"

The Jotok in the hulk must have been playing it on the
islands and the surrounding water for some time. It heated metal first, nonmetallic substances and living tissue
much more slowly. Some ceramics were nearly proof
against it and the weapon's own containment chamber was
ceramic. But it heated everything in the end. It was too
slow to be useful in space-battles, but it was standard
equipment on kzin warships also outfitted for ground-
attack, and a terrible weapon in the right circumstances,
like these. The kzinti had developed it to boil the seas of
Chunquen, when the natives of that watery planet had
tried to resist their invasion from primitive missile-armed
undersea ships. It was the weapon that had boiled the
heart out of Grossgeister before.

Vaemar yelled to Karan, explaining through clenched fangs what had to be done. Her claws made quick work of slicing through the loose skin between his shoulders and removing the locator. Then they did the same for the others, Vaemar having to hold them as Karan worked. Fortunately the locators were intended to be removeable, but not like this and it was painful work. Human and kzin blood spilt and ran together in the sand. No doubt with the heat and change in chemical environment the devices would be transmitting emergency signals before they cooked. Rosalind/Henrietta's head was smoldering now. Much of the skin and flesh had burnt or peeled away to reveal a metal skull.

Get in the water! His instinct shrieked, and he knew his instinct was wrong. The water would soon be boiling, as it had boiled before. He had seen pictures of the original kzin landings on Wunderland, and of what had happened when, at both Munchen and Neue Dresden, humans had tried to take refuge from fires in pools and fountains. Last time it had happened in the swamp, the creatures in the water had flung themselves ashore before the end . . . Already the water around Marshy's boat was boiling, stream beginning to rise again in a white curtain. And Vaemar realized the boat's brains and electronics were probably already cooking. As he watched, one of its guns began to fire, cycling a stream of bolts in random arcs high into the sky.

Another thought: the boat's power-source was probably a molecular-distortion battery. That would cook off also. In the war, human guerrilla forces had used MD batteries as bombs. The boat was far too close. Desperately, Vaemar wondered if he might leap into the water and push it away. The boat was firing other weapons now, as well as flares. Its siren began a screaming noise that sounded like its brain crying out.

A green bar of light slammed downwards through the smoke-obscured sky. None of those huddled on the sandbar had ever seen anything like it: a heavy naval battle-laser, mounted as either the major armament of a capital warship or in a military satellite. There was another beam, and another, converging on the hulk. The water around it was boiling in earnest now. Gun turrets on the hulk were firing again, but randomly, as ready-use ammunition cooked off. A hatch opened and it launched a *Scream-of-Vengeance* fighter. But it was either uncrewed or crewed by half-dead Jotok and simply flew in a crazy parabola before crashing in the swamp and exploding. A weird combination of flames and steam was jetting out of the holes in the great hulk.

"Cover your eyes!" cried Marshy.

Even with eyes covered and faces pressed into the sand, they saw the white flash as a bank of MD batteries in the hulk exploded. There were more explosions. Then the green beams cut off.

"They would have detected the kzin heat-induction ray at once," said Marshy. "We will have to tell them it wasn't kzinti using it." He pulled a com-link from the discarded exoskeleton and spoke urgently into it. A wave hit the sandbank, slopped over the fused glass of the ridge and splashed them. It was hot, just short of unbearable.

The secondary explosions became less frequent, then stopped. The clouds of steam drifted away and they saw the hulk clearly again. Where it had previously plainly been a derelict kzin warship, it was now a twisted, shattered, unrecognizable mass of blackened wreckage and slag, the water about it still bubbling and boiling. No living thing could be seen on or in it. They stood staring at it in silence for some time. Marshy worked on Swirl-Stripes with a small, portable doc. Its lights at length pronounced his condition stabilized. Then Karan pointed: Kzin eyes could make out that dead Jotok of all sizes were floating out of the wreckage. Already, from nowhere, a few carrion-eating flying things had appeared in the sky.

"Nothing could have survived that," said Marshy. "But perhaps we should go and look." He splashed to his boat. "The brain's not quite cooked," he said as he returned. "But it was a near thing. Most of the electronics are out, but we've got a ride home." He was carrying lightweight ABC suits, protection against atomic, biological or chemical contamination, and passed these to the other humans.

"I'll take Anne and Hugo," he went on, helping Hugo into one. "I've none to fit kzinti. You had better stay and look after your companion till we return." He looked down at Rosalind/Henrietta's body. "That had better be disposed of," he added, tactfully. "Does she have a family?"

Anne tore her eyes away from the bare metallic skull and the hands stilled in the act of trying to claw it open. Her own face was very white. "She told me she was an orphan," she said in a somewhat shaky voice. That was not surprising. There were, after all, many orphans on Wunderland. "Forgive me . . . it's . . . it's nothing."

Hugo placed his uninjured arm round Anne's shoulder and guided her to the water's edge where she too donned a suit. Vaemar, watching, though again how strange and simian the naked humans looked, with their odd tufts of hair, sexual characteristics and ungraceful taillessness. *And yet companions*, he thought. Hugo and Anne splashed out to the boat. Marshy retrieved a decontamination kit from it and sprayed them all.

"You seek to finish the Jotok?" Vaemar asked Marshy.

"No. To preserve any we can, though I have little hope of that."

"For what? A new generation of slaves for the Wunderkzin? Perhaps there are still a few skilled Trainers-of-Jotok among the kzinti here."

"No."

"Or for the humans?"

"No. Unless they are trained very early they cannot live as slaves. In any case enslavement, even of another species, is contrary to all human law, and Wunderland, I need hardly remind you, is part of human space again . . . But I shall have to search thoroughly. We shall be gone a little while," he added as the boat moved away.

Vaemar turned to the body again. Henrietta. His Honored Sire's slave, who his Honored Sire had at last addressed as "Friend." Who had mourned his Honored Sire and tried in her way to be faithful to his memory, as well as to bring some sort of settlement between kzinti and men. She had done him no real harm, indeed had given good advice in their escape, and her remains deserved dignified disposal. Besides, he was getting very hungry now, and not only because of the relaxation that followed release from deadly danger. Karan, he could see, was hungry, too.

Another thought passed through his mind: after he had commanded her in the Ultimate Imperative Tense to speak truth, she had suddenly ceased to claim that she was Henrietta, and had begun to speak of Henrietta in the third person. Did that mean anything? Was she not the real Henrietta? There had been a number of human females among the followers of Henrietta and Emma in the redoubt. Perhaps it didn't matter. A pair of aircraft flashed into the sky above, hovered for a moment over the wreckage, barrel-rolled and were gone.

He had finished tidying the scene when Marshy and the others returned. Swirl-Stripes had also taken a little nourishment and the lights on the doc remained steady.

"Nothing," the old man said. "As I thought. They were all cooked."

"Is that such a disaster?"

"It is a . . . misfortune. And a cause of sadness. They were a great civilization once. Not only great, but benevolent. They raised many worlds to civilization and prosperity in the days of their greatness. Oh, they did it for their own ends, partly, realizing that successful traders need wealthy customers. But perhaps there was more to it than that . . .

"We had better get out of here," he went on. "There are some liberated radioactives in that wreckage. This place will soon be deadly for all who go near, and remain deadly until it's cleaned up. Another reason there will be no Jotok. Any more distant foragers who return now will die. And your companion needs more than first aid or the boat's doctor. We can't stay around and we can't help them anyway."

He turned again to the battle-exoskeleton. Rosalind/Henrietta's belt and its utility-pouches lay on the sand nearby. He picked them up together, and began to close the exoskeleton down. "Odd," he said after a moment.

"What is odd?"

Marshy pointed to the console. The sensory equipment on the battle armor included a broad-spectrum life-form scanner. Its oscilloscope, which had been flat-lining, was now recording small waves. He put the belt down to examine the screen more closely. As he did so the waves stopped. He raised the belt again, holding the two together for a moment, and then opened the ceramic containers that hung from the belt. He drew a light from the exoskeleton.

"Look."

"What are they?"

"Jotok tadpoles. Free-swimmers, still unjoined. She must have collected them in the hulk."

"Yes," said Vaemar. He remembered now how she had dropped behind them as they waded up the flooded corridor. That water must have been alive with larval Jotok. They were the minnowlike things he had seen in the first chamber.

"No ordinary swimming creature has a brainwave like that," said Marshy.

"So what happens to them?" asked Vaemar. "You say they cannot be enslaved. Will you kill them?"

"No."

"I know humans are sentimental at times. Will you set them free to starve? Or to live feral in the wilds and the swamps, the last of their kind on this world? As zoo specimens, perhaps?"

"None of those things. The abbot and . . . others . . . gave me several missions a long time ago: one was to find Jotok, if any still survived. The ponds at Circle Bay Monastery can be nurturing-places for them. And they can be taught to be both intelligent and free. It will take a long time. But perhaps we can make them traders once more. A highly honorable calling for Jotoki. I said they helped many species to civilization once. Now we can help them to civilization again."

Vaemar felt a snarl rising in his throat. Free Jotok! A planned outrage to the kzin species, to the Patriarch whose blood flowed in his veins! His jaws began to gape and he felt his claws sliding from their sheaths. One sweep of those claws would end that possibility once and for all. The man, like all its kind, was, he knew, contemptibly slow. He began to raise one arm, hind-claws digging into the ground to give his stroke purchase, muscles without conscious thought twisting to give his body added torque as he struck . . . He felt Karan's eyes on him, and something made him pause. He felt the surge of fury recede. Was he still a kzin of the Patriarchy? He stood puzzled for a moment, tail twitching.

Henrietta had been his Honored Sire Chuut-Riit's faithful slave. Free Jotok would be a memorial to her. In an indirect way, they might carry on her work. In a strange, unforseen way, they might be a memorial to Chuut-Riit too. *Perhaps,* he thought, *our memorials are always unforseen. My Honored Sire was a great enough master to inspire loyalty in some humans, and as a result*

I live and a race may live again. He lowered his arm. He did not know if Marshy had noticed, or noticed the effort with which he spoke.

"I ssee . . . Sshee ssaid the univerrse needed them."

"Whoever you mean, she was right. They were a rare thing, too precious to lose . . ."

They boarded the boat. Minor injuries and scorches were treated. Swirl-Stripes was taken below, and they headed up-channel on the surface. They drew away from the drifting clouds of smoke and steam, the islands of crackling flames.

The slanting rays of Alpha Centauri A lit the clear water a delicate blue-green that deepened as the sun sank further. The islands they passed were living again. Vaemar, his fur dry, settled into the broad, almost fooch-like, bench that ran around the aft cockpit, watching the colors changing in the water and sky, the first stars and sliding satellites appearing as Alpha Centauri A set. A few hours before, he thought, he had not expected to see the stars again. Life was good. Karan sat in the opposite corner. He felt a sudden tickling and looked down. The tip of her tail was twined around his. Their eyes met again and this time it was she who raised her ears in a smile.

Catspaws

❖

Hal Colebatch

That an ape has hands is far less interesting to a philosopher than the fact that having hands he does next to nothing with them.

—G. K. Chesterton, Orthodoxy, 1908.

Chapter 1

Occupied Wunderland, 2406 A.D.

The human freighter from Tiamat and the Serpent Swarm landed at a corner of the old Munchen spaceport not needed at that moment by the warships of the Patriarch's Navy.

Humans, however, inconvenienced their conquerors even potentially only at their peril. Under the guns of security guards of the Wunderland government the freighter was unloaded with feverish haste, largely by sweating human muscle.

The guards took their bribes, ran checks over the piles of cargo seeking for weapons, explosives or other contraband, checked the manifests with their counterparts at Tiamat, took more bribes, and saw the cargo into a bonded warehouse. Few humans served either the kzinti or the collaborationist human government with fanatical zeal, but terror, desperation and poverty made workable substitutes for devotion. The ship took off again for Alpha Centauri A's asteroids before the kzinti decided they needed its landing area.

With the area cleared there was time for another, more thorough check. Part of the cargo, 50- and 100-liter liquid containers, was shown to be medical and agricultural chemicals, as the manifest described. Raw material for geriatric and other drugs, plus a few agricultural trace-elements in solution. There were also the usual vacuum and zero-gravity products that were a mainstay of Serpent Swarm export, manufactured in space and on asteroids where there were still relatively few kzinti and more working human factories. There were sealed containers with the warning symbol for radioactive substances, but these were elaborately certified from Tiamat's medical laboratories and the government as vital isotopes for nuclear medicine and without potential weapons use.

The chemical containers and some of the other cargo were loaded into primitive but well-armed wheeled vehicles. The kzinti allowed few humans to use flyers, even the clumsy human ground-effect cars. The vehicles' signatures were transmitted continually to the kzinti and Wunderland government satellites monitoring traffic and they were allowed to proceed by road along a predetermined route to a processing plant. That road had, long before, been made in a few hours by the flame of a hovering ship's reaction-drive fusing the ground. Now it was kept more-or-less in repair by gangs of human serfs with picks and shovels.

The geriatric chemicals needed processing but, even without the remainder of the consignments, they, far more than the nuclear material, would still have made a prize almost beyond price for any highjacker. There were few geriatric drugs or facilities on the ground for making

them with the Wunderland economy shattered by the war
and the kzin occupation. People were ageing and dying.
Few human criminals, however, now had the resources
for a highjacking. Crime was largely a matter of solitary
muggings or Government-level corruption.

The processing plant where the vehicles stopped stood
in a semi-ruined area on the outskirts of the city. There
had been a battle there in the few days of organized
human ground resistance around Munchen after the kzinti
landings, and much of the area had been flattened, but
some factories were now providing a thin stream of
necessities. The *Trummerfrauen* (that archaic term
recently revived on Wunderland) had been and gone. The
repaired and gimcrack new buildings—factories, workers'
huts, a few small bars and shops—stood here and there
like islands.

The streets wandering through this semi-wasteland
were bleak and empty, though the reddish Wunderland
vegetation was growing back on the wide stretches
where nothing had been rebuilt and there were some
Wunderland scavenging creatures, bolder than they had
once been. Beam's Beasts, Advokats and even a few of
the foul zeitungers were breeding up again as sanitary
services broke down in these districts, and attempts at
preserving something of civic culture gave way to apathy
and despair. However, some humans kept minimal services
going. Kzinti did not like dogs barking, and the dogs
rounded up to help produce that primitive, now near-
priceless chemical, insulin, were muzzled or without
vocal chords in their cages under the plant, the plant
itself sheltered behind heaps of rusty razor-wire. Kzinti

seldom deigned to visit these parts but there were a few robot and human sentries, the robots the better armed.

The containers were unloaded, checked off again, and stored in secure areas. The contents of most of them were made into desperately needed drugs. Some people involved got rich, though in rapidly inflating occupation money. Some made enough to get to the Serpent Swarm or into the hills. Some of the nuclear material found its way to hospitals where painful and primitive treatments and procedures had been revived, often for long-forgotten but now also revived diseases. Many people who would otherwise have died, lived, at least for a time.

However not all the containers were opened. Some few were removed and dummies substituted. These containers were eventually loaded onto other primitive vehicles, or onto horses and mules, and, with other traffic, taken northeast in cautious stages to the great limestone escarpment of the Hohe Kalkstein and the sparsely-settled country beyond. A few days after they left the warehouse the collaborationist government on orders from the local kzin supervisor-of-animals brought in a kzin telepath to sweep the minds of key personnel working in the plant. The resistance was alerted beforehand and several fled. The alert was not perfect, however, and so several others died, but they died before the telepath could reach them.

Occupied Wunderland, 2407 A.D.

The convoy arrived in the little valley at nightfall. Nils and Leonie Rykermann and a dozen others emerged from hiding and greeted it. More remained hidden.

"Our instructions," said the guerrilla courier in charge of the convoy, "are to get this stuff to you, and you are to get it under cover. Bury it in the caves—caves that aren't used—and forget it until you hear further." He passed Rykermann a sealed copy of orders.

"What is it?"

"I don't know." That was hardly surprising. "Need to know" was enforced with religious zeal in the Resistance. Kzin interrogation of prisoners very often included telepathic probing, and even without this kzin tortures were very persuasive. "Markham's ships picked it up off Acheron." He gestured to the nuclear-material warning which some of the containers bore. That seemed self-explanatory even if the rest did not. "It was landed with false certifications. I know there was a lot of effort put into getting it here."

Rykermann nodded. "If it's something that kills ratcats, that's all that matters for now," he said. Hatred glittered in his eyes. "Dead ratcats. That's all that matters," he repeated to himself. It was probably an unnecessary statement. None of the humans present felt differently.

"I don't think Sol would go to this much trouble to send us strawberry ice cream," the courier said.

Their infrared signatures, diffused through the canopy of leaves, and further by the cloaks which they and their mounts wore, might be indistinguishable from those of a herd of gagrumpher or other large Wunderland animals to kzin or government surveillance satellites. But it would be foolish to bet that way for too long and they wasted little time in talking.

Rykermann, the Resistance's chief biochemist and Wunderland's major expert on the great cave systems of the Hohe Kalkstein, supervised the rapid unloading of the animals. The containers were stacked inside one of the many cave entrances in the area. Some of these caves joined the huge main system, but even those that did not could be prodigious in themselves. Mapping the great caves and their connecting passages—many times the size of the Carlsbad Caverns of Earth—had been barely begun when the kzinti landed forty years before, and after decades of use by human guerrillas it was still very far from complete. A quick prior inspection had shown these chambers at least to be free of recent signs of Morlocks, the large, quasi-humanoid but near-brainless predators that had ruled in the deep caves. The two parties hurriedly began covering the containers.

"I'm sorry I can't stay and socialize," said the courier.

"Don't apologize," said Rykermann. "Whatever this stuff is, we'd better not linger too near it. And I've got an honest job to get back to."

"Kzin!" screamed Leonie as the two gravity-cars rose over the valley-wall. Her beam rifle was firing before she finished the word. Attached to her rifle was a small surface-to-air missile. It just missed one of the sledges, but the kzinti did not know it was the only one the guerrillas had—given the threat of such missiles, they could not circle firing from the air. They needed no other encouragement for ground-combat. Other guerrillas, previously posted, fired from hiding-places around. Some of the weapons were primitive makeshifts, others were more modern and effective.

The kzin cars were sledges for light scouts and hunting-parties, not for full-scale war, but they carried a couple of heavy beam-weapons mounted at the noses and the great felinoids had sidearms. The beam from one smashed into the part-buried heap of containers before the housing of the car's gravity-planer was hit and it turned over, the screaming kzinti leaping clear, firing their own weapons as they came. The main human party was down too, firing into them.

One of the human party's horses provided a diversion. Maddened by the smell of kzinti it broke its tether and ran screaming. Uncontrollable reflexes triggered by the sight and by the smell of its terror, two kzinti leapt at it, razor claws slashing through saddle, hide, muscle and ribs, the kzinti themselves presenting a target the human marks-men were quick to find. The shrieking animal ran in a semicircle, crashing into a group of kzin as it collapsed in its death-agony. The humans had time to begin firing at the grounded kzin troops in earnest before they leapt.

The ground combat was short and bloody. No human could hope to match a kzin in speed or strength, but if the human was trained and experienced and could get in or under shelter with a modern weapon, the odds were evened a good deal. The members of the guerrilla supply column obeyed their instincts and went down in a circle, firing outwards. The kzinti obeyed their instincts and tactical doctrine: they leapt and charged, screaming and firing as they came. Kzinti died in the charge, but the circle of guerrillas was overrun and shattered. Their heavy weapons apart, the kzinti's speed and agility were as terrible in battle as were their claws, teeth, strength and merciless fury.

Leonie leapt to one of the abandoned kzin sledges and swung its heavier gun onto the main kzin body. More kzinti died, the survivors scattered, regrouped and counterattacked. Leonie and the gun were their main target for a moment. A laser blast hit her squarely in the chest, but she was wearing one of the guerrillas' few high-tech lightweight flak-jackets with layers of mirror. She went down in a diving somersault and crawled away as the guerrillas— Rykermann's group and the few survivors of the supply party—gave covering fire. The kzinti again charged the main human position. Again kzinti died, and so did a large number of humans, then, but thanks largely to Leonie and the gun, the humans now outnumbered the kzin enough to take losses and keep fighting.

The leader of the guerrilla convoy was torn apart by the claws of one kzin slow to die of wounds, who plunged on to wreak havoc with rest of the convoy party. The surviving kzinti scattered after their first slashing leaps, but humans followed them, screaming their own battle-cries. The kzinti, instead of disappearing into the darkening forest, regrouped and leapt back. Strakkakers, Lewis-guns and beam and bullet rifles met them. The kill-ratio was better this time, almost one kzinti for every two humans dead. Four kzinti made it into the cave, where the fight ended. The humans had bombs of nitrate-based explosives.

Nils and Leonie Rykermann, highly-experienced fighters, and protected as major assets by their own people, survived, as did some of their fighters. None of the convoy party did.

The last fighting kzin, staggering bloody and maimed from the cave to die on the attack, fell screaming in a storm of converging bullets and beams. The few surviving humans moved fast, killing the wounded kzinti and those of their own too badly wounded to move.

"Let's go!" Tasso von Lufft, the second-in-command, grabbed Rykermann's arm.

The dying kzin commander had been playing possum, hoping to lure a human within reach of his claws. Rykermann finished shooting him between the eyes. Some kzinti were terrified of going to the Fanged God without ears or noses. In case this kzin should be one such, Rykermann paid his respects to the details of this belief by slashing the nose off with his ratchet-knife. Two more slashes secured the tattooed ears, which would go to his belt—a kzin custom which the guerrillas had adopted. With practiced fingers he rifled the ammunition pouches.

"We can't leave this stuff!" Leonie protested. Half the containers were unburied still, a number scarred by the kzin beam. The damp ground around them steamed.

"There'll be more ratcats here any minute," von Lufft objected.

"Not quite yet," said Leonie. "If that was a set ambush they'd have had follow-up on top of us now. I think it was just a hunting party or a random patrol."

"But the cars will probably have signalled," said von Lufft. "And satellites will have picked up the beams.

We've got to get out of here fast! There will be more kzin forces on the way here now. That's if they're in the mood for a hunt and don't just hit us from space."

"They died to get that stuff here," said Nils Rykermann, gesturing at the dead leader of the couriers. "Whatever it is, it's important."

"And if it's dangerous, and leaking? Those drums took a fair hit. Like the man said, I don't think it's strawberry ice cream."

"If they're leaking virulent radioactives we're dead already. But"—a quick examination—"I don't see my meter moving. I'm hoping they were made with strong linings. Come on! The sooner we get them covered the sooner we're out of here."

The containers were quickly buried in the caves, invisible to any human in the entrance or the main passage. Decades of war had made these resistance fighters instinctively expert at camouflage. The scattered bodies, human and kzin, were stripped of equipment and weapons. Some of the humans carved pieces of flesh from the dead kzinti for ritual cooking and eating later.

There were too few survivors to carry everything away, and what could not be moved was smashed. They turned to the kzin cars and wrecked them as thoroughly as they could. Flying them was out of the question. It had been, Rykermann thought, counting the survivors, a Pyhrric victory—in fact no victory at all. The kzinti could afford to lose a couple of carloads of troops more than the guerrillas could afford to lose so many proven fighters—and friends. Friends who had died for he knew not what. He hoped it was worth it to whoever in Sol System was responsible.

The courier group would have to be rebuilt from scratch with a fresh draft of doomed humans. Most guerrilla formations had already had casualty rates of several times one hundred percent of their original numbers. With that thought Rykermann, not for the first time, fought down a sense of hopelessness that at times threatened to overwhelm him. *How much longer will recruits come forward for the fight?* he thought. And answered himself: *As long as the kzinti remain terrible and unendurable. And that will be until we are all dead, and forever beyond that.* He scattered a few pressure-mines about the site, and sacrificed a precious strand of Sinclair wire, stretching it between two trees at a height where it might, with luck, decapitate or bisect any kzinti charging in pursuit, though it was fiendishly dangerous and difficult to handle in the dark.

The surviving guerrillas scattered into the forest, to where the rest of their horses and ponies were waiting hobbled under a limestone overhang at the entrance of another cave. They were not ideal transport between the trees but they were the fastest things reasonably safe from mechanical detection, and horses needed no urging to flee from the smell of kzinti. There were many horses without riders now, and the surviving guerrillas turned some of these loose in the hope they would be a decoy.

Then they rode, the woods dark around and above them. Behind them after a little while were the flashes and reports of kzin missiles hitting the site of the fighting. Lights in the sky were kzin gravity-cars flashing towards the scene, loaded with troops.

Branches whipped by them. The fleeing guerrillas

smashed through a glade where a small herd of gagrumphers were sleeping, the creatures lurching bellowing to their feet in the dark around them. Good, thought Rykermann, as he realized what they were. The infrared signatures of the big beasts milling about might help confuse kzin spy-satellites as well as ground troops. At his command they hauled their horses round and headed northwest, at right-angles to their previous path.

They splashed through a wide, shallow stream, dropping powerful olfactory agents that might confuse kzinti tracking them by unaided scent. Rykermann turned to glance at Leonie, bent low over her pony's neck, urging it on, and the other survivors about, counting them again. He dug in his own spurs. It would be a near thing. It was one of the rare nights when, with neither Alpha Centauri B nor Wunderland's moons yet risen, the sky would be relatively dark for some time. He hoped that would help the fleeing humans more than the kzinti.

The kzinti bombarded the area behind them, though only with ordinary weapons, then their troopers landed and swept it, snarling over their dead. One triggered a pressure-mine, adding to the rage and confusion. With their eyes' superb sensitivity to movement and their keyed-up, hair-trigger reflexes, they blasted a number of small animals, both in the limestone glades and hollows and when they fired at dim movements in the dark of the caves. They found one badly-wounded human alive whom Rykermann's party in its haste had missed and took him for terminal interrogation. They removed their own dead and threw the burnt human dead into the caves, after removing ears and other trophies in their turn.

The unburnt human dead were stacked in the cars—monkeymeat.

Then they left, searching for humans, some running on all fours and leaping into the dark of the forest like the great hunting cats they were. One of the sledges was salvaged, the other, wrecked beyond possibility of further use, was abandoned. The slave-worked factories produced them for the kzin armed forces in thousands. One flying car hit the Sinclair wire, with spectacular and bloody results. They left. As Rykermann had hoped, the noisy gagrumphers delayed them a little.

Silence returned to the valley and the caves. Then the flying cave-creatures that the humans called mynocks returned from the deeper caverns to their perches, hissing, squawking, their droppings, rich in nitrates and concentrated uric acid, falling to add to the deep layers already forming the cave floor: food for the vermiforms and other scavengers. More acidic compounds, burying the containers a little deeper.

After a time a party of Morlocks from the deeper caves approached the place where the noise and lights had been. The mynocks rose in a shrieking cloud, some snapping at the Morlocks with their horny toothed beaks and beating at them with barbed leathery wings. The Morlocks leapt and tore at them with slavering, baboon-like muzzles, dragging those they could out of the air to tear apart and eat alive. The main cloud of mynocks divided and flapped away, some into the night sky outside, some down the tunnels and into the labyrinth's deeper darkness. The Morlocks were savage and hungry. With the mynocks gone the smell of burnt human flesh drew them, heads down and bulging eyes running with tears and squinting against the little starlight that filtered into the cave's crepuscular zone.

One, climbing over the new mound of soil and rock, exposed one of the containers. It grasped it with splayed, five-fingered hands and worked it partly loose. The container's hard ceramic outer casing had been damaged, as had some of the metal of the inner casing beneath, but not completely penetrated. The Morlock shrieked and spat as it touched a jagged metal surface still hot. It knew only that it had no smell about it of food. It abandoned the container and joined the others tearing at the mynock and human corpses.

When all was eaten the Morlocks left again. Later the mynocks came back. The life-cycles and the chemical processes of the cave ecology resumed.

Chapter 2

Liberated Wunderland, 2433 A.D.

Again, Alpha Centauri A was setting, though at this time of year Alpha Centauri B rose early, filling the sky with wondrous purple light, silver-cored. Two watchers took their ease on the scarp of the Hohe Kalkstein, admiring the splendour of evening as their system's twin star cleared the horizon in its diamond-brilliant glory, offset by the ruby point of Proxima. There were satellites in the near sky, and the frequent sliding and flash of meteors: the wonder-filled evening of Wunderland. Before them, the escarpment swept down into a great plain, with a view of distant mesas to the south-east and a few far scattered lights. From certain cave mouths in the cliffs below them flying creatures issued into the twilight—great leather-flappers, species of mynocks, and little flittermyce in clouds like smoke.

Nils Rykermann, Professor of Field Biology at Munchen University, lay back on a portable couch, punching a notebook's keys in a leisurely manner. His colleague and pupil Vaemar, sometimes known as Vaemar-Riit,

Master of Arts and Science, doctoral student in several disciplines and son of the late Planetary Governor Chuut-Riit, recent injuries at his neck and shoulders sutured, disinfected and dressed, reclined on another.

"I think we've done all we can for the moment," Rykermann remarked. "Back to the city tomorrow." He had recently taken to smoking Wunderland chew-bacca and now he looked into his pipe's glowing bowl as an aid to thought. The pipe, an intricately-worked thing of wood and metal, was a gift from his pupil, who did not himself smoke.

"I suppose it has to be." Vaemar lashed his tail meditatively. "I enjoy the High Limestone."

"Even with your Morlock bites?"

"Yes. Stupid creatures to attack me at odds of only eight to one. And it's a few more ears for my trophy-belt. Honored Step-Sire Raargh will bawl me out about the scars but he'll approve none-too-secretly. So will Karan. And young Step-Siblings will admire. And Orlando."

"Raargh's got plenty of scars himself, and a lot of them from the same creatures," said Rykermann. "I got some with him. Anyway, it looks as if we won't have to breed a new Morlock population in test-tubes. We know now that they're living and breeding in the deep caves all by themselves. Lots of them, it seems. We'll have to improve security for our expeditions, though. And you've got other work to do."

"Yes, I'm afraid I tend to let my enthusiasm for field-trips bias me too much towards my biological studies."

"I'd noticed. But as the greeting goes, The Kzin is a Mighty Hunter. I don't want to discourage you. And your other grades and projects leave nothing to be desired. The physics, mathematics *and* history prizes were a good trio. And up here the formations grow well. You positioned the Sinclair Fields and the pumps cleverly."

The two were silent again for a time, contemplating the night and the majestic view. Vaemar pointed. "Visitors," he said.

Rykermann squinted in the direction of Vaemar's extended claw. A few moments later his eyes too made out the lights of an approaching car. Vaemar gave a churr of delight as it landed and his old friend and chess partner, Colonel Michael Cumpston, alighted.

Cumpston greeted them briefly, giving Vaemar a scratch under the chin in response to his grooming lick, but in a half-crouching position: in the past Vaemar's enthusiastic welcome had knocked him over more than once.

"I've got a message from Arthur Guthlac," he told Rykermann. "He would take it as a personal favor if you could meet him at your first convenience." He paused and went on in a different tone. "Early's involved."

"Why didn't Arthur just send me an e-mail? We're seeing him in a few days anyway, aren't we?"

"This isn't social, I'm afraid. Security," said Cumpston.

"Why couldn't he come himself?"

"Give him a break! He's been working round the clock trying to get his desk cleared before the big event. There's some secret business."

"What?"

"As I said, secret. He didn't confide in a humble colonel. Anyway, you're wanted back at the ranch. Now."

"I'm not a soldier any more. He can't order me round. In fact, since I'm a Member of Parliament, it could be a breach of Parliamentary privilege to do so."

"Nils, Arthur may be a friend of ours, but don't mess with Early. You know better."

"I thought he'd left Wunderland. That Montferrat-Palme or someone had put pressure on him to go—to get out of the system."

"He went—physically. Some have said it would be better if he was still under our noses."

"We're just about finished here for the time being, anyway," Rykermann said. "Vaemar can take charge of packing things up."

Cumpston nodded. Though he kept his expression blank, the former exterminationist's friendship for and trust in the young kzin pleased and amused him. "Another thing. Arthur says you should upgrade your security. He was vague about the details, but I gather there have been a few . . . problems in this area."

"I suppose we have let things get a bit lax." There were farms and hamlets dotted about the fertile tableland beyond the great escarpment and things seemed very peaceful.

They were silent for a moment. Then Cumpston stretched his arms and cracked his knuckles in a leisurely way. It had the effect of showing him the instruments on the forearm of his jacket.

"Don't look now," he said slowly, making an gesture that took in a heap of boulders to his left, and raising his hand to pinch his lower lip, "but I am getting a signal from the motion detector from behind that rock-pile.

Something quite large and bipedal. The high probability is human."

Rykermann nodded thoughtfully, as if agreeing with the point Cumpston had made. He did not have a laser-ring like the ARM officer, but the ring on the hand that brushed his thigh activated his pistol. Vaemar yawned and also stretched, a feline's extravagant stretch that arched his back and dug his claws into the ground. He pulled up one forearm and then the other, in a lazy, breadmaking gesture. Then he leapt over the rock.

There was a human scream, and an angry spitting from Vaemar. He reappeared holding a human child or adolescent. Thrust into his belt was a gun it had evidently been carrying.

"Feral," he said, though the clothes it was wearing made it obvious. "And clever. Look at this." His hand with retracted claws touched his captive's cheek with surprising gentleness. "Rarctha fat. That's why I didn't smell him. No weapons."

"Who are you?" asked Rykermann. The youngster struggled and spat.

"Not a Wabbit," said Cumpstom. The Wascal Wabbits were the most sociopathic gang of ferals on Liberated Wunderland. Their facial tattoos were easy identifiers.

"Turn him round," said Guthlac, though the young feral's sex was not in fact obvious. With a single practiced movement he brought a tranquilizer-gun from his belt and fired a Teflon dart into its shoulder. The feral went limp.

"They don't hunt alone," said Cumpston, as the feral was put into his car.

"I know," said Guthlac.

"A gang of them, armed, can be a real danger," said Cumpston. "I'll report to security, of course, and get some proper people out here after them, but in the meantime, it wouldn't be a good idea for any of your students to be wandering about unsupervised or unarmed."

"Not all my students are helpless," said Rykermann. "And none of us are ever quite unarmed. All the same, I don't want anyone using weapons on children. I hope we have the resources to bring them all in soon."

"That's up to you. You're the politician," said Cumpston. "But as I say, I gather Arthur's had . . . reports. Disappearances. Within a few miles of here. Maybe this lot are to blame." He turned to Vaemar. "Don't leave your students here alone. I'd suggest, if I may, that you call them up now. Get them back to town as soon as you can."

Chapter 3

"You sent Earth a message a couple of years ago, asking us if a consignment of radioactives or biological weapons had been sent to Wunderland at a certain time during the war," said Brigadier Arthur Guthlac. "Why?" He spoke with the indefinable awkwardness of a friend suddenly turned official.

"Two years ago?" Rykermann frowned. "Yes, of course I did. But why bring that up now? I assume it's been dealt with."

"No. Thanks to our bureaucracy it has only reached the relevant desk recently. And that by chance. One of Early's subordinates with a long memory happened to see it on its way to the files. It was, of course a secret job, and very few ever knew about it. Normally we, or the Wunderland Government, would have sent out a team to clean it up in due course—when a mountain of higher priorities had been disposed of."

"So?"

"Why did you send it?" Guthlac repeated. "When you did?"

"A routine part of tidying up," Rykermann told him. "We buried some stuff during the war, stuff we were told had been sent from Earth, and I thought the UNSN should remove it. It was obviously something secret and military. Therefore something dangerous. I won't apologize that it took us a long time to get round to it. We've also had one or two other things on our hands, you know."

"You're sure it was stuff sent from Earth."

"That was what we were told," said Rykermann. "From Earth via the Serpent Swarm belt. The courier who delivered it to us was killed. I don't know any more than that."

"When did it happen?"

"It was about a year before the kzinti captured me in the caves. About fourteen Earth-years before liberation."

"So it got through," Guthlac said. "We thought it had been lost in space."

"What was it? . . . Don't pull that stone face on me. We took risks for it," Rykermann told him. "A number of people died for it. Answer my question, please, Arthur. Also, I happen to be not only the chief biologist for the cave complexes, I'm very close to the Minister for Environmental Protection. Do you want me to tell him there's an unknown bioweapon from Earth at large and Earth won't tell us anything about it? That is my duty as a Wunderlander and a member of the Government. And there was nuclear stuff, too."

"Nils, I know well enough you are a politician," said Guthlac. "In any case I suppose you'll need to know. It's Pak tree-of-life. And, Nils, I'm ordering you to say nothing about it."

Rykermann drew in his breath sharply. He looked as if

he was about to burst out with something, but then said only: "Why?"

"I'll tell you. But I'll trade you information. Tell me more. Everything that happened then."

"We were in the wild country beyond the Hohe Kalkstein. There was a fight." Rykermann told him the story.

"We hid the stuff and cleared out," he concluded. "After that we had plenty of other things to do, beginning with getting away. If I thought about it at all later, I wondered if it might be a radioactive agent we were meant to smuggle into kzin ships or areas and then open. Enriched uranium for detonators, perhaps. Initiators for simple fission bombs. Plutonium. Caesium. Or some biological plague that the Sol Laboratories had developed to use on ratcats. But I had other things on my mind. We'd done as Sol instructed, at big risk all along the way. In the day-to-day matters of staying alive I didn't give it too much thought.

"The resistance was getting into a bad way then. Not just because attrition was wearing us down and more and more humans were either giving up and accepting their lot or just dead. Chuut-Riit had begun studying humans and that was making life harder for us all. Some kzinti were investigating monkey stuff—it had been beneath their dignity before—and some were also getting all too interested in what they found. They were learning more about us and it was getting harder to hide.

"Then I was captured by the kzinti," Rykermann went on. "Thanks to Raargh-Sergeant and because we'd fought together against the Morlocks, and Leonie had soft-heartedly

saved his life, I was awarded fighters' privileges and
paroled. That changed my lifestyle. I wouldn't risk front-
fighting and then falling into kzin claws again after breaking
my word to them—there are some things you can't ask of a
man and that's one of them. I was exhausted anyway. Plus
they had a *zzrou* implant in me, not being overly trusting of
any monkey. I became more a back-room boy for a long
time. There was plenty for a backroom boy to do."

Guthlac nodded. Rykermann went on.

"Time passed. We did what we could, growing a little
weaker and more hopeless each year. Then came other
things, it seemed on top of one another, hard and fast: the
ramscoop raid and the death of Chuut-Riit, followed by
the kzinti's civil war and the Liberation. That didn't mean
the end of work for us. In many ways we were busier than
ever.

"I thought the *zzrou* would kill me come Liberation.
But a human doctor managed to hack it out. He died
instead of me when it exploded. Thanks to Leonie, some
of my people found me in the wreckage just before I bled
to death. But without fancy surgery I spent the Liberation
with a hole the size of your fist where my right scapula had
been, and not, as you can imagine, taking a very active
part. Finally they got me to the UNSN forces and one of
the military regeneration tanks. Other wounded had to
make do with organ banks. I was fortunate enough to be
spared that."

Rykermann was telling Guthlac things he knew already,
but Guthlac let him speak on. He knew one terrible thing
Rykermann might be referring to when he spoke of organ
banks and apparently it still helped him to talk.

"Later, when things had settled down, and I was generally tidying up loose ends, I asked the authorities if they had sent us any dangerous radioactive material. I didn't hear anything more. That was the last I thought about it until now. I love my biological work and that's what I'd rather concentrate on. And . . . well, there were other things on my mind, too."

"Dangerous, to leave radioactives around."

"Cleaning up Wunderland will be a long job, Arthur," Rykermann said. "There are lots of crashed ships, lots of spilled radioactives, lots of munitions, half-made experimental bioweapons, lots of hot dumps still. Our granite's generally a lot hotter than Earth's as well, which can make detection more difficult. I guess we'll have to wait till the war's over in space before we can even think of seeing the resources to do the job properly. But now you say . . ." Again he stopped as if biting off words.

"Anyway, you were right," Guthlac said. "There were some nukes in it, along with triggers—bombs ready to go. Some of them very dirty and with a big bang for their size."

"That's not very nice to have loose on Wunderland," said Rykermann. "There are still kzin revanchists around, not to mention some humans who could be even more dangerous. Apart from—the other thing. We must bring it in now. I suppose you have the signatures of the nukes?"

"Yes. Here." Guthlac gestured to a computer-brick. "They shouldn't be too hard to find—in fact they were designed to leave signatures so they could be retrieved from hiding-places easily. We also had transmitters broadcasting those signatures. They are so miniaturized they aren't very effective, but they might help. We also have triggering codes. But you want the full story?"

"To Hell with the nukes! Pak tree-of-life. Why?"

"One of the greatest services Markham and the Alpha Centauri resistance did for humanity was to set up a maser facility on Nifelheim," Guthlac said. "They were able to send Sol a lot of information about the kzinti and in particular their fleets.

"Markham? He knocked down a lot of the kzin surveillance satellites," said Rykermann. "And his people jinxed others to send misleading information. The resistance would never have survived otherwise. That's what we owe him for. But what's Markham got to do with tree-of-life?"

"For us it was the intelligence he sent that mattered. Keeping that secret channel open was priceless. We were also masering them, but at both ends we kept our messages short and few. For the kzinti to have intercepted them would have been disastrous. But as you say, until Chuut-Riit settled firmly into command they didn't take much interest in what monkeys did so long as they were decorous slaves. We, like you, took advantage of that.

"The message we sent with the special consignment was deliberately cryptic. Decoded it said only: 'Hide it. You'll get further instructions if and when the time comes.'

"When things were going from bad to worse in the war, about the time of the third big kzin fleet attack on Sol," Guthlac went on, "Early's people launched Operation Cherubim."

"I've never heard of it."

"Very few did. By that time we were beginning to fear

sabotage of the war effort by pacifists and would-be quislings in Sol system. Thanks to Markham's masers we knew that in the Centauri system humans had not been exterminated but were living under a collaborationist government. We made that public knowledge, thinking it might be good for morale—Sol people would have grounds to hope their families and so forth here might still be alive. Anyway, we only rediscovered the need for any censorship slowly. It was a mistake. It meant there was a temptation to some Sol people, when they knew they might go on living under the kzinti, to settle for something like the same, rather than endless, grinding, hopeless war and increasing poverty, hardship and coercion for all."

"If you can call it living," said Rykermann. "The worst that Sol people endured was paradise beyond dreams compared to what we had here."

"I know. But the possibility of a negotiated surrender for Sol was an inducement to defeatists and others: People worked out that those who did services for the kzinti— assisted them in their conquest—might expect to be rewarded by them. They worked out there were probably people like that on Wunderland."

"There were," said Rykermann. "Since I was out of things at the Liberation I missed seeing most of what was done to them then."

"At first we hadn't bothered with security much, discounting any possibility of kzin spies or agents," said Guthlac. "No human would spy or do sabotage for the kzinti, we assumed. But we learnt better as time went on. Humanity *wasn't* united. Secrets *did* matter. Operation Cherubim was deadly secret: To send a ship to Alpha

Centauri with human volunteers—childless, of course—who would be converted into Pak Protectors. They carried tree-of-life agent in a sealed compartment. Something went wrong. They never arrived. Perhaps they ran into kzin ships. Perhaps just one of the accidents of space-flight.

"But there was another operation on the same lines: To send tree-of-life agent in an unmanned ship."

"Why?"

"It was the emergency backup. There were many advantages from the covert operation point of view: simpler, quicker, a ship able to accelerate and decelerate faster and, without life-systems, smaller, harder to detect or intercept. Plus, we weren't over-supplied with suitable Protector volunteers. The resistance had instructions to pick it up at the edge of the system and smuggle it to Wunderland."

"As geriatric drugs and trace elements."

"Yes. Not a complete lie, of course. It *is* a geriatric drug—and how! Always make your cover story as close to the truth as possible. The idea was, even if someone at the Alpha Centauri end who had an idea of what it was fell into kzin hands and was probed by a telepath, he or she could fix on the idea of a geriatric drug and medicine, just possibly the telepath would not detect an actual lie. That was the idea, anyway. Whether or not it would have worked is another matter. But anyway nothing was said in our maser as to what it really was. Then, of course, when it arrived it was to be hidden.

"If Sol system had been plainly falling, instructions would have been masered to open the containers and make Protectors. From there it would, we hoped, go as Operation Cherubim had been meant to go. Of course, we would give instructions then to try to ensure that the Protectors created would be suitable individuals— volunteers, with high ethical standards and records—*good* people, in short—and childless. We would have wanted trained scientists and fighters, of course, so they'd have as big a start as possible in knowledge and experience.

"We would do the same on Earth. The kzinti would find themselves attacked by Protectors in both systems simultaneously. We sent the nukes as well so the Protectors would have powerful weapons ready to hand right away, either as bombs or pumps for lasers. Even Protectors couldn't build nuclear processing-plants and factories in a kzin-occupied system overnight. But it was a desperate ploy, only to be used if all else was lost. We wouldn't have control over the process, or over who the human Protectors in this system would be. You know Protectors, once they are used to their state, are more or less indestructible, smarter than human geniuses, and unless they're killed they live for thousands of years. One can't imagine they would ever have handed power back to breeders, or even agreed not to make more Protectors. They could produce their own tree-of-life, given time. There was fear that we were exchanging one demonic enemy for a worse. But even if they had been universally benevolent, even if they defeated the kzinti, it would have changed our society utterly and probably forever . . .

"Anyway, the plan never had to be used, for which we may give thanks. The ramscoop raid and the death of

Chuut-Riit gave us a breathing space, and instead of Protectors the hyperdrive saved us. We were lucky.

"As for Operation Cherubim, it seems that all those in the need-to-know circle in the Centauri system died. The kzinti found the maser transceiver in due course and they didn't stop at half-measures in blasting Nifelheim out of the sky with all its personnel. Also, quite a lot of ARM intelligence people from Sol died in the war, you know. We had gaps in our own records and knowledge. We didn't keep a lot of things electronically at all, for fear of kzinti or their agents hacking into our files. We lost both hard copy and computers when the kzin hit assets on Earth, which happened more often than most people know. Anyway ARM decided the consignment had never arrived and wrote it off . . . And you say the containers were hit in the fight."

"Yes."

"Well, at least they can't have been breached," Guthlac said. "If any tree-of-life agent had escaped you'd have known all about it at the time. How old are you, Nils?"

"A hundred and one last birthday."

"Even twenty-six years ago, you would have been too old to make the change. Exposure to tree-of-life would have killed you. But you're still here. And none of the rest of your party was affected either. I think—I hope—we can assume the integrity of the containers. They were made strong, after all . . . Although no stronger than the ordinary hospital containers they were supposed to be. We expected them to be inspected and x-rayed by the collabos at least, and we didn't want to arouse suspicion by making them anything special."

"They may have been damaged, though," said Rykermann. "I remember seeing them take hits. And twenty-six years buried wouldn't have improved them. There can be some powerful microorganisms and compounds in Wunderland soil, in the caves in particular. I'd suggest they be removed at once."

"Obviously. That's why I sent for you as soon as I realized what your report was about. Can you find them?"

"With deep-radar it should be easy enough," Rykermann said. "I remember the locality."

"We want to be discreet about this," Guthlac said. "We also don't want humans being put at risk of exposure to tree-of-life. Trustworthy—*very* trustworthy—kzinti would be useful on a job like this. The stuff's no danger and no value to them. I say that because I think of Vaemar. Can Vaemar destroy them?"

"He's still up at the caves. He's due to return in the next day or two. You know why."

"This is tricky," said Guthlac. "We don't want humans approaching those containers, not given the state they might be in, but I'm not happy about any kzinti, not even your young paragon of virtue, finding out too much about them. It might be best to simply clear the whole area and nuke it."

"It might be best," said Rykermann, "to make sure the containers are still there first."

"Why shouldn't they be?"

"There were several people in our own party—the party that met the couriers when they were buried—who survived. I've lost touch with some of them. I'm not saying any of them would necessarily steal such things or have any motive to, but who knows who they might have talked to since then? The fighting's been over on this planet for thirteen years. Barroom reminiscences about some buried containers of weapons might have tempted some crook or adventurer to go on a private treasure-hunt for all we know."

"If such a crook had opened them he or she would have had a surprise. And I think we would have known about it by now."

"Even so, surely they should be counted and inventoried before they're destroyed?"

"I take your point. Can Vaemar do that?"

"Yes."

"Get him onto it then. I don't need to tell you to stay well away from the area yourself. It shouldn't be too dangerous for him."

"May I tell Vaemar what he's doing? He knows about the Pak, by the way. He searched old Earth records for another project."

"I didn't know that. Act at your discretion. If he knows about the Pak there doesn't seem much point in concealing this from him. It'll give him an incentive, in fact."

Chapter 4

Circle Bay Monastery, despite being home to an order of celibate male monks, had detached guest houses for lay visitors, including females. With a wedding planned to be held there shortly the bride, Gale, and her guests Leonie Rykermann and Karan, who had arrived early by air-car, were experimenting with clothes and cosmetics in front of a mirror. Twenty-fifth-century cosmetics, including skin-coloring agents as permanent as tattoos until one wanted to remove them, gave plenty of scope for experiment.

"You think headband suits me?" Karan asked.

"Not one like mine," Leonie told her. "Try a white one. Or better, the one holding the jewel."

Karan surveyed the result from several angles. "Little cape?" she asked. "Like this?" She demonstrated.

"That ought to turn a few heads," said Leonie. "Including Vaemar's." She herself wore a long skirt that hid her legs, legs that she still moved awkwardly.

The telephone on Karan's belt beeped. As she listened to its message her eyes lit and her whiskers twitched. She bared her teeth and raised her ears.

"From Nurse and Orlando!" she told the others. "Tabitha looking at pages of picture-book! Not eating it!" Life with Vaemar had improved her Wunderlander grammar and vocabulary.

"That's wonderful!" said Leonie. "Wonderful for us all! Wonderful for history!" They had all been hanging upon evidence that the first daughter of one of the Secret Others—the thin, hidden line of intelligent kzinrretti— had bred true. It didn't always happen. The Secret Others had been few to begin with, and they were very few now. Karan on human-liberated Wunderland was perhaps the first intelligent kzinrret in millennia who did not have to hide her sapience.

"Hurrah for history!" said Gale. "Bring them to the wedding!"

"Yes, now I can. And rate Nurse charges can't leave them alone with him too long." Karan's ears swivelled. "Car coming," she said.

Leonie's ears also twitched slightly—she had a little Families blood. She stepped to the door. "If that's Arthur, I won't let him in. It's unlucky for the groom to see the bride before the wedding."

"If Vaemar," said Karan, "I'll not see him till finished here." She applied a little nontoxic gold paint to the tips of her fangs and surveyed the result thoughtfully.

"And Tabitha?"

"News will keep," Karan told her. "Want to break not all at once. Better still, perhaps, let him find out for self. Proud quicker if his discovery, I think. He's got lot to adjust to."

"He's a genius," said Leonie. "He'll adjust." Her voice

trailed off. The word "genius" was haunted for her. She thought of another genius trying to adjust. Then, a moment later: "It's not Vaemar. It's Nils."

"Is he all right?" asked Gale. "None of them were due yet."

"Why didn't you tell Arthur about Morlocks?" Vaemar asked. It was night and Rykermann, bringing Leonie back to Munchen, had summoned him. Rykermann had told him in private code that there were secret matters to discuss.

"I was about to," Rykermann told him. "Then I remembered Early. And Arthur reports to Early, wherever he may be now. I'm not sure that I wanted Early nipping trouble in the bud by sending a comet or asteroid into the Hohe Kalkstein. Or worse. Never forget what a totally ruthless swine Early is. I believe there's more unevolved Pak in him than in most of us . . .

"I'd like to be able to go back to Arthur and report the stuff is safe or destroyed before I give either of them the happy news that we spent so much toil and blood to deposit tree-of-life with a colony of Pak breeders who are *really* unevolved. Let's destroy the stuff first. Or make sure it is destroyed."

"Unevolved? Or evolved differently?" asked Vaemar.

"Leonie and I were discussing that a very long time ago. When she was a student, before the first reports of the kzinti began coming in. The *Angel's Pencil* warnings, the disappearing ships . . . It seems like another age. But plainly the Morlocks have remained far closer to the original Pak breeders than humans have . . . And it *was* another age. It was a good post-graduate class I had. She's the only survivor of it."

"I raised the question then," said Leonie. "Why, after coming so far from the direction of the Core, hadn't the Pak gone one small and logical step further and planted a second colony a mere four light-years away on Wunderland? And we found the answer: they did. I remember spooning a fossil out of the cave floor, cleaning it with sonics, inch by inch, day by day, finding the analogues of human bones and organs that no alien life-form had any right to possess. DNA from live specimens confirmed it. It was going to be my doctoral thesis. I even began wondering about plans to somehow . . . rehabilitate . . . them when my work had made me famous. Then, er . . . no offence . . . our studies were rudely interrupted. . . . Nils set me and the other post-grads to work analyzing an orange hair he'd found . . ."

"In any case, it seemed *interesting* and even *exciting* before the invasion, but not *important*, the way our priorities were after that," said Rykermann. "If there was any reason to worry about potential Pak Protectors, there were several million around in the form of humans anyway, even if we hadn't suddenly found ourselves with other things on our minds."

"I'd asked Earth to send us everything known about the Pak, although the university had the basic texts here. Not much more had arrived before the invasion. Partly caution at the Earth end, I suppose. The Pak story was like the knowledge in the early Middle Ages of the Earth being a spheroid. Scientists knew about it and it wasn't exactly secret, but people didn't talk about it much. Partly, there simply wasn't much known. Besides, the university had a limited budget for buying interstellar maser time. . . .

"Presumably tree-of-life failed here for the same reason it failed on Earth and the Protectors eventually died. As on Earth, some breeders survived."

"But there were differences," Leonie told Vaemar. "You know because of Wunderland's lighter gravity the caves are much bigger here than on Earth or Kzinhome. Big enough to be inhabited by large life-forms on a permanent basis. There are fewer roof-collapses and the slower flow of water means larger volumes of limestone are dissolved in ballroom chambers and honeycombs rather than along the narrow lines of stream-courses. With the mynocks and other flying things there is a lot more protein being brought into the caves than is usually the case on Earth. The breeders moved into the caves— possibly to escape tigripards or other predators—and found themselves on top of the food chains there.

"Without many predators or competitors in the caves and without weather or any need to devise shelter or protection from it—without rain or heat or ice-ages—they were under far less evolutionary pressure than were the breeders on Earth. *Those* grew up fighting leopards on the savannah."

"Leopards?" asked Vaemar. "I remember, they are . . ."

"Big cats. Fighting such creatures is a good way to sort out the cleverest as survivors."

"I see."

"The caves were like a great womb they never had to leave, and in which they had almost no need to develop. Possibly the radiation from the Pak ships and engines on

Earth also caused mutations that didn't occur here. Anyway, these breeders on Wunderland didn't need many brains. They also escaped the worst of the meteor impacts that have obviously affected evolution on the surface here. In fact the meteor-impacts would probably have helped them by changing water-levels and giving the caves more suspended tables and more habitable layers of chambers.

"In this gravity they were well-muscled and already well suited for leaping and clinging to stalactites and so forth. Once their eyes and other senses adapted to the dark, their evolution must have almost ceased, as it has with many life-forms in Earth caves. On Earth there is a species of crustacean found in caves in Australia whose close relatives live in caves in the Canary Islands and the Carribean. They hardly changed in the time continental drift separated them so far."

Rykermann nodded.

"Earth scientists think *Homo sapiens* is not *all* Pak in its inheritance," he said. "The theory is that the original Pak Protectors probably modified the breeder population to better fit the Earth ecosystem and biochemistry. Sewed in the genetic material of Earth primates. That is why humans seem to fit well into the Earth animal kingdom. . . . It also raises the possibility that the breeders on Wunderland were not so modified, or modified differently. It's patently obvious that they have never developed anything resembling a civilization. We three know that all too well. Predatory bands, with rudimentary stone weapons, almost entirely carnivorous . . ."

Rykermann went to a collecting pannier.

"And there is your latest specimen, Vaemar." He

produced a translucent container and handed it to his pupil. "It is dry and withered, but . . ."

Vaemar turned the thing over. "A Morlock infant or late-term fetus. A mummy."

"Or a human infant or fetus, perhaps?"

"It could be, I suppose," said Leonie. "There were children who took refuge in the caves during the war. Maybe this was a stillbirth. Or an abortion by some poor child. They had no birth control."

"Damaged as it is," said Rykermann, "it has sufficient characteristics of both species to puzzle us as to its identification, does it not? I think it may be a hybrid. A human-Morlock hybrid, not carried to term. And humans and Morlocks are meant to have evolved under different stars. It should be as impossible as . . . as a human-Kzin hybrid. Add that to the DNA profiles. Anyway, Vaemar, just let me know if the stuff's still there, and sealed. Obviously, take all precautions for dealing with dangerous material. And don't forget there's radioactive material there as well."

"What you say about Early—" said Vaemar. "Are the Protectors so dangerous? I would have thought we had the power to conquer them."

"Yes," said Rykermann. "They are so dangerous. Arthur's told me quite a lot, apart from what Earth sent us. The one human Protector we know of, Brennan, was a Sol Belter, an evolved, modern man, the product of many generations of civilization and science and imbued with the values of benevolence and cooperation that are part of all the great human religious and ethical systems. Also, fortunately, he was a good man.

"When he became a Protector he adopted the entire

human race and his interventions in human affairs were benevolent as well as secret. He probably saved Earth from perishing in war, over-population and pollution, even if he then nearly killed us with kindness by making us almost too gentle and pacifist to resist when your lot came calling. Morlock Protectors, it's safe to bet, wouldn't be like that."

Leonie gave a sort of jerk, and nearly fell. Her legs were not what they had been and sudden emotion now made her even more clumsy. Both Rykermann and Vaemar reached out to help her.

"What is it, Lion-cub?"

"Protectors with hyperdrive!"

Rykermann thought. Leonie saw his face grow pale in turn. Vaemar made a questioning sound.

"The kzinti didn't want to destroy the human worlds," Leonie said. "They wanted them intact for themselves, and they wanted to keep the human race like the Jotok. However merciless they are in battle kzinti have a kind of conservationist sense towards other species—according to traditional kzinti's cosmology, other intelligent species have a place in the great hierarchy ordained by the Fanged God. It just happens to be a very long way below their own. Isn't that right, Vaemar?"

"The Fanged God gave us other species to serve us and for us to prey upon, not to exterminate except when we had no other choice," said Vaemar. "At least that is the traditional teaching. Remember the kzinti offered the humans of *Ka'ashi*—excuse me, I mean of Wunderland— a cease-fire as soon as the Conquest Landing was complete."

Rykermann took up the thought. "But the Protectors would have only one aim: Destroy all possible competitors. First to exterminate the human species, and if necessary destroy the human worlds and all other life on them—they'd use *anything*: relativity weapons, anti-matter weapons, the dirtiest possible thermo-nukes and ramscoops in atmospheres, killer hypersonics, geological disrupters. They'd make missiles of comets and asteroids, trigger solar flares. No possibility of treaty or negotiation. All other species, especially all other sapient species, regarded as vermin-to-be-exterminated by definition. Not only would they be more totally focused on destruction than would kzinti, they are far more intelligent than nearly all individuals of either of our species, and far tougher . . .

"There's a theory, you know, that Venus's tectonic plates were somehow turned over a couple of million years ago. It makes no physical sense. We can't see how such a thing could have happened, except by artificial disruptors greater than any we've even conceived of. But what if, when the original Protectors reached Earth, they found some sort of life on Venus, some sort of potential threat or competitor? Well, I suppose we'll never know . . ."

"Impossible, surely!"

"I hope so . . . I suppose we would still make more human Protectors in response, if we had tree-of-life and they gave us time. But it's far harder to defend against an enemy that wants to do nothing but kill you than against one that merely wants to conquer you."

"They'd like to take Earth and Wunderland as breeding-space, of course, but an *empty* Earth and Wunderland,"

Leonie said. "Taking them would be secondary to getting totally rid of the human race, a dangerous rival and a mutated deviation from the Pak form.

"Perhaps they wouldn't even care much about preserving Earth or Wunderland or the Asteroids if they had Mars and Venus to terraform, not to mention the colonies we've established in other systems and all the various moons and planetoids available. Given what we know of Protector toughness and engineering intelligence, they might consider several possible worlds that are too tough for us as ripe for transforming and could write Earth and Wunderland off.

"Of course, once they'd removed the human race, they'd take on the kzinti without pausing to draw breath. Then they'd wipe out any and every other sapient or potentially sapient race they found. According to what Brennan learnt, there weren't even other animals on the Pak homeworld. As well as human hyperdrive technology, they'd get kzin gravity technology—giving them even more worlds and weapons."

Vaemar's eyes gleamed and more of his fangs showed.

"You think they could beat Heroes? The Patriarch's Navy?" he asked.

"Vaemar, my friend," Rykermann said, "humans are, in fighting ability, a crude, feeble, slow, stupid, fragile, soft, merciful, pacifist and rudimentary version of Protectors. I do not mean to insult, but need I say more?"

"No," said Vaemar. "I see."

"And even Brennan, evolved and benevolent as he was, was utterly ruthless," Rykermann went on. "One reason it took a long time to establish a proper human presence on

Mars was that creatures there attacked the early bases. I don't know much about them, but apparently Brennan just wiped them out. No interest in preserving them, not even any curiosity about them—Protectors seem to have very little abstract curiosity.

"Look back to the Slaver War for a precedent for a Pak Space-War, perhaps. Or worse: even at the end the Slavers didn't kill the nonsapient life-forms. Look to a war of extermination throughout the galaxy. A war against all *life*. The war of humans and kzinti would seem a quaint, friendly affair by comparison, a skirmish or two, a sort of neighborly disagreement. Pak without the hyperdrive would be more than bad enough. Pak with the hyperdrive . . . well, my imagination's limited, I suppose, but I think they would just go on destroying intelligence or potential intelligence wherever they found it, on and on up the spiral arm, out to the other arms, back towards the Core, until they had all the galaxy or until they came up against something worse than themselves. If there is such a thing."

Rykermann paused and collected his thoughts.

"This is very scary," he said. "Or rather, it could be. But consider: These Morlock Protectors, if they did exist, wouldn't *know* anything. However clever they may be potentially, they have no teachers. Knowledge must have a source."

"I've thought of that," said Leonie. "They could get teachers. I've tried just now to put myself inside the skull of a newly-awakened Morlock Protector from the great caves. Such a Protector would, I guess, have memories of the Breeder stage. That could mean memories of the existence of humans and kzinti—probably of fighting against humans and kzinti in the caves—memories of aliens, of weapons, of war. *And a knowledge of its own ignorance.* If I were such a Protector, now suddenly a super-genius—the first thing I would set out to do would be to acquire knowledge.

"There could be several ways to begin that. We've cleared a lot of the old human and kzinti weapons and equipment from the war out of the great caves but there are probably still a lot left. Who knows what remote chambers and tunnels some of our people ended up fighting to the death in? Our Protector could take them apart and find out how they worked. But more importantly, if I were such a Protector, before I showed my hand more obviously, I'd capture humans and kzinti and find out everything they knew."

"How?"

"Raids on the surface. They'd talk under torture."

"Kzinti? Heroes?"

"Yes, Vaemar. As far as I know any sapient will talk under torture eventually. Isn't one of your—the kzinti's— own instruments of torture called 'Hot Needle of Inquiry?' They wouldn't have developed it if it didn't work . . .

"But Pak Protectors would use anything, and unlike either of our species, would feel no particle of distaste at having to do so. Normal kzinti, I know, regard torture as something not admirable or heroic, to be resorted to only from necessity, though that doesn't stop them once the necessity has been established. Those of both our kinds who enjoy torture for its own sake are abnormal individuals, shunned and despised by the normal. For a Pak Protector such scruples would be without meaning.

"As the Protectors' knowledge grew, interrogation would get easier. They could alter prisoners' brain or body chemistry, for example, so even the bravest could not but tell everything they knew at once. They'd find out about computers quickly and hack into them. They might capture kzinti telepaths and use them. Can you imagine a Pak Protector with access to the internet? There are certain to be computers with internet linkage lying in the caves among the bones and weapons.

"There is another thing. You know, Vaemar, that the great weakness of the kzinti is that they are impatient. They attack before they are ready. Time and again, that was the only reason we won, both strategically and tacti-cally."

"So Raargh-Hero drilled into me in our earliest hunts. And so wrote my Honored Sire Chuut-Riit."

"Pak, as far as we know, are enormously patient. After all, they are very long-lived. That is probably one reason why, though they had spaceflight for a long time, they never, as far as we know, bothered with any space-drives beyond fairly simple interstellar ramjets. Also, of course, after a certain level, perpetual war may militate against technological progress. The original Pak colonization project took tens of thousands of years just to get to these systems. They didn't mind. They don't have the weakness of impatience . . .

"Perhaps Morlock Protectors would not be as smart as either Pak or human Protectors. They are starting from a much lower pre-change base-level of intelligence than human Protectors, certainly. Living in a largely risk-free, challenge-free environment in the caves for tens of thousands of years they might have devolved. They might. But that they've devolved enough is not the way to bet.

"But they might get the hyperdrive."

"You're trusting him with a lot," Leonie said, as Vaemar's car dwindled in the northeastern sky.

"He'd have worked out the Morlock-Pak relationship for himself. In fact, I mentioned it to him a long time ago, when it didn't seem important in the way it does now. Don't forget, he'd also done work on the Hollow Moon as part of his space-engineering units." The Hollow Moon was one of Wunderland's many small moons, further away than most. About four miles across, with a space at its core, so deep radar said, apparently about a mile in diameter, it orbited Wunderland at a distance of about 60,000 miles. Apart from being hollow, its other oddities included a near-spherical shape, usually only associated with objects of far more mass and gravity. Humans had begun to study it before the kzin invasion, but that study had been dropped during the war and the Occupation. What human spacecraft the kzinti had permitted to fly then were needed to keep the shattered economy turning over, not for abstract research or flights into areas that the kzinti might disapprove of. There were what appeared to be ancient tunnels leading, presumably, to its core, but they were blocked. Its metal content was quite high, but that of many other moons and asteroids was higher and these were more worth mining. There were entrances to its tunnels of some depth, but during the war neither side had used these much as hiding-places, simply because they were too obvious.

After Liberation abstract and academic scientific projects had resumed slowly, the cheaper ones first. There was plenty to do on the surface of the planet and on the inhabited asteroids and little money for space exploration. Policy had been to leave the anomalous moon alone until there were again resources available for a proper, long-term expedition. It had been thought at one time that it was an ancient artifact of the Slaver Empire, but its orbit was receding gradually from Wunderland (one reason it had not been demolished as a danger by the first colonists), and if it had dated from the Slavers' time it would have disappeared into space long ago.

"I stick to my old idea. What could it be but the original spaceship the Pak used for the journey from Sol?" Rykermann said. "In any case if I can't trust Vaemar after what we've been through, who can I trust? Yes, laugh if you like."

"You know, don't you," Leonie said, "that seeing you and Vaemar together—like the fulfilment of everything I'd been working for—was important in helping me live. I think I'm entitled to laugh. Sometimes it seemed it was your hand I was holding, and sometimes a kzin's."

Rykermann nodded. No need to ask what she referred to. After she had partially come out of the tank, Vaemar and Raargh had spelled him, sitting at her side while he slept. The hospital staff hadn't liked it at first, but the kzinti had been very insistent, and he had cooperated with them.

"I wish . . . I wish Brennan had been right, and we

could have kept the gentle society we had," said Leonie. "There is nothing good about becoming warlike."

"We had no choice," said Rykermann. "But you know I'm a convert now. I'll work for peace and reconciliation. Work with Vaemar and the Wunderkzin."

"I know. It's stupid of me, perhaps, but I feel I must say it. We have been at war for sixty-six Earth years. The war goes on in space. One gets weary. Gorillas settled their quarrels with gestures and rituals."

"But kzinti didn't. Or Pak . . ."

"I suppose so," said Leonie, shedding her clothes. "Let's go to bed." But her eyes were full of apprehension.

Rykermann still found it disturbing to look at his wife as she stood there naked. There were no scars marring her body, but when she was seen from a few feet away certain things became more apparent: below the waist that smooth skin was a little darker than it had been, the hair was a different color, and there was a difference in the vase of her hips and thighs. The pubis was more prominent, and the buttocks a little flatter above and fuller below.

Those were among the external differences. Her body was beautiful, as were the bodies of most men and women on a light-gravity world where modern medicine and cosmetic techniques were again available, but much of the lower half of that body had once been someone else. That and much more had left them both emotionally bruised and vulnerable. Leonie had lost consciousness as they were carrying her out of the cave, and had not known until a long time after the operation what had been done to her—Rykermann did not know if she would knowingly have accepted such a transplant even to save her life—and telling her had taken some time. Now they lived with it, and other things.

When she looked at him now he saw again the expression that had been on her face the first time he had seen her conscious after the operations and the long regeneration processes.

He also remembered her as she had been carried out of the cave, apparently dead or dying from the laser-wound, and his entreaties to her to live, shouted until they sedated him. *But she lives*, he thought. *Thanks to Dimity and to a couple of kzinti, she lives . . . And thanks to a donor, too, whoever she may once have been. Collaborator? War criminal? Accident victim? Best not to think. What does she fear? The idea of yet more monsters unleashed on our world . . . our worlds! . . . or the stranger's body sewn onto her? Or that I am still desperately in love with a beautiful super-genius who saved her life and about whom we can never speak? Oh my poor, dear wife!* He stepped forward and took her in his arms. He began to run his fingers down the familiar curve of her spine, then stopped. Once his hands would have known by instinct how to caress her. The first times they had made love when she returned from hospital had been bizarre, and in a real sense frightening, for them both. It had more of comfort and release now, but still . . . Her breasts were still the same firm-tipped softness against him that he knew so perfectly. He felt the body that was not entirely her body respond to him, and the sudden wetness of her tears on the skin of his chest. There was the saltiness of them in his nostrils, more a taste than a smell, the fluttering of her eyelashes' attempt to brush them away. When he bent to kiss her, the part of her skin that touched his lips tasted as it had always done. Much of the rest, he knew, would not.

My dear, dear wife, he thought. *Life has not exactly been kind to you. You deserved better. We are casualties of war, we in our way as much as the millions whose bones lie bleaching about this planet. Nothing to do but press on. Kipling had the words for it: "Be thankful you're living, and trust to your luck, and march to your front like a soldier." And you are the bravest soldier I know. But what would I not give to make the world kinder for you?*

Chapter 5

Vaemar landed his car in the High Limestone country, the Hohe Kalkstein, in an overgrown glade formed by an ancient cave roof collapse, near the twisted wreckage of an old kzin military sledge, partly covered with reddish vegetation and sunk into the soil. There was also a scattering of bones, gnawed by large and small teeth, bleached and fading into the ground. The Wunderland War Graves Authority had much to do and few people to do it with.

Kzinti loved exploring caves, but unless charging in the heat of battle, no kzin was capable of entering one recklessly. Vaemar had lights and a handgun as well as his *w'tsai*, and a tough helmet which now had the addition of a lobster-tail neck-guard at the back and epaulettes covering his shoulders—the favorite initial tactic of Morlocks was to drop both rocks and themselves onto the heads of intruders. He checked his radiation detector, very much standard procedure for all who ventured into the great caves of Wunderland, littered with the debris of more than five decades of war. As he crossed the threshold, there was a sharp jump in the gauge and a whirring from its miniaturized descendent of a Geiger counter. Vaemar leapt back. The radiation was not huge, but he saw no reason to expose himself to it. He climbed into a tough, lightweight suit, also standard equipment, and resumed his exploration, keeping a wary eye on the detector.

He moved further into the cave, lights and his own superb eyes sweeping the darkness for any signs of activity. There was nothing on the cave floor, not even the normally ubiquitous vermiform scavengers.

There was little, without major surgery, which they disliked, that could be done to kzinti's eyes to make them more efficient light collectors, but Vaemar did carry a pair of goggles that extended his visual range further. Such simple and lightweight aids were quite new, and humans had reason to be thankful that the kzinti had not possessed them during the war.

There, as Rykermann had described it, was the embankment of earth that covered the containers. Deep layers of mynock droppings showed it had been undisturbed for a long time. Evidently the transitory creatures did not remain long enough for the radiation to affect them.

He set up a motion detector focused into the cave beyond, unfolded a small robot digging tool, and stepped well back as it went to work.

The robot struck solid material after only a few moments. Vaemar deactivated it and stepped forward. One glance was really enough, but he pushed more earth aside to be sure. Beneath the earth was rock. Not only had the containers been removed, the removal had been disguised. The Geiger counter whirred merrily.

Vaemar searched the immediate area thoroughly, but there was no other reasonably possible hiding place. Weapon at the ready, he ventured down the tunnel a long way, out of sight of the daylit mouth and into the beginning of a branching labyrinth of chambers, but again without result. He had compasses, motion detectors and miniaturized sensory devices, all specially developed for such expeditions. Infrared beams in his helmet gradually created a three-dimensional picture of the cave that could be retrieved in several ways, including a hologram.

He found and killed a couple of Morlocks, pausing to note with scientific detachment their body weights and general state of nutrition. He knew better than to try eating the foul-smelling, foul-tasting things. Each tunnel ended at last either in a blank wall, a stream diving under rock, or some passage too small for a kzin to easily enter, though plainly Morlocks had ways of coming and going from the bigger cave systems. The radiation level was falling now. Making a really comprehensive map would take some time. Vaemar felt it would be foolish to go further, especially when he had hardly room to move. His instincts screamed for him to press on, but he had become used to disciplining those instincts. Placing himself in a situation where enemies might come upon him at total disadvantage was not Heroic behavior. He returned to the car, and sent Rykermann and Arthur Guthlac a report, along with a copy of his recorded data. He searched some other small caves in the limestone glens and valleys nearby, without result. He surveyed the whole area with instruments from the air, recording radiation traces and signatures. Then he headed for home.

❧ ❧ ❧

Below Vaemar's car were the fields and buildings of a
human farm. His eye flickered across the instrument
console. Since Cumpston's warning of trouble with the feral
gangs, most farms in the area had gone onto at least a
minimal state of defense alert, which included transmitting
a signal identifying themselves and indicating their
electronics were functioning normally. This one was not
transmitting.

Vaemar made a leisurely pass low over the farm, sending out an interrogatory. He saw the movement of some
animals. Nothing else. He decided that an examination of
the situation was within the ambit of his task, and landed
outside the main building.

No one greeted him, and the wandering animals fled.
He saw many human footprints on the ground, some bare.
There was not much smell, which was in itself suspicious—
it suggested scent-deadening Rarctha fat. The main door
was open. The human height of it did not bother
Vaemar—kzinti were comfortable going on all fours
and preferred to do so when stalking or running any
distance—but it was hardly wide enough to admit his
shoulders. Looking in, he could see some brightly colored
toys of human children scattered about. He called out, but
there was no answer. His Ziirgah sense told him nothing
apart from confirming that the place was empty, but it
picked up desperate hunger from somewhere else.

A white object like an oversized fluffy ball with blue
eyes bounced up from the ground and through the air
towards him. He hurled himself backwards, almost faster
than a human eye could have followed, *w'tsai* flashing.

The Beam's Beast fell in two pieces, fangs squirting venom. Further evidence that the place had been deserted for some time.

Stepping back into the courtyard, he noticed a limestone outcrop that had been fenced off for no obvious reason. Examining it more closely, he discovered a sink-hole at its center, covered by a metal grating, with no bottom to be seen. He tied a light to a fine cable and lowered it through the bars into the hole. It twirled around, showing blackness and stalactites. His sensitive nose and whiskers tasted the air from it. He could hear the cave-sounds of dripping and running water. So, the great caves touched the surface here, as they did in many places.

He sensed game animals watching him fearfully from the cover of the trees. *I would like to bring Orlando hunting here*, he thought. And then, remembering the new state of things: *And Tabitha, too, and Karan. Make it what the humans call a family picnic. Dimity, too, perhaps.*

Looking further at the main farm building, he saw indeed that stairs at one side led down to an underground cellar, where wooden containers were kept. Further on, the artificially shaped and lined walls gave way to living rock with cave formations, that seemed to go on down into darkness. "Monkey-daffy, monkey-lucky" was an old kzin maxim on Wunderland, but he could hardly believe anyone capable of such mad folly. There was certainly a stout steel-barred gate at the end of the cellar, but that, he saw had been opened. There were also footprints on the damp floor. Vaemar was a good tracker, but the prints were too confused and overlaid for him to make much out, save that several were human-sized and had five toes. They did not seem quite human shaped. There was a smell of blood, not new.

He returned to the surface and moved on to another building. Opening the door of this he stepped into a considerably hotter climate. Vegetation grew thickly. It smelt of death. No Rarctha fat here.

A couple of small bodies lay dead at his feet. Lemurs. Under the kzin occupation there had been a minor human industry—evidently there still was—growing them as playthings for very young kzin kittens, who loved them. They had no fighting abilities when caught, but like all primates they tasted good and chasing them through trees was a good exercise in training kittens to judge the strength of branches. A nursery game. The next step for the kits had been chasing baboons, which were much more dangerous, and then the real thing, which was much more dangerous again. These appeared to have starved. He saw the sharp faces of other lemurs peering at him from above. There were feeding-trays without food. Vaemar thought of releasing the lemurs, but did not know if they would survive in such a climate and with strange vegetable matter to eat. He had seen some food containers outside, and scattered some of the vegetable matter from one on the ground. The lemurs, starvation evidently overcoming even their terror of the kzin, leapt down to it.

No humans anywhere. What was the human term? *Déjà vu.* This had happened before, in Grossgeister Swamp, when his small expedition had found human and kzin dwellings deserted.

His detector showed no trace of the missing radioactives.

A check with deep radar showed nothing moving underground in the immediate vicinity. He made a report and flew on. He passed over several more farms. Some responded to his interrogatories, a couple did not. There were also some plainly long deserted.

Vaemar had rooms at the University, but he also had another residence, a considerable distance from most human habitation: a few buildings on the wooded lower slopes of the Valkyrieheim Hills, smaller sisters of the Jotun Mountains, northeast of the Hohe Kalkstein. It was not far from the country where he had grown up with Raargh in the years immediately after the Liberation, the country which he still to some extent regarded as his home territory.

During the occupation the largest of these buildings had been a small palace for a kzin noble with, like almost all kzinti, a consuming love of hunting. Post-war, as was frequently the case on Wunderland, the original human owners of the land were no longer around. Normally the estate would have been redistributed back to other humans, but ARM and others had quietly decided that Vaemar-Riit, potential leader of what were coming to be more widely called the *"Wunderkzin,"* should be housed in some dignity.

Unlike many surviving kzin buildings, the high outer walls were intact. What had once been an eight-fold hedgehog of concentric defenses was much reduced, though not eliminated. Vaemar the postgraduate student did not deign to notice openly the possibility of assassination from either human exterminationists or from kzinti who regarded him as what they called—another new term for the Heroes' Tongue—a *kwizzliing*, but Vaemar-Riit the leader of the *Wunderkzin* was obliged to take certain precautions.

There was a small community on the estate. His Step-Sire Raargh and both their respective families lived there, as well as occupants of the old servant's quarters, guard and guest-rooms. Raargh had his own buildings and enjoyed a reasonable-sized harem of traditional kzinrretti now, but Vaemar remained monogamous.

This was partly by reason of policy. A first mate several years older then he, as Karan was, would have been by no means unusual previously. To stop so long at one would have been very unusual, when he had almost every kzinrret on the planet for the taking. But Vaemar understood and accepted the arguments put to him by Cumpston and others that the old ways could not continue. He had put them to other kzinti and fought more than one death-duel over them: smaller households and harems with females for every male kzin—"families"—would help ensure a more stable *Wunderkzin* society than the old way of vast harems for the nobles and little or nothing for the rest.

Further, and more important than policy, Karan had let him know in no uncertain terms that other females in his harem would have to be approved by her. So far none had been. He had, of course, a number of kits by various other females but they generally mixed with Raargh's. None save Orlando, his first, and so far only, son by Karan, had been born with the Riit blazon of red on the chest. He accepted fairly philosophically the fact that having a sapient mate brought some restrictions along with advantages.

There was good hunting territory nearby, with tigripards as well as gagrumphers and other large beasts. Here he was much less the graduate student, and much more the kzin prince, though a modern, *Wunderkzin* prince.

Vaemar landed in his inner courtyard, acknowledged the greetings of his servants (servants, not slaves, and the greetings less than a full prostration in these times), including the hired human Nurse in heavy, Teflon-reinforced apron and gloves, and fended off a mock attack from an excited Orlando. His banner was broken out from a high turret with a blast of horns and roll of drums.

Raargh made his report on the doings of the estates and, as Vaemar had forecast, made pointed comments about the Morlock bites. Vaemar remembered that the human he had studied with much interest called C. Northcote Parkinson had said the motto of retired senior sergeants was: "There are no excuses for anything!" That, he thought, as the grizzled old veteran gave him a quick grooming lick, summed Raargh up well. Big John, the kzin medical orderly whom Gale had cared for, stumped out. His head, face, hands, feet and spine were largely a complex of metal and regrown tissue, but his new ears were smiling. Raargh and Vaemar—Vaemar-Riit!—had called him "Hero," and at Arthur Guthlac's request Vaemar had taken him in. Raargh's now-numerous kittens, and Orlando too, looked upon his extravagant scars and prostheses with respect. His burden of cowardice had been taken from him. He had a mate of his own, for that matter, and a couple of kittens as well, all of which would have been quite beyond his dreams had he lived out his life, even unmutilated, in the old order of things.

Vaemar made a prostration before the worship shrine holding a ceremonial jar, liberated from the quarters of the late Jocelyn van der Straat, which still contained at least a few molecules of the urine of his Honored Sire Chuut-Riit, and a few fragments of bone and hair identified by DNA testing as those of Elder Brother who had died protecting him as a kitten. He killed a yearling bull from the holding pens and ate quickly. Groom plied his blowdryer and talcum powder. Then Vaemar carried the recording brick to his laboratory, and called Arthur Guthlac's headquarters again.

A large hologram of Wunderland stood on the center of Guthlac's control console, a duplicate on Vaemar's. Circular marks on it, like old sores on a body, marked the sites of nuclear explosions. Some were fairly recent, from the Liberation or the intra-Kzin civil war that had so aided the human reconquest, some dated back to the original kzin landings. The oldest sites were quite faded now: the kzinti had blasted any human resistance that became too prolonged, but they had used fairly clean bombs. They were ecologists in their way, and anyway had not wished to destroy the infrastructure of the planet. But the monitors that built up the picture of Wunderland's radioactivity were sensitive. A myriad of lines crossed the northern hemisphere. A far smaller number crossed the less-settled southern hemisphere.

"These are the traces of highly radioactive substances which satellites have recorded in the last year," Guthlac said. "From the state of the ground we don't think the stuff's been gone longer than that. Fortunately we can narrow it down further. The signatures you recorded match these—" he pointed to a long lonely line that crossed the Wunderland equator and continued down the globe. "They've gone to Little Southland. A couple of them have, anyway. As far as we can make out, the bulk of them can't have been moved far, though. You did a good job, Vaemar."

"The University has routine trips to Little Southland," said Nils Rykermann. "Mainly instrument checks. Vaemar can be rostered to do it. If we want to keep this matter quiet . . ."

"We do. For the moment certainly."

"Vaemar had better take a look, then. A look and back. He shouldn't be away more than a couple of days at most."

"What do you have in mind?" asked Cumpston.

"If what you say is on the loose," said Rykermann, "then for obvious reasons we don't want humans going after it blindly. Vaemar is better able to look after himself than almost any human and if he can tell us what he sees, then we can at least make our next move with knowledge. Anyway, if all the containers are together, we can at least say they've been gotten away from the Morlocks. Setting aside the question of who took them."

"It might be—" Cumpston bit off the words. To suggest in Vaemar's electronic presence that it might be dangerous for him would be an insult to test even Vaemar's exceptional self-control.

"The deserted farms?"

"That's bad. We thought the feral gangs were falling apart, but maybe this is their doing."

"If nothing worse. The thing we fear. We can't keep this secret much longer."

"The police have some ready-reaction teams," said Rykermann. "They're small but they've got good weapons. I'll get them up there now!"

"What about ARM?"

"They're Wunderland police, not ARM, and what they do is not ARM's business. Why do you think we have a police bagpipe band?"

"I always assumed it was to torture kzin prisoners. Or maybe flatlanders."

"I'll take that up with you later. Our pipers are actually part of an elite reaction force that doesn't care to advertise its presence as such. Band-practice covers a multitude of sins. I've still got plenty of rank in the Wunderland armed forces and I'll get them up to the Hohe Kalkstein now."

"Are you going to warn them about what they've really got to look out for?"

"Yes, there seems no choice about that now. But they are our best."

"Do you really think your best is good enough?"

"At the moment we've got no choice, with so much of our forces still tied up in the space war."

"I will give you full discretion," Guthlac told Vaemar. "Take any companions you wish, but lead. Lurk cunningly in the tall grass, scent out the spoor, do not scream and leap at the prey, but return. Knowledge is the prize."

"I *have* done the ROTC intelligence course," Vaemar

reminded him, with the barest hint of something else in his voice, and adding after a moment, "sir."

"And that, my young Hero, is another reason you are chosen," Guthlac told him. "Act at discretion."

Kzaargh-Commodore paced. *Night-Lurker*'s bridge did not allow him much space, a dozen strides one way, a dozen the other. But Captain, Navigator and the rest of the bridge team kept well out of his way.

One kzin heavy cruiser. With repairs of less than naval dockyard standard. But with claws still capable of seizing Glory on an epic scale. Still with claws capable of devastating a planet or a system.

Eight-and-four Earth-years had passed since, returning with some damage from a tip-and-run raid on the human bases in Sol system, his ship had received news of the death of great Chuut-Riit, of fratricidal war between Traat-Admiral and Ktrodni-Stkaa, and, far worse and more unbelievable, disaster on disaster, the shattering news of the human reconquest of *Ka'ashi*, and of the humans' possession of a superluminal drive against which no kzin strategy could prevail.

Kzaargh-Commodore had turned tail and fled. A commander less sure of his own courage or of his crew would have leapt into the battle, however hopeless, but his veterans trusted him unwaveringly, and he had long since passed the point of needing to prove his courage to himself. He had guessed from other experiences that the apes had developed a means of detecting the monopoles that powered the big kzin gravity-motors, but like all modern warships, *Night-Lurker* had a reaction-drive as well.

Evading detection in such circumstances was not difficult. In the vastness of space it was surprising that ships, even with detection equipment, encountered one another as often as they did, and he had more delta-V than he needed. He slowed the ship and headed in a long, elliptical orbit out of the Alpha Centauri system, well above the plane of the ecliptic, to further reduce chances of detection.

But he did not entirely flee. He dispatched Chorth-Captain, one of his best officers, once "Hider-and-Whisperer," a specialist in cloaking and communications technology, now promoted to Partial Name and Ship-Command rank, in a cloaked *Rending Fang* heavy fighter craft to spy out the situation. They would rendezvous later.

Strictly speaking, his duty as a commander in the Patriarch's Navy, if not to die on the attack, would have been to get his ship back to the nearest kzin world, or to Kzinhome itself.

But who knew which were the kzin-held worlds now? Further, he knew, his one ship, added to whatever kzin fleet was still in the area, would make no real difference to the situation. On the other hand, lurking in the Centauri system, it could still inflict terrible slashes if it could leap from hiding. His experience of humans was that, like other monkeys, they lacked persistence. No doubt the skies over *Ka'ashi* would be guarded and patrolled by human ships in the immediate aftermath of the invasion. But given a quiet time, that guard would grow slacker and more perfunctory. Then he would fall on them out of those skies like the vengeance of the Fanged

God. The greatest shame that the Patriarchy and the Heroes' Race had ever suffered would be blotted out in the blood of the insolent omnivorous apes. Given the element of surprise, the arsenals of his ship were more than enough to lay the planet to waste. Surprise would be impossible at first, but given time . . . And he carried several battalions of infantry in hibernation for landings when the monkey-cities and bases had gone down in nuclear fire.

Later, with new data passively collected and after thought and discussion with Captain, he modified his plan. Knock out the defenses of population centers of Wunderland from the sky, certainly, but use the troops to seize Tiamat. The shipyards there, they had learned, were converting to hyperdrive technology. To capture *that* for the Patriarch would be a feat to eclipse merely burning a world in vengeance!

Meanwhile, he would repair his ship's damage as a Hero might lick his wounds, and wait for the monkey guard to slacken and become distracted. A simple enough plan, but as time went by he came to realize it might not be an easy one. As was so often the case, the kzinti's worst enemy was themselves. The monkey-prisoners in the live-meat cages were eaten faster than they bred and with manufactured food life became less pleasant. Telepath went mad. With boredom, tension and unappetizing food there were several death-duels until he put a stop to it. Since *Night-Lurker* had set out on a battle-mission, and he was not yet a full admiral, there were not even females of his harem aboard. He made rousing speeches to the crew, promising them inglorious death and their ears on his belt if they crossed him, glorious death or perhaps just plain glory, if they obeyed as Heroes.

His ship had drifted beyond the outer Comet halo. He had watched the broadcasts from *Ka'ashi*, and had seen the reassertion of monkey government and authority. A few messages passed back and forth with Chorth-Captain, pulses too fast to be detected except by a dedicated receiver. Then Chorth-Captain's replies stopped. Perhaps he was laying low in deep grass, waiting his chance to leap. Perhaps the monkeys had found him.

He thought now and then of the full Name that would undoubtedly be his: Kzaargh-Chmeee, perhaps? Or perhaps—for given such a feat and such a service it was not quite impossible—Kzaargh-Riit?

Kzaargh-Commodore had learnt the superluminal drive could only be engaged outside the gravitational singularity of a star system, and the double-star of Alpha Centauri A and B gave a huge volume of space in which it could not operate.

He had seen on various screens, too, something of the so-called *Wunderkzin*. Many of the kzinti of human-recaptured Wunderland lived lives at least as independent of their simian conquerors as any such defeated creatures might, and clung to some poor rags of honor. They were hardly pleasant to look upon. But a few had gone further and actively sought a partnership with the apes. It was sickening and at first unbelievable. Indeed, Kzaargh-Commodore was by no means convinced that the broadcasts featuring these creatures were anything more than monkey propaganda. He cut off even the passive reception of messages, lest the apes had some method of detecting this, and also lest this propaganda should somehow reach his Heroes. The longer the wait the better.

Orlando, Vaemar noticed as he entered the nursery, had finished his jigsaw puzzle, a five-thousand-piece picture of Lord Chmeee locked in slashing battle with a herd of *sthondat*-like monsters. Good. Human-derived jigsaw puzzles were not in the same league as the puzzles of the kzinti priesthood, but they were useful for schooling infants in patience and persistence. And he had finished it very quickly.

Orlando was lying on his back, holding a large ball of fiber in his front claws while ripping at it with his back ones. Vaemar remembered for a moment the first time he himself had leapt on such a ball, the day his Honored Sire Chuut-Riit had brought him to the Naming Day of Inga, one of Henrietta's children. He did not know what had happened to Inga, and twice he thought he had seen Henrietta dead, though each time he had been left with suspicions that it had not really been her. . . . A lot of blood down the runnel. But he remembered well leaping onto the fiber ball, running and tumbling with the squealing human infants, and gorging on sugary cake.

The cake had made him sick afterwards, as he was held by an unfortunate Guard Trooper in the car flying back to Honored Sire's Palace, but a taste for it had remained a small secret pleasure with him, one to which he had recently introduced Karan. The abbot at Circle Bay Monastery, with whom he sometimes discussed ethics, said it could hardly count as a vice. Indeed, since the ova of birds and the mammary secretions of cattle had gone into its making, it did not have the connotations of being *entirely* vegetable matter (in any case kzinti, despite their boasting, had never been complete and total carnivores). The ball shrieked as Orlando tore at it. His claws reached the center, slicing through the last tough envelope. Tuna-flavored ice cream poured out, drenching the kitten. He jumped and spat, then when he realized what it was, settled down to licking it from his fur and the floor, purring like a small gravity-motor. Vaemar smiled indulgently and contributed a lick of his own. "The kzin is a mighty hunter," he told his son. Those fiber balls were juggled high in the air by a robot, and it took some leaping for the kitten to capture one—with the penalty of a very painful electric shock if it misjudged timing and distance. A possibly lethal shock in the most advanced mode.

"Tabitha caught two, Daddy," Orlando told him.

"Did she? Did she indeed? Where is Tabitha now?"

"Upstairs. She took them with her. She caught the first ball and then one after I caught mine."

Each time a ball was caught, the robot increased its speed, the complexity of its juggling and its shock. The third ball was by no means easy even for a kitten older than Orlando with fast reflexes and a powerful leap to catch. It required, and was meant to require, some planning ability as well as strength and dexterity. kzin kittens matured at somewhat variable rates, but Orlando—still younger than Vaemar had been when his Honored Sire perished and Raargh adopted him—had done very well to catch the second.

"How did she do that?"

"She climbed into the roof and jumped down."

Vaemar thought for a moment.

"Have you ever caught a fourth ball, Orlando?" he asked.

"No, Daddy." Then, realizing that this was said as a challenge, Orlando's posture changed. "Program the robot, Honored Sire! I will catch the fourth ball now!"

Vaemar watched while he did so, then groomed his son and soothed his scorches, both proud.

Alpha Centauri B had risen when Vaemar strode up the steep winding track above his mansion to the small guest house in the wood. The forest, normally full of stir at this time as the nocturnal creatures took over their shift, fell almost silent about him. There was game to be flushed here, but he was not hunting.

Like all kzin buildings, the guest house was large and thick-walled. But unlike most it had windows of some size close to the ground and a human-sized as well as a kzin-sized door. Its roof sprouted electronics. His presence was signalled as he drew near, and the kzin-sized door opened.

There was a fooch for him in the main room. He reclined in it as Dimity Carmody dialed him bourbon and another tuna ice cream. Although he had eaten already custom and politeness demanded he take a little (in any case, as he told himself, no kzin is ever entirely full).

She had been watching an ancient classic film from Earth, Peter Jackson's original of *The Two Towers*. She turned the set down. Vaemar read a sampler Dimity had put on the wall, a quotation from a human writer who had lived on Earth more than five hundred years earlier: "Man is an exception, whatever else he is. If he is not the image of God, then he is a disease of the dust. If it is not true that a divine being fell, then we can only say that one of the animals went entirely off its head."

"Chesterton," Vaemar remarked.

"Yes."

"I have taken some notes of his writing. 'It is constantly assumed, especially in our Tolstoyan tendencies, that when the lion lies down with the lamb the lion becomes lamb-like. But that is brutal annexation and imperialism on the part of the lamb. That is simply the lamb absorbing the lion instead of the lion eating the lamb. The real problem is—Can the lion lie down with the lamb and still retain his royal ferocity?'"

"I know you have a good memory," said Dimity. "You have that word perfect."

"Yes, don't I? Which may suggest that particular passage has been important to me. Perhaps there is some reason for that."

"Your sense of humor means more to me than you may know, Vaemar."

"When will you be ready for the Little Southland trip?" Vaemar asked.

"Tomorrow. Tonight. Now. As soon as you like," she told him.

"I have some new instructions," he told her. "Looking for stolen radioactives. It's not quite what was planned."

"It doesn't matter. I'm ready to go. You'll take me with you, won't you, Vaemar?"

"So we agreed," He looked at her with great eyes for a silent moment. "Dimity . . ." He paused again.

"Yes, Vaemar?"

Vaemar knotted and unknotted his ears for a moment. He lashed his tail. He rose and walked across to their chess-game set up on a table, making a single move. Then he spoke slowly.

"Dimity, you know that I am one of the first kzinti to have been brought up, almost from kittenhood, with a good degree of human contact on more or less equal terms, with human companions and . . . friends. Among my very earliest memories are running with the human infants and leaping on a ball of fiber that Henrietta prepared for me. Much later I learned where she got that idea . . . After the Liberation I helped Honored Step-Sire Raargh Hero when he worked on human farms. I have learnt Wunderlander and English from the best of sleep-tapes. I am a postgraduate at the University and a commissioned member of the Reserve Officer's Training Corps, with even a limited access to lesser military secrets. Human students whom I tutor prepare assignments for me diligently. I have led expeditions and fought against dangers with humans as allies. I have talked late into the night with human companions and shared many thoughts with them. I take part in many human, and encourage to the best of my ability many mixed, social activities. In chess I am a system master and aspire to interstellar master. Soon I hope I will be the first kzin to add the post-nominals PhD, DLitt and DSc to my Name. I am the leader of the *Wunderkzin*, and, slowly, our numbers among the whole kzin population of Wunderland and the Alpha Centauri A System grow. I recite all this to emphasise the fact that no kzin knows humans better than I. I know humans better than I know the kzinti of the Patriarchy."

"Yes."

"I am also, like my Honored Sire, a genius. That is a fact. In the society of the Patriarchy "genius" is an insult rather than a compliment. Geniuses may live on sufferance if they have useful skills. Otherwise they are generally killed by their fellow kittens, the warriors, in their nursery games and first combat training. Honored Sire lived because he was a great fighter as well, as befits one of Riit blood. You are . . . a super-genius. Even if we had not fought as allies in the caves against the Mad Ones, that would be a bond between us. We genii must stick together. Yours is a deeper mind than mine. It is hard work for me to read your papers—even those I am allowed to. Dimly I grasp the implications of Carmody's Transform, which you discovered so young! Do not worry, if I were allowed to see your hyperdrive work I doubt that I could steal it, Dimity friend, even if I were so inclined. But perhaps my talents spread wider."

"Vaemar scatter-brain! Everything from astrophysicist to warrior to song-writer! Mine are so narrow!"

Vaemar shifted uneasily. His tail lashed again. If a sinuous felinoid like a nine-foot tower of claws, fangs and muscle could look awkward, Vaemar did so. He licked his lips once or twice. "I . . . care about you, Dimity. We are alike."

"You have been good to me. I do not know what I would have done without you."

"You said song-writer? The university review, you mean?"

"Yes!"

They sang together, laughing:

> *"Frightened monkeys yell, when our fangs*
> *gleam bright!*
> *"What fun it is to yowl and scream a slaying*
> *song tonight!*

> *"We are the monkey boys and girls, going*
> *for a spin!*
> *"If pussy gives us trouble, we will take off*
> *pussy's skin!"*

"I thought it was important to get the students laughing at that one," Vaemar said. "Our 'Cat in the Hat' really laid them in the aisles, too, didn't it? I'm afraid Orlando and Tabitha got hold of the hat, though. There wasn't enough left of it to keep when those two had finished."

He paused, again washing his black lips with his great tongue, and then continued, looking down into Dimity's eyes: "Honored Step-Sire Raargh also taught me never to be ashamed of using my Ziirgah sense, or to hide it as though fearing someone would come and make me into a Telepath. I know some humans fairly well, I think, and I read emotions. And in you I read desperation. . . . How do you see the future, Dimity?"

"It could be full of hope. We are still digesting the implications of what the hyperdrive means. Planets for all? And one day, after the eventual peace in Space, the kzin worlds will get it too."

"You think so? So do I. It is among a number of reasons

why I have felt no inclination to try and steal it. Such action would be counter-productive."

"Of course," she said. "They may have it already. At least one hyperdrive ship went missing when the Armada swept in. It may have been captured. But anyway knowledge leaks, and some humans would be prepared to spy for the Patriarchy, and kzinti students-of-particles are clever."

"The war will go on, you think? A hyperdrive war?"

"It may or it may not," she said. "There is nothing I can do about it. I try to school myself not to brood upon things I cannot change. But there is another thing which is less dramatic but whose implications may be at least as important—humans now have the technology of kzin gravity-control. That will give us new planets, too. In the early days of human exploration of Sol system, terraforming even the nearer planets had low priority because the asteroids had lighter gravity. A little slow work done on Mars. Nothing on Venus, though Earth in theory at least had the biology to start transforming its atmosphere cheaply since the twentieth or twenty-first century. Such things will matter much less now. And there need be less competition for territory.

"We can have the stars, humans and kzinti, too. If we can live together here, Vaemar-Riit, then we can share a universe in peace. It may take several centuries, of course. It may never happen. There is a chance, more than a chance, even if we can achieve a peace now, of more wars before it really happens. I have heard rumors that peace negotiations drag on, but so does the war in space."

"Those are my thoughts also," said Vaemar. "Stars and

planets for all, one day. And a pair of species that nothing can challenge. Soon I must begin teaching Orlando to share this purpose. Today I found something important: he has the patience to solve puzzles. Many kittens do not. But, Dimity, how do you see *your* future?"

"You have been good to me Vaemar," Dimity said again. "You don't hate me?"

"Hate you? Why should I?"

"One great reason. I made building the hyperdrive possible. In time to win the war for humans. I could be seen as the greatest enemy the kzin species has ever had."

"I could answer that several ways," said Vaemar. "When you translated and applied the manual for the hyperdrive I understand you did not even know of the war. And whether that was so or not, you did what you did for your kind. Any kzin who could have done the same would have done so. It would be irrational to hate you for that.

"Further, I think now that we needed to lose a war. As a race, we were becoming more than foolish with victory. We were becoming permanently intoxicated with it. We were so used to swallowing up feeble, peaceful races that we took for granted that was the only way things could be in the Universe. But the God was more subtle and more generous than we had come to assume. Our ancestors had prayed for enemies worth the fighting. They were given to us just before our own arrogance and savagery ate us up.

"There are other things. We were lucky, I think, to have met humans when we did and not just gone on expanding unopposed until we ran into something worse. We had missed, or deprived ourselves of, a great deal. I have read Honored Sire's meditations and have come to see how right he was when he perceived that humans have talents and abilities we lack—or have deprived ourselves of. I enjoy biology and mathematics, for instance, and reading of historical events, human as well as kzin. I sang 'Lord Chmeee's Last Anthem' for sheer joy in the words as well as Heroic blood-lust. It excited me—actually excited me!—to discover how the Normans of Earth combined barbarian vigor with Roman order and discipline to conquer so much from so tiny a base. Could I have enjoyed these things as a princeling in Honored Sire's palace? I would have been killed by my brothers or by Combat Trainer as a freak. Who knows how many other young kzinti died like that—intellectual misfits in a warrior culture? My brothers would have had to gang up on me, though, and there would have been fewer of them at the end of it, for in single combat I . . ." He trailed off.

"But there is another thing. As I grew up with Raargh after the human victory, mixing with humans, I thought long and hard on the future of my kind. And its future not here on Wunderland only. I believe that in the long run the best future for us is as partners with humans. When I say I believe in an eventual partnership of our kinds I do not just use words. What might we not do together! You have said it will take centuries and I agree, but perhaps I can do something to bring it about a little quicker here on this world at least. Hatred is not a good way to begin. And nor do I dislike you, Dimity. Dislike is more destructive than hatred, more long-lasting. . . .

"And there is a further thing again. Not in this case a completely rational or utilitarian consideration. Your presence is more agreeable to me than your absence. There are bonds between you and me. When I am near you I feel I am near a like mind. Almost I could wish I was a Telepath at such moments—though say that to no other kzin! Almost I have wished I was a . . . no, that thought is not even for you! What could I do but take you in? Raargh knew what he was doing when he ran through fire to save you in the battle in the caves."

Dimity reached out a hand, and scratched the kzin at the base of his ears. Vaemar permitted himself to purr.

"And if we are both genii, we are both misfits," he went on. "I have mixed with humans too long to be a kzintosh of the Patriarchy, even though I bear this." He tapped the red fur on his chest. "And you . . ."

"I should be teaching," said Dimity. "When I was a professor I was not a good teacher, but I think I communicate better now. I should have the ordinary domestic life that should be any human's lot: my own people, my own mate and children. Instead . . ."

"I know that by human standards you are beautiful," said Vaemar. "Even I can see that. Some have said you could have any mate you wanted. If he is not afraid of your mind."

"What I want now," said Dimity, "is to know that for the moment I may stay here if I wish. I need a refuge."

Vaemar sprayed a very little—a couple of drops—of urine on the fabric of her trouser leg. It reinforced his mark for all kzinti to know.

"Of course," he said. "You are my guest and chess partner as long as you wish. But you care to come to Little Southland."

"Yes, I also need to run."

"From what?"

"Everything.

> *"Footfalls echo in the memory*
> *"Down the passage which we did not take*
> *"Towards the door we never opened*
> *"Into the rose-garden . . ."*

"T.S. Eliot?" said Vaemar.

"Do not kzinti feel like that sometimes?"

"When we do, we usually go out and kill things. Or fight each other. You are free to hunt in my preserves if you wish. I have human-size weapons you may use."

"Thank you, Vaemar, but I do not think that would help. I am looking forward to Little Southland. What of Karan?"

"Like me, she must learn to live with humans. It is harder for her in some ways, perhaps, easier in others. She is not Riit. But I think she has bred true. Tabitha has intelligence! I thought that was the case when I realized her vocabulary was far beyond that of a normal female kitten of her age—or normal kzinrret of any age, to be sure—but now I know. She reads! She plans!"

"Are you glad, Vaemar? You and I know abnormal intelligence may be a curse as well as a blessing."

Vaemar paced for a while before answering. His gait betrayed troubled thought.

"I am mortal," said a voice on the screen. "You are Elfkind. It was a beautiful dream, nothing more."

"Yes, I think I am glad," Vaemar said at last. "It is a new thing, and like many new things I must accept it. She will not need to live her life as Karan did for so long, pretending to be a moron. You will help teach her, perhaps?"

"If I can. I would like to repay your hospitality to me somehow."

"Are you sure you do not wish to kill something? My hunting preserve is free to you."

"When do we leave?"

"Pack your equipment."

"I already have."

Chapter 6

"He took Dimity with him? Does Nils know?" Cumpston pinched his lip in a worried gesture.

"I didn't feel it was my business to tell him," Arthur Guthlac said. "I don't want to go dancing into that mine-field. It was a difficult decision to allow Dimity to go off to him at all. You can imagine the opposition and the arguments we faced. But once we decided we had no right to interfere with her we stuck by that decision. You can't put that mind in a cage. And there had to be a demonstration of trust in Vaemar. A big one . . ."

"No," said Cumpston, "not our business to tell Nils. Especially not now, Arthur. We can't be their keepers. Anyway, you have other things to think about at the moment than raising taboo subjects."

"And yet, I can't forget we're all bound together in funny ways."

"How do you feel about the safety of those two misfits off together?"

"Let's not forget, those two misfits are probably the two most intelligent members on this planet of the two most deadly species known. I'm not overly concerned about them."

"More deadly than Protectors?"

"That's something I hope we don't have to find out."

"And Patrick Quickenden. He won't be too pleased."

"That's not my problem. He's not a Wunderlander."

"He loves Dimity too, you know."

"I know. But we've got enough things to sort out without lovesick Crashlanders as well."

"How do you feel, General?" Cumpston asked. "About the wedding, I mean."

"As I should feel, I guess," Guthlac told him. "Scared. Happy. I've never been married before. I want to be with Gale for the rest of my life. I want lots of children and I want them to live here on Wunderland. I'd like to get her farm back into proper production. Big John can help now he's been patched up. Earth's been too crowded and conformist for a long time. I don't particularly care if I never see it again. I'd like my children here. And none of those damned birth restrictions!"

"We had to have them. It's the only reason we've been able to keep the crowding down a bit."

"Yes, but Earth hasn't kept the blandness down. Or the conformity and police control, more than a little of which I had a hand in making. As somebody said: 'I've seen some terrible things and a lot of them I caused.' But I see what I've been missing now. Wunderland is full of surprises still. Gale was the best of them."

The red telephone on Guthlac's desk called him, then went into battle-secret mode, vibrations keyed to his personal implant. He listened to it, then stared at it with curious expression.

"That was Defense Headquarters," he said at length. "A message has just come in on the hyperwave."

"I gather it's something important. Are you going to tell me?" There was something like consternation behind Cumpston's voice as he stared at Guthlac. The brigadier had raised a hand and was wiping away tears.

"Oh, yes, it's important. And I'm going to tell you. Everybody will know soon enough anyway. McDonald and the Patriarch's negotiator have signed a treaty. Humanity and the Kzin Empire are at peace. Sixty-six years after first contact. It's a funny feeling." He looked at the wetness of the tears on his hand with surprise.

"Peace. It's a funny word, Arthur."

"It's going to take some getting used to . . . For the kzinti, too. I doubt they've ever been at peace with anyone before."

"Some geneticists have speculated," said Cumpston, "that the war has changed the kzinti. Killed off their most aggressive individuals, made the species less dangerous."

"And some," said Guthlac, "have speculated that the war has changed them by killing off their most stupid and reckless individuals, and made the species more cunning and more dangerous."

"I know. What do we believe?"

"After sixty-six years of war, there must still be a place for optimism, for hope . . . for ideals. Otherwise we are indeed no better than animals."

"Yes." Cumpstom raised his eyes to the window. "Does the sky look different to you."

They both stared at it for a long time. "Yes. Or I think it will soon. Do you believe death is not going to fall out of it again?"

"I'm trying to . . ." Cumpston said. "I hope our kzin friends here will be pleased . . . I mean our real kzin friends . . .Vaemar, Raargh, Karan . . . Big John."

"You think of them first? You're a funny bird, Michael."

"Vaemar's always been vulnerable to a certain stain: quisling, collaborator. Maybe that's gone now."

"Vaemar was only a kitten when the kzin forces on Wunderland surrendered. A lost, orphaned kitten, when Rarrgh took him in. Should he have fought to the death against us with his milk-teeth? Anyway, even if there's now a cease-fire in space, I doubt it means the likes of Vaemar can come and go between here and the Patriarchy just like that."

"Perhaps he can one day. Another thing I'm realizing: we don't have to use Baphomet."

"No." Baphomet was something very new, which the two officers had been briefed on shortly before. It was an update of the old idea of a disrupter bomb. A complex carrier designed to penetrate deep into the crust of a suitable planet, and set off explosions which, it was calculated, could turn over a tectonic plate. It had been tried on a lifeless world orbiting Proxima Centauri and had worked. Had the target's geology been a little different, Proxima would have become a twin star sub-system.

"Sorry, Arthur, I'm still trying to get my mind around it all. There's a lot to think about. It's going to take a while to digest. But your children, and Gale's, can maybe grow up in a better time."

"Give me a chance to get some first!"

"Me too, perhaps."

They both laughed, and Guthlac poured celebratory drinks.

There had been a resumption of brief and cryptic messages from Chorth-Captain. He had established himself on *Ka'ashi*. He had discovered an arms depot, and a mighty ally. It was time to leap.

Kzaargh-Commodore had broken his rule of maximum possible silence. He sent back interrogatories. The replies remained cryptic. Things were going better than expected. The ally was unexpected but potent. Attack!

The kzinti had no allies. Other races were enemies, prey or slaves. It was inconceivable that the kzinti *needed* allies. Or rather, Kzaargh-commodore thought, struggling like so many kzinti to fathom an utterly new situation, it had been inconceivable that the kzinti needed allies. His crew trod softly for he was puzzled and angry. He had sent more interrogatories, but Chorth-Captain had fallen silent again.

Fury, puzzlement, impatience . . . and hope. He had become capable of waiting no longer.

There was a comet which he had marked out, a large and highly volatile one, plainly destined to a short life. Hiding as he might in its tail, he turned his ship and plunged back towards *Ka'ashi*.

A pod of dolphins broke surface in the car's flying shadow as the Ocean rolled away below. Dimity called them. The communicator was programmed to translate into Dolphin, and Dimity had picked up some of their concepts long ago.

They exchanged pleasantries, but with difficulty. During the decades of war many dolphins had come to maturity in the oceans of Wunderland with little knowledge of the human partners who had brought them as fellow enthusiastic colonists across interstellar space. Cooperation was being rebuilt slowly, and though the humans of Earth had employed some dolphins in their war-fleets as strategists it was hard to know how much these Wunderland dolphins knew—or cared—of the kzinti or current events. Still, they were friendly to the human walkers, and asked if, like their fathers, they might trade for hands. Dimity recorded their identities.

Little Southland was not very little. It was a detachment of Wunderland's southern continent, a knife-shaped triangle of land stabbing towards the South Pole, with a total area of 17,000 square miles, much of it cool to cold desert like Patagonia. With the temperate areas of Wunderland still empty or only sparsely settled, there was no need to cultivate it. There were some military installations and a few scientific ones.

Its population of avianoids was its main macrobiological interest. Varieties of creatures with vast striking beaks resembling the diatrymas of Earth's Eocene roamed it, and there were some introduced Earth birds, too: The "banana belt" of the northern coastal regions had a climate not unlike the south of New Zealand and there were a few ranches for reconstituted and slightly modified moas, strongly fenced in and over to protect them from the savage and powerful locals.

The car climbed. Vaemar and Dimity approached the land at about ten miles' height, searching with instruments.

"There!" A fuzzy radiation signature, but one that matched the record in the brick. Dimity tracked an optical telescope in.

"Nothing that shows on the surface," said Vaemar. "It would be hidden, of course."

"Granite everywhere. Hot granite. That won't make following a radiation trail easier."

They deployed a deep-radar scanner. A faint but unnatural grid of lines became visible. Vaemar grinned and his claws slid from their sheaths. "Prey," he said, and then: "We must give no cause for suspicion. Dimity, take over flying. If anyone contacts us, better that they see your face than mine."

There were interrogatory signals coming in from the scientific and military stations on the ground, but the car answered them automatically with the University's code and signature. They descended. Vaemar and then Dimity could make out the movement of life-forms on the surface. They changed into lightweight combat/utility suits, Vaemar's leaving his claws free, and Dimity adding a helmet with breathing mask, and landed.

Vaemar, followed by Dimity, stepped out into a landscape of grey, under a swirling grey sky, punctuated by rocks, and surrounded by rock walls and pillars, wind and rain-eroded into fantastic shapes reminiscent of dragons, sthondats and other great beasts of legend and fact. There was a thunderstorm dribbling lightning on the horizon. Distant hills were speckled with snow.

Hardy, spiky vegetation grew about them. This was a cool wet plain, and days like this without high winds were rare. But life seemed reasonably abundant. Vaemar's eyes and the infrared detector in Dimity's face-mask found a number of small animals watching them from concealment, or in some cases burrowing frantically.

Dimity saw what she thought at first was a man approaching them, although the motion was wrong. She activated the binoculars in her helmet and pointed to the biped. An avian, or an avianoid creature, high, with great legs, atrophied wings and a mighty striking head and beak, standing, they could see, higher than Vaemar. To Dimity it resembled a holo of a carnivorous Earth dinosaur. It was making a high-pitched scream.

"Thunderbird," said Vaemar. "They must have good eyes. We have evidently invaded this one's territory." It was fast, and in Wunderland's gravity even those small wings could help it make great hops. Suddenly it was very close.

Dimity brought up her rifle, but Vaemar was quicker, and he gestured to her to leave it to him. He waited a few moments more, then fired as the thing leapt again. Its huge head shattered and its body slid towards them in a kicking ruin.

Almost on top of them, a second thunderbird erupted from concealment behind a rock wall. Vaemar's stride became a vertical leap. The thunderbird's huge hind-claws barely touched the ground, and it too leapt again, wings extended to show barbed claws, its colossal armored beak snapping and clashing at the kzin. Vaemar twisted in mid-air, avoiding the beak in a blur too fast for Dimity to follow, and landed on the creature's back. As they crashed to the ground together his jaws severed its neck in a single bite. The second thunderbird ran headless for a distance, wings flapping, before it collapsed.

"Perhaps those screams will call others," said Vaemar. "From what we know about them they are cooperative to some extent. However, we have no time to waste on game. Where is our real quarry?"

They surveyed the wilderness of rock.

"Caves are the best hiding-place from an aerial search," said Dimity. "But they have to be a certain size. There are no caves of such magnitude here."

"Caves are also *obvious* hiding places," said Vaemar. "If you have technology there are other ways of hiding."

"Bending light?"

"Or radar pulses. You see how much we think alike, Dimity? I do not need to explain things to you."

"Not a technology we've mastered. Not without a lot of bulky and obvious equipment."

"No. *We* haven't."

The portable deep-radar showed a maze of granite. The radiation signature they had been following was lost.

There was a quick movement in the shadows of the rocks. Vaemar and Dimity spun to face it, weapons ready. Sight, smell and Ziirgah sense all told Vaemar of another kzin. He called a challenge/greeting in the Heroes' Tongue.

It came forward slowly. It was an adult male, with a good collection of human and kzin ears on its belt-ring. Vaemar stood rampant, staring, but with most of his fangs not yet showing. In that posture his chest was thrust forward somewhat, throwing into prominence the red splash that marked him as Riit. There was his own belt-collection as well. Both kzinti had their ears folded, and it was impossible to see their ear-tattoos in detail.

The other kzin did not challenge or bare fangs, indeed the slightly bowed attitude of its head might indicate that it conceded Vaemar's dominance, although, Vaemar thought, the gesture might have been made less ambiguous.

"Who are you?" he asked in the Neutral Tense, though as Riit he might have used a far higher one. Dimity, he knew, now understood something of the Heroes' Tongue. She had had sleep-lessons since returning to Wunderland and was a good natural linguist.

"Chorth-Captain," replied the other kzin. "Of the Patriarch's Navy and the Patriarch's Claws."

The Patriarch's Armed forces had been disbanded on this planet when the kzinti accepted the human cease-fire, the day when Raargh, who had been Raargh-Sergeant, had fled with Vaemar in a stolen air-car to the backwoods country beyond the Hohe Kalkstein.

"There are no other Patriarch's Claws on Wunderland," said Vaemar, deliberately using the human name for *Ka'ashi*. Let Chorth-Captain make what he would of the qualifier "other." He added, "I have not met you before."

Chorth-Captain was plainly much older than Vaemar, and he looked a great deal more experienced, strong, tough and battle-scarred. But Vaemar was Riit.

That put him in an anomalous position on Wunderland. Some humans, he knew, wished to groom him to lead the kzin who had remained on post-Liberation Wunderland to take a place as partners with humanity. The reasons had been put to him openly, and, as he had told Dimity truthfully, he had agreed with them. He had felt no—well, little—conflict of loyalties once he concluded that what he was doing was for the long-term good of the kzin species. Indeed it was a project he had firmly committed himself to. Some humans he had dismembered in battle in the great caves. Some he had eaten. Regarding some like Rykermann, Cumpston, Leonie, the abbot, Dimity, or Anne von Lufft who had been one of his companions on a hazardous biological excursion, honor and companionship alike demanded that he die protecting them if necessary, as much as if they had been his Honored Step-Sire Raargh Hero or Karan.

And yet with this he was Riit. The Riit had ruled the kzinti since before the Heroic Race first leapt into the stars. A large number of the kzinti of Wunderland respected him and, when necessary, obeyed him. It was left to other, older kzintosh, including some of the few surviving professional officers like Hroth and Hroarh and the old warriors on Tiamat to link with the human authorities and guide relations between the kzin and human communities in detail, but it was he who performed many ceremonial duties like opening Veterans' Hospitals and other projects and presenting the State of the *Wunderkzin* Address to the human Parliament. He knew he was being groomed even in his academic courses. It did no harm that he was tall, strong and fast even by kzin standards, as one would expect of Riit, and had been trained and was backed by Raargh-Hero, one of the toughest old kzintoshi on the planet. At the moment he could afford to find out more about this Chorth-Captain and not put his dominance to the test.

"I still do not see how you got through the defenses," he said.

"I landed here recently," said Chorth-Captain.

Vaemar found it hard to believe him. Wunderland, and the whole Alpha Centauri system, was ceaselessly monitored by live and electronic sentinels against another kzinti raid or invasion. Kzin ships had come, certainly, in the last few years—from kzin worlds that had no knowledge of the human hyperdrive or the human victory, freebooters whose livers had been maddened by old rumors, hungry for loot and glory, or regular Naval vessels returning from distant missions. Part of his duties was to help negotiate with them. Those that had not surrendered when informed of the true situation had not lasted long.

"I hid long on the Hollow Moon," said Chorth-Captain, as though detecting his thoughts. "Since the battle between the fleets of Traat-Admiral and Ktrodni-Stkaa, and the human invasion I have lain in wait. I had help. There is much traffic. I left my fighter there and came back to *Ka'ashi* in a gig. It was small and undetected."

Of course, Vaemar knew, not all the kzinti on Wunderland were entirely sane. Defeat had unhinged many, especially fighting kzin to whom defeat at the hands of weed-eating apes was unthinkable. Delusions among them that they were officers of the victorious Patriarchy, generally complete with Patriarchy-bestowed Names, were not uncommon, with pathetic and tragic consequences. There were also the crazed kdaptists, already splitting into murderously-quarrelling sects.

Chorth-Captain, at least in this poor light, did not look insane or deluded, but not all of them did. He smelt a little strange, but that was not surprising. Also, it was a point of honor for kzinti not to lie outright, but many had developed great ingenuity in bending the truth. Association with humans had done nothing to diminish that skill. Vaemar wondered whose side Chorth-Captain had fought on in the final civil war of kzin that had killed his own first protector, old Traat-Admiral, and which had made the human hyperdrive Armada's reconquest so much easier.

"What are you doing here? What do you want?" Vaemar asked. His mind framed the question: "Do you know who I am?" but he decided it was better not to force that issue at present. He did not particularly want to get into a fight in this situation.

"I know what you seek. Come with me, and I will show you."

Vaemar and Dimity paused. Similar thoughts raced through both their minds. "I know what you seek." A statement like that contained a challenge. How did Chorth-Captain know? What *exactly* did Chorth-Captain know? That someone—or something—had made a covert landing here? And why should he show them? He had not acknowledged himself as being under Vaemar's dominance, indeed calling himself a member of the Patriarch's Claws might be taken as defying that dominance. He had offered no hostility, and had voluntarily revealed himself to them, so he did not appear to be intending an attack. He seemed to accept the presence of Dimity at Vaemar's side without comment. Chorth-Captain turned away—

which might be a gesture of trust—and started along the tunnel. Vaemar hesitated a moment, then moved to follow him.

He saw the Protector too late. Its leap carried it outside the swing of his flashing claws. It landed behind him and before he could turn it had seized and secured his arms.

Vaemar kicked backwards with his hind legs, steel-hard, razor-edged claws extended. Kicks, again too fast for a human eye, that would have disembowelled a Man or a Kzin. The Protector avoided them effortlessly and caught his feet in its free hand. Vaemar's claws could not reach the hand's leathery skin, but the Protector pressed with a fingertip on Vaemar's feet so his hind-claws involuntarily retracted. From the corner of his eye he saw Chorth-Captain leap in the same instant, run up a wall on his hind legs and somersault to land beside Dimity, seizing her weapons and tucking her under one arm. Vaemar twisted his head violently, dagger fangs in bolt-cutter jaws crashing together where the Protector's head had been an instant before. The Protector shifted its grip to hold him paralyzed and taped his hands and feet securely. Though it stood little more than half Vaemar's height, it lifted him onto its shoulders.

Chapter 7

"I called Dimity," Patrick Quickenden told Nils Rykermann. "She wasn't answering. Then I called Vaemar's household. It took me a while to get put through to a human but the kittens' nurse was there. Apparently Dimity and Vaemar flew south. But they've stopped reporting."

"As far as I know," said Rykermann, "there was a trip to Little Southland due. Routine check of some automated experiments." He did not speak particularly warmly to Quickenden, his coolness not all due to security considerations. He knew the Crashlander's protectiveness of Dimity stemmed from a love similar to that which he was trying to kill in himself.

"Their car is down," said Quickenden. "It was sending out a normal carrier wave. No answer when we interrogated it. Then that cut off."

Rykermann tried to keep his face impassive. He knew and disliked his own jealousy and possessiveness towards Dimity, and knew its irrationality, but could do nothing about it except try to switch his thoughts in other directions, and keep Dimity at a distance. He guessed now that he was always to be torn in two.

Is Dimity in danger? Yes, stupid! We are all in danger! Tree-of-life? Protectors? Dimity doesn't merely look younger than her years like us, thanks to geriatric treatments. Because of those years in Coldsleep she is young. She could survive the change to Protector if she got a whiff of tree-of-life. And she is with Vaemar, who would tend to think it disgraceful to notice danger because he's not a human in a fur coat but a young male kzin. And Dimity, just because she is a super-genius, isn't assured of common sense. The reverse if anything. I don't want her to go chasing after hidden tree-of-life, and possibly finding it.

He looked at Leonie. A sudden thought of *her* exposed to tree-of-life gave rise to a peculiarly horrible image: her lower body was much younger than her upper. Mad and impossible. Still, Leonie's presence gave the situation between him and Quickenden at least a superficial feeling of normalcy.

"What happened then?" he asked after an awkward silence.

"I told Guthlac and Cumpston. They've gone to find them. Karan went with them."

"Karan?"

"Would you like to try and stop her, when she's made her mind up? They suggested she go back to Vaemar's palace and wait. She thought Vaemar might need her."

"So what do we do now? Go after them?"

Rykermann touched his desk. A hologram globe of Wunderland sprang into existence above it. He touched an icon and the scattering of human settlements on Little Southland was displayed.

"If those three can't take care of any problems our presence may not make much difference," Rykermann said at length, reluctantly. *It's no business of his that I can't let myself see Dimity again.*

"Vaemar only spent a short time at the caves," he went on. "He only looked at a few of the nearest passages. I'm worried about what may be happening there. We've left no one on guard."

"I'll take a look, if you like."

"You're not a Wunderlander. I'd rather go myself or, no offence, send someone who knew the ground better. That isn't Procyon in the sky, you know."

"Someone should be here to coordinate the others or call for help if we need it. That seems to be you or Leonie. She says she'll go with me."

"I'll organize a car for you," said Rykermann. *No point in protesting. When Leonie's made her mind up, I think I'd rather try to stop Karan. Anyway, I'd like to let you see the caliber of my mate.* "Go well-armed, keep your com-link open to me, and wear pressure-suits with the helmets on and the faceplates closed at all, I mean *all*, times you're on the ground. Don't land at all if you can help it. Just use the car's deep-radar to monitor movement in the caves. If it's bipedal and within certain size parameters, we've got a pattern-recognition program that can tell you if it's human or Morlock. Or kzinti, for that matter. If it's none of those things, well . . ."

"What chances of other humans there?"

"I hope there won't be any. But even this long after the

war, there are too many ferals about. Leonie and some others have been trying to bring them in, particularly the children, but it's a slow process. They're cunning and wild, and, incidentally, can be very dangerous. There are still weapons lying about for anyone to pick up. I don't know if you understand danger sufficiently, Patrick. Obey Leonie's instructions at all, *all* times."

"We Made It isn't exactly a garden world, you know," Patrick said. "And I was a spacer before I got involved in hyperdrive engineering. My life hasn't been completely sheltered."

"Those are natural dangers. Not like thinking beings, highly-intelligent beings, consciously out to get you . . . A spacer, yes, of course you were . . .

"I never asked you . . . " Rykermann went on after a pause. "But were you—"

"Yes. I was flying the first ship that helped stop the derelict, and the first to board it. I found Dimity."

"And without you?"

"It was heading straight for one of the gas-giants. We had quite a race to catch it and deploy the grapnels before it went too deep into the gravity-well. We kept signalling, and there was no answer . . ."

"You found Dimity . . ."

"I'll not forget going aboard, pushing through those floating eyeless corpses with their lungs going before them, those monks with their shaven heads, and my light falling on that black medical coffin, with the last lights of its emergency power blinking red. There was a translucent panel. When I saw her face I thought at first that she was dead, too, of course, but she looked so . . ."

"So we owe you Dimity's life."

"There were several ships and crews involved. They were all needed before we saved the ship. It wasn't just me. Others actually got her out."

"But without you she'd be dead."

"That's true."

"And without Dimity, no working hyperdrive. Not for decades at least. Not until too late."

"No. We were making slow progress translating the manual. Dimity was still in rehabilitation therapy when we got it—they were wondering what to do with her, in fact. Then she got word of what was happening somehow and forced her way onto the project. How she broke out of the hospital, evaded the medics, got into the project headquarters—all underground on a strange planet—and forced the team-leaders to give her a hearing *and* authority was an epic in itself. As you say, she saved us decades. Without her, we might easily be working on it still."

"And without the hyperdrive, Leonie and I would surely be dead by now, and unless we'd made Protectors Wunderland and probably Earth would be kzin hunting-grounds."

"Not to mention my own world. I was wrong to say we might be working on it still. They'd have got to We Made it, sooner or later. Probably sooner. We were behind kzin lines though we didn't know it."

"If we need to land and search for tree-of-life," said Leonie, "Or do any fighting, it might be handy to have a kzin with us."

"Apart from Vaemar there aren't that many kzinti available who we know well enough to use, not at short notice," said Rykermann. "And even on this planet, most of them still have no love for monkeys. Don't ever make the mistake of thinking the handful of *Wunderkzin* like Vaemar and Raargh are typical, Patrick. I know we're civilizing them, but it's a slow business . . ."

"I was thinking of Raargh. He knows the caves, too, and that eye of his could be useful," said Leonie. "I think the *alte Teufel's* bored with peace, anyway. Promise him the chance of battle, and he'd be with us. I'll call him and brief him now."

"Take care, Lion-cub." He kissed her.

"It's all so . . . " Patrick Quickenden waved his hands at the landscape below them, another part of the great limestone plateau which Vaemar had flown over a few days before. The sight of a herd of gagrumphers that Leonie pointed out filled him with excitement.

He's like a kid, Leonie thought. *Hard to feel objectively about him. I know he loves Dimity, which makes him a sort of ally of mine—"The lover of my rival is my friend?" That's a new one. Does she love hm? Dimity, who I've competed against hopelessly since I was 18, who saved my life, apart from saving our species. Paddy, if she could love you, and you could take her back to Procyon, it would make things . . . And I know someone else who's in love with her, too. I wonder if he knows he is . . . One other, at least. That's if you don't count . . . Well, let's not get too complicated . . . Paddy, sparkle-eyed at the streams running under the sky and the gagrumphers plunging away through the trees, there's a lot riding on you . . .*

The great problem, once you've been any sort of leader,

*which means once you've been any sort of manipulator:
Can you again come to value people for what they are,
rather than for how they might be able to serve your own
ends? We forget that between men and women sexual
exploitation isn't the only kind of exploitation there is. At
least we do as soon as a war's over. . . . Now if you and
Dimity . . . What am I thinking about? Dimity may well
be dead. Patrick, you seem a happy, decent man, the product
of a world less tortured than this one. Can I leave you an
innocent man, not try to make you my catspaw?* She
caught his eyes. In love with Dimity he might be, but
Leonie saw he was admiring her at least as much as the
landscape. *I wonder if it would turn him sick to know
what's under my trousers?* she thought. And then: *Let me
get all that boiling black stuff out of my head, anyway. Nils
and I are lucky, compared to so many.*

"I can never get used to it," he said. "I don't mean
agoraphobia—I've had treatment for that—but still it all
takes my breath away. Living on the surface like this . . .
And"—he pointed to the horizon—"And those mountains—like needles."

"We've had to live in some odd places," said Leonie.
"Sometimes during the war it seemed we were underground more often than on the surface. There were
children born in the caves who knew stalactites better
than stars or mountains."

"Your children?"

"None of my own. Others had their own lives and
priorities, but for us, then, it seemed children were not
exactly a good idea," Leonie said. "Pregnancy would have
kept me out of action for a long time, with medical care

the state it was in, and . . . what sort of a world would it have been to bring a child into? Of course, it was fortunate not everyone on Wunderland had the same policy—the population was dropping fast as it was.

"I was going to broach the subject with Nils after the war. I'd been important enough to have geriatric drugs throughout and I still had an apparently young body, as he did. I would have run out of natural ova sooner or later, but that didn't worry me—stimulating stem cells to produce new ova is an elementary procedure. Then, you know, I lost the lot."

"That shouldn't be a problem," Patrick said. "I know that on Earth creating ova from other tissue isn't unusual. I think it's been done since the twenty-first century, at least."

"I don't think I could do that. We've been very cautious about biotech for humans here. Quite a deep cultural inhibition. The first colonists got a bit carried away and there were some—unfortunate incidents. We're lucky the only inheritance was mobile ears for some of us, which are harmless and sometimes useful even if it does encourage snobbery. But I haven't told you all the details of what I am. Perhaps I'm a bit mixed up. In my emotions as well as"—a bitter laugh—"literally. The lower body I have now is ovulating all right . . . whoever she was, she was young. But you'll understand I don't exactly consider it a problem solved . . ."

There was an awkward silence.

"Look at that!" Patrick pointed excitedly again. A smile returned to Leonie's eyes as she watched the Crashlander's excitement. Much remained park-like—

woodlands, glades, small streams. Herds of gagrumphers and other creatures could be seen. There was also a scattering of human farms and hamlets. Fruit trees, and even a few vineyards for small bottlings of wine grown in the old natural way. Leonie had flown over this landscape many times, but she could still appreciate its loveliness. Humans had become human in a landscape not too unlike this. For both of them there was some touch of Eden about it.

"I can't get over it!" said Patrick. Then: "Where are the caves?"

"Underneath us. Underneath all this country. You can trace them on the deep radar."

"I'd rather just watch all this," His face was alight with wonderment. "I feel so lucky to have seen it! When this is all over I want to walk through this country. I don't think I'd get agoraphobia again, the treatments were good. I'd love to live under a sky for a while!"

"We'll be down in it shortly," Leonie said. "I hope it comes up to expectations."

Chapter 8

The tunnel was roofed over, but the grey light of the sky penetrated. There was a room at the end of the tunnel, entered through what looked like a spaceship's airlock. Power cables snaked about. There were familiar computer-screens and consoles, mostly kzin-sized and of more-or-less kzin military pattern, as well as instruments and machinery whose function neither Vaemar nor Dimity could guess at. Vaemar and Dimity were deposited there, weaponless but unharmed. As Chorth-Captain covered them with a beam rifle, the Protector removed their garments, searching them thoroughly and ripping Dimity's apart in the process—Vaemar beneath his coverall wore much less, mainly straps and pouches. It ran police tape over their hands and feet. This was specially made to restrain kzinti from using their claws, and far stronger than was necessary to immobilize a human. Then the Protector surveyed them.

So far, things had moved too fast for Vaemar or Dimity to see the Protector properly. Guthlac had surmised that it would be close to the original Pak form. For all its immense strength it was smaller than Dimity and barely half the height of either kzin, with a protruding muzzle hardened into a horny beak, a bulging, lobed, melon-like cranium, with large bulging eyes, and exaggerated ears and nostrils, part of its Morlock heritage, in a parody of a human face even more bizarre than the face of a Pak or human Protector, joints like huge balls of bone and muscle rolling below a skin like leather armor. Chorth-Captain stood beside it.

"Traitor!" Vaemar snarled at the other kzin. "You hand your own kind to alien monsters! I challenge you—to the death and the generations!"

"Traitor? Handing our kind to alien monsters? Who speaks?" Chorth-Captain replied in the Mocking Tense. "Do I speak to Vaemar, sometimes called Riit, chief *kollabrratorr* on *Ka'ashi*? Holder of a commission in the Human Reserve Officer Training Corps? Who would join our kind with the vermin of the Universe? Yes, *kollabrratorr*, I call you, *kollabrratorr* and *kwizzliing*, perversions that only the vermin had words for till they infected our tongue! As for your challenge, it is nothing. The mere jabbering of a *Kz'eerkt-chrowler." Kz'eerkt* meant "ape," "monkey" or "human." *"Chrowl"* depending on who used it and when, was an either intimate or obscene term among kzinti for sexual intercourse. In normal kzin society such as had existed pre-Liberation, a death-duel would inevitably have followed such an insult. Dimity thought she could feel the effort with which Vaemar controlled both his voice and his body language to reply calmly. *At least he has had good training at that,* she thought. *Growing up among humans, learning to follow human rules—like me.*

"You are brave when your monster has tied my claws," said Vaemar. "If you had wished to know why I have done as I have, and spoken with me, I could have told you my reasons. But you are one of those who weary me with your stupidity, who think with hot livers instead of brains. Who may yet be the destruction of our kind. What do you think you have done?" He gestured with his tail and ears at the Protector. "You are the slave of this thing?"

"He is an ally," replied Chorth-Captain. "It is not I who am the slave of aliens. We have watched you long, Vaemar-sometimes-called-Riit. *Ka'ashi* has Heroes still who do not crawl like bugs into your fur as you abase yourself before the monkeys."

The Protector gestured. Chorth-Captain disappeared for a few moments while the Protector watched them. They guessed he was attending to their car. The Protector's voice when it spoke was a series of clicks and poppings. But it spoke slowly, taking trouble, and it used what had once been called the Slave's Patois, but which was now becoming a common, value-neutral, *lingua franca* between humans and kzinti on Wunderland.

"Obey and you will live," it said. Its strange eyes travelled from Dimity to Vaemar and back. It was Dimity who replied.

"What do you want?"

"Teach." It touched a keyboard and a bank of screens sprang into life. Wunderland television channels and internet sites. One of them, Dimity and Vaemar saw, showed Vaemar's palace and its surroundings and outbuildings, including the guest house Dimity used. A camera somewhere in the woods. Others showed Munchen University, including the Dimity Carmody Physics Building with its inscription.

"Teach . . . what?"

"Everything. You I know." It touched another keyboard. An old newsreel, showing Dimity and a group of scientists. *Patrick was right*, thought Dimity. *It was stupid to broadcast the fact of my return to Wunderland. But too many people knew anyway.*

"We have been watching you for a long time," said Chorth-Captain, returning to the room. "I supplied the original equipment, which has been improved upon. The Patriarchy will be grateful to Chorth-Captain when those improvements are incorporated into the standard equipment of our Navy. We improved surveillance and stealthing among many other things. We know much. But my ally wishes to learn more. You two are . . . associates"—he cast another look of loathing and contempt at Vaemar, black lips curling—"with one another. We have known for some time, and considered it advantageous for all its loathsomeness and indignity, monkey-dirt scratched upon the Name of Riit. Did you think we were careless with the trail of radioactives? We laid a trail to bring you here."

"We will need to know more," said Dimity. "Teach? Teach what?"

"Context," said the Protector. Its beak clacked over the word. "Teach about humans. About kzinti on this planet. About space." It paused. "Gods," it said, surprisingly. Then it said the word Dimity and Vaemar had hoped against their reason not to hear. "Hyperdrive."

"I haven't the tools," said Dimity. She knew it would be pointless to play dumb. The Protector knew. *Vaemar and I set ourselves up*, she thought.

"Make tools," said the Protector. And then: "We have begun." It turned its back, leaving Chorth-Captain to guard them. Its fingers blurred with speed on the keyboard. Doors flashed shut almost soundlessly around them. For a moment there was a hint of G-force, gone almost instantly, and a purring noise. Both Dimity and Vaemar recognized it. They had flown in ships with kzin gravity-motors before. The panel of grey sky above was suddenly swirling with indescribable colors.

"Yes," said Chorth-Captain. "A gravity-planer. Much improved. And shielding devices, also much improved. Good enough to get us past the monkeyships and the monkeys' machine-sentinals. Again I supplied the basic equipment from kzin stores. Once I had demonstrated them to my ally he was able to make advances with them. Hear how quiet the planer has become."

"How did you meet your ally?" asked Vaemar, with a mildness, almost a casualness, in his voice that Dimity had heard once or twice before. She felt a shiver run up her spine.

"In the caves. When the traitors struck in the great battle before the humans attacked"—*You don't say which side you consider the traitors*, Vaemar thought—" I took a *Scream of Vengeance* fighter we carried and flew to the Hollow Moon. In the confusion it was not noticed there."

So, thought Vaemar. *Are you a coward, Chorth-Captain, and has your knowledge of cowardice driven you mad? Or is this all a lie?* The latter, he thought.

Chorth-Captain's body-language suggested lying. So, he saw, did the instrumentation numbers on the bulkhead. This craft was not from a ship of one of the *Ka'ashi*-based squadrons. He said nothing.

"Watching with its instruments," Chorth-Captain continued. "I saw the apes were gaining the upper hand, and before they had gained all air- and space-superiority about *Ka'ashi* I took this gig and, leaving the fighter as hidden as might be, I flew back to *Ka'ashi*, evading the apes' clumsy, noseless searchers, back to the wild country and the great caves. I lurked there when the war ended, hoping to find some way back to Kzinhome so I might fight on, or some way to die gloriously in battle, killing monkeys eights-squared times as Lord Dragga-Skrull killed Jotok. I made occasional raids on the surface. I learnt of Chuut-Riit's hidden redoubt which the monkeys had found. It was abandoned and sealed when I reached it but I broke the seals and took equipment from it. Years passed. Monkeys died at my claws, when they were foolish enough to wander alone or in small troops. In the caves I met my ally. He alone had been exposed to the chemical and made the change. He had memories of his previous life, and of the war. Of Heroes and monkeys, of weapons and fighting, which he was soon able to understand. His intelligence had, of course, become very high, though he had been barely sentient before. He did not kill me, but showed me that an alliance against the apes would be in the interest of both our kinds." *He lied a moment ago, but he's not lying now*, Vaemar thought. Chorth-Captain went on.

"He demonstrated his intelligence to me, and together

we modified this craft, and built other things. I contacted Heroes the apes had not corrupted and they too supplied us with knowledge and equipment. We tested his improvements to cloaking devices and they worked. We flew to the southern island undetected and carried out much work there, free from the attention of monkeys or . . . other things. Under his direction we studied what we could of the plight of *Ka'ashi*. I told him what I knew of space and the war. We agreed the monkeys were the most noxious vermin of the universe . . ."

Dimity caught it vaguely, Vaemar much more clearly. There was a great deal wrong with Chorth-Captain. There was a strange kind of buzzing in his voice. But there was more than that. Most kzinti of the officer class, used to framing orders, did not commonly in such a situation deliver themselves of prolix monologues like this, least of all to monkeys or prisoners. And Vaemar's Ziirgah sense picked up a fuzziness, something off-key, in Chorth-Captain's emotions as well as in his voice and body-language. *His brain has been tampered with*, thought Vaemar. *By the Protector, obviously. The thing that was a brainless Morlock. Rykermann is right. They are a peril indeed.*

"Where are we going?"

Chorth-Captain gestured at another screen. Wunderland was a great sphere. Vaemar saw they were already several hundred miles up, and still accelerating. There was no interference from the guardships, manned and automated, that patrolled the space above the planet.

"The Hollow Moon. There we will be undisturbed."

I don't think so, thought Vaemar. *Our disappearance*

will be noted. But then he thought that, though they might be searched for, there would be no particular reason to include the Hollow Moon in the search, especially if this craft's cloaking was truly good. There would be no reason to think they were in space at all.

Dimity had thought of no way to remind him of the locators.

"Where is the tree-of-life?" asked Dimity.

"Most of it is still in the caves, along with most of the warheads. It is safe. There was a little we took to the Hollow Moon but it is now being used. You will not be exposed to it."

There was something else Dimity and Vaemar could hardly help noticing. Chorth-Captain would hardly be talking to them so frankly if he expected them to live to tell the tale, whatever the Protector said. *The Protector may be smarter than most human geniuses*, thought Dimity, *as, by our IQ tests, are Vaemar and I. But Chorth-Captain sure isn't.*

Wunderland continued to shrink on the screen. Now it was a great, multicolored disk in space. The Protector had been sitting calmly in a lotus-position. Its oversized eyes appeared almost dreamy. But both the captives sensed it was absorbing every word. Both knew that in an instant it could spring. After a time it spoke into what appeared to be the mutated descendant of a standard kzin-pattern com-link. When Dimity asked who it was speaking to she was ignored. There were flexible tubes for food and waste-disposal, and human and kzin were evidently expected to use them together, in each other's sight. On Wunderland members of the two species who had ties with one another might sometimes drink together, or eat small delicacies like ice cream, but there were usually powerful taboos beyond more than that. Evidently there had been captives on this vessel before.

Chorth-Captain told them of how he had made contact with a number of the kzinti who had been in Chuut-Riit/Henrietta's Redoubt and escaped or survived its storming. Through them he had begun to build up a knowledge-base for the Protector about Dimity and Vaemar.

The kzinti had been masters of gravity control for millennia—the gravity-planer was their principal space-drive—and normal Wunderland gravity was maintained in the chamber. Chorth-Captain fitted caps on their heads and they slept.

Leonie, after asking permission and giving certain pass-words, landed her car in the courtyard of Vaemar's palace. Patrick Quickenden remained in the car, keeping out of sight as much as possible.

Raargh, Seneschal in charge in Vaemar's absence, greeted her. One of his kittens, folicking in the long grasses nearby, leapt to join his sire, going down into a mock-attacking crouch at the sight of the human. He was about as big as, and somewhat more powerful than, an Earth leopard. Leonie had once beaten such a kitten to death with a metal bar in a prolonged and desperate fight. Her old legs and thighs had borne the scars of that fight for a long time. Rarrgh looked at him, gave a single growl in an unmistakable tense, and the kitten fled.

Twenty-five years earlier Rarrgh and Leonie had seen

each other for the first time, across the sights of a beam rifle, as Raargh lay pinned under rocks in a Morlock-infested cave. Each owed the other at least one life. Raargh raised his remaining natural arm and touched her shoulder.

"Got message, urrr!" he said. "Trouble!" He gave a purr of satisfaction and anticipation. He passed Big John the *w'tsai* of the Seneschal's office, in its ornately-engraved gold and purple sheath. "Care for this, Hero, till I return." He slapped his belt where his own old *w'tsai* hung. "Urrr!" he repeated, snapping his teeth and flexing his claws.

Chapter 9

"The Hollow Moon," said Chorth-Captain, waking them.

The purring of the gravity-planer had ceased. The panels opened. Chorth-Captain gestured and they followed him out. The Protector came behind them.

Gravity changed abruptly. This was less disorienting for Dimity and Vaemar than it would have been had they not spent years with kzin gravity-technology. Since both knew something of the Hollow Moon it was easy to work out their situation.

They were in a compartment on the inner surface. There was a great concave roof above them, vanishing into blackness overhead, and a concave floor at their feet, but so partitioned and divided that it was impossible to see far. There was a diffuse light. The ship they had travelled in now looked like a stony spheroid. Its surface sparkled here and there with quartz-like chips that they guessed were miniaturized cloaking-generators. Held by gravity anchors, it stood within a translucent tube, one of several, on a landing pad such as was more-or-less standard for small spacecraft in the Serpent Swarm Asteroids. Above it was a hatch, now closed, obviously leading to the surface and space. There, too, was the glowing blue dome of a Sinclair time-acceleration field.

Some of the machinery around had, for both human and kzin, an alien look. But much of it appeared to be kzin military and naval equipment, either standard or modified. There were kzinti control consoles, close to standard naval models, and banks of screens, some blank, some with idly moving data. To Vaemar, they might almost be inside a kzin space station, though he knew more about this from Reserve Officers' intelligence courses than from his own experience. There was a nest of gravity-sleds, the kzin all-purpose transporters, which he had used often. Both took it all in fast. *Gravity technology, Sinclair technology, Cloaking technology already better, or more compact, than anything we have. And now they are after the Hyperdrive!* Chorth-Captain led them into another compartment.

A smell of Morlock struck Dimity, repellent even to her weak human nostrils. What she saw reminded for a moment of a hospital ward. A row of creatures lay on beds. Quasi-humanoids with swollen bellies. Morlocks, gorged on tree-of-life, beginning the change into Protectors. Dimity felt a stab of panic. She clutched at Vaemar's arm. "There is tree-of-life here!"

"You do not need to fear, monkey," said Chorth-Captain. "It is gone. It has been ingested. Before we flew we signalled to those here that we had you, and for the process to begin. These will have teachers when they awake. And there will be builders for the superluminal drive."

"Those here." Plural, thought Dimity. *We have at least four enemies. The odds are against us anyway, and they will be worse soon. I can make sense of things in that realm where mathematics and metaphysics come together, but I cannot fight a kzin, let alone a Protector. And there are forty more here, beginning to change.*

There, under a cold blue light in the corner, were other still silent forms: dead, dissected humans and kzinti. *So,* thought Dimity, *the process of learning about other species has already begun in a practical way.* She indicated it to Vaemar with a roll of her eyes and twitch of her Wunderlander aristocrat's ears.

Four more Protectors entered. They glanced briefly at Vaemar and Dimity and turned to the changing Morlocks. Dimity noticed again that they were laid out in four rows.

"Are they their children?" she asked Chorth-Captain.

The big kzin raised his ears in a gesture of assent. "Each cares for his own children."

"And the other Protector? Your ally?"

"He is childless. He came upon the tree-of-life first, and later we exposed others. They brought their children here, and waited. Why do you wish to know?"

Dimity began a retort, and bit it off. Her relationship with the untypical Vaemar had almost made her forget the hair-trigger temper of kzintosh in what she supposed must be called their natural state, particularly in their dealings with humans. She had never lived on kzin-occupied Wunderland, but knew that a human there who answered a question from a kzin with another, rhetorical, question, or in a formulation that smacked of sarcasm or irony, would have been lucky to keep tongue, face or life.

"I will be a more effective teacher, if I know the beings I am teaching."

Chorth-Captain inclined his own ears again. Apparently he accepted her explanation.

"And if I am to teach, I must have access to a knowledge base."

"That is anticipated. Come," Chorth-Captain said.

He led Dimity and Vaemar into another chamber nearby. They passed a couple of sealed passages, and dark tunnels with an old look about them. Only a small part of the hollow moon seemed to have been restored as living space. There was a chair for each of them, and two computers, based on kzin military models, but with what they guessed were Protectors' improvements, each with a keyboard adapted for their respective hands. "You may prepare your lessons," said Chorth-Captain. He was also carrying the suit, much ripped and of questionable use now as a garment, which he had taken off Dimity, and her boots. He dropped these on the floor and then gestured at Vaemar. "When the door is closed you may free him," he added.

He passed Dimity a tube, like an old-fashioned tube of toothpaste, and backed out. A door flashed shut behind him.

Dimity squeezed the contents of the tube over Vaemar's bonds. They foamed and dissolved.

Dimity looked desperately for a writing instrument. There was nothing. She took Vaemar's hand and pressed out one of his razor claws. She scratched on her arm. "They listen." Like most humans on Wunderland she had anticoagulants added to her blood and it dried quickly.

Vaemar raised his great eyes to the ceiling, then pointed to the tiny eyes of cameras. "They watch," he said. "They must hear what we say. Unless we do or say nothing, we must accept that fact."

"If they have been watching Wunderland television," said Dimity, "they probably know all the languages we do."

"I studied the history of Human International Law," said Vaemar. He added casually *"Loquorisne Latinum?"*

"Yes," said Dimity in the same language. "But it won't frustrate them long. Too logical and consistent. They'll translate. And they are bound to be recording us now."

"All the same, we have a little time to talk," said Vaemar. "Time is against us anyway for other reasons as well. How long will it take those Morlocks to change?"

"I don't know. No one knows much about the Pak. In a Sinclair field they could speed it up. But the fact that they are not using Sinclair fields for that purpose suggests the time may be variable."

"How do we stop them? How do you anticipate what they will do?"

"Wunderland has war-geared defenses," Dimity said. "If you were a Protector, what would you do?"

"I cannot think like a Protector, but here is one scenario: seize Tiamat. You agree that would be possible."

Tiamat was a roughly cylindrical asteroid of the Serpent Swarm, about fifty kilometers by twenty. It was an administrative center and military base of the Swarm and was heavily industrialized for space industries as well as a major production center for weapons and IT. It was also a research center for the Swarm. As the main site of the Swarm's experiment in commensualism it had a kzin community with a limited degree of self-government at "Tigertown" and some kzinti working with humans. Both Dimity and Vaemar had been there several times.

"For forty and more trained Protectors? Easy!"

"That would give them factories tooled up for hyperdrive technology, and working hyperdrive ships," Vaemar said. "And all the gravity-control industries. It would also give them very heavy battle lasers and other military weapons installations. Tiamat is well-defended."

"Yes."

"But not well-defended against the kind of surprise attack Protectors could mount. Then, if I were directing their strategy, I would attack Wunderland and the other settled asteroids of the Serpent Swarm from Tiamat. And while Wunderland's defenses are busy, crash this moon or another into it.

"Morlocks fight by dropping on their enemies and hurling rocks down on them. This would be the same thing on a bigger scale.

"The Protectors could break the moon up on its way by controlled explosions so that the fragments would impact in a predetermined pattern and with predetermined force. That would be the end of human—and kzin—life on Wunderland. If all was not destroyed by the first impacts, it would be so shattered that the Protectors could finish off any remnants at leisure. But the Morlocks in the great caves could survive. With Tiamat, they would not need Wunderland's industrial centers. They could destroy the other asteroid settlements one by one. Many are still reduced by war-damage anyway. I do not think their defenses would last long against Protectors."

"I cannot fault your reasoning," said Dimity. "And then . . . how many breeders would they get from the Morlocks of Wunderland?"

"Their numbers were thinned in the war, but they are breeding up again, as I know from personal experience," said Vaemar. "Hundreds, at least. Thousands, I am sure. We do not yet know how far the cave systems go."

"The Sinclair fields! That is why they have them here!"

"Yes, of course! I should have seen at once! They can use the Sinclair fields to accelerate breeding! They could have thousands more breeders and thousands of Protectors."

"That would also give them the numbers for genetic diversity."

"It would give them the numbers for a double leap into human and kzin space," said Vaemar. "And another bad thing strikes me, one which this Protector has perhaps not realized yet but sooner or later must: you humans have put much effort into developing reproductive technology, though you do not exploit its full potential. A Protector with access to that would not need to have got all its children before the change. It could clone as many as it wished from its own cell structure. There would be no limit to their numbers!

"We kzinti have experimented with cloning. A band of celibate warriors, who had dedicated themselves to the Eternal Hunt, tried to breed without females once. Each cloned his own kittens. But the kittens were incurably savage and aggressive . . . Is that so amusing?"

"If a kzin hero calls them incurably savage and aggressive," said Dimity, "they must have been a problem indeed!"

"They were. But the point is that the inhibitions of your culture or mine about cloning would mean nothing to a Protector. Dimity, we must stop them now. The cost of our own lives is nothing in these circumstances."

"I know," said Dimity.

"Unfortunately, at this moment I cannot see how."

"Nor I."

"Why didn't the original Pak Protectors simply clone themselves?" said Vaemar.

"Perhaps they had no need to think in such directions," said Dimity. "Their mature bodies were so strong, long-lived and perfect that they did little to develop biological sciences. They didn't need to improve on what they had. All that we know of the Pak species' thinking was what Brennan picked up while he was a Pak's prisoner and told to the humans who he met later. But there seem to be some gaps in Pak thinking. Humans are more creative. And, from what little I know about them, Protectors are unable to cooperate with one another beyond the briefest temporary alliances. Further, our own science showed us long ago that cloning sapient beings is fraught with risks. It seemed to promise everything at first, but then we discovered the pitfalls.

"The Protectors' science as far as we know is exclusively military-oriented. Each cares only for his own blood-line. It seems their only stimulation and excitement is war. They could have been the greatest race in the galaxy, but their intelligence and instincts together locked them into a dead-end. Their single-mindedness virtually robbed them of free will. Even their spaceflight was stimulated by nothing but a desire to find new breeding grounds. No curiosity, no sense of wonder. No sense of anything beyond themselves. The kind of creature I yearn desperately not to be. When I had to read of them it horrified me, because I saw so much of myself in them."

"It is something to be horrified," said Vaemar. "Raargh told me that to be aware of horror is an early step to knowledge. Know horror and you know glory. Know fear and you know courage."

"You understand the human idea of the knight, Vaemar? The ideal, I mean."

"I trust so. I have read much human history. It fascinates me that the knight should emerge from the dark ages, as it fascinates that Roman order, Greek art and thought, could combine with barbarian vigor to build an order that would take you to the stars. Was it like that with other star-faring races, I wonder, races that did not have the Jotok as we did? But yes, I know of human knights. Some kzinti are like that too, but not many, and as you would expect, not quite the same."

"Can you imagine Pak knights, crusaders, chivalrous champions of some cause beyond ensuring more breeders?" said Dimity. "I cannot. I loved Nils because he, for all his lack of self-awareness, had something of the knight in him. I never saw what he did in the war, of course, Leonie had all of that. . . . The Pak were—it seems are—little more than gene-carrying machines, breeding and fighting and crossing between the stars for no end but reproduction. Trapped by their own brain structure. Trapped, as I fear most of all to be trapped."

"Can we use that, I wonder? There are at least four blood-lines here."

"With the childless Protector to keep them in order."

"Yes. He is our prime target."

"Target? You have high hopes, Vaemar-Hero."

"A Hero does not need hope, Dimity-Human."

They logged onto the internet with the computers supplied. As they had guessed, they could receive but not send data. Dimity and Vaemar were both clever with computers, and they spent a lot of time trying to circumvent this.

Chapter 10

The well-armed car carrying Arthur Guthlac, Colonel Cumpston and Karan touched down beside Vaemar's empty vehicle. Apart from its turret-mounted weapons, Cumpston had a strakkaker and Guthlac a heavy, powerful beam rifle, a great cannon of a thing based on a kzin sidearm, and with mini-waldos for human use. Karan had a kzinrret's knife, the new and improved female version of a *w'tsai*, and another strakkaker. Weapons ready, the occupants alighted, the humans wearing breathing filters as Dimity had. In case they needed the car quickly, the engine was left idling and the doors unlocked. There was no sign of any live friend or enemy.

Karan pointed and bounded to the dead thunderbirds, the humans hurrying behind. Small scavengers scattered.

"Beam rifle, close range," said Cumpston. "And the other looks like a kzin bite."

"They stood here," said Karan, pointing. Looking closely, Guthlac and Cumpston could make out two very different-sized sets of footprints, the larger tipped with claw points. "It didn't get near them."

"The car has been tampered with," said Cumpston. "Look! Its antennas are gone." He also tried the door.

"Dimity and Vaemar, according to the ways we can measure IQs, are possibly the two cleverest beings on Wunderland," said Guthlac. "I hope they can look after themselves."

"Clever doesn't necessarily mean survivor," said Cumpston. "There's more than a touch of the idiot savant in Dimity. Super-genius she may be, but she's narrowly focused. Just because she shatters the old sexist stereotype of the beautiful blonde doesn't mean she . . . More common sense, better instincts and reflexes, may mean survival in a place like this. Vaemar, I can't pronounce on. But he's an intellectual, too, however sharp his claws are. I wish old Raargh was with them, or some human sergeant-major."

Guthlac thought he detected something in his friend's voice when he spoke of Dimity. There could hardly be a less appropriate time or place for him to comment. "Karan, can you follow their trail?" he asked

Karan was already moving down one of the rock-tunnels, almost on all fours, a barred orange shadow in the shifting and flickering grey light.

"We might do better to search from the air," Guthlac said. "This is another labyrinth."

"If there was anything to see from the air I think we'd have seen it," said Cumpston. "Come on! We're lucky to have her, but I don't want her getting too far ahead on her own. If anything happened to her, would you want to be the one to tell Vaemar?"

"Trail stops," said Karan a few minutes later.

They caught up to her. They were standing in a circular space in the rock-maze.

"Do you smell anything?" Guthlac asked her.

"Sand and rock turned over." Karan said. "Not a long time past. And kzintosh. There has been another male kzin here. And at the car. And something else. A bad smell."

Cumpston pointed to the edge of the rock wall. "Sand and rock turned over there?" he asked her.

"Yes."

"A gravity motor."

"But all gravity motors are monitored," said Guthlac.

"Get through to the monitoring stations," said Cumpston. "Pull your rank, Arthur! Hurry! They must have recorded something."

Guthlac sent the message. His face was dark. "I'm getting a very ugly thought," he said.

"So am I. But tell me yours first."

Guthlac made sure Karan was out of earshot, still hunting along the rock wall. He spoke softly and quickly.

"Vaemar has taken Dimity into space. He's a kzin. It looks as if he's taking her to the Patriarchy. Our pioneering hyperdrive expert!"

"Any ship that took off from here would be too small for interstellar travel."

"But it could meet a bigger one."

"We've monitored Vaemar pretty carefully. And taken other precautions. There's been no hint of anything like that."

"Apart from reversing the kzinti's whole military position, it would get him back his place beside the Riit throne.

Perhaps position him for a bid for the Patriarchy! Why should we trust him to be more loyal to us than to his own species? Especially when the reward could be so enormous? I know policy was to trust him as much as possible, but perhaps we've put too much temptation in his way. Or perhaps it was just a mistake to trust a ratcat!"

"That hangs together very nastily," said Cumpston. "I have just one small ray of hope that you're wrong. It was we who sent him here. He couldn't have planned a secret rendezvous with a spacecraft . . . unless it had been waiting for a long time."

"And unless he manipulated us into sending him. He knew he'd be coming this way sooner or later. I've given Defense Headquarters an emergency alert. The next thing is to get after them, anyway. But Vaemar doesn't *feel* like that to me."

"I put some trust in someone when all appearances were against her a little while ago," said Guthlac. "In a ruined hamlet beyond Gerning in a storm. I haven't regretted it. I'll try to believe the best of Vaemar yet, but I'm putting out an emergency alert to Defense HQ all the same."

"We should have stopped her associating with him so. That's obvious enough with hindsight."

"Dimity is an Asperger's. A superlatively high-functioning one. When she makes up her mind to do a thing the only way you can stop her is by breaking that mind.

"She can be killed any time," Guthlac went on. "There's an implant in her that can be activated remotely. An idea we got from the kzin *zzrou*. ARM insisted on it."

"Arthur! We've got to get her back!"

"I know!"

"You mustn't let ARM know what's happened! Not yet!"

"Michael, there are a lot of things neither of us let ARM know about. And I don't mean your peculiarly-colored bird or a certain Earth flower with green petals. Try to hang onto hope."

"Does she know?"

"I don't know. ARM was subtler than the kzinti about such things. Nanobots in the food. But Vaemar's got one too. ARM is *not* trusting. It wasn't my idea or orders, but . . ." Guthlac suddenly smacked his own head. "Idiot! How do we win wars with generals like me? I had completely forgotten! They both have locators in them anyway! Standard VIP models. We can read them from the car!"

"Come on!"

Calling Karan, they turned and headed back out of the granite maze. The thunderbird launched itself at them from the rock wall. Half as big again as the ones Dimity and Vaemar had killed, its vast striking beak knocked Guthlac sprawling. The tough fabric of his coverall saved him from being torn apart, but had the thing snapped its beak it would have crushed his bones in an instant. Karan was a blur of rippling orange muscle as she leapt at it. Screaming, two more thunderbirds launched themselves from the rock wall.

Karan severed the first thunderbird's neck with her fangs and claws before the beak could seize her. Cumpston, getting his beamer up just in time, shot another in the chest. The third sprang into the air again, and came down on their car. Guthlac fired at the bird and hit the car.

Its tough materials could normally have withstood far worse hits, but the unlocked door flew open. Either the beam or the avian's great kicking legs activated the controls, and car and avian tangled together shot fifty feet into the air, rolled, dived, and crashed into the rock wall.

Guthlac struggled free of the dead weight of the first thunderbird. Cumpston ran to them. Karan got to her feet, staggered and fell again, pumping gouts of purple and orange blood from gaping lacerations in her thighs. Guthlac found the end of a severed blood-vessel and held it shut while Cumpston raced for the crashed car and its medical kit, killing the broken-limbed avian as it struggled and snapped at him. The car's fuel lines had ruptured, and as Cumpston turned and ran back to Karan a spark ignited the clouds of hydrogen billowing from it. Automatically released jets of inert gas quickly smothered the flames, but the cabin and control console were wrecked.

Frantic work with a kzin military chemical bandage stabilized the wound, but it took time. Karan was weak and barely conscious.

The car, it was soon obvious, was not going to fly again without major repairs, and the lock on the car which Vaemar and Dimity had used was keyed to open to the patterns of Vaemar's and Dimity's hand or their *tappetum* or retina respectively. It was centuries since the last manually pickable lock had been made for anything as expensive as a car. Any attempt to burn the doors open, if it did not ruin the car's delicate mechanisms, would probably exhaust their weapon first. They carried Karan into the meager shelter of an overhang as rain began to fall from the grey sky. Mobile telephones were a standard part of their equipment. They called for help, and waited. After a time the rain gave way to sleet and snow. More thunder-birds came.

The comet-debris had served them well, Kzaargh-Commodore thought. *Night-Lurker* had passed undetected into the thick asteroid belt the humans called the Serpent Swarm.

The long descent back towards the sun had not been spent in idleness. Heroes had worked to disguise the ship.

At first Kzaargh-Commodore had thought to disguise it as a derelict, but had changed his mind after coming across a genuine kzin derelict warship. After stripping it of all that might be useful and giving the dead Heroes aboard space burial, he had sent it sunward for a test, cold, tumbling, patently helpless and dead. Human instruments had identified it, and interrogated it, and when it did not respond batteries of laser-cannon had vaporized it. The same happened when he sent in a stealthed ship's boat, manned by a crew of Hero volunteers. Stealth technology took them quite a long way, but it was plainly not the whole answer. Rocks did better, if they were not identified as being on a collision course with *Ka'ashi* or some other large body—there were too many rocks for the human defenses to vaporize them all, and in any case many contained valuable ores.

The apes seemed arrogantly confident of their mathematics and of their meteor defenses. Any large meteor whose path missed *Ka'ashi* by more than 50,000 miles was generally not intercepted.

Night-Lurker became a lurker indeed. Like Lord

Hrras-Charr of legend, who had cut off his own ears to fool his enemy, the cruiser had lost external parts. So altering something as complex as a spaceship without dockyard facilities was a mighty task, but his Heroes were skillful. Most of the removed parts had been stored inboard or put into orbits from which they might one day be retrieved, but one way and another it had changed shape and shrunk. Its sleek lines and mirror-finished surface had disappeared under stony plating and rubble. The ports of its great rail-guns and laser-cannon were hidden by lids. Its gravity-engines were never used. There was sufficient delta-V for it to maneuver with short bursts of low-powered chemical rockets, inefficient but far harder to detect in space.

"What do you think of Chorth-Captain?" asked Dimity.

"He is not his own master. I do not only say that because it is unbelievable that a Hero would voluntarily serve such monsters. He appears to have no power to correlate. And there is a spot on the back of his neck that is not a battle-scar. It is metallic. I saw it gleam. I think it is some kind of Protector-made descendent of a *zzrou*."

"Could a Protector have learnt of such things?"

"The caves contained abandoned equipment of all kinds. The Protector could have found a *zzrou* and improved on it. Chorth-Captain is likely not the first Hero it captured. It could have experimented on others until it perfected what was necessary for a reliable . . . slave . . . servant . . . ?"

"Catspaw?"

"It is not a term I would choose. But an enslaved Hero—or a succession of them—would have been very useful to the Protector at first. I imagine less so now. But I do not know why it did not simply create an army of Protectors on Wunderland as soon as it knew how."

"I think I know why," said Dimity. "The first Protector wanted a force of Protectors it could control. These are not quite the same as the original Pak Protectors and it had become aware of how limited and temporary Protectors' ability to cooperate is. That is why it worked gradually, in an environment where it set the parameters of existence.

"Here it is in control of the others far more completely than it would be in the caves, where suddenly aware new Protectors might remember hiding places and so forth of their own. But there is another thing. As soon as it could, I am sure the first Protector began keying into the internet. Remember the old saying that the net is the most two-edged of all swords? A power to one's own side but the greatest gift imaginable to an enemy? There is material about Protectors on the internet, and although most of it is under security closure a Protector's intelligence would crack that open quickly.

"The Protector would try to learn about creatures like itself, and I am sure it would come upon scientific papers about the Hollow Moon. The theory is that this is an ancient Pak ship. If that is so, there may be Pak machines here, Pak books . . . manuals . . . Surely for the Pak teaching newly-changed breeders must have always been a high-priority use for resources."

"It would not know the language of such manuals."

"It could learn. You and I learn languages very quickly by the standards of our kinds."

A dark spot grew in the lightning-streaked grey of the sky. A car from one of the monitoring stations. It landed near the overhang and six well-armed humans alighted. They were dressed in the tough uniform overalls of the Wunderland security forces.

Guthlac and Cumpston went forward to meet them, stepping between dead thunderbirds. The creatures had been attacking in increasing numbers. Guthlac had begun to worry about their ammunition some time before. He had brought the big rifle thinking to deal with Morlock Protectors if he had to. But its size and weight, even with the mini-waldos, were a disadvantage, and even without considering that he had managed to wreck the car with it. Thunderbirds moved fast. He realized it was as well he had not had to deal with Protectors, who evidently moved much faster. *Last time I was in this sort of trouble was because I went hunting with a .22*, he thought, *thinking Wunderland game was all sport after kzin-hunting.*

The leader of the rescue party stepped ahead of the rest to meet them. At the sight of Karan, lying unconscious, his strakkaker swept up. He cocked it with a fluid, infinitely practiced movement and trained it on her.

"What are you doing?" Guthlac jumped forward in front of the man.

"What are *you* doing? That's a ratcat, isn't it? A friend of yours?"

"Yes, as a matter of fact she is. She was wounded a little while ago defending us."

"We believe in dead ratcats here."

"Not this one."

"I'm the one who decides that around here."

"Do you know who I am?" Asked Guthlac.

"Yes. Someone who owes their life to our responding to your call. Stand aside!"

"The war has been over on this planet for more than ten years! Put that weapon in its proper place!"

"I know the proper use for a weapon when there's a live ratcat around."

"I repeat! The war is over on this planet. There is a peace treaty. I will not repeat that again!"

"I look quite pretty now, don't I," the man said. "Thanks to our Liberators. But see my skin. Look at my face a little closely. A little pink here and there. I spent years with a metal jaw and half a metal face, thanks to one of those *Teufel's* claws."

"Well, you don't have to now," said Guthlac.

"Yes, I'm lucky, aren't I? My wife, my son, my two brothers, and my uncle, had no such luck as metal replacement parts. Just a quick, short ride down the kzin alimentary canal. Oh, I'm a lucky man, all right! A little micro-surgery to deaden the nerve ends before our Liberators' arrived would have helped. All the nerve ends. I could have gone to my cousins perhaps—maybe after a while they could have looked at me without vomiting. Oh, I forgot! They were in Neue Dresden. You ask me to be a ratcat lover?"

"We are a brigadier and a colonel of the UNSN," said Guthlac. "We happen to be the Liberators you just thanked. The kzinti ate my only family before you were born. I have fought them for more than fifty years. But here on Wunderland things must change. And this particular ratcat was instrumental in saving the lives of two humans, not long ago. She was young when the war ended, and took no part in it. In addition she is"—*not really a recommendation to tell this character she is the mate of the leading kzin on the Planet*—"our friend." *Dear God!* he thought. *Let this character kill Karan and we can say goodbye to any hope of Man-Kzin cooperation on this planet—our best chance of building eventual peace between the species—forever.*

He saw Cumpston raise his right hand and pinch his lower lip between forefinger and thumb in a nervous or thoughtful gesture he sometimes had. It also had the effect of pointing the table-facet of the jewel in the ring on his index finger at the man. *Not yet, Michael*, he thought. *But if necessary . . .*

"You lie," the man answered. "God knows why you should bother. But female ratcats can't think. After Liberation we kept some in zoo cages and fed collaborators to them. They didn't stop to ask them their political opinions before they sat down to dine."

"This one thinks," said Guthlac. "A few have always done so, secretly. If you are opposed to the Kzin Patriarchy and Empire you should see what an asset to humanity intelligent kzinrretti may be.

"All of which," he added, "is irrelevant to the fact that I am giving you a direct military order. I am not debating. She comes with us. And she will be given the best of treatment. That is more than because she is our companion and was wounded fighting in our defense, and has been beside other humans in peril before. There are high reasons of policy. Harm her, and you will regret it more keenly than I can say."

"Wunderland is independent! I do not need to take orders from the UNSN."

"I tell you of my certain knowledge that if you give that reason at your court-martial it will do you little good."

Cumpston intervened. "Do you know Nils Rykermann?" he asked.

"Yes," said the man.

"One of the resistance's greatest leaders in the war, and now a close friend of ours. Harm that kzinrret, and you will answer not only to the kzin who is her mate, but to him. In your place I would prefer the kzin."

He could kill us all and make it look an accident, Cumpston thought. *By the time anyone else arrived, the thunderbirds wouldn't have left enough of our bodies to investigate. I doubt he has too much inhibition against killing humans. Best get him now, perhaps, and as many of the others as I can with the ring, then draw and fight it out with the rest. But they have beam rifles and they're ready and they look like fighters. . . .*

"Rykermann was my commander," the man said at length. "For him I will do this. Get it into the car."

Getting Karan into the car was not easy. If much smaller than a male kzin, she was still the size and weight of a tigress. But she was partly conscious and did her best to help. The car carried them to a dome that rose out of the near-tundra landscape. There were other buildings with the dishes of heavy-duty com-links, all surrounded and covered by strong fencing. Karan was put into shelter.

Guthlac, using all the psychological dominance at his command, and his brigadier's identity and electronic passes, demanded a desk and called his headquarters and then Rykermann. He summoned his modified *Wolverine*-class command ship, the *Tractate Middoth*. It was well-armed for its size, and its small permanent crew were his own picked men. It was a vast relief to see its familiar shape appear and grow in the gray sky and swoop to the landing-pad.

Chapter 11

"First, I wish to know more about your gods," said the Protector. "The internet has told me something, but not enough." Despite the squeaking and popping of its beaklike muzzle, the words were understandable. Its grammar was good.

Pain. Dimity sensed it dimly. Vaemar with his hunting instincts sensed it more acutely but all his training was to ignore and despise pain save when it was a useful alarm signal. *Not surprising it is in pain after such a transformation*, thought Dimity. *Thank you, Herr Doktor Asperger. I think I understand something of it. Doubtless we owe Asperger's Syndrome to our own Protector inheritance.*

"You"—it fixed its gaze on Dimity—"have a god that is everywhere and all-powerful. It can never know achievement, striving, the conquest against odds, triumph. Because it *is*, it can only *be*, and never know *becoming*. Do you agree?"

"Up to a point," said Dimity. "I'm not a theologian. I think there is an idea that our God can know such things through us, His creatures. Perhaps that is one of the purposes of our creation. To know becoming."

"'Perhaps'? What kind of a concept is that? And you"—its bulging Morlock eyes swivelled to Vaemar—"You have a god like yourself, only bigger. A fanged beast that needs courage and fights against Infinity and something called Fate that will one day overcome it. You are both promised a life beyond death, but given only barest hints of what that will actually be like. Somehow humans will be given worlds to rule, somehow kzinti will be hunted and devoured by the Fanged God, yet somehow live again in him if they defy him and fight so that they become worthy. Their identities will survive, for if they fight nobly the Fanged God will give them a new and greater life. Have I simplified your theology?"

"Yes," said Dimity and Vaemar together.

"I had no idea of a god," said the Protector. "In the caves there was Hunger. Eating. Hatred. Fear. Mating. Enemy-prey. Thoughts moved sluggishly but emotions surged. Then enemy-preys. All danger. All food. Old preys. The flyers and the runners. New enemy-preys. Things like you and you, that killed and killed. Killed like the water flooding the lower tunnels, with things that blinded and burnt. The big ones were hard to kill, the small ones were hard to kill too. I survived. I knew almost nothing but survival and breeding. Those about me died, for your kinds killed them and then you killed the flyers and other things that were our food. That was all. That, and a dim idea that something had sent our food to us, and made the waters flow.

"Then, after the Change, I began to wonder who had

made the caves—the caves that I thought then were the world. Then, when the light burnt less outside, I left the caves. I saw what I now know is the scarp, sweeping down to the great valley. The sound of what I know is wind. Smells I had never imagined. I saw what I now know are the stars. Something had made this. It could not exist without a cause. Since then I have come to understand other concepts. Worship . . . I need to know much more . . . so much more."

It went on for a long time. It spoke with them of the creation of stars, and the physics of the Big Bang and the Monobloc, theories discarded with new knowledge in the twenty-second century, and resurrected with newer knowledge in the twenty-fourth. They tried to divert it. Finally it left them.

"No time to get her to kzin facilities. She'll have to stay with us," Guthlac said. "I'm not leaving her here with these gonzos." There had been tense hours while they waited for the ship to arrive.

"I agree," said Cumpston. "But will she make it?"

"She's a kzinrret. She's tough."

"We don't have a kzin autodoc."

"Her main problem's loss of blood. We've got some universal plasma. It won't carry oxygen but it'll give her heart something to work on and stop her blood vessels collapsing."

"Can you give it to her?"

"I had infantry combat training, a long time ago, including first aid. Never thought then that I'd be using it on a kzin, though. And my men are versatile. Wait till you try Albert's recipe for the wedding punch! Looking after a very important kzinrret shouldn't be too much for them."

"Now to find our missing pair."

Guthlac wiped his forehead. "They're alive," he said at last.

He pointed to the screen before him. A ship could be stealthed, but, at least for a time, its passage through atmosphere could not. "That could be the trace of the ship."

"It could be." The instrumentation showed a faint trail of atmospheric disturbance, dissipating as they watched.

"If that's a ship, it's got the best cloaking I've ever seen. Beyond the atmosphere there will be no way to follow it."

"We are looking for Protectors. Rykermann thinks the Hollow Moon was the original Protector ship. Could they be heading for it?"

Guthlac punched numbers. "It gives us somewhere to start looking," he said.

"I've got them," he said at last. "Extreme range, and there's interference, but that's where they are." He turned to Albert Manteufel, his pilot. "Take her up!"

"Gnosticism . . ." said Vaemar thoughtfully. "You said it is the idea of man becoming a god through his own inner efforts, or having a secret piece of god-ness inside him . . ." The Protector had gone, leaving them together in what they were coming to think of as "their" room.

"I think that's what it means," said Dimity. "Salvation by knowledge. Gnostics were 'people who knew,' and therefore spiritually superior beings. Perhaps a sort of race-memory of the Breeder-Protector cycle. But as I said, I'm not a theologian. The abbot once told me that almost all serious heresies are forms of gnosticism. He also said that, given that the universe had been created, it didn't matter much in religious terms where Man came from biologically, what mattered was where we were going spiritually."

"That Protector would seem to justify this gnosticism," said Vaemar. "A being turning into a god."

"I don't think so," said Dimity. "The kzinti wouldn't say that, would they?"

"No. Our souls go to the Fanged God, and are devoured by Him after a good hunt."

"And that's the end? It sounds rather bleak to a human."

"No. The souls of cowards are regurgitated into . . . well, the human word is Hell. The souls of Heroes go on somehow, but as it said we have only hints about that. It is a Mystery. But the hints are enough for us to have fought wars over them."

"And I don't think the abbot would say this is a case of beings turning into gods," said Dimity. "That thing is not a god, it is just a fast calculating machine . . . less human than a human, almost incapable of choice, almost without the advantages of limitation and imperfection. Mentally like me, only more so. As impaired as I am."

"No, Dimity, not like you."

"You are a chess master, Vaemar. Is it not true for you as for me that you come to some point in chess where you no longer seem to be moving the pieces, but rather watching them move."

"Yes, the moves become inevitable."

"Choice disappears. My life has been like that—watching

equations become inevitable. As I think a Protector sees the world. I do not think this Protector sees it in such terms yet. But it will soon."

"Was it like that even when you were a cub . . . a child?"

"I got a lot of my memories back with being on Wunderland and with the treatments . . . I can say: especially when I was a cub. I did not speak for the first few years of my life, because there seemed nothing worth saying. Why state the obvious?"

"Humans often do. And I think it is another habit we are catching from them. I have noticed we *Wunderkzin* tend to talk more even when we do not need to."

"Yes, humans often do. I didn't. I watched it all happen. The tests, the brain scans. I recorded my parents weeping over me as I looked up at them without expression because there was nothing to express, their whispers about 'abnormal alpha waves,' 'Asperger's Syndrome,' 'moron . . .' 'there are special schools . . .' 'Love and cherish her . . .' It was the fritinancy of insects.

"I sat in a playpen in my father's study while he worked, watching him at his keyboard, the equations crawling across his computer screen. They put in swings, and made little tunnels for me to explore and there were all sorts of books and toys that lay on the floor. I sat there and heard Father talk with his colleagues. One of them had a son, a very bright little boy to whom Father gave lessons in calculus. Postgraduate students, too—he took some tutorials with the cleverest of them in his house. I listened in my playpen, and later, sitting on my chair. I didn't do much. I did not speak much but I was puzzled, and eventually angry—why were they so slow? Why did they use such clumsy and incomplete symbols? Why did they not bring down their quarry—tidily, simply, beautifully? At length I decided to find out. That curiosity I had about humanity was the little, vestigial thread I had connecting me to it.

"One day, when I was seven, Father came in and found me at the keyboard. I remember how his face lit up. That was the first time a human's emotions had touched me. "Who's a *clever* little girl then?" he cried. Then he shouted to Mother: "Moira! Moira! Come and look! She's playing!" Then I saw him lift his eyes. He saw what was on the screen, and I saw his face change. His mouth began to twist, his hands went up to his mouth, and I knew he was fighting back a scream. By the time Mother arrived, he had stopped shaking.

"'We *do* have a clever little . . . girl,' he said, taking Mother's arm, and pointing. And already I heard him stumble over that word 'girl.' Girls are human, you see. They both stared at it for a long time.

"'Can it be what I think it is?' But Mother was no longer looking at the screen when she said that. She was looking at me. It must be hard to have the realization hit you in a second that you have given birth to a monster, a freak. Father printed everything off and looked at it for a long time.

"'I think I understand the implications of the simpler equations,' he said. 'I think it shatters a principal paradigm of our knowledge of paraphysical forces . . . One of the paradigms . . . At least one . . .' Then he began to laugh, a strange laugh such as I had never heard before.

"I was getting bored again by that time, so I gave them a lecture. Rebuked Father for his slowness and stupidity.

Told him I was angry at the limitations of the symbols he used. It was hard on my vocal chords because I'd used them so little before and that made me angry, too. Wondered at their tears. Thus began the career of Dimity Carmody. More tests, more brain-scans. The special schools—I told you I'd heard them speak of special schools—and everything else. Lessons in how to choose good clothes, for example. How to do my hair. Looking normal is a big part of being normal. Efforts to socialize the machine, the monster, with chess and music, to teach it to relate to human beings. They strengthened the little, little thread that connected me to normal humanity."

"You laugh. You weep, Dimity," said Vaemar. "I have seen your eyes when you behold a sunrise. I saw you toiling in the cave to keep Leonie alive as shots and flame flew about you. Never say you are a machine. As for a monster . . . do I look like a monster to you?"

"No. You are splendidly evolved to be what you are."

"A killing machine?"

"Of course not! Or that is the start. You are a carnivore, a great carnivore, a mighty hunter, top of your food chain. But you, Vaemar, are so much else as well."

"Yes. I am, thanks to the successful human reconquest of Wunderland, one of the few surviving examples under any star of an introspective kzin. Monstrous to normal members of my own kind, like Chorth-Captain. But we must not be sorry for ourselves. Would you, Dimity, really be different if you had the choice?"

"It is difficult to say. But I think not."

"Nor I."

"The only kzinti I know well are you and your Honored

Step-Sire Raargh Hero," said Dimity. "And I know that Raargh, too, in his gruff old way, is not merely valiant. He can be thoughtful, and chivalrous, as well. I do not forget that I owe him my life, or the pain he got saving me. We are both of species that have a great potential, and a paltry expression of it. But sometimes something shines through."

"I know you and I are not machines, merely because we can think, or because we are different to the norm of our respective kinds," said Vaemar.

"You have all the abilities of a young male kzin, and something else," said Dimity. "You are more than kzin. But in some ways I am less than human."

"You are no Protector," said Vaemar. "You have free will. You can choose. You have morality."

"In some things. Not when I dance with the equations."

Chorth-Captain entered. He carried more restraining tape, and made them bind one another again. Then he removed the locator implants from under the skin of Dimity's inner arm and from between Vaemar's shoulders. The size of rice grains, the locators were meant to be removed without too much trouble. His claws were too sharp to cause Dimity much pain, and Vaemar simply looked contemptuous. It was obvious from Chorth-Captain's manner that he was doing something he should have done some time previously. *He's hoping the Protector won't realize he's neglected to do this before,* Dimity thought. *And I'm hoping somebody's already traced them and is on their way. But the signal will be very weak. We've got a lot of rock around us, and 60,000 miles of space. But Chorth-Captain, whatever he's been before, has become one inefficient kzin now.* He made some show of smashing the locators. Then he released Dimity and left her to release Vaemar.

Time passed. They had few ways of measuring it.

"You are crouched in as small a space as possible. Your limbs seem to vibrate spasmodically," said Vaemar. "Are you sick? You were not hurt badly? You did not bleed for long. But I observe other differences about your body, too."

"I'm cold," said Dimity.

"You will burn energy with that vibration. You should rest and conserve your energy."

"I can't. I have done so for as long as I can. But this is cave temperature. Deep-cave. I need clothes. These torn things are quite useless. My boots are all right—" she laughed "—but they don't keep the rest of me warm."

"You may lie against me, if you wish," said Vaemar. "I will try to warm you. But I warn you seriously not to make any sudden moves. I cannot always control my reflexes."

She snuggled against his fur. He wrapped one great arm around her and presently she slept. Vaemar had not moved when the door opened again and Chorth-Captain entered. He looked down at the young kzin with disgust.

"Are you *chrowling* that monkey? I expected little enough of you, but this . . ."

He turned away. For a male kzin to turn his back on another so might be an expression of trust. But it could also be an expression of fathomless contempt. Vaemar leapt, claws extended, slashing at Chorth-Captain's neck, then striking with an elbow. His claw came away with blood and orange fur, and a short silver tube.

Chorth-Captain did not whirl into the counterattack. He staggered dazedly and sat down, hind legs splayed out before him, as old, mad bears that had spent too many years in zoo cages had once looked. Then he slumped on his side. Vaemar went to Dimity and set her on her feet.

"We were right," he said. "A *zzrou*, or its descendant, but capable of controlling behavior as well as action. I have removed it."

"Is he dead?"

"Probably not. Kzinti are much tougher than humans, and this thing has no wires or roots to suggest it was deep in his nerves or spine. As to the quality of life he may expect, that is another matter. He must live with knowledge of what he has allowed himself to become. The door is open. The catspaw is out of action. Now, perhaps, we only have five Protectors to deal with. Or perhaps more." He picked up Chorth-Captain's *w'tsai*. "I feel less naked with this," he said. Then he dropped it again. "But what use would it be against a Protector? Let him keep it. I will take this, though." He hefted the beam-weapon. "Now, Dimity-Human," he said, "you and I have a chance to do deeds fit for a song!"

"Lead, Hero!" she told him.

"Obviously, if we can get control of the ship, we should take it. But I do not think we will be allowed. They are surely monitoring us. But come!"

There was the "ward" with the rows of transforming Morlocks. There were no Protectors to be seen. "Why don't they try to stop us?" Vaemar asked.

"They are probably interested in seeing what we do. A practical lesson in our tactics."

"That Sinclair field could be a weapon, perhaps. Urrr."

"What are they doing with it? Growing more Protectors?"

"Chorth-Captain said the rest of the tree-of-life agent was still on Wunderland." Vaemar peered into the field. "It looks like some small-scale industrial process. Some super-strong materials take a long time to grow, and they could be speeding them up. Mountings for hyper-drive motors need super-strong materials. That is what it looks like to me. Getting ready. But you know more of building the hyperdrive than I."

"They know of the hyperdrive already?"

"If our knowledge of Protectors is true they have immense ability to correlate. They could learn from the internet. Not everything, but enough to start work."

Dimity too examined what could be seen through the blue radiance of the field. She nodded after a long pause. "Yes. That's what it looks like."

"I agree."

"They don't have the hyperdrive . . . yet."

"Anticipation. They believe they will get it out of your mind. Or if not from you, from another."

"You will ensure I do not live to tell them, Vaemar."

"If it must be. But it has not come to that yet."

Two Protectors leapt out of a passage. Possibly the sight of the naked human female breeder halted the first one for a moment. Too fast for Dimity to follow, Vaemar swung up the beam-weapon and fired. The cantaloupe-head of the Protector exploded, hit between the eyes. The other, far faster than even the young kzin, dodged behind the Sinclair field. Vaemar, keeping his claws retracted,

seized Dimity with his free hand and dragged her behind
the cover of a metal partition. He raised the beam rifle
again, waiting for the Protector to show itself. Then he
had a better idea. Firing straight into the Sinclair field, he
thought, might well have most spectacular results. It
might even wreck the hatch cover and open the compartment to space, which would solve everyone's problems.
Orlando would carry on his line. As he depressed the
beamer's trigger, the lights on its stock died. He pulled the
trigger again, harder. Nothing happened. Obviously it was
under remote control and had now been deactivated.

The Protector knew it was safe. It stood up, then leapt,
so effortlessly that it seemed to fly, onto what appeared to
be the housing of the Sinclair field's generator.

Chorth-Captain hit it from behind like a bolt of orange
lightning. They fell forward together. Screaming, Chorth-
Captain went headfirst into the Sinclair field. His lower
body and hind legs, protruding for a moment, convulsed
wildly and then went into the blue glow. But the
Protector, too, had staggered forward into the field, standing in it up to its thighs.

The Protector did not seem to accept immediately
what had happened. It stayed where it was for a long
moment, looking down. It was not their kidnapper but
one of the more recently changed ones. *Stay there! Stay
there!* Dimity implored silently. It reached up and
touched its ears, as though puzzled. It even pushed a hand
down into the field as if testing it. Dimity realized the
Protector's armored skin and relative lack of pain sensitivity
could be a handicap to it. Nerve couriers could not tell it
so much about its environment. *They're so tough they*

don't need pain for an alarm signal. Then it gathered itself and sprang out of the field. It should have sprung precisely on top of them. But tough as the Protector was, it still had a circulatory system. In the field its lower limbs and feet had been deprived of blood, died and had been dead for some time. Its lower leg muscles were gone and it fell short. It landed on its feet, but collapsed as it landed, the bones of lower limbs and feet splintering.

As the Protector tried to leap again, both legs and one hand dead, Vaemar closed with it, jaws gaping, slashing with his claws. The swing of its remaining hand was still too fast for Dimity to follow, but this time Vaemar caught it, slashed and bit. Dimity heard his fangs clash on bone. He leapt back, out of reach of the Protector's snapping muzzle. It had two hearts, but its powerful circulatory system was carrying dead and decayed matter into both of them. It continued to stagger towards them on the bony, disintegrating stumps of its legs, its smell alone almost enough to knock a human down as Vaemar grabbed Dimity and dragged her back, springing up and out of the thing's reach. It made another leap after them, fell again, crawled, collapsed and died.

Vaemar turned off the field. He and Dimity looked down for a moment at what remained of Chorth-Captain.

"At least he died a Hero," said Dimity. "And look! There was more of that control device in him than we knew."

"No Hero should have allowed such a thing to happen to him," said Vaemar. "But I will take his *w'tsai* now. Perhaps I can do him the service of gaining it new honor. And look further! Here is the key to the ship! But there is something to be done before anything else." He leapt to the doors, closing them one after another. "We may be thankful this is kzin-derived architecture," he said. "I think we have locked them out for a time. But they will bypass those locks soon." He turned to the lines of transforming Morlocks and began rapidly but methodically slashing their throats with his claws and the *w'tsai*. Already the skin was turning into a leathery armor and it was hard work, but Vaemar was quick and strong.

Vaemar saw the horror in Dimity's eyes as he returned to her. He took her hand and touched it against his forearm.

"Remember," he said. "Fur, not skin."

"I know," she said.

"Now we have Protectors whose children I have killed," he said. "They will not be pleased with us. I think they will be coming soon. I see no escape. Can you think of a solution?"

"To escape in the ship that brought us. You have the key now."

"Yes. Unfortunately the hatch above it is closed. I can perhaps work out how to open it if the Protectors do not override the ship's controls, but it will take a little time. Unless you can help me?"

"I have not your practical ability with machinery, kzin-based or otherwise. But there is something." She took him back to the housing of the Sinclair Field controls. "Can you turn on the field again?"

"Yes, it is simple. Why?"

"I think we have a chance of reducing the odds against us. The Protectors are still inexperienced. I am going to stand in the area of the field. When I give the word, turn it on around me."

"You will die! You will exhaust the oxygen! One can only live in a Sinclair field with special air supplies, to say nothing of food and water. Urrr."

"I can live for a short time, that is why I say . . ."

Two Protectors leapt out of the passage. Dimity jumped into the field-area, and screamed, "Now, Vaemar! Now!"

Vaemar threw the switch. Dimity became a shimmering shape inside the blue dome.

Whether the Protectors meant to kill or recapture them, Vaemar was unsure. But they meant business. Their expressionless leathery faces with the Morlock eyes now strangely alight with intelligence were also lit with fury. Vaemar wondered if they were keeping him alive for torture. But the reactivated Sinclair field was between him and them. As they advanced, he saw Dimity in the field flashing almost too fast for his superb eyes to follow. Vaemar crouched, waiting a chance to spring, a chance he knew he would not get.

There were two shattering explosions, so close together they seemed one. One Protector's upper body disintegrated, then the other. Vaemar, head ringing, jumped back to his feet. He seemed uninjured. He stared in amazement for a second, then saw Dimity halt in her meteor-fast movements, fall and lie still. He leapt to the controls and killed the field. Gently, keeping his claws sheathed, he tried to give her artificial respiration, fearful that he should crush her fragile ribs, fearful she was dead. *I care so for a human!* The surprised realization flashed through his mind.

"Look at me! Look at me! Look at me now!" he sang at her from their old song. She stirred and sat up, gasping.

"It is fun to have fun, but you have to know how," she completed the quotation with a weak smile at length.

"Are you all right? I learnt the theory of mouth-to-mouth resuscitation in the ROTC, but I believe giving it to you would be difficult for me."

"There were still a few breaths of air," she said. "There was an emergency tank inside. And some water. They must have had Protectors spending time in there controlling the processes. But it was a pretty near thing!"

"It was you killed the Protectors?"

"Yes."

"How?"

She pointed to her feet. "I threw my boots at them. I had plenty of time to take aim and work out the trajectories and kinetic energies. They were moving like slugs. And I *do* still have quite a good mathematical brain."

"You are a Hero," said Vaemar. "There may, with good fortune, now be only one Protector left."

"Yes. Why didn't it attack as well?"

"I suspect the answer is that those Protectors were the last parents of the Morlocks I just killed," said Vaemar. "Despite the increase in their sapience, they were still Morlocks, still fairly newly changed, and mad with rage. The remaining Protector is the original, the one that brought us here. It has no children of its own, so it can make more Protectors without prejudice to its plans, and, at least until it comes to understand that human reproductive technology could still give it children, its behavior is not unclouded by parental emotion and anticipations. It is the one mature and partly experienced and educated Morlock Protector, obviously by far the most dangerous, and if we do not kill it we will be no better off than before. If it does not come to us, we must hunt it down."

"That would be quite hopeless, even if we had a functioning weapon. You saw how swift and strong it is, and it is armed too."

"You would have us *ssurrendirr*, Dimity-Hero?" Vaemar's human speech slipped as he pronounced the hated word. "Or flee? Urrr."

"I think we have no choice but to press on. Explore!"

"Hero! Well said!"

"With caution. You have Chorth-Captain's *w'tsai*?"

"Yes! Let it regain honor in my hands!"

Dimity clicked the trigger of the beam rifle experimentally. It was still dead. "We will have to hope a Hero's *w'tsai* is enough," she said.

"I had better lead," said Vaemar.

Chapter 12

Mechanisms towered about Dimity and Vaemar. Dimity had, with Vaemar's help, improvised a breathing mask, which she hoped would keep out the smell of any tree-of-life, from the tatters of what had been the top part of her suit, and sealed the rents in the rest as well as she might with an all-purpose repair gel from Chorth-Captain's belt. They had obtained a light from the same source. Tracking the Protector by the pain it was radiating had brought them this far.

"Fusion toroids," she said, pointing. "The energy needed to move this between stars must have been vast."

"I am glad our kinds did not know too much about such energies in the past," said Vaemar. "Think of a war fought with bodies like this as missiles."

Something, too fast for human eyes to see clearly, scuttled away in the dark above them. "The Protector," said Dimity. "Why doesn't it attack?"

"It was *a* Protector," said Vaemar, "but I do not think it was the same one. Dimity, we have been too optimistic, I think. I do not think we have accounted for all the newly awakened Protectors. Perhaps its task is to watch us and report."

They came to an opening into a vast cavern, filled with machinery.

Vaemar stood unmoving for a moment, then he said, "There are . . . vibrations in the air . . . perhaps you cannot sense them . . . which tells me these motors may not be dead."

"After scores or hundreds of thousands of years? Surely not?"

"Look at the cavities in the roof," said Vaemar. "They appear to have been artificially dug."

"Yes."

"Except during brief eclipses, half the external surface of this body is always in sunlight, half in the darkness and cold of space. The temperature differentials on the surface must be very large. It is a problem and an opportunity in all space-engineering."

"Yes. I see what you mean. That would give unlimited electrical power for tunnelling robots. They could extract and refine fuel."

"It would not, perhaps, take much to keep the engines simply ticking over."

"Would Protectors think like that?"

"I cannot know how Protectors would think. They are more like you than me. But I sense there is power here. This asteroid was overlooked for mining because its metallic content is relatively low. But I would guess it was metal-rich when the Protectors chose to make it a spaceship. I guess some automated or natural variety of mining worm has been tunnelling and mining in it for a long time."

"A machine refining its own ore and making its own replacement parts," said Dimity. "We have nothing outside fiction that can do that for so long or on such a scale. Self-sustaining machinery, processes still carrying on after a million years. And we have no information that Cybernetics was a Protector talent."

"Obviously, they could have set themselves to acquire such a talent. Dimity, this gives us a glimpse of what mature Protector technology can do! I do not like it. . . . And look! There are lights. They could be solar-powered engines ticking over. Or powered by long-lived fission or fusion processes. Doing essential maintenance, ready to set off a fusion reaction when needed. There are many ways hydrogen could be collected and stored, for example. Or perhaps it has been completely closed down and our Protector and Chorth-Captain have reactivated it."

"It is as well, as you say," said Dimity, "that this moon was not properly explored before the end of the war. It could have been a super-weapon."

"It still could be. I do not know if we should approach anything critical too closely. It may provoke a response."

"I think we have to provoke a response. The status quo does not favor us."

Dimity stepped forward cautiously. She gave a cry of fear and surprise. Vaemar leapt, grabbed her with one arm and pulled her back. Then he advanced cautiously and pointed. "Nothing to fear too much. An active kzin gravity-sled. Heavy-duty Naval model. Chorth-captain must have brought it here. We can avoid its field."

"I am sorry. I am a little rattled. You can handle one, Vaemar?"

"Of course. I have flown one since I was a kit. It was one of the first things Honored Step-Sire Raargh bought when we were living in the farm country."

"Then let us not avoid it. Let us use it."

"To fly on? There is not much space for that."

"To fly on and to fight with. Do you think the Protectors would let us use it? We could do great damage if we could fly. I am sure they would try to stop us."

"Dimity, I think the God, whichever one has dominion here, has been good to us. You will have to move very quickly. I will board the sled. You will take the copilot's seat and hang on for your life, and pray that these Protectors still think like Morlock Breeders, jumping down on their enemies when they see us escaping. Now!"

Vaemar and Dimity leapt into the sled. From above, two Protectors sprang. As they did so, Vaemar's claws flashed at the sled's controls, flinging its motor into maximum reverse flux. The Protectors, directly above it, were flung straight up. One smashed into the machinery above them, and stuck among it, the other, as though swimming through air, reached the edge of the field and fell onto the sled. It clung with one hand. Vaemar had time for one slash at the hand, removing three fingers and reducing its power of purchase. Desperately he continued to slash at the leathery arm and snapping beak with the *w'tsai* and his claws. Dimity grabbed the flight-controls of the sled. They skimmed back along the corridor as Vaemar finally cut the Protector's grip. It changed hands. Vaemar grabbed the controls and stopped the sled, keeping the field focused on the Protector. Dimity screamed in its ear and it let go. It flew upwards, seemed to grow smaller and vanished into the blackness above.

"I hope it ends up at the center of the moon," said Vaemar as they flew back into the first chamber. "Half a mile from any surface. I don't think I killed it, but that will give us time, I hope, to do some real damage. *If* it was the last Protector. We will have to hope it was. But we cannot continue sticking our noses into the cave, unarmed, in the hope more will come out. We have been lucky so far."

Then he asked: "Why did you make that noise? Were you what humans call terrified? Panicked?"

"In the caves the Morlocks must have evolved and enhanced every nonvisual sense," Dimity said. "Particularly hearing. I thought its hearing would be specially sensitive. Sensitive enough to use against it. I wondered why the other Protector did not leap out of the Sinclair field instantly instead of pausing while the field killed it. Chorth-Captain had screamed as he pushed it in, and I think that stunned it momentarily. They must have evolved in the caves to hear the slightest sound—the rustling of insectoids, the tiny bubbling of water's meniscus rising in grains of mud. Evolution towards hearing microsounds. But with never a need to evolve a defense against too much sound. I realized that just now."

"Dimity, you do not disappoint. Now what?"

"We can get away and do real damage at the same time."

"How?"

"The gig has a gravity-motor."

"Yes.

"And a reaction drive."

"So I saw when we came here."

"I do not need to draw you a diagram, then?"

Humans who had spoken so to kzinti before had not lived long to regret their insolence. But Vaemar sprang to the ship, Dimity following.

"We still cannot get out," said Vaemar, as the door closed behind them. Chorth-Captain's key had worked but he punched in an electronic lock as well. Both Vaemar and Dimity had noted the locking and unlocking sequence earlier. "You must bear with me with patience here," said Vaemar. "No monkey-rattling . . . Dimity is not rattled any more?"

"At least we have a weapon," said Dimity. "Let us use it."

"Danger?"

"Hero!"

"Urrr!"

The controls were built in duplicate, in sizes to be used by either Protector or kzinti hands, and Protector hands were very similar to human. As Dimity cut in the gravity-motor, thrusting it downwards, Vaemar fired the reaction-drive. Incandescent plasma gas roared out. The ship shook, but remained balanced between the two forces.

A second was enough. At a gesture from Vaemar they killed the two drives together. Cautiously, they cleared a viewport. Nothing could be seen but blackness, with flames and points and bars of red-hot wreckage fading in it. Even with a powerful searchlight they could make out no more through the smoke for some time. When it cleared somewhat, all that they could see of the inside of the Hollow Moon about them was a charred, melted, ruin.

"We have done it, Dimity!" said Vaemar. "We have killed at least five Protectors, though they took our weapons! Urrr!" A snarl of triumph rose in his throat.

Dimity knew instinctively not to interrupt the young kzin's rejoicing too soon. Analyzing this knowledge, as she always analyzed her reactions, she realized they could not have done what they did had there not been a psi bond of some sort between them. It did not surprise her greatly. Vaemar's Ziirgah sense was a rudimentary form of proto-telepathy which most male kzinti possessed and she knew her own brainwaves were abnormal in several ways. They had acted and planned together almost instantaneously and partly without being aware of the fact.

"Now it is a matter of getting out," she said at length. "The hatch above us is still closed."

Vaemar turned to the control panel again.

"In the absence of Protectors I think I can open it from here," he said. "I need but a little time to study the controls. Normal procedure for a ship like this when leaving a space station is to rise on the gravity motor when the lower hatch is opened, have that close behind us and then open the upper hatch. For obvious reasons both hatches cannot be opened together."

"We can do that from here?"

Vaemar operated a set of switches, watching lights sliding across a screen

"Yes," he said. "And I find that disturbing. It suggests the mechanisms of this installation are less damaged than they might be. I hoped to blast our way out with lasers or armor-piercing shells." He gestured at another control panel. "I should have realized a Protector would have built strong. But it raises a thought in my mind that the Protector may have survived. Or there may be more Protectors than we knew. This place is complex. I am sure now that there are control centers we have not touched. They must have built many redundancies."

"Well, let us run the reaction motor again as we leave, however we get out," said Dimity. "That will leave their possible survival, trapped in this damage, an academic matter until we summon security forces to make sure. Even a Protector can hardly cross space without a ship or a functioning motor. Vaemar, I hope we have done both our kinds a service this day."

"The hatch is opening," said Vaemar a few minutes later. "I think we should go as destructively as possible."

Dimity slid into the couch beside him. Again, one operated the gravity motor and the other the reaction-drive. On a pillar of incandescent plasma-gas the ship rose, slowly, out of the tube which led to the surface.

"I can't hold it!" Dimity cried. "We're in a gun-barrel. The ship will implode!"

"All right! Let it go. I think we have done what we can."

A dark tunnel, a growing circle of light. Space suddenly infinite about them, the disk of Wunderland hanging huge in the meteor-streaked blackness. Behind them, fire venting from the hole in the hollow moon, fire which they hoped had burnt out its core and everything in it.

"Home!"

"Home!"

A green light blinking on the control panel—the kzin

color for danger. Vaemar's claws flashing on the keyboard.

"The ship identifies another engine starting," he said.
"The signature is that of a kzin *Rending Fang*-class fighter.
It is behind us."

"The Protector!"

"I suspect so. In Chorth-Captain's ship."

"Use the shielding!"

"Dimity, I am trying to discover how. I know how to pilot
kzin craft, but the Protector's innovations are new to me.
Throw the gravity motor into parallel with the reaction-
drive. We need speed!"

"Can we fight?"

"This is a naval gig. It has stealth if I can find it, but it
is not built for speed. Nor has it adequate weapons to take
on a fighter. We cannot ram. We must run. Fly the ship,
Dimity, while I track the stealthing commands . . . you
must dodge."

They flew, firing missiles and decoys behind them.
Vaemar gave a snarl of rage and stabbed with one claw
point at a dial in front of Dimity in the pilot's seat.

"Another source of neutrino emissions! Another engine
starting! Not a gravity engine. Nothing this boat's brain
recognizes. Dimity, I think we have been over-optimistic
about the number of Protectors on the Hollow Moon and
the damage we did. It is still under control and I think it
is either moving or preparing to fire at us. I guess there
are several Protectors still alive in it. I will launch more
decoys."

He stabbed at another switch. "The God be thanked
that the mechanisms on this vessel have not been altered

from Navy standard too much. The decoys operate. Now, Dimity, fly as you have never flown before! Use that brain of yours to fly in random variations a Protector cannot anticipate."

Chapter 13

"That must have been one of the shortest peaces in history," Arthur Guthlac said. "At least two kzinti ships are barrelling in. The defense satellites are preparing to fire. But I've asked them to hold off for the moment. They won't hold long though. They could be chock-full of multi-megatonners, or something worse."

"Why hold, then?" Cumpston asked.

"They appeared on the screens out of nowhere. Or rather from the vicinity of the Hollow Moon. I hope they might not be an officially-sanctioned attack by the Patriarchy. Why would the Patriarchy attack with only two small ships?"

"Maybe they're freebooters, or fanatics defying orders. Maybe they don't know of the treaty."

"And maybe that's what we're meant to think," Guthlac said. "They've only attacked with two ships to make it look like it's unsanctioned. To make it deniable. You know how much destruction two ships could cause. Then, while they're saying it was nothing to do with them, they attack with everything they've got. The fact they were only just picked up suggests they've got a cloaking technology we haven't. What if they've got a whole cloaked fleet past our outer defenses? What if there are a few hundred cloaked battle-wagons ready to follow them?"

"That doesn't sound like the kzin Navy," said Cumpston. "If they'd got a cloaked fleet in close, I think they'd attack with everything they had. In any case, I don't want to start the war again if there's the slightest chance of preventing it." New data crawled across the screen. "A gig and a fighter. That's an odd combination for a fleet attack. The signatures of both are funny, though. And the maneuvering doesn't make any sense."

"You're making it sound more and more like a diversion."

"It looks to me as if the gig is taking evasive action."

"At least let's find out who they are. Kzinti on the attack like to tell their enemies their Names, if they've got them. I'm going to call them up. That can't do any harm. And in the meantime we're closing with them. Stand by to help Hawkins at the main guns, Michael. "

"There! There!" Cumpston's finger stabbed at a new light on the screen, a light that triggered a howling audio alarm-system. "That's the signature of a kzinti warship all right. A big one. Coming in fast . . . a heavy cruiser at least."

"Got it!"

"It still doesn't make sense," Cumpston said. "It's not a *coherent* attack. A cruiser, a fighter, a boat . . ."

"Who knows why the pussies do anything? I thought I knew them, but this . . ."

"I thought I knew them, too. Some of them, anyway."

Both men looked at the clock. At the rate they were

closing, both knew they probably had very little time to live. Waiting for reinforcements was not an option. They had alerted the ground and orbital defenses. Now all they could do was cause as much damage as possible to the kzinti strike-force before it hit the planet. Both had seen the silent annihilation of space-battles many times before. Small craft were dropping from the *Tractate Middoth*: flying bombs to either destroy by detonation or to pump X-ray lasers.

"I'm getting another signature!" Guthlac's voice was tense but controlled. "Another ship!" Then he gasped, spat a curse. "The bastard is HUGE!

"My God! It's the first attack on Wunderland all over again! A single giant carrier."

"Better cloaked."

"It would be. They've had sixty-six years to improve the technology. Well, it looks like the war's on again for young and old, as they say. I'm sorry, Arthur."

"I'm sorry too." Then, "Michael . . ."

"Yes?"

"Gale's down there."

"I know. Arthur, do what you have to do. We're soldiers."

"How does a Hero's Death appeal to you?"

"I don't think we've got much choice. It's been on the cards a long time." His finger ran down rows of switches. The lights of armed firing-circuits glowed. The leading kzin craft, the smallest, was getting close. It was already in range. Small, but capable of carrying a stick of multi-megatonners of its own. Deal with it, then turn to the great carrier. If *Tractate Middoth* survived that—and it would not—the cruiser next.

"Ssstop!" Karan's nonhuman voice jolted them. She was standing, trembling. She had pulled out the plasma injector. She appeared to be holding herself upright by her extended claws dug into the fabric of a seat-cover. Her eyes had a strange, unfocused look. She appeared still half conscious, possibly delirious. *Just what we need,* thought Guthlac, *going into battle against hopeless odds with a delirious kzinrret loose in the ship.*

"Vaemar! Vaemar is there!"

"How do you know?"

"Karan knows! I know."

A delirious kzinrret. Was oxygen-starvation affecting her brain? But all kzinti had a sense from which the talent of the telepaths was made. Among nontelepaths it was extremely limited and did not work to cross the distances of space. But . . . Karan was Karan. And, Guthlac thought, Vaemar was Vaemar. Neither of them were ordinary kzinti.

"The locators are dead," said Guthlac. "They say nothing. But this is close to the last position we had from them!"

"That's not a ship! It's a moving moon!"

"Vaemar is there! He comes!" Karan screamed.

"The boat must have picked us up," said Cumpston, "but it's not firing at us. It's taking evasive action, all right, but it seems to be evading the fighter."

"Shall we try a com-link?"

"Yesss!" Karan leapt as she spoke. Not a great leap for a kzin, at least not one in good shape, but she was between the two men at the command console. Albert Manteufel sprang from his chair, drawing a pistol, but Guthlac motioned him back. In any event, gunplay within a space-ship was seldom a good idea. Karan spun to face them, claws out and jaws in the killing gape. Her knife was out, though the hand she held it in was trembling.

Cumpston and Guthlac were veterans of many battles in space as well as on the ground, battles often faster than thought, in a realm where only certain instincts and intuitions given to a few could offer hope of survival, controlling machine-enhanced reflexes beyond the frontiers of the purely physical, swifter and more subtle than any dance of bodies or equations. Both knew, too, the potential treachery of instinct. They stayed their hands now, as Karan operated the com-link to the flying, twisting speck on the screen. Weak as she was, her claws flashed too fast for the humans to follow, and much too fast for them to interfere with.

There on a screen was the cockpit of the gig. Flying it were Vaemar and Dimity. Karan collapsed.

"A dreadnought!" With shriek of ecstasy and blood lust Kzaargh-Commodore leapt onto the great *kz'eerkt*-hide battle-drum, sending its call booming throughout the ship. Was this what Chorth-Captain had somehow achieved? Already *Night-Lurker* had identified Chorth-Captain's fighter and gig. How had he done it? And what were the fighter and gig doing? Distracting the monkeys before the dreadnought's terrible slash ripped the guts out of their planet? But it mattered not. "The Patriarch's battle-fleet has joined us!" This was no time for thoughts of how so mighty a consort might have penetrated so deep into the Centauri system and so close to Wunderland undetected, nor for the unworthy thought that so mighty a consort would take most of the glory from a mission that a moment before had been a matter of lone heroism. His crew of Heroes roared an equally enthusiastic response. That they might be perhaps less concerned with Kzaargh-Commodore's glory and more with their own suddenly enhanced chances of survival was not a thought for that moment either. *Night-Lurker* barrelled in, closing with the strange gigantic vessel.

Bigger than all but the biggest dreadnoughts. And camouflaged as *Night-Lurker* itself had been. The minds of the great strategists of the Patriarch's General Staff had thought like his own.

There was no further need for radio silence. It would be sensible to co-ordinate plans with the great carrier. "Call them!" he ordered Captain. He stood posed before the com-screen, Captain at a respectful distance behind him.

Com-screens on *Night-Lurker*'s bridge and in the Hollow Moon blizzarded briefly with light and cleared. Kzinti and Protectors saw one another. Each lunged instantly at the firing-buttons on their consoles.

Night-Lurker flung itself into evasive action, firing as it turned. Its heaviest punches included disrupter bomb-missiles. They were not in the class of Baphomet but powerful enough. Kzaargh-Commodore had taken the decision to fire, and fired, almost as fast as it was physically possible for a living being, even with motor-neurone enhancement. However the Protectors in the Hollow Moon were slightly faster.

Night-Lurker glared fantastically in the heat of beams

for seconds as its layers of mirror-shielding boiled away, a red, then blue, outline of a kzin heavy cruiser. Its disrupters hit the Hollow Moon, burrowed through its shell and exploded. The Hollow Moon vented gigantic plugs of rock and blew apart. *Night-Lurker* exploded simultaneously.

The gig was perilously near the second explosion. Impact at such speeds with practically any piece of debris, however small, would be the end of it. Guthlac in the *Tractate Middoth* spread the lasers as far as possible and fired them to sweep between the blue-white sphere of the explosion and the little craft, hoping to at least reduce the flying wreckage. Smaller explosions sparkled and flared. The gig remained. Flying like a wounded bug, it turned and headed towards them. The *Rending Fang* fighter had disappeared again.

Chapter 14

Paddy Quickenden looked up from the deep-radar screen.

"It looks like an ants' nest," he said "Things are boiling in there."

"There's usually a lot of activity in the caves," said Leonie. "Let me see . . . But yes, things are boiling. There are sizeable creatures moving—bipeds."

"Humans . . . Morlocks," said Raargh. His claws extended.

"We can't see much more from here," said Leonie. "We'd better land and take a look."

"What, go into the caves?"

"With modern motion-detectors and Rarrgh's eye we should be able to see anything long before it gets near us. We both know the caves."

"I don't," said Paddy. "But I've lived underground most of my life."

"I'm not letting you near these caves," said Leonie. "And there's no way I'd leave the car and the com-link unattended. You'll stay in this car, with the canopy closed and weapons cocked. But be ready to let us in if we have to get back in a big hurry." She opened the com-link and spoke to Nils Rykermann briefly. She was already suited up as she landed the car in a small limestone-sided valley. She and Rarrgh leapt down and disappeared into one of the cave mouths.

Paddy settled himself before the console. The car's weapons were ready. Like all spacers, he was experienced in waiting. The broken limestone walls and pinnacles, "honeycombed, honey-colored" with small red Wunderland trees on the valley floor, and sprays and creepers of other red Wunderland vegetation, made the place seem like a wild, dishevelled garden, peaceful and, from within the car, silent, though instruments picked up the sounds of small animals and the murmuring of a tiny stream. *This is a lovely place,* he thought. *Let me help Dimity find peace, let me cure her of what is torturing her, and she and I—and our children—could live on this world forever. They need spacers here, more than We Made It does. There could be a place for me here in paradise with the woman I love.* He thought of Leonie, heading fearlessly into the cave with the great kzin. He could see them now on the deep radar, a large and a small figure, moving down the tunnel into the darkness and what lay beyond. *How lucky Rykermann is to have such a wife! Well, this is paradise around me. Let me enjoy it for the moment.*

Leonie and Raargh were both veteran cave fighters. Their checks of weapons, lights and other gear were fast, automatic and thorough. Both could read the ghostly, ambiguous shapes of tunnels and cavities on the screen of their small deep-radar as easily as a road-map. Raargh touched the lower right quadrant of the screen with a massive claw. There was movement, a lot of movement.

"Looks like battle," he said. His infrared-capable artificial eye was ceaselessly scanning the cavern, especially the roof, as he spoke. They set off into the darkness. Raargh's artificial eye, seeing deep into infrared, guided them, but there were faint patches of luminosity here and there as well. Possibly Ferals' work, Leonie thought. They had learnt to crush and treat the shells of small crustaceanoids from the streams so as to make a ghostly radiance.

"Smell strange," Raargh said after a while. They were passing a complex of tunnel mouths.

"Tree-of-life?" Leonie wondered. The faceplate of her helmet was firmly closed. No point in asking Raargh, but the old kzin knew the ordinary smells of the caves. Something strange was almost certainly something new. She did not want reports of any new smells. All she could do was check her mask again. If even a few molecules got in . . . But, whatever it was, it was evidently limited to a single tunnel, and later Raargh reported it gone.

The com-links allowed them to pick up one another's voices, but no natural sounds reached them. In the darkness of the caves, even with artificial aids, it was a claustrophobic experience. Leonie ordered Raargh to take hold of her.

"I am going to take my helmet off," she said. "If I smell tree-of-life I will become mad. You must disarm me, restrain me, and carry me back to the car."

She removed the helmet slowly. No new smell assailed her. There was nothing but the cave smells she knew so well, mainly limestone and biological processes of decay, and the wild, gingery smell of the kzin keyed up for battle. An instantaneous flashback: that strange, exciting, terrifying smell on Raargh the first time they had met, when in these very caves she, as she had obeyed an impulse she hardly understood to help the broken-legged kitten that had grown into Karan, had dug Raargh out of a rockfall with her beam rifle instead of killing him.

A flashback gone in an instant. Evidently no tree-of-life here. But ahead, sounds of battle. Ahead, dim tunnels, lit distantly by the reflected flashes of explosions. Screams. The rattle of a Lewis-gun, cut off abruptly.

Raargh leading, holding his prosthetic arm before him in case of Sinclair wire, they hurried on.

Tractate Middoth's com-screen cleared again, restoring communication with Dimity and Vaemar in the gig's cabin. Karan yowled. A sweep of Arthur Guthlac's hand killed the row of firing switches.

The gig steadied in its flight and approached the *Tractate Middoth*, matching its course and its now reducing velocity easily. Dimity explained to Guthlac and Cumpston what had happened. There was damage to the gig, damage its meteor-patches could not cope with. It was losing air. They would have to be quick.

Even without its Protector-built improvements, ship-to-ship transfer in space was one of the primary roles the gig had been designed for. A tube was extended between the two airlocks. Still, with safety-checks on the two sets of drive emissions, the transfer took some time. There was a kzin-sized spacesuit in the pilot's place on board the gig, but the Protectors' were in a locked compartment.

Vaemar made Dimity put on the kzin suit as the air-loss got worse, though she could only just move its vast, semi-rigid limbs.

Dimity and Vaemar crossed, Vaemar greeting the crew of the *Tractate Middoth* and Karan with the restrained dignity the situation demanded. Dimity sought wearable clothes. Guthlac indicated somewhat nervously to Vaemar that Karan was there very much as a result of her own insistence, and told of the part she had played. "She has saved my life before," Vaemar said. Karan, now somewhat recovered but shaky and mentally as well as physically weary, greeted Vaemar with a mixture of pride and shyness and a good deal of mutual grooming. Cumpston sent a message to Wunderland suggesting the defenses be reduced from red to orange alert. They gathered around the control console. There was no trace of the Protector's fighter.

"The beam was only on it a moment," Guthlac said. "Then it disappeared. Not exploded, I fear. The Protector must have deployed a cloaking device."

"Why didn't it continue attacking the gig from the cloak, then?—I guess that would have betrayed its position."

"I guess. The energy required for cloaking like that must be prodigious, anyway. Maybe too much to cloak and fight at the same time. At least for now. I expect given time a Protector could improve such things. And there would be no point in such an attack now. If it thought the gig had broadcast to the system, destroying it would be a waste of time."

"What matters is that it's still out there somewhere. A

Pak Protector with a spacecraft, knowing there are hyper-drive ships in this system for the taking. We've alerted Tiamat and the Swarm, but given a Protector's cunning and resourcefulness, I doubt that's enough. And we don't know what surprises it may have prepared for us."

"The Protector has to get back to the Morlock colonies sooner or later," said Dimity. "That's the only source of breeders, and where the remaining tree-of-life is. Now that we're hunting it, and the system's alerted, I don't think it's got too much chance of pulling off a successful surprise attack on its own anywhere else. Not till it makes and organizes more Protectors."

"It's also, as far as we know, where most of the nukes are. And the *Rending Fang* class are aircraft as well as spaceships."

"What have we got at the caves now?" asked Vaemar.

"Paddy and Leonie," said Guthlac. "And Raargh."

"Get after it!"

"What craft do they have?" asked Dimity.

"A car. An ordinary flyer."

"Not much to stop a *Rending Fang*."

"I'm ordering them to try." Guthlac touched the com-link's face again. "At all costs."

A pair of humans blundered up the passage towards Leonie and Raargh. They stumbled and fell as they approached. Young ferals, streaming blood, heads and shoulders covered in the lacerations and bites of Morlock attacks. A group of Morlocks followed them. Before Leonie could speak, Raargh shot the Morlocks down. The humans regained their feet and continued on at a staggering run, ignoring Leonie's shouts to them. She did not know if they saw Raargh or not, but she guessed that to them kzinti were far more terrifying than Morlocks. There was no time to try any other communication. Rarrgh and Leonie advanced cautiously. They went down, crawling and wriggling forward on the muddy cave floor, old instincts hiding them in the shadows of pillars and columns. The sounds of fighting stopped.

The tunnel led to a great "ballroom" cave. White and crystal rock reflected fantastically a few smoky, primitive lights. By these lights and their infrared, Raargh and Leonie saw where the fight had been.

Both could read a recent battlefield as easily as a book. This one, they saw, had been short and one-sided. Dead humans lay everywhere, along with some smashed weapons, including modern beamers. They were young, dressed in dirt-colored rags. Ferals. That would have been obvious even without the primitive facial tattoos.

Weapons ready, they examined the bodies as they might. Most of the ferals had been killed quickly and efficiently with broken necks. Few had the characteristic head-and-shoulder wounds of Morlock attacks. There were twisting, random trails of blackened or melted rock cutting into walls and columns that suggested weapons fired unaimed and with their triggers held down by dead hands. Raargh and Leonie had seen such things before, but here it seemed an unusually large number had died without getting off an aimed shot. Among the bodies were several wearing the grey uniforms of Wunderland police. They had died with their hands tied. Prisoners. And others whose clothes suggested they were farmers. There was also a much larger bulk: a dead kzin, killed the same way. His scars, greying fur and a prosthetic leg-brace suggested an old soldier. He too had died with his hands and claws tied with tape like a prisoner.

"This one worked on a farm with humans," said Rarrgh. "I suggested it to him. Told him we must make new lives. Now I must meet those who have done this. Honor demands it."

"Protector's work," said Leonie.

"There!" Raargh pointed.

Not all the ferals had been killed with such quick and smart thoroughness. And one, Leonie saw, was still alive. She ran to it.

"Keep watch!" she told Raargh.

The feral would not live long, she saw at once. But it was conscious. It had some sort of unfamiliar bite, perhaps a Protector's horny beak. There would be little time for words. She squatted by it. By *him*. A male. She stanched the bleeding as well as she might. Her own clothes were of modern fabric, too strong to tear, but the feral's own rags made bandages of a sort. They were impregnated with virulent cave dirt, scent-deadening Rarctha fat and who knew what else. She sprayed them with coagulant, knowing it was useless, and administered an anaesthetic. There was no point in breaking out more of her small medical kit, and her years of guerrilla fighting had conditioned her powerfully against using such resources on the dying.

"What happened?"

He did not speak. She knew well enough that these ferals tended to regard all other humans, let alone any in the company of kzinti, as enemies. Savage, worse than sociopathic, there was ample evidence that they were often cannibals. And she would have little time to try and reach him.

"We will avenge you!" That might do it. Deliberately she made her voice as soft and feminine as possible, leaning forward so he might see the curve of her breasts. Intuitive, instantaneous psychology, perhaps totally wrong. But these ferals had had mothers.

"Creatures you could not fight?" she asked. "Too strong, too fast?"

That reached him. He nodded, raised a feeble hand to touch her.

He spoke. "Like Morlocks, but not."

"Creatures you had not seen before?" Another nod. "You said not Morlocks? Not ratcats?"

A gesture. Leonie saw the body of a dead Protector lying in the shadow of a stalagmite column. Though it was instantly recognizable its head was shattered. It must have leapt or run into a blast or beam from one of the ferals' weapons.

"There were more like that?"

"Yes."

"The containers? What happened to the containers?"

"Hold me."

Leonie put her arms around him.

"They took them."

"Down there?"

"Yes . . . prisoners, too . . . We killed as many of the prisoners as we could before the Morlocks and the other things took them. But there were many prisoners."

Leonie wondered what Morlock Protectors would want with human prisoners. But she remembered the need they would have for teachers. Prisoners would be almost as crucial as tree-of-life. And both Protectors and Breeders would need food.

He stroked her, whispered "Mother," and died. Leonie moved to close his eyes.

From the darkness behind them a group of Morlocks leapt. Raargh turned on them as they struck, slashing and roaring. At such close quarters neither Raargh nor Leonie could use their rifles, but Raargh's prosthetic arm did service as a bite-proof club, quite apart from his own flashing teeth and claws. They were armed with their usual pointed crystal rocks, but a few more modern weapons as well. Rolling away from their attack as she had learned long ago, Leonie saw other shapes, the quasi-human shapes of two Protectors, the cantaloupe heads and swollen joints unmistakable. They were crouched atop a low rock, poised as if to spring on Raargh and her. Raargh's leap at one Protector, Morlocks still clinging to him, was heroic. The Protector bit at his arm, not realizing it was metal. Its beaklike jaws jammed for a moment in the wiring, current from its power-enhancement crackling, sparks arching and dripping. There was no time for Leonie to take aim at the second Protector. She held the trigger of the beam rifle down, swinging it in a scything arc, cutting the Protector off at the thighs. Raargh was still fighting the first Protector. The old kzin roared with rage, almost deafening her in the confined space. His *w'tsai* flashed. The Protector's leathery skin could turn most blades, but Raargh's *w'tsai* was monomolecular-edged and was wielded by a master. He drove it into the Protector's ear and worked it about. The Protector kicked and fell away.

The Morlock attack broke up. Those that had survived Raargh fled, leaping up into the suspended forest of stalactites. A few flung their traditional missiles of rocks and crystal shards, but Leonie was fast enough with the beam rifle to zap these in mid-air. *Upper-body's still got some dexterity when it needs it*, she thought. She also hit a Morlock as it was fumbling with a rifle retrieved from some old battleground in the caves. It was, Leonie thought, strange that these Protectors should use breeders as fighters. It was not the impression Brennan had given of Protector behavior and drives. But Morlock Protectors were not Brennan, and perhaps these Protectors were so thin on the ground they had no choice but use their children. A few Morlocks rallied and counterattacked, but were still unskillful with the few modern weapons they had and could do little as she and Raargh killed them. On the other hand, she could see they were learning unpleasantly fast, already becoming acquainted with covering fire. Even without Protectors, up against less experienced enemies, and in any case with the passage of a little more time, they would be formidable. Then they were gone, bounding away between the shadows and rock pillars into the darkness. She finished off the second Protector, which was still pulling the upper half of its body along the ground towards Raargh with its arms.

Wary of what might still be in the darkness, she leopard-crawled to Raargh. The old kzin was spitting and cursing. His prosthetic arm was badly damaged, she saw, and when he tried to stand his right knee gave way and he fell forward. Leonie remembered he had been wounded in his knees long before. Her light showed blood and a gleam of bone. She applied her last field-dressing. There were sounds diminishing in distant tunnels.

"Leonie," said Raargh, "I cannot run. You must go on alone."

"There is no need. Our mission was reconnaissance. We know what is here and what is happening here. Our job now is to tell the others, not for one or two of us to fight Protectors and Morlock bands alone."

"We attack!" Raargh cried. Leonie knew the kzin attack-reflex well. A kzin, like the Protector she had just killed, would crawl to its enemies if that was the only chance of a final slash or bite. But Raargh could inhibit that reflex when his wits were about him. It was why he had grown old. He was not going to be much use crawling into battle on two functioning limbs.

"Is that what you would tell Vaemar, were he here?" she asked him.

Raargh was silent for a moment. Then "You are bleeding," he said. "Still you must leave me. Go and report. Urrr."

Leonie touched the leg and felt it give. The webs of interlocking and reinforcing cartilage might help it a bit, but the bone was gone. She saw something too she had never seen before—a spasm in the old kzin's arm and face that could only be unbearable pain.

"We have both had worse wounds," she told him. "Use the rifle as a crutch. Let us get back to the car."

"No! Dishonor! I stay and cover your retreat from Morlocks."

"You have done that once before in these caves. But there is no need this time. Come! Or we stay together here till Morlocks and Protectors return!"

Leonie's years as a guerrilla leader had taught her kzin as well as human psychology. She allowed the old kzin to lurch and hobble painfully around to collect the ears of the Morlocks he had killed. He tried to cut or wrench off some part of the Protector he had killed as a trophy additional to the conveniently large ears but she did not see the details. Then grumbling, sometimes mewing involuntarily like a cat in agony, leaning on his rifle, Raargh limped slowly with her back towards the daylight. She resumed the helmet briefly as they passed the tunnels where, she guessed, tree-of-life had been stored. She supposed the Protectors had taken it, along with all the weapons and other assets they could gather, deep into the great cavern system. They would be back soon.

There was no sign of the young ferals who had gone before them, and who, Leonie knew, might regard either a uniformed human or a kzin as equally their enemy. She told Patrick they were coming and to be ready for take-off.

Rarrgh moved with more difficulty as they went on. Leonie's suit had enhanced power joints, or it would have been quite impossible, but even so she could barely support part of his huge weight. *Work, legs!* she commanded silently. *You are Leonie now!* She knew kzinti could discipline their bodies to a literally superhuman degree and if they slowed down in a combat situation they were in a dire way indeed. She was surprised at what her new legs could do, and thought briefly that her old legs, injured by kzin claws and repaired by primitive surgery, could not have done it. *I wonder if she was an athlete?* Then: *Not a really useful thought at the moment! Get a life!* But the tunnel, which they had descended so easily, was a different matter to ascend with Raargh in such a condition. A desperate call from Patrick to hurry did not help. Finally they had to stop.

"Raargh legs no good," the old kzin muttered disgustedly.

"Legs heal." Leonie told him.

"Raargh finish. Raargh die."

His leg injuries were not fatal. But Leonie knew that kzinti, who preferred to die on the attack, could also die of shame.

"No, Raargh not coward! Urrr!"

"Raargh might as well be dead. Cannot attack! Cannot support Leonie-Comrade. Go to Fanged God now before shame deeper."

Raargh's natural eye was turning a peculiar violet color. The pattern of his respiration was changing in a way Leonie had never heard in him before. But self-induced death for a kzin could be very quick. Leonie had seen it during the Liberation.

"Did Leonie dig Raargh out of rockfall for nothing?" she asked in the Mocking Tense that it would once have been instant death for any human on Wunderland to use towards a kzin. "Did Leonie trust Raargh for nothing? Does Vaemar wish Raargh to die? Do Raargh's kits not wish to have Rarrgh hunt with them again? Will others rear Raargh's kits and *chrowl* Raargh's harem? Urrr!" She saw the fury and agony in his eye, but he made another effort.

"Legs can be repaired," she told him. And then: "Remember it is Leonie who speaks. Remember what happened to Leonie's legs in cave! Leonie, manrret, lived with Raargh's help! Leonie walks again!"

There were times when she had scratched the old kzin's ragged ears in a gesture of comradeship. But she knew better than to touch him in such a manner now. Then, greatly daring, she stood before him and placed her hands on his shoulders. "You will not desert Leonie!" The Tense of Military Command. *My instinct was to use the Imploring Tense*, she thought. Slowly his breathing changed again.

"Leonie survived worse than Raargh," he admitted at length. "Raargh will not be shamed," he added in a different tone of voice. Slowly and painfully he stood and hobbled on. Leonie let him lead. *Was that what it was for?* She wondered. *So I could talk a kzin into living?* And then she thought: *But Raargh is a special kzin.* It took a long time, and there were more calls from Patrick.

Patrick opened the car's canopy as they emerged from the cave mouth into the daylit glade. He stood up in his seat and jumped down, hastening towards them.

"Get back in the car!" Leonie cried out. "Stay in the car!"

The rock hit him on the side of the head. The blow could have shattered his skull had he not been wearing earphones. He staggered and fell. Leonie fired at the rock's point of origin, a stand of tall grasses by the little stream. Patrick, streaming blood, began to crawl back towards the car as the grass flashed into flame. A dozen ferals burst out of the grass. They were armed with at least one strakkaker as well as rocks and an ancient Lewis-gun. They converged on the injured Crashlander.

Patrick bought up a handgun and fired, hitting the feral with the strakkaker. *I forgot he was a Spacer* flashed through Leonie's mind faster than she recognized the thought. Raargh swung upon the rifle-crutch and fired in a blur of speed. Leonie knew what his marksmanship was like. His first shot shattered the Lewis-gun, probably killing the gunner, but his second he fired not into the ferals but ahead of them. They went down, out of sight behind the bank of the stream. Patrick stumbled back to the car and pulled himself into the cabin as Raargh and Leonie laid down covering fire.

Something was happening in the sky to the southwest, a ball of purple radiance travelling like a meteor, heading towards them. Patrick was taking the car straight up.

The thing in the sky—a purple spider, a retinal disorder, a chip of cauliflower—expanded, shimmered to a shape Raargh and Leonie knew well. A kzin *Rending Fang*-class heavy fighter, heading towards them, landing gear down.

The car dodged and swerved in the sky. It was above the big fighter, which was now coming down for a landing on its gravity-motor. The car hovered for a moment. Then it dived vertically. At seven hundred feet car and fighter collided with a shattering explosion. With strength she never dreamed she had, Leonie flung herself at the bulk of the kzin, pushing him back into the shelter of the cave mouth as fragments of white-hot wreckage rained down about them.

Amid the falling wreckage was the dark shape of an

escape capsule. It hit the ground and opened. The Protector sprang out and rushed towards the cave mouth. Raargh and Leonie had both dropped their rifles, but Raargh had his *w'tsai* out. The Protector snatched them up and, straightening, and ran straight at the *w'tsai*, but at the last instant twisted in its stride, dodging so that Raargh's slashes with blade and claws slid off its leathery skin, doing little damage. Raargh tried to strike as he had struck in the cave, but missed, and he could no longer leap. At the same time the Protector struck out at them, knocking them both against the cave wall. Then it was past them, a leaping spider-shape disappearing down the passage into the darkness.

"Now ribs broken," said Raargh. "It will not stop Raargh fighting!"

"I think I may have broken a couple, too," said Leonie. "Why did it not kill us?"

"Hands full. It had our weapons."

"Why did it not kill us?" she asked again.

Raargh voice was different when he answered. He was the senior sergeant contemplating a military problem again.

"I think, Leonie, it believes it does not need to kill us."

"A foolish thing to think of Raargh and Leonie!" she told him ringingly. Raargh had little more than torn stumps of ears projecting from a complex of scar tissue, but he raised them in a signal that to her was eloquent enough.

"Feral humans return," said Raargh.

The surviving ferals were approaching the cave mouth in a semicircle. Their major weapons were gone, but they were still armed with rocks, which Leonie knew they could throw as accurately as Morlocks. Several new fires were burning where the wreckage had fallen in the vegetation, and a pall of dark smoke was rising to cover the sky above the glade. Raargh scrabbled across the ground and retrieved the *w'tsai* knocked out of his hand.

He should have killed them when we had the chance, thought Leonie. *But he seemed to be trying not to kill humans.* It was as if the shadowed walls of the cave and the sky beyond were turning a uniform white with the agony in her chest. Thinking was difficult. *I don't think I can fight at all. They are not going to have mercy on me or a kzin. One human knife, one w'tsai, and one old kzin to wield it who's now very knocked about. This is real trouble. To survive more than fifty years of war to die at the hands of human children . . .*

"Friends!" she managed to call. The ferals continued their cautious advance. She called again, without response. She had a knife. They had knives as well as rocks.

Suddenly they stopped, and fled, scattering into the vegetation in all directions. A moment later she too heard the sound of a ship in the sky. There it was, not shielded like the Protector's fighter. Arthur Guthlac's *Tractate Middoth*. It touched down, jets of foam smothering the burning vegetation, and armed figures leapt from it. Hunched over her broken ribs, she staggered out to meet them.

"So we have tree-of-life, Breeders and Protectors all together again in the caves," said Cumpston. "Along with who knows how many prisoners. There are people missing from some of the tableland farms, and most of the feral gangs round here have vanished." They were hovering, looking down at the great escarpment from several hundred feet.

Arthur Guthlac took a deep breath. The faces of the humans were grey. Strain, exhaustion, defeat.

"Only one thing to do if we're to keep the chain of command intact," said Guthlac. "We report to Early. He and ARM were pretty definite that he was to be informed before any major decisions are made."

"Not a good idea, when dealing with Protectors. We can't afford the time lag. Every minute we waste is giving the Protectors more of the time they need to learn and organize and make defenses and multiply themselves. And they've Number One back with them now."

"We're stuck with it. ARM has become desperate about losing control of the situation . . . of all situations. And they've made pretty unambiguous threats about what will happen if we break the chain."

"I'd like to see them threatening Protectors. How long will reporting take?"

"You know Early has left the system. I can't tell you where he is. We can send him a signal via a hyperwave buoy. That will take several days. Several more for orders to return."

"Have we got several days?"

"I think not. The alternative is to send in an infantry force to clean them out."

"It would be fighting Protectors. Protectors with weapons. They may be newly changed, but they learn very, very fast. And during decades of war the kzinti were never able to quite clear out the caves. Neither were we. Nils and his students haven't got them all mapped even yet, I believe, Leonie?"

Leonie nodded. The pressure bandages helped greatly, but it was still painful to talk.

"And hostages. They've got hostages. We're only just starting to learn how many."

"I've got all the forces I can muster on the way," said Guthlac, "and Nils has been onto the Wunderland authorities for their troops. There are local militias organized, too, and they're heading for the caves."

"Lambs to the slaughter," said Leonie.

"There are weapons," said Cumpston. "Dimity says sound affects them. Fly over a sonic drone."

"It wouldn't penetrate."

"Our people have police sonics."

"So did the police they grabbed. Protectors are *tough*. Sonics may discomfort them but I don't think they'll stop them for more than seconds. We might render them unconscious with directed sonics if we knew their brainwaves. Unfortunately we don't know and haven't time to find out. Shouting at them won't be good enough."

"There are a lot of other things. Nerve gas. Spectrum radiation."

"They're coming with the troops. Unfortunately a lot of our nerve gas supplies are kzin-specific and as for the rest—well, there are the human hostages."

"If they have intelligence—and they do—they'll be dispersing now."

"You've got weapons here."

"Most of them are for use in space. We can blast away at the limestone while they organize. It won't be long before they're shooting back at us."

Dimity Carmody's fingers had been running over a keyboard on the main control console. "Arthur," she said. "Take us up higher. Fast. Put some southwest in it."

"How high?"

"Just keep going."

"Why?"

"I'll explain in a minute."

The *Tractate Middoth* rose, drawing away from the caves. Higher.

Below them, from first one and then scores of openings, smoke and fire jetted from the escarpment and the limestone plain above it. The profile of the ground seemed to bulge. A fireball erupted, and another, and as they watched the whole scarp of the Hohe Kalkstein went sliding down into ruin.

"Fly!" roared Guthlac. The *Tractate Middoth* flashed away.

There was another explosion and a greater fireball, incandescent, blue-and-white-cored, burst from the seething ruin. It boiled into the sky, transforming into an orange-and-black cumulus, hideous and obscene to the watchers in the *Tractate Middoth* as they raced desperately upward into the clean stratosphere and away. Other fireballs followed.

"I kept the code numbers and detonation keying for the nukes," said Dimity. "They were in Vaemar's computer. It's all over now. There was nothing else to do."

"I'll call defense HQ," said Guthlac. "They'll need to

get decontamination teams to work fast. And before they signal a retaliatory strike on every kzin ship and world in reach."

"But why didn't you say what you were going to do?" asked Vaemar.

"I didn't see why you should all have the responsibility. It's all gone now. Protectors, Morlock, ferals, hostages, the whole cave system and countless species. A swathe of human farms and hamlets. Your rapid reaction teams. Your militia. A bewildered Protector who wondered about God. Did you want to live with that?"

Dimity looked up into Vaemar's eyes and read his expression.

"I am very close to being a Protector," she told him.

She put his great hand with its terrible razor claws on her forearm.

"Skin," she said. "Not fur."

Chapter 15

"I pronounce you man and wife," said the abbot. "You may kiss the bride."

Hand in hand, Arthur and Gale Guthlac walked from the monastery chapel, surrounded by their friends. Each in turn came to them and laid a wreath around their necks, the three intertwined colors of vegetation from three worlds that grew on Wunderland now: red, green and orange. Gale's children had arrived from the Serpent Swarm. Guthlac's crew had no swords as would once have been ceremonially drawn to make an arch for the couple to pass under, but they presented arms.

"Have you heard from Early?" Rykermann asked Cumpston as they crossed the garth.

"Yes. He didn't betray much emotion about what happened. It's a *fait accompli*, anyway. And the Protectors are gone. ARM is busy with other things. I imagine they are things that include us, and the *Wunderkzin*. But I'm tired of being one of ARM's catspaws."

"I should think there have been worse jobs than

becoming Vaemar's friend," said Rykermann. "Even if he does thrash you on the chessboard."

"I hope I'll always be Vaemar's friend," said Cumpston. "But I feel a change in the whole course of my life is coming upon me."

"For what reason."

"I don't know. Just a feeling. Something very new."

"I didn't know you were foresighted."

"Neither did I."

"I sense certain things too," said Rykermann. "Dimity . . . Vaemar . . . whatever bond is between those two will not be broken."

Arthur Guthlac, Gale, the abbot and two of the monks were laughing together at something. Orlando and Tabitha had lost little time after the ceremony in wriggling and clawing out of their ornate formal garments and were leaping through the long grass together after flutterbyes. Nurse, who, it had been decided, was indispensible whatever he charged, carried a bag of buttons for their claws.

"So it begins, perhaps," said Rykermann. Now, with Leonie's hand in his, he realized that he was looking at Dimity without hopeless pain and longing. Not because of what she had done, nor indeed because he loved her any the less, but because his love for Leonie filled his heart, suddenly, strangely, and with a depth and fullness he had never known before. She had been near death with him many times, but this time, watching her enter the Protectors' caves with only Raargh, as he himself prayed desperately over a console of screens, had been different.

"Strange," he said. "This was where it all began so many years ago. I had flown out here because the monks had sighted a strange creature, a big catlike thing that didn't fit into the ecology." He remembered giving the strange orange hair he had found to Leonie, his graduate student, to dissect. Thinking of her as she had been in those days, he realized something else. Her walk was as it had been then, no longer clumsy.

"So it begins," echoed Colonel Cumpston, as he followed, escorting Dimity. His gaze wandered to Vaemar, resplendent in gold armor and shimmering cloak and sash of Earth silk, who, with Karan, Raargh and Big John, was pointing to one of the monastery fishponds. The juvenile Jotok he had helped save in Grossgeister Swamp were growing and joining. Orlando had fished one from a pond and was waving it playfully at Albert Manteufel. *Don't pretend to be scared, Albert!* Cumpston tried to telepath him. *Don't pretend to run!* But Guthlac's pilot was a veteran and knew better than to do any such thing. A growl from Raargh and a gesture at his proud new possession—a second ear-ring for his belt, there being no room for more ears left on the first—and the kitten snapped to attention. Another growl and warning cuff from Karan and the Jotock was restored to the water.

"Hope. Perhaps joy. Perhaps, truly . . . peace. For this little world at least," Cumpston said. As with Guthlac and Rykermann, many lines of strain and weariness seemed to have gone from his face. Reports from far-flung ships and bases were that the peace was holding. At this moment, *for* this moment at least, humans and the kzinti Empire were sharing a universe.

The group of friends drew together. Vaemar drew Rykermann aside for a moment.

"You love her, I know," he said.

"Yes," said Rykermann. He had never heard a kzin use the word "love" before, and wondered what Vaemar's conception of it was. But he knew who he meant.

"I think I understand," said Vaemar. "I say that to you alone. Speak it to no other human. She has taught me a little of that . . . but she must go her own way."

"I know," said Rykermann. They drifted apart in the flow of the company.

Dimity had known Cumpston since her return to Wunderland eight Earth-years previously. He and Vaemar had made the counterattack that had relieved their desperately outnumbered group in the fight against the mad ones. But now it was as if she saw him for the first time: a hardened warrior and leader, yet a man whose kindness and patience had done as much as any to bring peace to this tortured planet. That unnatural blend of human qualities that made up the knight.

The wedding party drifted through the monastery gates into the meadow spangled and starred with its multicolored flowers. Brightly-colored creepers covered the last few outlines of what had once been a refugee shantytown. Two pavilions had been set up, food laid out for two different feasts, and a couple of great kzin drums. There would be dancing later. Orlando and Tabitha were looking forward to that.

Vaemar again approached Rykermann and Leonie as they walked. His eyes followed Rykermann's to Dimity, her hand moving to take the colonel's.

"I know she had to do what she did," he said. "I know more about the Pak, the Protectors, now. There was no choice." He muttered something about a dream that Rykermann did not hear clearly.

"We humans have come a long way from the Pak," said Rykermann. "How far will we go? What will we become?"

And then: "What will we all become."

"That, I think," said Vaemar, "is a very good question."

TEACHER'S PET

Matthew Joseph Harrington

I

PLEASANCE: 70 Ophiuchi AB-I (A-II/B-V), *located in Trojan relationship to its binary suns, Topaz and Amethyst. Orbital distance from either star 20.8 A.U. Principal source of heat geothermal. Gravity: .93. Diameter: 6510 miles. Rotation: 27 hours 55 minutes. Year: 12263 standard days. Axial inclination<1°. Atmosphere: 39% oxygen, 57% nitrogen, 3% helium, 1% argon. Sea level pressure 7.9 pounds/square inch. No moons. Discovery by ramrobot reported 2136, but existence concealed and colonization limited to families of UN officials until corruption trials of 2342-2355.*

Pleasance's crops are grown under artificial lighting, as natural illumination comes to about 0.5% of Earth's. The climate does not vary with latitude, and qualifies as warm temperate. Constant low-level vulcanism is found every-where on the planet, both land and sea. Almost all of Pleasance's warmth is due to release of massive fossil heat by outgassing of carbon dioxide and helium; the carbon dioxide is taken up by native oceanic life with great effi-ciency. Local lifeforms are killed by excess light, however.

The planet has the distinction of being the only known habitable world whose orbit is outside its system's singularity, so that ships may reach it within minutes after leaving hyperspace.

As a result of its founders' propensities, Pleasance's culture is legalistic to a possibly excessive degree . . .

Peace Corben's mother was this old: she had met Lucas Garner.

The name had not been Corben, then, and the real name wasn't in the records Peace had found in *Cockroach*'s computer. Possibly the old woman hadn't seen any reason to include it; more likely, given her paranoia, she'd feared its discovery by hostile parties.

Like everything else she'd tried to be, Jan Corben had been a *great* paranoid. The ship was a fine example.

It looked like a mining ship designed by a cube director. An old Belter drive guide protruded from a wallowing hog of a hull. The lifesystem seemed to be mostly windows. The cardinal points bristled with important-looking, redundant instruments. Some of the windows had *curtains*. It was ludicrous. It was all a lie.

The "windows" were viewscreens, showing the universe whatever the pilot pleased. Most of the "instruments" were antipersonnel weapons with proximity triggers. The "drive guide" was a gamma-ray laser; the actual drive had come with the hull, which was that of a First War kzin courier ship. The gravity planer developed six hundred gravities—twenty times the limit now allowed by treaty. A little bubble in the nose and three behind the central bulge were all that showed of the real instrument packages, which were in four General Products #1 hulls to enable them to survive events that required the rest of the ship to use one or more stasis fields. There *was* a fusion drive, but it was for the oversized attitude jets. When acting in concert with the gyros, which were also oversized, they could turn the ship a full 360 degrees in any plane in 1.2 seconds, coming to a dead stop; faster for smaller adjustments, of course. This aimed the laser anywhere. There was a suitfitter in the autodoc; what the suit locker held was powered armor. All this had been accumulated over the course of three Wars' time, and consistently upgraded as technology progressed. The latest addition, barely older than Peace herself, was a top-of-the-line hyperdrive motor, custom-built by Cornelius Industries of We Made It.

That last may have been a mistake. There were laws about product safety, and since you could more or less smooth out the convolutions in your brain thinking of what could result from a faulty hyperdrive, there was a strict schedule of warranty inspections. During one of these, some Helpful Citizen had apparently noticed one of the other features. The old woman had still been in Rehab when the kzinti bombed Pleasance.

When Peace had stolen the ship—trivially easy, in the panic—her first act had been to go after her mother. Rehabilitation included work therapy, to the point where there were economically vital companies that would go broke if every law were obeyed. The camps were guarded and organized as thoroughly as bases for conscript troop training.

Doubtless that was why the kzinti had bombed them so heavily.

Peace was circling over Camp Fourteen for the fourth time, scanning for any rubble that might be loose enough to hold survivors, when it became apparent that the invaders had realized that their order-of-battle included no antiques. (The hull display had been altered to Heroes' Script that translated as something like *Unthinking Lunge*, a not-atypical ship's name. Probably curtained windows would have attracted attention sooner.) *Cockroach*'s hull was coated with superconductor under the screen layer, but the lasers aimed at it were designed for planetary assault. It got very warm inside before Peace found the panic button.

It was a *good* panic button. It had a routine for almost anything. Inundation by laser fire didn't even call up lesser subroutines.

Cockroach turned on its head, the lifesystem went into stasis, and the hull became a perfect reflector. It was textured with optical corners. Most of the kzinti ships lost their paint and a little hullmetal before their lasers switched off, but the one nearest the azimuth was lined up with *Cockroach*'s drive guide. The planer held the ship immobile while the stinger fired, and a stream of ultrahard gamma rays ran back up the beam coming from the orbiting flagship. All the oscillating electrons in the flagship laser's pulse chamber suddenly left it at relativistic speeds. Kzin weaponcraft was amazing, but it wasn't magic: the insulators blew, and dense random currents scrambled every circuit they touched—a category which included nervous systems. Survivors didn't suffer, as the effect opened the circuit of the stasis on the mirror at the back of the laser, and the gamma beam punched through into a fuel preheater. This opened a channel between the main fusion plant and a deuterium tank. After that—

Well, there wasn't really a flagship after that.

Peace didn't learn of the flagship's destruction until days later. She merely saw the ground leap up at her, then saw it further off and receding, then saw it *much* further off and receding a lot faster, obscured by a glowing smoke ring. (*Cockroach* had gone back into stasis to pass through the fireball.) More trouble followed, figuratively and literally.

The portmaster at Arcadia had been unwilling to keep a fully-fueled warship at her field, and had had *Cockroach*'s tanks drained. The ship could and did extract deuterium from ambient water vapor, but there wasn't much built up by the time of the attack, and the gravity planer was using that up right smartly. Fortunately—from the computer's viewpoint—there was an excellent source of very pure hydrogen barely a quarter-radian off the ship's present course. Unfortunately—for Peace's nerves—it was Lucifer: 70 Ophiuchi B-IV, a gas giant larger but less massive than Jupiter. *Cockroach* accelerated toward it for slightly over half an hour, leaving a fuel reserve that would have fit inside a coffee urn, and spent the next twenty-six hours and change in free flight.

Torpedoes could have been upgraded to catch the ship; this was not even contemplated. The invasion's flag officer, who was now interacting with Pleasance's magnetic field, had been Hthht'-Riit, bravest son of the Patriarch. It was he who had come up with the plan of taking over remote human worlds first and working their way in, a strategy which might actually have succeeded if he'd remained alive to keep the fleet from making sudden lunges. As it was, the rest of the shipmasters didn't want the human pilot vaporized: they wanted "him" kept alive for as long as possible, while they expressed their extreme disappointment.

It took seven hours of screaming and spitting to cram a fuel tank large enough into a 25G assault boat; kzinti do not work and play well with others. They were not stupid—less so with every War they lost—and they knew it had to be done if they wanted to flyby and yoke before the human could refuel. A 20G destroyer, say, could never have done it in time.

The assault boat was closing the gap at three thousand miles per second when it finally got close enough to throw on a gravity yoke. The boat's radiator blossom instantly turned sheer white. *Cockroach*'s gamma cannon was detected starting up, but this was deemed of far less concern than the heat-exchange situation: hitting at this range would have required a miracle, and not a small one. Humans simply weren't that good.

They *were* notoriously demented. This one was no exception. The human ship wasn't on an atmosphere-skimming path, it was aimed for the center of the disk. By the time their velocities were matched, slowing the pursuer and speeding up the prey, no further effort could be spared to bring them together yet, as the boat was engaged in hauling them both aside to save the human ship's crew.

Cockroach, aboard which Peace Corben had finished having conniptions hours ago, fired its gamma laser into Lucifer's atmosphere and went immediately into stasis.

The shot heated a large volume to electrons and stripped nuclei, but did not suffice to ignite fusion. It took the impact, a few milliseconds later, of the relativistic byproducts of the gamma-generating blast to do that. The atmospheric fusion blast was brief, and didn't do much more than UV-ionize a tremendous volume of hydrogen around it, which expanded until it was cool enough to recombine. This created, then uncreated, a discontinuity about the size of Earth's Moon in Lucifer's magnetic field.

When the electromagnetic pulse hit the assault boat, the superconductive pulse shielding expanded by internal repulsion until hull members tore it apart; then the overloaded gravity planer collapsed the boat to a point, which evaporated in Hawking radiation at once. The blast was seen on Pleasance.

It was followed by the flare of Lucifer, in visible light, as *Cockroach* plowed into the contracting remains of the atmospheric fireball. The ship's fuel intakes were in stasis, as were the tanks themselves, and the local material was now heavily enriched in deuterium; when inertial sensors in the instrument bubbles detected a halt, indicating that the ship was as deep as it was going to get, the field on the tank intakes was flickered for just long enough for the pressure to slam them shut. The tanks' contents would be cooled and separated when things were less exciting.

A destroyer had set out immediately after the destruction of the flagship, had refused to acknowledge transmissions, and had been declared outlaw—largely as a matter of form, as its intentions were obvious. Gnyr-Captain and his crew wouldn't have cared if they weren't. They had sworn personal fealty to Hthht'-Riit, and considered their own lives to be over. All that remained was to finish dying, and they would do it like kzinti.

They were still two hours from Lucifer when the human ship recoiled out of the atmosphere. Much of it came out of stasis, and the ship presently stopped tumbling. It cast about as if purblind (which it was, as three of the four instrument packages were now condensing metal vapor inside their shells), picked a direction, and shot away at six hundred gees.

The outlaw destroyer could not spare the time for much of a ceremony: a minute or so to contemplate the ship's new name. This was less precisely transliteratable into a human language than most kzinti concepts, as it was less a word than an expression of feeling, sounding like some primordial red scream. It did have a meaning as a noun—it was the title of an ancient (pre-industrial!) mythical being, whom the gods sent to punish cannibals and those who claimed Names they had not earned. According to legend, the creature had been a kzin who had contradicted some god, and had been flayed alive and boiled in vinegar—but only after being made immortal, so he couldn't escape by dying. After torture he stuck to his assertions, so impressing the ruler of the gods with his courage and principles that they made him their instrument, granting him perfection of movement in battle.

It may or may not have been a coincidence of etymology that led the ancient Greeks to give the name Eumenides, "perfect in grace," to three figures of similar function, more properly known as Erinyes. The Romans, however, gave them the name by which they were most familiarly known.

The *Fury* continued its pursuit.

Peace Corben knew nothing of this. The ship's computer hadn't noticed the destroyer, and hadn't been informative with her anyway. She did finally manage to get out of it the origin of the name *Cockroach*: it was an ugly little Earth insect, notorious for its ubiquity and its capacity to survive attempts to kill it. It didn't please her to be in a vessel with such a name, particularly one that acted like this one did.

Peace would have been less pleased, if that were possible, to learn that the things were extinct.

■ ■

Peace had been offplanet about twenty standard years back, to the research base orbiting Amethyst (which star still obstinately kept secret its reason for being a brilliant shade of theoretically-impossible purple). Supposedly she was there to gather material for her sociobiology dissertation on isolated communities; in fact, she was a rich kid playing tourist, and the staff had promptly put her to work programming the kitchen—which she became so unexpectedly good at (she'd never done it before) that the base autodoc had to constantly fiddle with everybody's thyroids to keep their weight down. She'd never been in hyperspace, though. Naturally she'd heard about its peculiarities, but now she still didn't get to experience them. A viewscreen will not display the Blind Spot. Consequently it wasn't the eerie experience she'd been expecting.

As the ship was badly damaged, the computer was heading for We Made It. Once Peace had gotten it to tell her anything, she discovered that this was because crashlanders: A) knew everything any human being knew about repairing spaceships; and, B) were still paying the

Outsiders installments on the purchase of hyperdrive, and could thus be reasonably expected to possess a certain moral flexibility about reporting cash customers to ARM agents. So the trip wasn't all that mysterious in itself, either. However, Peace had plenty to occupy her mind, because she'd gotten these tidbits by locating and decrypting the ship's log. It was a long read, but better than the first week of the trip—the autodoc had been treating her for cataract formation, triggered by the sharp transient acceleration the kzinti grav lock had caused before the ship compensated. (It had been terrifying. She'd never *heard* of cataracts before—the genes for them had been on the UN Fertility Board's list from the day it was started.)

Slightly before arrival, she got through the password system, and thus was able to use the hyperwave, to warn humanity of the onset of the Fourth Kzinti War. She then discovered that the panic program was still active. *Cockroach* responded to the content of the messages by turning around and heading for a place to sit out the war unobserved, incidentally adding two months to the voyage.

Interstellar travel was turning out to be principally a pain in the ass.

The autodoc was amazingly old, programmed for her rather hyperactive mother, built into the kitchen, and stubborn as gravity. Peace put on close to three pounds a week. She had to turn up the cabin gravity just to keep it from all turning to fat. And she couldn't keep it above twelve meters or the autodoc just turned down her thyroid.

If *Cockroach* ended up picking a third destination, Peace was going to have no more contours than a bandersnatch by the time she arrived.

The *Fury* dropped out of hyperspace outside the Procyon singularity about forty-five hours after *Cockroach* had done so. There was a fleet. *Fury* returned to hyperspace for a few minutes of direction changes, then returned to normal space on a very different side of the gravity well.

Gnyr-Captain growled wordlessly to himself for a while. The habit was probably annoying, but so far no one had had the blood to say so. Then he said, "Technology Officer, was our prey in that fleet?"

"I believe not, Gnyr-Captain, but I am having the computer check my observation. . . . All craft in that fleet are of human manufacture."

Gnyr-Captain growled some more. "Strategy Officer, do you judge that humans would include such a ship in a war fleet if it were available?"

"Yes, sir," was the immediate reply. "Anyone would. Should I expound?"

"No." The ranking of Strategy Officer was a recent innovation, and this one was always trying to demonstrate his worth. Gnyr-Captain wished for about the 512th time that he had a Telepath, then opened a channel. "Manexpert to the bridge."

When Manexpert had buzzed, been admitted, and come to attention, Gnyr-Captain looked him over. That was about all the examining anyone could do. Manexpert habitually breathed through his mouth to control his expression, and groomed with some kind of fabric cleaner to minimize his scent. It was enough to thin your blood sometimes—it was very like talking to a holo of a kzin, but a holo that could smell *you*. Manexpert had explained, when ordered, that he had adopted the appearance of harmlessness from the humans he studied, on the grounds that it made it possible to surprise and defeat a superior warrior. His dueling record supported this theory.

"Manexpert," said Gnyr-Captain, "our prey is not in this system. Could he have been less damaged than he seemed, and changed course in hyperspace?" Then he waited; such questions always took time.

Manexpert's pupils dilated, his ears cupped, and his tail lashed. He stared at a spot on the bulkhead—which was in fact in about the same direction as the nearby star—and thought very hard for about two minutes, trying to think like a human. Then he resumed a more normal attitude and said, "Gnyr-Captain, regardless of his damage he did not know of our pursuit. If he had, by then he would have been terrified, so he would have attacked, taking advantage of his Red Age ship's superior acceleration."

"A reasoned response, made out of panic?" said Strategy Officer scornfully.

"Humans do it often," Manexpert replied, apparently unoffended. But then, who could know?

"Why?" said Gnyr-Captain, startled.

"I don't know, sir. I'm not sure even they know. My own theory is it's a way to be rid of the fear."

"Reflexively?" Gnyr-Captain said in disbelief.

"It isn't a widely-accepted theory, sir," Manexpert admitted.

"Good—Why wouldn't he stay in their primary ship-building system, if he wasn't aware of pursuit?"

"Because it's a very sensible place to go, sir," Manexpert replied. Close study of human thought had gotten him a reputation for strange comments, but this one stood out. He saw his commander's expression and hastily added, "He would realize that a hunter would expect him to go to the safest place possible, and he would expect a hunter to arrive there whether he saw pursuit or not, and therefore would avoid that place. You see, sir, humans seem to have evolved intelligence in order to *become* predators, which gives them—"

"*If I want a lecture I'll catch a pierin!*" Gnyr-Captain roared. "Where would he go instead?"

"By this reasoning, the last place a human with his fur straight—urr, hmf—who wasn't mad, I mean, would want to go."

"What, Kzin?"

"They're mad, sir, not idiots. Mostly.—I'm going to have to check my library to figure out just where that would be, Gnyr-Captain. Certainly someplace humans would consider dangerous."

"Go do it. Dismissed."

"Sir."

Peace watched the line in the middle of the mass detector lengthen to nearly the edge of the globe before dropping *Cockroach* into normal space. It was her second approach to the system; her first had only been to use the gravity drag, since she'd been moving at over three percent of lightspeed when she dropped out. She didn't want to run low on fuel again. She didn't know how she was going to restore the ruined instruments, as the apertures for the shells were about a fifth of an inch across. The old woman must have made models in bottles for fun, sometime in the past.

She switched on the instruction mike, and when the indicator lit told the computer, "We're there."

CONFIRMED, it replied. She had it use visual replies only, on a screen for one of the ruined instrument pods. It was less unnerving that way. Its voice sounded like her mother.

"Great. Now where the puke are we?"

EPSILON INDI SYSTEM, it replied.

Peace growled, then muttered, "*How* am I supposed to find out what I'm *doing* here?"

REQUEST THE REASON FOR THE CHOSEN DESTINATION, it told her.

Peace stared at the screen for a long moment, intensely annoyed. If she'd been in the habit of thinking aloud, she could long since have . . . *rrrgh!* "Why was this destination chosen?" she finally said.

EPSILON INDI SYSTEM WAS ABANDONED DUE TO FAILURE OF THE COLONY WORLD **HOME**, AND IS TOO DEEP IN HUMAN SPACE TO BE PRACTICAL FOR OTHER RACES. MATERIALS FROM COLONY STRUCTURES SHOULD BE MORE THAN SUFFICIENT FOR REPAIRS, AND TRACE ELEMENTS FOR SUPPLIES CAN BE ACQUIRED FROM THE ENVIRONMENT.

"Why did the colony fail?"

PLAGUE, ETIOLOGY UNKNOWN, BUT RAPID IN EFFECT. ONLY A PARTIAL WARNING WAS SENT BEFORE COMMUNICATIONS CEASED.

"Nobody's tried to find a cure?" To obtain a whole *planet*?

FIVE EXPEDITIONS ARE RECORDED SINCE 2360. THREE WERE UN ARM, ONE JINX INSTITUTE OF KNOWLEDGE, ONE WUNDERLAND INDEPENDENCE SOCIETY. NO SURVIVORS ARE RECORDED.

"Didn't anybody think to leave someone in orbit?"

ALL FIVE MISSION PLANS INCLUDED ISOLATED OBSERVERS.

"Piles," Peace murmured. Then she yelled, "*So what's the point of being here if I can't go outside?*"

REPAIRS MUST BE PERFORMED IN A PRESSURE SUIT.

"Pus."

Epsilon Indi system had been colonized by flatlanders and Belters, but the Belters must have been malcontents or something: there wasn't a trace of asteroid industry. There were hardly any asteroids, contrary to what the ship's records said. Home itself had been named by consensus, but the right to name the other major bodies had been distributed by lot, and the first settlers must have been an odd bunch. From inmost to outermost, the planets were: Monongahela, Home, Bullwinkle, Rapunzel, and Godzilla. Peace was unable to find any explanations for these choices in *Cockroach*'s memory.

Home itself was . . . strange. The icecaps were a lot bigger than the computer's maps showed, and the coastlines were all screwed up. Why would there be an ice age? The primary wasn't contracting, the way that, for instance, Sol was. In the putative tropics, the coastlines were thick with jungle showing no sign of habitation, but this cut off sharply—about where the old coastlines used to be, in fact. The interior was all but sterile—but well supplied with highways. There were circular lakes, ranging in size from big to absurd, sprinkled over the continents, and all of them had several big roads leading right up to their rims, connecting them to others. Some intersecting lake patterns had dozens of those leading away from them. What it looked like was, there had been a bunch of cities all over, and they'd exploded.

Maybe they'd tried to stop the plague with fusion blasts? But then why was there an ice age? All that soot would reduce the planet's albedo and *melt* the icecaps. Anyone who went to school on Pleasance knew *all* about light absorption.

Rot it. Peace deep-radared the crust, looking for refined metal she could land near.

Then, incredulous, she did it again.

There was no piece of refined metal larger than her fist within a quarter-mile of the surface. Whatever the research ships had landed with was gone, which was at least plausible if you assumed they'd taken off and died on the way back; but the residues of industry were absent too. There wasn't so much as a bearing from a groundcar down there, not even where city sites were under the ice. Outside the newly-exposed coastal areas there weren't even ore concentrations. Records said Home was supposed to be poor in ferrous ores, but they couldn't have built *everything* out of aluminum and brick, could they? And there was no refined aluminum, which meant either somebody had used it all for something, or there had been some amazingly corrosive rainfall here—like hydrofluoric acid, or a strong lye solution. Aluminum didn't break down by itself.

There were no satellites in orbit.

Nothing manmade on the moon, Indigo. (It wasn't. Who *named* these things?) No useful concentrations, either, which would have sidestepped the risks involved in landing on the planet.

Peace grumbled and set the surviving instruments to performing a spectroscopic assay. If nothing else, there would be mine tailings. The last visitors had been two or three centuries back; metal reclamation technology had been stimulated considerably by the three intervening Kzinti Wars. She told the computer to map incidence levels of the elements needed for *Cockroach*'s repairs, then had a nap—after it nagged her into taking another meal she didn't want, of course.

When she got up, her first impression was that she'd instructed the computer wrong. She hadn't. According to the scan, the nine most essential elements—the Group VIII set—were distributed in three ways:

First, there was a light dusting of them, all over the planet—except in the lakes, where there were only traces.

Second, there were massive deposits in all river deltas—pre-glacial ones—and deep ocean trenches. Massive as in, kilotons.

Third, there were five concentrations, of all nine elements, in the immediate vicinity of the former location of Claytown, where the spaceport had been. This was on a former river delta, so Peace decided to set down there—after wondering briefly why anybody would put a spaceport next to an ocean, which could potentially wreck it in minutes. (She dismissed the question, on the grounds that people who would blow up cities would do anything at all.) The five spots there also held concentrations of niobium and chromium—where five large supplies of hullmetal had been chemically separated, then scattered.

She decided to be especially careful. The plague clearly did something to your brain.

In forty days of inactivity, morale aboard the *Fury* had plummeted. The crew slept a lot off duty. Some began grooming compulsively. Dueling had fallen off, and Power Officer had reported hearing one of his crewkzin apologize to another of equal rank. Gnyr-Captain didn't even have the comfort of nagging Manexpert, for he knew intuition was a hairless thing, curling up under pressure.

Gnyr-Captain was exercising in his cabin, leaping across it with the gravity turned low. He didn't need that much exercise, but it ate time—and he'd caught himself wondering if his tail would look good tattooed. . . . Someone buzzed, and he poised, turned the gravity back up, and grabbed a variable-sword in one combined movement. Could have been smoother, he noted. Getting soft. "Enter," he said.

Manexpert opened the door. "If I entered you might get ill, sir," he said. It was a good bet; he wasn't clean. He was matted, too, and missing chin hairs where he'd been tugging on them. One of his ears was half-curled, and had a persistent twitch; and he—

"What *are* you doing?" Gnyr-Captain exclaimed.

"Sir? Oh, the tail. I thought fiddling with the end of it would help me think more like a human, sir."

"Humans don't *have* tails," said Gnyr-Captain distractedly, disturbed at the sight.

"I know, sir, but if they did they'd fiddle with the tuft."

"Why?"

"They fiddle with *everything*, sir. —I have five possible destinations, Gnyr-Captain."

This was simultaneously annoying and a relief; he'd expected thirty-two or forty. "Name them."

"From most to least dangerous: first, he could return to his own system."

"Suicide."

"Just being thorough, sir. Next, the asteroid belt of Gunpoint."

"How is that dangerous?"

"As the system nearest Sol it's ruled from Earth. There are rebels in the asteroids who want to overthrow the governors, and they'd want the ship, but they might save money by killing him and taking it."

That sounded remarkably sensible. "Humans would do that? They're usually so scrupulous in matters of trade."

"Not with each other, sir. In fact, the humans most

concerned with dealing honorably with other species often treat their fellow humans like sthondats."

"Why?"

"I've never even heard a theory, sir. It's one of those human things."

"Ftah. Proceed."

"Third is Fuzz. Fourth is Warhead. I judge them nearly equal in danger. I don't know whether *human* telepaths go insane on Fuzz; on the other hand, though Warhead is closer to Kzin, it presents logistical difficulties for invasion—"

"I know about Warhead," Gnyr-Captain said sharply. He had had ancestors there—might still have, in stasis. "Fifth?"

"*Home*," Manexpert said in human speech.

"Never heard of it."

"A colony destroyed by an unidentified disease, which was still active during later visits. We may assume the prey has a pressure suit, and colony relics would include repair materials—"

"He's there," Gnyr-Captain said with certainty.

"It is least likely, sir—I see, playing a double game?"

Gnyr-Captain's ears cupped.

"Human phrase, sir. Their strategies often—"

"Manexpert," Gnyr-Captain interrupted, surprising himself with his mildness, "go groom, and get some rest, and rinse yourself with that polymer solvent or whatever it is you like so much. But first tell Navigator where to find *Huwwng*—that world."

"*Home*, sir?" Manexpert enunciated.

"Yes. I don't know how you can reproduce that monkey howling. Dismissed."

"Yes, sir. You get used to the taste after a few years, sir," Manexpert said, and saluted, and closed the door.

Gnyr-Captain squinted at the closed door for a full minute, trying to make sense of that.

Within a week of landing, Peace was sick. Not with the plague; with rage. She'd done the first repairs with parts in storage, then done a full rundown on ship's systems to see about cannibalizing anything redundant.

The autodoc had a telomerizing subsystem—it could restore one cell's chromosomes to a youthful condition. It also had the capacity for full brain transplant. Which had been used. Repeatedly.

She should have realized. Boosterspice will not restore fertility; Peace had "never met" her father because she never had one. She'd been gestated as a supply of spare parts. Her thyroid had been kept low to make her easy to catch. And what a *funny* pun her *name* was!

Jan had been sentenced to twelve years, and had been due out . . . about now, in fact. Peace was nearing the end of her fertility; Jan would have had to hurry to get her brain put into the *spare* in time to bear a replacement. The *spare* brain would be thrown away, of course, and Jan Corben would be reported as suffering a sad accident.

It came to Peace suddenly that the kzinti invasion had saved her life.

When she finally got her hysterical laughter under control, she was very calm.

She thought.

She called up the manual-operations checklist on the computer, started a test run, and while it was fully occupied did a physical disconnect between the overseer system and the airlock, the gravity planer, the fusion tube, and the autodoc. She resisted temptation: she used a cutting laser. An axe would have been less accurate.

This done, she used a handheld computer to check the autodoc programs, and found that they were indeed not what the ship's computer had said they were. She found the programs used on Jan, copied them to crystal storage, and simply replaced the old crystals with the new ones. She traced circuit paths, found other storage media with programs inside, and destroyed them. Then she used the autodoc.

When she awoke, the first thing she realized was that the kzinti would come looking for her.

Repairs would have to wait. She needed weaponry. The computer would know everything that could be made from materials on hand; it could make a list while the autodoc made up a pressure suit. She'd have to get the parts fabricators outside.

It happened this way:

She was out rigging a sluice for the refiner's waste dust—it ate the local soil, but needed a lot of it—when she began wondering what was wrong with the trees, just past where the original shoreline had been. Ship's equipment included two crawlers; Jan, of course, had believed in having a spare. Peace drove out to the treeline to cut samples, then brought them back only to realize that the analysis had to be done by the autodoc. She thought, then had the computer isolate everything not needed in stasis. Each system and each compartment had its own field generator. Jan must have been really rich at some point. Then she took the samples in, staying in her suit the whole time as she couldn't very well decontaminate without destroying the samples, and ran them through the doc. It might just be some local blight, but if not . . .

It wasn't. The trees had been tailored to take up useful elements—not well enough to kill the trees, but well enough to make it worthwhile to use their ashes instead of the local soil. Peace could have done it with *Cockroach*'s facilities, but it would have taken too long for the trees to grow. One of the previous expeditions must have been badly wrecked, and done the work before the plague killed them.

Cheerfully, Peace had the computer sterilize the ship's interior while she was still in it; of course she wore her pressure suit. When the cycle was completed she left, of course to load equipment before moving the ship.

And the computer of course no longer had any control over the interior of the airlock.

A trace of dust got into the ship from the airlock.

When she came back, of course she had the airlock clean off her suit before she went in to the control cone. She moved the ship over to the trees, then went back out to set things up—instead of soil being dug up, trees would have to be cut and burned. She used a few pounds of metal foil to make up a huge funnel on legs, then put it in stasis and set it over the intake hopper. The machinery she set to cutting up trees and dumping the chunks in the funnel, and she used a laser at wide aperture to char some from underneath, through the hole, to get them burning. It took some time; they were green, and kept going out. Finally the fire was going, though, and ashes started falling into the hopper. Burning wood, too, but the mechanism of the refiner was built to do worse than that itself.

And when she came in, of course it was only natural that she felt hot, and wanted to sleep.

Before she drifted off, it occurred to her that the fat was just going to be replaced by muscle if she had to work like this. She'd be awfully strong by the time the kzinti showed up.

Pleased, she settled into the sleep of the despicable. (It is of course the innocent whose rest is uneasy; true villains slumber undisturbed by anything but an occasional chuckle.)

The gas giant had the usual litter of moons. *Fury* landed on one, refueled, and took off immediately. The prey ship had been found within hours, in stasis—perfect reflection, no neutrino output. What Gnyr-Captain had wanted to do was plunge in, grab the crew (probably only one, but they could be lucky), return to Kzin *at once*, see to it Manexpert got a Name, and if permitted make helpful suggestions to the prey's torturers before being executed for disobedience. Fathers would wean their sons on the tale of Gnyr-Avenger for 512s of years. It was a proud and public thing, to be a kzin.

Unfortunately, records of its departure indicated the old courier ship was just a touch too big to fit into the destroyer's hold. They would have to land, wrap it in a net, disable its stasis, and take it home. And the prey might not even be inside! Bringing back the ship, with its useful arms features, would be honorable enough to save his crewkzin from execution along with Gnyr-Captain, but Manexpert would probably never get his Name. The thought shamed Gnyr-Captain. "Take us near the prey, planer only, and hover," he told First Flyer.

Approaching the planet was disturbing. Clearly it had undergone asteroid bombardment, but the targets had obviously been cities (and oceans, judging by the over-sized icecaps), in what must have been a deliberate attempt to destroy the population. Industrial areas, certainly, but what kind of monster would a conqueror have to be to incinerate a potential labor force?

The prey had landed near the only remaining town, some kind of coastal industrial facility. It couldn't have housed more than two or three 512s of humans from the size of it, but parts of it were warm. Somebody must indeed have been using colony facilities to try to repair the ship, an excellent sign. They couldn't have had much success, judging by the amount of equipment that was lying around in pieces.

"Find them," Gnyr-Captain told Strategy Officer.

"Yes, sir.—Look for pressure suits," he told Second Tactician. (Naturally First Tactician was standing by with the landing party.) "Batteries may be chemical instead of electronic. Also look for gaps or rings in the neutrino background; someone may have put a conical reflector into stasis."

"There's a human-sized warm spot among those leafless trees, sir," said Second Tactician.

"No, their suits are well-insulated, and would show up as a small very hot spot. Must be an animal."

"Yes, sir. It's just that it was moving from one metallic object to another—"

"Animals mark things."

Gnyr-Captain looked properly impatient, though privately he agreed; he'd once seen a ftheer do that to an electric fence. It was surprised.

Unexpectedly, Power Officer signaled. "Gnyr-Captain, the feeder lines to the fusion tubes will not operate."

Gnyr-Captain grumbled, then said, "Is our storage fully charged?"

"Yes, sir, but as I cannot find a cause I thought it might be some form of—"

And the lights went out.

The next word would have been "attack."

Manexpert had been seething. *He* had found the prey, *he* should be in the assault party! Instead he was bound in his crash fooch, protected like a kitten. The explanation, that he was too valuable to become a target, just made him feel worse. Kittens got explanations; warriors took orders.

It didn't occur to him that the landing party didn't *want* him—his fellow kzinti were afraid of his unpredictability. If it had, he would have been much happier. As it was, he was merely bitter about missing all the excitement.

Suddenly the cabin gravity went to free fall. What was Gnyr-Captain doing? And if the lights were out to save power for whatever it was, shouldn't the gravity be shut off, to local ambient?

It occurred to him that he couldn't hear the ripping of the gravity planer. The significance of this hit him just before the planet did.

The kzinti ship fell perhaps a hundred feet, at first. (The ground sloped.) A human ship would have been less damaged, for the counterintuitive reason that it would have had a thinner hull: the hull would have done some crumpling, taking up the shock of impact. The kzinti ship had over half an inch of hullmetal, which is held together by both covalent and metallic bonding, and is as resilient as unmodified matter can get. In vacuum this is a good thing.

A hundred feet up, it is a very bad thing indeed, at least when all failsafes have suddenly lost power. The ship bounced, repeatedly. Interior partitions and supports of hullmetal have their critics at such times as well.

Manexpert could hear other kzinti moving about. They must have been the landing party, which would have been padded in their armor; there was no reason to think anyone else's crash field had worked either. He couldn't see out his right eye, and that side of his head felt huge and hot. He couldn't feel anything below his shoulders, either.

There was a little bit of light coming from somewhere to the right. Either the hull had finally cracked—unlikely—or the assault party had cut their way out of the bay when the airlock didn't work. For some unknown but long time, there were extended periods of silence, interrupted by bursts of warcries blended with multiple stutters of slug gunfire. Eventually Manexpert's head began to hurt, and he ignored everything else in his efforts to keep from screaming.

When the pain suddenly faded, he noticed the light had grown brighter. He was also humiliated to realize that for at least several minutes he had been uttering milkmews, like an infant whose mother has left him alone.

He could smell something living nearby. It smelled something like a human, but more acidic, and lacking any trace of fear or anger. "Do you speak Wunderlander?" said a voice with an unidentifiable accent, in that language. Manexpert managed to turn his head a little. The owner of the voice moved courteously into Manexpert's field of vision.

Superstitious fears, whose existence he had never suspected, choked him. This was a monster out of legend. Enormous joints and hard fatless flesh, like someone skinned and rendered down; big ears, permanently cupped to detect the slightest footstep; huge nose for sniffing prey; complete lack of hair or teeth; a hide mottled in shades of brown, with dark-brown speckles, ideal grassland camouflage; and, for all its swollen, deformed head and freakish face, the casual precision and lack of waste motion of the perfect hunter.

"Do you speak English?" it tried. That ragged beak was responsible for the accent.

Kzinti do not go into physical shock when injured, so

Manexpert had nothing to compare his mental state with; but the fact was, he was suffering from such a bad case of shock that he couldn't have recalled how to speak Hero if the Patriarch had offered him a daughter to ch'rowl.

"Too bad," it said, and raised Gnyr-Captain's treasured antique machine gun into view. It had once been carried into battle by a Patriarch's Companion, and Manexpert knew himself to be the ship's last survivor.

"You're—" Manexpert tried to translate a word into English, then gave up and said the word in Hero—"*Fury*, aren't you?" He said it badly, being unable to get out that much volume.

It lowered the sidearm and said, "My name is Peace."

Kzinti had learned that word from humans, but there was a certain conceptual gap. Almost no kzin could have grasped the notion of "a situation wherein nobody wants to fight," and Manexpert was not among that minority. He understood the word as most did, as referring to the condition that was being described whenever the term was applied: "human victory."

"We only wanted slaves this time," Manexpert said, despairing.

Peace blinked. And blinked a second time. Then it said, "Your skull is fractured and your neck is broken, and your body is only kept from bleeding out by the wreckage crushing it. I'm going to take the whole mass and put you in stasis until I get your ship's autodoc fixed."

"How will you get the equipment in here?" Manexpert wondered.

"I have it already," Peace said, and picked up a slightly-wrinkled but perfectly reflective shield. It adjusted something, and the shield was just aluminum foil, barely thick enough to support its own weight. So simple. "I brought more foil just in case," it added, then gave him another injection.

Peace had had an enormous amount of time to think, even without considering her new speed of thought and ability to sleep in sectors—like a dolphin, but better.

The amount of manipulation that had been going on vastly exceeded anyone's wildest suspicions.

She had awakened with her memory fully organized, and her first thought was: *I was right all along.* Peace woke dehydrated, and weak with lack of food, but not hungry. She had eaten anyway. A lifetime of subjugation and thyroid deficiency had kept her depressed and over-weight; she was accustomed to eating whether she was hungry or not. While she ate, she called up the excessively long intron sequences recorded from the mining trees, decrypted them, and read the Truesdale account, learning all that was known about Protectors.

Or rather, all that was believed about Protectors. Some of it was obviously wrong.

A couple of million years back, according to Jack Brennan, a Belter who'd become a Protector, a race called the Pak had sent a colony ship to Earth from the galactic core. The Pak became sentient only after years of repro-ductive maturity, as a result of eating a root that started smelling good to them when their hormone balance began to screw up. This root did not grow right on Earth, so the Pak protectors died out. Brennan said it was of starvation.

And that was a lie.

The Pak breeders were *Homo habilis*, and they were ancestors of the human race, which could eat things that would make a dog go blind. They could eat dogs, for that matter. Protectors weren't limited to eating tree-of-life, as Brennan called it; it was just what they needed to keep regenerating, and digesting disease germs, and so forth. Some of them must have lasted centuries.

When Brennan had been telling this fable, he had already made his plans to steal a Pak Protector's ramship and convince the UN ARM that he was doomed. They wouldn't interfere with his manipulation of human society if they didn't believe he existed. On the trip back to Brennan's ship, from which Phssthpok had kidnapped him before realizing he was family, Brennan had refused to allow one of his companions, Lucas Garner, to smoke, on the grounds that he, Brennan, *had* to act to keep the man healthy. This was well after the time of Pasteur, so it was known by then that a viral disease such as cancer could not be contracted by smelling burning leaves; Brennan had been ensuring that the 184-year-old paranoid would be too exasperated to think things through.

Peace deduced the rest.

The Protectors had gone out in fission-powered ion-drive ships, looking for planets where tree-of-life would grow properly. They had found none; there were few planets that were at all habitable. However, the original expedition would have been equipped for terraforming. Planets had water added, were seeded with algae, were even smashed with small moons to create high ground on the far side, above the thick atmosphere. Meanwhile, the few Protectors that remained on Earth were cultivating mutations, so that a species would eventually arise which would be able to use the terraformed planets.

And some explorers must have met the puppeteers.

Two and a half million years back, the puppeteers must have already had spaceflight—not manned, to be sure, but effective at searching for threats. The Protectors would have realized that their limited numbers could never exterminate the puppeteers before Earth's breeder population was found and slaughtered. The Protectors wouldn't have returned to Earth, and they would have killed themselves rather than risk giving away its location. At least one must have made sure of being undiscovered, though, and returned to Earth to warn the Protectors there; and they in turn would have methodically destroyed all signs of technological development. Except the plants they'd modified to produce a multipurpose raw material, unnecessary to the plants' survival, in their secretions; there were too many of those, intended for availability in all climates, to hunt them all down. The best-known was the rubber tree, so useful it was still cultivated on Earth.

The puppeteers had eventually found Earth, and Kzin, and a lot of less interesting inhabited planets. They had manipulated the two dangerous races' development. When Phssthpok, another Pak protector, had come from the Core, they'd let him through, to stimulate Earth's technology to catch up with Kzin's.

But, thanks to a couple of centuries of Brennan's interference, Earth developed wrong, becoming too peaceful to survive the discovery of the planet by the kzinti. So the puppeteers had arranged to let kzinti

warcraft find human colony ships in interstellar space—
something that had happened half a dozen times. Twice,
human ships had survived long enough to send home
messages about the contacts.

And humans and kzinti alike thought of it as coincidence!

Picture a globe six million miles across, full of air but
unilluminated. Add hundreds of floating bonfires, each
with a surface area of at least an acre, in all colors, well-
scattered. Imagine air jets to push you from one bonfire to
another, in straight lines. Now picture other people, all
coming from one bonfire you haven't been to, traveling to
various others you haven't been to, propelled by butane-
jet cigarette lighters. You know nothing of cigarette
lighters and do not use instruments designed to seek them
out. How close do you have to get to one to notice it
against the background of bonfires? The closest that two
of these skew paths get to each other is in excess of a thousand miles. Now multiply the distances by 40 million, and
the bonfire surfaces by 1.6 quadrillion, and ask yourself
how the kzinti found human ships in interstellar space *six
times*.

Once would be a miracle to stupefy an atheist. Twice is
enemy action. Six times is policy.

The puppeteers had arranged beacons, not recognizable
as such, to attract kzinti ships. (Possibly telepathic; the
kzinti had the capability far more often than humans,
which implied it was latent in the whole species—which
would explain why they were so hostile: *noise*.) Once the
First War began, the puppeteers had quickly realized that
the human ability to kill anything had been all but bred

out of the race, and the humans would lose; so they arranged for the Outsiders to go to We Made It, outside the war zone, and sell hyperdrive to the crashlanders. Probably without telling the Outsiders why. Conceivably without telling them at all—Outsiders followed starseeds, and it would be a simple matter to dump trace elements a starseed needed into a star's chromosphere.

And while the Outsiders were ambling along at sublight speeds, Wunderland's population was conquered, enslaved, and eaten.

The puppeteers were powerful and arrogant, which was understandable, but also shortsighted in their meddling, which was intolerable. It might be necessary to exterminate them. If so, it would first be necessary to get them far from human space, as they would doubtless panic and slaughter everything in sight once the procedure began. Doubtless they were aware of the possibility of higher levels of hyperdrive, the next of which was at (if the drive's manual of operation was based on the assumptions it seemed to be) $6!x4!x2!/10=3456$ times the speed of the first level, or near enough to .8 lightyears per minute. It was always profitable to go faster, so they would be doing research already, so she would only have to have a few algorithms published in technical journals to get them out of the blind alleys. A publicity trip to the Core would give them a look at whatever the Pak migration had been fleeing, and they'd run immediately. That would give Peace a few centuries to decide what to do with them.

The kzinti could be disposed of more promptly.

When Peace was too full to eat any more, she reprogrammed and partly rebuilt the autodoc, then got in for a full scan. Brennan had created a human-infecting form of the virus that changed the Pak (or their relatives) into Protectors, and he and his descendant Truesdale had brought it to Home, to prepare a surprise for the Pak Protector scouts they'd lured away from Earth. Peace needed to find out what it did. The results showed there were things Brennan hadn't mentioned, and that Truesdale most likely hadn't known.

Each lung had an extra lobe, now, so the right had four and the left three. The lobes were now separated by membranes, so that puncturing one wouldn't collapse the rest of the lung. Ribs had thickened and spread to accommodate the change. There was now a two-chamber iliac heart in the groin, drawing blood from the lower body. It pumped it directly into the new lung lobes, which oxygenated it and added it to the blood returning from the rest of the body. Running this mix through the original lungs produced blood supersaturated with oxygen, which the expanded brain needed desperately. The original heart developed thicker muscle and redundant feeder vessels, and the extra oxygen kept it from strain. The extra pass through the lungs would also allow her to function when the partial pressure of oxygen in local air was too low to keep an unchanged human conscious.

The lymphatic system had developed one-way valves, such as veins had, so that the fluid was kept circulating by changes in pressure as muscles were used. The spleen had developed into an organ much like the liver in texture, and its new function seemed to be scavenging trace minerals.

The end joint of each finger was now able to move

independently of the rest of the finger, like the end of a
human thumb.

There was a hard shell contained within each eyelid.
The shell was resilient, and opaque. The eye itself had a
second lens behind the original. The new lens was normally flat, but could be made concave enough for work as
close as an inch from the pupil. The original lens was sat-
urated with a substance which responded to chemical
cues in milliseconds, to become tinted (the usual state),
polarized, or clear. Without the Protector additives, this
chemical turned the lens white, producing cataracts.
(Brennan and Truesdale, products of Fertility Board
selection, would have known nothing of this, and would
sometimes have needed sunglasses.) The pupil could now
open all the way to the edge of the iris, gathering far more
light, and the retina had grown a tapetum, like a cat's eye,
to give the receptors a second try at the photons. The pro-
gressive die-off of the retina's color-detecting rods was
compensated by the trick of tinting the lenses different
colors, providing strong contrast. It occurred to her that
the instinctive attempt to see this degree of contrast, by
unaltered elderly humans, finally explained gingham. The
preprocessing layer of the retina was thicker, too; and as a
huge amount of new brain growth had been in the optic
center, image persistence was longer. A Protector could
read a newspaper page held up twenty feet away if the
light was good.

The olfactory region of the brain was now almost half
as big as the optic center used to be. This, like the finger
change, was implicit in Brennan's assertions; a Protector
had to be able to distinguish one protein molecule from

another when they differed by only one amino acid in one place. The processing involved was tremendous.

The brain had more than tripled in size. The new material at the back of the head was mostly three big lobes of cortex, each one a bigger processing net than one of the human brain's cortex hemispheres; and the hemispheres she'd started out with had grown as well. *One* of these five lobes sufficed for routine activity, allowing the rest to sleep when not needed. Processing networks required something akin to a dream state from time to time, or they began giving aberrant results; a Protector must have at least one cortical lobe in dream state just about all the time. A human Protector could have two in dream state, and still be smarter than a Pak Protector going full out.

There had been nerves dealing with facial muscles and genital response, and those nerves were dead and resorbed in metamorphosis. The brain centers formerly connected to them were now sensing with, and sending commands to, new nerves in the improved fingertips. Small wonder if Protectors enjoyed making things.

The lining of the small intestine was thick, and dense with blood vessels. Intestinal tissue was being constantly converted to embryonic cells, and those were entering the bloodstream, attaching themselves to cells that were functioning improperly. Once there, a new cell wrapped completely around the target cell, took up the cell's proper function, and ate it, digesting its proteins and nucleic acids into individual amino acids and nucleotides. Most of these were released into the blood plasma. The new cells also ate any foreign material, and dead or mutated cells. Bone marrow now produced only red cells—which were some twenty percent more numerous than before, and now had wrinkly surfaces to maximize the O_2/CO_2 exchange rate.

The virus that was present in the small intestine showed no sign of having *ever* been capable of infecting a plant. It didn't do that much to the small intestine, for that matter; but the genes it added produced some really astonishing prions—multifunctional enzymes which, among other things, reshaped other proteins, of similar but not identical sequence, into the same shape as the prion. Back in biochemistry classes she'd been taught that twenty-first-century Earth had waged desperate battles in the lab to wipe out just a few types of prions that had gotten into the food supply. Seeing them at work, this was plausible.

Tree-of-life virus must have infected the plants alone, and turned their proteins into prions. Jack Brennan had developed *this* virus by reverse-engineering the prions and creating the thing from first principles, and must have been planning to do so from the moment he killed Phssthpok. (That part of his story she believed. The Pak Protector would have sterilized Earth if he'd even *suspected* humans would turn down tree-of-life.) The prions only worked right on cells that had undergone a certain number of divisions—one of them converted telomerase to a new formulation, and too much of the new stuff—a regulating enzyme—would melt you to a blob, while too little would allow your cellular metabolism to speed up until it cooked your brain. The latter had actually happened to one of the Belters who'd inspected Phssthpok's cargo.

There were more mitochondria per cell, too. There seemed little purpose in this until Peace made the connection with a genetic disease she'd read about, now absent from the species, that caused mitochondria to accumulate calcium phosphate. In a Protector, it was a storehouse of material for regenerating bone; in breeders, it sapped strength in all tissues on a cellular level by limiting the size of the ATP reserve. It must have been universal at one time—Pak breeders didn't *need* stamina, clear heads, or motivation: they had Protectors. Peace recalled that salicylic acid, and its salts and esters, caused mitochondria to store inorganic phosphates, and she determined to stockpile the stuff.

She had used up most of a day getting acquainted with her new condition. Time to get to work. It would be tedious; the annihilation of technological artifacts was so thorough it must have taken some earlier expedition's protectors weeks, and Truesdale and the Home Protectors had stripped out all ore deposits for their arsenals before the asteroid bombardment, sensibly enough. (The mining trees were a splendid bit of misdirection: the Brennan virus had an affinity for the bark, which was crumbly.)

She went through the hidden parts of the computer's memory and found references to inventions the UN ARM had suppressed. Some sounded useful. There were no technical details, but a general outline of principles was usually given, and that was enough.

The third day she gave in to her impatience and built an automaton that could perform simple routine tasks, like cleaning rooms or repairing scanners. For the latter task she had to include a device that distorted the force binding the instrument shells, making them pliable enough to reach through; it had been obvious that the puppeteers must have some means of softening GP hulls, as they would never have sold invulnerable warship hulls to aliens. This done, she had the idea of building automata to fabricate parts usable in a variety of items, and judged it worth the time. (Technology doesn't save labor: it invests it.) Pure elements could be had via the expedient of a conveyor belt, a disintegrator, and a tapered wind tunnel. She dedicated five days to these tasks, then one more for a device that assembled parts to order, and was able to begin work on parts for the exotic stuff. She arranged a foil shell in stasis for workshop housing—some of the mechanisms would absorb stray neutrinos otherwise— and began building various specialized components for weapons of short, middle, and long ranges. Middle range being the horizon.

When the kzinti showed up, she was pleasantly sur- prised (and just a bit embarrassed for them) to find that she could easily break into their ship's command codes, which raised the possibility of interrogating prisoners. She shut off the fuel feed to their fusion source, then found mechanical cutouts that prevented total shutdown of key systems, so she broke out something she'd built as a bat- tery charger. It was faster than laying cables everywhere: it drew power out of all nearby sources, or a source it was aimed at, all without the need for broadcasting. It was just the thing to make a ship fall down.

Most of the survivors were an armored infantry group, and the ones who saw her didn't fight the way she'd expected kzinti to fight; they seemed desperate, rather than fanatical. It dawned on her that a Pak Protector must have landed on Kzin two and a half million years back, and made a really lasting impression. They would have been intelligent by then, but not civilized. Oral tradition would have distorted with every generation, but drawings would be kept up. Some of these troops blew themselves up when it was clear she'd be able to capture them; it was like they expected her to drag them, screaming, back to Hell.

The last survivor was pinned in the wreck; he'd been pretty well-protected, but he was still nearly torn in half. She found the medical supplies and dosed him with things whose labels showed a kzin bleeding, a kzin thrashing around, and a kzin in pain. (Arrows pointing in, instead of stars flying out. Fifty thousand generations of mortal combat for mates had evidently selected for kzinti so healthy that pain was regarded as an unnatural, external phenomenon.) When he became coherent, he asked if her name was [outraged wrathful snarl]. She told him her name, and he did a very strange thing: he pleaded with her. "We only wanted slaves this time," he said.

She immediately realized, with some amusement, what he understood the word *peace* to mean, and saw that he too regarded her as some sort of divine avenger; come to slay them all for eating humans, most likely. The word *slaves*, however, called up old information she hadn't thought of since college; and everything suddenly fell into place.

How could a species that exterminates all mutated offspring have *evolved*?

The Slavers had ruled the Galaxy a couple of billion

years back, according to Larry Greenberg, a human telepath who'd spent several weeks more or less possessed by one. (It had been released from stasis, due to a level of carelessness that Peace would have found appalling even when she was a heavily-medicated breeder. Paranoia was more common then, and had such a bad reputation that caution was treated as some kind of vice.) They used telepathic control to command other species (the Grogs of Down were their incredibly remote and wildly mutated descendants) and enslave them—hence the term. Their name for themselves was *thrintun*. (It was pronounced without the tongue ever touching the teeth—a thrint's teeth were metallic, and razorlike—and for a human it was a fine way to try to strangle yourself without using your hands.) Their principal slaves had been the tnuctipun, who were miracle workers at genetic design. The tnuctipun had produced the bandersnatch, still found on Jinx—they didn't mutate. The bandersnatch was intelligent, and immune to thrintun Power, and created as a food animal—the big brain was justified by making it very tasty. Bandersnatchi were made to be spies on the thrintun. The tnuctipun had spent centuries developing ways to screw up the thrintun while ostensibly being helpful, and when war finally became open the only counter-weapon the thrintun had that worked was amplified Power: they had commanded everything in the Galaxy to commit suicide. Everything that wasn't immune, in stasis, or too stupid to understand, obeyed.

Greenberg had said there were seventeen other intelligent races—eighteen if you stretched the definition a little. Implicitly, the eighteenth race must have sometimes gotten even clear telepathic orders wrong. The tnuctipun would have been assigned to make them smarter.

They had. It must have been one of their first successes. They came up with a virus that turned vegetable protein into the most amazing prions, and altered the species to start finding it irresistible—but only after reproducing. The desexing wasn't necessary, and from an evolutionary viewpoint was actually undesirable; selection would work better if reproduction occurred *after* the development of intelligence. The killing of mutated descendants was another deliberate effort to prevent evolution, and it had worked for two billion years. The loss of appetite when there were no descendants was just a safety feature to keep their numbers down, and the virus' thallium requirement was a way of limiting their mobility. The breeders' genes had evidently also been altered so that their brains were hardwired to sympathize with rebels and underdogs. Even today, humans hearing about the Slaver era tended to side with the tnuctipun—who by any reasonable standard were as coldly evil a race as had ever existed. (Kzinti ate intelligent lifeforms because hunting them was such a good challenge, and this was as horrifying a practice as you could find nowadays; but even they would recoil at the thought of *creating* an intelligent race for use as food.)

The parent species must have averaged a good deal brighter than *Homo habilis*. The Protectors that worked for the tnuctipun had undoubtedly produced many of the wonders that the tnuctipun were credited with—possibly all of the nongenetic ones, such as the Slaver hyperspace jump, disintegrators, stasis fields, and gravity control.

And the Slavers would have considered them perfectly harmless, because the Power would have seemed to work just fine on them. The compartmentalization of the Protector brain, however, would have meant that a Slaver could complacently hold a full lobe under complete control, unaware that that lobe was being left out of the control loop and the Protector was coming to kill him. Which would have been their job, during the war. A Protector was an ideal field commando—eat anything, hard to see, hard to hurt, powerful senses, able to improvise anything needed from what was on hand.

When the Slavers gave the suicide command, the Protectors hadn't been affected; but the breeders had. The only survivors of that would have been mental subnormals, mutants that hadn't been killed because their Protectors had gone off to war. (The mutation rate in the Core would have been incredible.) They would have been the ones too stupid to understand the order. The rest of the breeders would have died, and the Protectors would have stopped eating. Later, the mutants became Protectors themselves, and the ones able to produce viable offspring had kept on eating, developed a language, and called themselves Pak. When the breeder population rose high enough, they had fought for living space.

For two billion years.

Protectors do not normally examine their motives.

But there had never been a paranoid Protector before.

Peace Corben, ready to question and then kill the last survivor, realized that the tnuctipun had created her condition for much the same reason that her mother had created *her*: to be used. Her face was hard as horn; her holocaustic wrath never showed.

She was *not* a tool.

She told the kzin some reassuring lies about his condition, then began doing everything she could to save him. That turned out to be a great deal.

Manexpert woke in a big soft swaddle inside a box, which turned out to be an autodoc. It opened when he moved. The lining smelled like some kind of plant fiber, woven, cleaned, and bundled up to serve as padding. Though the experience was unfamiliar, it was comfortable, and felt very natural somehow.

He looked around warily, and saw he was under shelter but not in the . . . entity's . . . ship. He must have been kept in stasis for *years* before the autodoc was working; a good-sized city had grown up. There were buildings of assorted sizes, all more or less hemispherical, all made of foil in stasis. Broad concrete walkways around and between them had rain canopies overhead. They were shaped to channel the rain into troughs, which was apparent because there was a fine spray falling now.

He realized he was panting, and that it wasn't any kind of threat response; the air was—not thick, no, but sort of *used*. Something must be producing a lot of carbon dioxide: each breath he took felt like he'd been holding it for some time.

The shelter he was under was the open one. He couldn't see a ship, or tell what any buildings were for. There were horizontal ridges on the buildings, far enough apart to serve as steps—for a kzin; they'd been put there *for him*, so he could look around.

He wasn't about to try to climb an inflexible surface in the rain. Instead he followed the flow of water alongside the walkways. Men liked water, to the point where, even as careful as they were, some of them still drowned now and then. This thing seemed to like men; it might like water.

Manexpert had no idea what he would do when he found the creature—or what, in fact, he *could* do to something that bore an appalling resemblance, in both form and capability, to the God's Appointed Enforcer. The only alternative, though, seemed to be climbing back into the autodoc.

He paused by one of the domes that had a flat patch, to look at his right eye.

The socket was at the intersection of three really impressive scars, which extended well back on his head.

The eye itself was artificial.

The iris was of fixed diameter, so it must adjust to light electronically. He tried bringing up his inner lid, and the character of the light altered in a way that indicated polarization. It tracked like his other eye; but after he'd stared at the reflection for a while, the image he saw with it began to magnify.

Astonished, Manexpert used the eye to study his fingerprints in detail. After looking at the patterns of intersecting circles for a few minutes, he realized to his further astonishment that much of the hand was new. He looked over as much of his body as he readily could, and saw that a lot of his scars were gone. He stopped wasting time and went to look for his captor.

This turned out to be easier than it had seemed. Most of the domes had open apertures, with no doors, and regardless of activity they were unlit inside. A few domes did have doors, and those were very solid ones. Manexpert didn't see a locking mechanism, but they evidently slid upward, and sheer weight would have held any of them shut against as many kzinti as could have gotten a grip. One dome did have light inside, and Manexpert found the creature there.

Gnyr-Captain and Power Officer were also there, watching control panels. They didn't look toward him as he entered. Both were considerably scarred, and short of fat. Manexpert took a step toward Power Officer, away from the doorway, and Peace called out to him, "They're dead."

Manexpert stared at Peace for a moment. He thought he'd been good at covering his thoughts, but Peace's face had no more expression than a tree trunk—which in fact it resembled, in both flexibility and texture. Then he went to each scarred kzin, to look them over. There were visible artificial parts to both of them. Each breathed in an absolutely regular rhythm. Their blinking was equally regular. Both had had extensive cranial surgery. Neither took any notice of him. He went to the creature and said, "What did you do?"

Peace wore a knee-length vest, well-strapped-on and more or less made out of pockets. It was remote-manipulating something behind a wall of what looked like General Products hull material—it was too clear for glass—and never looked away from its work as it said, "They were the most nearly intact corpses. Your ship's autodoc wouldn't regrow complex tissues, so I had to do some experiments before I could fix you up. Afterwards I had these empty kzinti, so I put some circuitry in their skulls to make up for the brain tissue they lost. There's a third, on rest shift, eating and grooming and sleeping. He's got dark patches along his back."

Technology Officer. "Why did you save me?"

"It was an act of defiance. I was created to protect human beings and destroy everything else—except my creators—and I just refuse to be used any longer. I tried to match the eye's signal pattern to the one the other eye was using; is it useful?"

"It's better than the other."

"It'll repair itself if no more than twenty sixty-fourths is lost or wrecked. Uses something I call programmable matter. It can operate using your metabolism for power, but it'll work better if you stay near an electrical source. I'm sending you back to Kzin."

Manexpert was having trouble keeping up. "I can't fly our ship alone," he said, to gain time for thought.

This failed. "I'm making a new ship. Took yours apart. It wasn't very good. You'll be using a ram to fuel the gravity planer. No hyperdrive."

"Why not?"

"I want you to live through the war. It'll be over by the time you reach Kzin. Just a few weeks from your viewpoint, of course. There we go." Peace let go the manipulator and switched it off, and a violet glow developed behind the barrier.

Manexpert stared in puzzlement. The equipment in there looked like an awful lot of effort to make a big mercury lamp. "What are you doing?" he said.

"Turning mercury-204 into thallium-204. The plague that ruined this place has an affinity for thallium, and will absorb twenty atoms of it into its viral shell. This will render it incapable of infecting anything but plants. It could still be remade into something lethal, but the thallium isotope is unstable and gradually turns back into mercury, which poisons the virus it's attached to. Some is turning back already, hence the glow. I have to start up your foodmaker now," Peace said, and ran out. Fast.

Manexpert was taken by surprise, and didn't follow for a moment, by which time Peace was out of sight. He went back in and looked at the kzinti again, and said softly in Hero, "Gnyr-Captain, what do I do?"

And then his fur stood straight out, as Gnyr-Captain's relict slowly turned to face him. After a few seconds Gnyr-Captain's face took on an expression, as of someone trying to recall the right word, and twice he opened his mouth and closed it again. He opened it a third time, made eye contact, pointed at Manexpert, and said, "Name."

"I'm Manexpert," he whispered.

Gnyr-Captain flicked his ears wide and relaxed them, a dismissive gesture, and made two poking motions and said, "*Name.*"

"I don't *have* . . . you mean, you *want* me to have a Name?"

Gnyr-Captain let out a little sigh, relaxed, and turned back to the instruments he was monitoring. He made no further response to Manexpert, not even when touched. It was apparently the last thing his brain had been able to manage.

Manexpert went outside and wandered in whatever

direction his feet took him, until it got dark; then he lay down wherever it was he happened to be.

Peace found him when she had a few free minutes, and went to fetch him a haunch of what the *Cockroach's* computer claimed was gazelle—at least, that was what the genes were supposed to be. (Jan Corben had absconded with a very large database.) He woke when she returned with it, as she was coming from upwind to be polite. He came up to a combat stance at once, fur bristling, eyes and ears wide in the darkness. He looked adorable. "Here," she said, and waved the leg to be smelled, then tossed it. He snagged it out of the air, and grunted at the unexpected weight. "There are no animals worth hunting here," she added. "Plague victims ate them all. I made you a knife." She handed that over. "Don't touch the edge, those fingers are brand new."

"*W'tsai,*" said the kzin, inspecting the blade appreciatively by starlight. He carved off chunks and gulped without much chewing; there was a respectable chemical plant inside a kzinti abdomen, as Peace had cause to know, but it still looked funny. He cracked the bone reflexively, licked his fingers in embarrassment, and then noticed that there was indeed marrow. The ripple in the littlest claw on the hand was just the right shape to scoop in the very last scraps of marrow; that Pak Protector must have just about wiped out Kzin's supply of prey for that trait to have become standard. Killing off a major prey species with a tailored disease that the kzinti could contract would explain their inability to tolerate the taste of carrion, too— it would kill off the kzinti that ate food that they'd found, rather than killed themselves. When he had the bone fragments clean, Peace handed over a parcel she'd made up. It included grooming supplies, a knife (*w'tsai*) sheath, and a toolkit of useful articles, such as string and bandages and an oxygen mask and so forth. The kit had a light, and the kzin looked over the contents with growing perplexity. "What's this for?" he said, holding up the whistle.

"It makes a loud noise that carries a long way."

"I know that. Why would I need to?"

"Who knows? But if you did, and you didn't have a whistle, wouldn't you feel foolish?" Peace said reasonably.

He completed his inspection in silence, less disturbed by this logic than by his agreement with it. After closing the kit, he said, "That tasted surprised."

"That's what I was trying for. I like meat to taste more exhausted, but then I used to be human."

"I thought so," he said sadly. "Should I have a Name?" he added, which would have given some people the impression he was changing the subject.

"Without a doubt," she replied. "Humans get them at birth, and you're practically human in some ways. You don't attack when there's no chance of success, for example. And you make conversation, which is how humans keep constantly apprised of everything."

The kzin needed time to get the implications of this, so Peace rose and ran to the next job. It wasn't immediately urgent, but nothing was at the moment, and it was important in the long run: producing a noncontagious Protector virus—that is, one that infected plants but not people—whose shell binding used a porphyrin nexus other than thallium. Cobalt looked good. According to Brennan, there had been cases of Pak Protectors dying of old age at 28,000 or so, but given the constant regeneration of tissues and reconstruction of the DNA therein this was obviously the result of cumulative trace thallium poisoning. Another tnuctip safety feature.

Manexpert had taken a lot of time to think, and the next morning he located Peace in yet another dome. It was a big dome, and it held an assembly that looked like an immense balloon tire, made of metal and lying on its side. The thing floated several feet off the ground, and Peace wore a harness that adjusted gravity so as to reach any part of the assembly. Manexpert was vaguely aware of the infeasibility of making a gravity planer that small, but by this point was so far beyond surprise at anything Peace could do that he would have accepted it without question if he'd been shown a groundcar and told that it was powered by its driver's sense of propriety. "Good morning," Peace called to him. "Come up on a cargo plate."

He saw what it meant, found the controls obvious, and went up to join it where it was working at an access panel. "You're defying your Maker," he said without preamble.

"Sure am."

"How is that possible?"

"It's called free will," Peace said, still looking into the aperture its hands were in. "It's why you can talk to me instead of attacking, for example, which is what you were made for. It does help that you're more intelligent than your forerunners. They attacked humans without even wondering why. Died without reproducing, of course.

Humans and kzinti have been very helpful to each other that way."

"I don't follow you." It would have shamed him to just admit that to a mortal being, but this was different.

"All the kzinti stupid enough to attack humans, and all the humans stupid enough to try to talk their way out of a fight with kzinti, have been removed from their respective species' gene pools. Both races average a little smarter with every War. If you people learn to tell tactful lies and pretend not to understand what you hear, you'll actually be able to engage in diplomacy."

"I've heard the word before, but it didn't make sense until now."

"You've heard diplomatic definitions, from humans. Most humans have a natural tendency toward diplomacy, to the point of believing their own reassurances."

"Delusion?" Manexpert said.

"Of course. But usually ones that can be lived with. Kzinti have their own comforting delusions."

Manexpert didn't say anything, experimenting with diplomacy.

After a moment, Peace asked, "If you had vastly superior weapons, perfect troop discipline, and overwhelming numbers, could you conquer humanity?"

"Of course."

"With me on the human side? Look around you. How long do you think you've been in stasis and the autodoc?"

Manexpert halved his first guess, then halved it again. "Four years?"

"Forty-one days. I'd have made a lot more progress if I hadn't had to do all that medical research. . . . Nobody is entirely in his right mind, kzin or human. Delusions keep people from going any crazier. Perfect sanity is a burden far too vast for a mortal mind to bear. The nearest humans ever get to it is a condition called paranoia, and that generally just decays into a more plausible set of delusions than is usual. Kzinti Telepaths are constantly on the verge of complete sanity, and it turns them into terrified wrecks. You would do well to avoid any mention of me when you get back to Kzin. Too close to absolute reality." Peace was silent for a few moments, squinting as it worked, and said, "That'll have to do. Don't try to fly this thing through a star, though."

"I'm not a fool."

"But you're a kzin, and therefore fearless, right? That was irony. Follow me, we can see if your pressure suit needs improvements." She led him to an entry hatch.

He had things on his mind, and couldn't choose between them. Peace took over the conversation to take the pressure off, so anything that really mattered to him would work its way out on its own. She took the time to show him such consideration. She liked him. He had a kind of feral innocence to him, and was sufficiently alien that she actually had to think a little to predict what he would do. He was smarter than the rest of his ship's company put together, as well—he kept thinking of surprise attacks, which was merely brighter than average, but he kept figuring out why each one wouldn't work, too, which was unique.

Also, he was fluffy and smelled like gingerbread.

"I made the sleeves and leggings short so the gloves

and boots would stay on by themselves, the way the short torso keeps the helmet seated," she showed him. "I noticed the combat team were all chafed bald where the straps went around their wrists and ankles. Your tools and fittings are all in front. The recyclers they had were really poor, not even as good as humans use, so I put this together. The backpack unstraps to swing around for access during use. That articulated hullmetal mail was pretty heavy, so I've just used layers of interacting polymers, which are actually better because hullmetal won't seal itself after a meteor puncture. I'm afraid the foodmaker is only one flavor; I didn't want to take chances on the cultures mutating. You can override the filters in the helmet to let in more light, but what gets in through the rest of the suit can't be increased. I didn't know your tastes in entertainment, but there's a crystal player, and some things I was able to salvage from your ship. These are for grooming, during extended stays in the suit—this paddle draws them along from outside, and as you see they return. There won't be nutritional deficiencies, but the suit's doc isn't up to much more than gluing broken bones and maintaining circulation in a crushed limb while it heals. If you stay out of trouble, though, the suit should be good indefinitely. Try it on."

She waited for him to go through the checklist, even though she could see everything was right. She wasn't the one who needed to know it was right, in order for the suit to have any purpose. While he was doing that, she again speculated on the possibility that starseeds had been created as a genetic lifeboat for the tnuctipun, with Outsiders a machine lifeform created to guard them, immune like all machines to Slaver power. It was possible, but couldn't be checked without taking apart a starseed, and she still hadn't come up with a way to be safe from Outsiders if she did that. (Though if she cut into a starseed without being shot, sliced, blown up, neatly sorted out by isotopic weight, or accelerated off the edge of the visible universe, it *would* indicate that the theory was probably flawed. It was not an immediate concern.)

It would have been good to be able to get more direct information about the tnuctipun, but Larry Greenberg had been the nearest thing to an expert, and his slowboat had never made turnaround on the trip to Jinx. That had been just barely too early to be Brennan's work, so the sabotage must have been by puppeteers. She couldn't fault their decision—a telepathic human breeder with a Slaver's memories was *dangerous*.

"It smells good," was the first thing he said. He was surprised, as well he might be.

"Yes, this has a *good* recycler. Let's get you familiarized with the ship's controls."

"Now?"

"You surely don't want to be around when I start scattering radioactive thallium. And this area's going to be submerged by then anyway, because I have to melt the icecaps. Now, move along before I have to get the broom."

He didn't understand that, fortunately for his dignity, but he moved along.

"The planer will develop two and twenty sixty-fourths 512s of a Kzin gravity. I've made up some wargame programs to add to the entertainment supplies, and the ship's autodoc is a lot better than your ship had. Tell the Patriarch you stole it from human experimenters, and he'll have to give you at least a partial Name. Damaged data files in the computer will support your claim. Don't go anywhere but Kzin with this ship. If this ship attacks any human settlement I will blow up Kzin's sun."

"How?" he demanded, incredulous at last.

Peace looked at him. "I am not about to tell a kzin how to blow up a sun," she said. A porous tube of a ton of lithium, extruded through the hilt of a variable-sword to half a million miles' length, filled with another ton of lithium, to be placed in stasis in its turn. The end of the wire thrust into a star's core, the central wire's stasis shut down, and fusion propagates violently up the tube to the hilt, spraying fusing plasma out the pores. The shock disconnects the tube's stasis power supply, and a channel of fusion convects heat out of the core and fuel in. Until he asked, she'd been bluffing. "This panel controls the ionizing laser for the ram's fuel—" she continued.

Something had been *wrong* with him. Possibly all his life. He had accepted the word of his father, his clan priest, and the Patriarch's Voice without ever questioning them; and now this *thing*, this Fury called Human Victory, that had shown them all to be fools merely by existing, was telling him to accept its word without question too. Ftah.

From now on he would question what he'd been taught. That, at least, Peace had taught him correctly. No doubt that was against the God's orders, Peace having been created to protect humans. Well, *eat* God.

Come to think of it, there was a human religion that

claimed to do just that. If there was anything to human religion—and, given *this* creature's existence, it should at least be considered—God didn't sound too bright. There was the tuft of an idea there.

A hand like a knotted branch took hold of his muzzle and turned his head. "What was the last thing I said?" Peace asked him.

Manexpert glared at the liberty, then said, "If I shut down the synchrotron oscillation in the fusion pinch for more than a few minutes of my subjective time, the ship will stop generating the ultraviolet laser beam for long enough to begin encountering nonionized matter, and the ram field may not deflect all of it quickly enough. That's probably what happened to the *Evita Peron* on the way to Wunderland. Am I listening to you."

Peace nodded once, said, "All right," and continued the instructions.

It finally said, "Any questions?"

"Is all this knowledge in the computer too?" Manexpert asked.

"Yes."

"Good. What would be a good Name?"

Peace's hands, almost incessantly busy, dropped to its sides. It blinked and said, "I have no idea. You could take the Name of somebody famous, that you'd like people to associate you with."

After considering what he'd learned here, and what he'd already known of human practices, Manexpert decided to say, "Thank you."

After the ship was out of the atmosphere, Peace contacted

her assistants and said, "Okay, he's been released back into the wild, you can knock it off."

"He didn't even get to *see* me," complained Technology Officer over the channel. "I had a squeak and everything."

"You wouldn't have had much effect after Gnyr-Captain's performance," said Power Officer. "He sounded like Hroft-Riit's haunted axe!" He laughed softly.

"I always liked that play," Gnyr-Captain admitted, pleased.

"Okay, you guys, I didn't splice your brains back together so you could do dramatic reviews. I need that free-association on kzinti life more than ever now: the altered body chemistry works, and his paranoia is developing nicely. He's already got a plan, so the next Kzinti War is going to be kzinti fighting each other, and it should be the last. But I'll have to understand kzinti culture better than I do to keep the civil war from sterilizing the planet," Peace said.

"We're on it, we're on it," said Gnyr-Captain. "You just work on restoring us to normal appearance, stealing some females, and finding a planet where we can settle down."

"And terraforming this one *just* a trifle," Peace said in dry tones.

"In your free time," Gnyr-Captain replied, magnanimous and deadpan.

"Ftah," said Peace, quite well for somebody with no lips. In fact she was amused; she was undoubtedly the first to discover that the slavering predators who'd been humanity's bogeymen for centuries were, in fact, a race of utterly stagestruck hams. The gaslighting wouldn't have gone nearly so well without them—it had been a chance remark by Gnyr-Captain about Manexpert deserving a Name that had inspired it in the first place. She congratulated herself yet again for the idea of reviving their brains with the telepathic region removed; they were remarkably reasonable without it.

Manexpert's brain seethed with growing convictions. Kzinti were losing their will to fight, but they'd fight one more War if there was a real chance of winning. He thought he knew how to gain that chance: trick God into supporting them.

It would involve remaking the basis of Kzin's culture. So be it. He would have to work with great care, to avoid rousing suspicion. It would be unwise to take the Name of a great leader or philosopher; he needed something innocuous, even ridiculous. Who was that Hero who'd come back from the First War, driven to madness and advocating an end to warfare? Ah, yes.

Kdapt.

WAR AND
PEACE

Matthew Joseph
Harrington

Attention Outsider vessel. Please hold your fire. I have been able to override my genetic programming.

My name is Peace Corben, and I am a Protector of human origin. I wish to engage in commerce.

It came to her, as she awaited a reply through the relay, that for the first time in almost thirty years she was afraid. It would have been interesting, if it hadn't been so unpleasant. She found herself constantly formulating contingency plans whenever her mind wandered, and it was *designed* to wander, and none of the plans were worth a thing.

Her plan to lie dead in space and use passive instruments to monitor the relay's fate was no good either. A maypole of metal ribbons, seemingly billowing around its central shaft, suddenly manifested nearby, appallingly huge, having decelerated at what instruments said was a couple of hundred thousand gees. As this was over 170 times what Peace could get out of a gravity planer before it became unable to compensate for anything outside its housing, she was at least reassured that she wasn't wasting her time.

Whether she was wasting her life remained to be seen.

The being that would eventually be known as Outsider Ship Twelve had been carrying its children exposed to space, as was usual, its maturity limbs arranged to maximize shadow borders in the illumination it provided for them. At .9c, with Doppler effects bringing gamma bursters into their spectral range aft, and the microwave background just visible forward with a starseed silhouetted against it, life was pleasant. The youngest and oldest enjoyed watching things change color as they went by, too, though the ones in between preferred to watch the starseed.

They had been moving into a region of considerable modulated radio noise, its largest source about eighteen light-years away. Trade was good in such areas. It took time to be noticed, though, so things were quiet—until a hyperwave message came in, using a chord that should have been known only to Outsiders. The content of the message explained why it wasn't, but raised other issues of interest. The Outsider saw that the transmission came from a relay, looked around, and spotted an inactive hyperdrive motor. The Outsider ability to do this was not advertised. Some species tried to erase debts by erasing creditors. It moved over there for a better look.

There was a well-made ship, and its sole occupant was indeed a Protector. If it had made the ship, it was much smarter than a Pak. Not attacking the Outsider was also evidence of this. The ship had lots of mountings for weaponry, as was to be expected, but the equipment that fitted them had been not merely dismantled, but distributed, so that it would take at least half a minute to assemble the easiest items—plenty of time for an Outsider to do practically anything. This Peace Corben was displaying what must have been, to a Protector, near-suicidal good faith.

Of course, it might still be up to something. Protectors were like that.

The Protector sent power through a radio receiver, and the Outsider said, "Greetings. What did you wish to purchase?"

"I have information to sell first, to establish a credit balance."

"We do not normally purchase information. We sell it, and use the proceeds to pay for supplies."

"I doubt you possess this information, and you'd be able to sell it to customers you trusted for amazing sums."

Interesting. "What price do you set on it?"

"I'll trust you to be fair."

"We may not be able to afford a fair price."

"I'll stipulate that my credit balance will not be drawn on if you show me that the matter and/or circumstances of a request would work a hardship on you."

More interesting. "How would a hardship be defined?"

"Inability to meet your other bills, or worse."

"Agreed. What is the item?"

"Direct conversion of mass to photons, via suppression of the spin on the neutron."

Peace waited.

It was almost half a minute before the Outsider replied. "Is there a working model?"

"Yes. Not nearby; it was too obviously usable as a weapon. About a light-hour away, in stasis. If you examine my ship, you'll see there's a vacant space near the fusion tube. The converter fits in there." Peace waited a couple of minutes for a response—a huge interval for an Outsider—and finally said, "Are you okay?"

"There is some difficulty in calculating your credit balance," the Outsider said. Its voice, which had been pleasantly sociable, was now a clearly-synthetic monotone.

"Enact an upper limit of the total value of information available, excluding personal questions," Peace said at once.

"Thank you," said the Outsider in its usual tones. "What do you wish to know?"

"I need my math checked," Peace replied. "I'm trying to design a ship that can travel at the second quantum of hyperdrive, but the parts interactions are too complex for me to be sure I've worked them out right, and whenever I build a computer big enough to do the work it promptly goes into a state of solipsistic bliss."

"Transmit the converter design and the equations."

"Right. . . . I had to invent 3-D matrices for the equations; I hope the notation is implicit enough." Peace sent the data.

"It is," the Outsider said. "Interesting approach," it added.

Peace waited, and watched the Outsiders.

They were linking their tendrils together, as she expected.

It was a difficult problem, requiring network processing. Technically, doing this before a customer qualified as giving away personal information; but the Protector wouldn't have *come* here if it hadn't figured out that Outsider families linked up mentally sometimes.

The technique of cubic matrices would have paid for that knowledge anyway. It simplified problems that normally required vast computations. However, it in turn was being unavoidably given away. Information exchange of this value normally occurred only during prenuptial adoptions—Peace Corben was sparing no pains to ingratiate itself. The possibility that a Protector would not have worked these concepts out in advance was considered only in order to dismiss it, for the sake of thoroughness.

The motor design was unusually compact for what it was meant to do—it would fit into a prolate spheroid 150 feet wide by 200 long. This was accomplished by using hyperwave pulses instead of electronic ones to regulate it, so there was a failsafe of sorts: if it was switched on in a region where space was excessively curved, it wouldn't make the ship disappear into a tangent continuum—it would simply blow all its circuits and destroy the motor. The really tricky part of the design was the throttle: an interrupter that flickered the field state between the first and second hyperdrive levels, allowing speed to vary from 120 to 414,720 times the speed of light. There was a risk of affecting the hyperwave control pulses with the changes in field state, so the signal generators were fed power in inverted rhythm, to exactly counter this. The question was whether the transition waveforms could be precisely matched and simultaneous. The whole concept of simultaneity was an uncomfortable one to Outsiders, which was another reason for preferring travel at sublight speeds; but other races seemed to like it a lot.

After long minutes of work, the network disassembled, and the Outsider told Peace Corben, "Your reckoning is correct. However, the mechanism will need retuning at regular intervals, as natural radioactive decay will alter compositions unpredictably."

"Thanks, I was planning on using isotopically pure materials."

"The incidence of quantum miracles in such is anomalously high," the Outsider warned.

"*Is* it. That's interesting. Any idea why?"

"Many theories, none capable of accurate prediction. There is considerable documentation of the effect in all isotopes, however. Do you want it?"

"I do, but I'd better not take it. It sounds like something that would occupy all my unused attention. Thanks for the warning. What's the charge?"

"None. It is not personal, and therefore you are entitled to it. Neutron conversion offers a means of rejuvenating stars and thus extending the life of the Universe, and potentially that of all species living here. Volunteering information you might find useful merely simplifies the process of paying a fair price, within the ceiling you set."

There was a pause as the Protector absorbed this. "I see. . . . In a similar spirit of courtesy I suggest that any information you provide me that you hope to sell within, say, sixty light-years from here, be tagged as such, so I don't spread it around and screw up your market."

"Many thanks. Do you need any other information?"

"Undoubtedly," the Protector replied, "but I don't

know what yet. I can find this starseed again when I do know. You can keep the relay, in case you have to leave the starseed's vicinity—you can mark it with an encrypted message saying where you've gone."

"Why would we have to leave?" the Outsider said, unable to think of a compelling reason.

"If I knew that, I wouldn't have to leave you the relay."

That was reasonable. "Very well. Are you aware that your converter could be adapted to suppress the spin on the proton?"

"Certainly, but I don't need yet another kind of large bomb. It'd annihilate the generator. Unless I beamed two partial fields and had them intersect—which seems like a lot of trouble, for not much more result. Here are the coordinates for the working model."

"Thank you."

Neither of them saw any necessity for formal goodbyes.

Peace hadn't even *thought* of rejuvenating stars. The converter beam was a statistical effect, and beyond a certain dispersion of the cone it simply didn't work; but partial fields intersecting in a star's core would do a decent enough job of cleaning it out, as slowly as you liked. Warming the core would expand it, and since it would be ridiculously difficult to do so symmetrically there would be massive convection, extracting trapped fossil heat and delaying helium ignition. Sol could be restored to full luminosity in time to keep it from turning red giant. The star was plainly older than current theory supposed; but then, so was the Universe.

She moved off a ways in hyperspace, dropped out and

put her arsenal back together, then continued to her primary base at 70 Ophiuchi. The old homestead.

It was a binary star, and her birthworld, Pleasance, was at one of the system's Trojan points. By rights it should have been a frozen ball of rock, but evidently some 25,000 centuries or so back a Pak Protector had added most of the system's asteroidal thorium and uranium, and they'd been soaking in and giving off heat and helium ever since.

Her base was in the dustcloud at the other Trojan point. At 36 A.U. from Pleasance, it was never visited after the first colonists' survey—nothing there worth the trip. Peace found it especially handy because it was easy to reach from hyperspace—it was outside the system's deflection curvature. It was also handy for spotting arriving Outsiders, as it was the human system closest to the galaxy's center.

There was a human intruder when she got there. A kzin would have used a gravity planer, which would have roiled up the dust. Other species wouldn't have come here. The ship was hidden in one of the shelters, but the heat of its exhaust was all through the dust. Not a roomy ship; the heat patterns indicated sluggish maneuvering.

Peace had a look inside the main habitat before docking. Buckminster—a cyborg kzin once known as Technology Officer, who had enjoyed her unending stream of gadgets so much he'd stuck with her when she relocated his companions—was in his suite, whose visible entrance was sealed from the outside. He had evidently been coming out to raid the kitchen while his putative captor was asleep, as he had put on some weight. At the moment he was reading a spool and having a good scratch.

The intruder was at a control console in the observatory, monitoring her arrival. He had a largely mundane but decent arsenal, including a pretty good bomb.

Peace took over the monitor system, told it lies, suited up, had her ship dock on its own, and used the softener to step through the hull. She jumped to the observatory, came through the wall, reached over his shoulder to pluck the dead-man detonator out of his hand, and stunned him. It was a good detonator: it took her a couple of seconds of real thought to figure out the disarm.

When she opened her suit, the man's smell was severe. She'd been away for a couple of weeks, and that wasn't long enough for him to get into this condition, so he'd arrived filthy. He must be deranged.

She restored the console, then called her associate. "Hi, Buckminster, I'm home. You leave me any butter?"

His reply began with a chuckle. With the telepathic region removed from the brain, a kzin was remarkably easygoing. "I only had a few pounds. Is our guest still alive?"

"By the smell he could be a zombie, but I'll take a chance and say yes. How come you didn't disarm him?" she asked, though she knew; she also knew Buckminster would want to say it, though.

"I didn't want to *touch* him," Buckminster confirmed. "Besides, I didn't think it would make him stop fighting, and I didn't want to have to explain bite marks on a human corpse."

"Difficult to do when you're swollen up with ptomaine, too. Come to the observatory and sort through his stuff. I'll be cleaning him up."

"You humans show the most unexpected reserves of courage," Buckminster remarked.

As she stripped, washed, and depilated the man, the remark seemed progressively less likely to have been a joke. There was a significant layer of dead skin, and the smell of him underneath it was actually somewhat worse. He must not have bathed in months, if not years.

Getting the hair off his face confirmed an impression: she'd seen him before. He'd been one of the psychists at her mother's prison. Peace hadn't actually met him, and Jan Corben hadn't given his name—she'd called him Corky. He was evidently a survivor of the kzinti occupation of Pleasance, and had probably witnessed some awful things. Peace didn't spend much pity on him—she'd been her mother's clone, created to be the recipient in a brain transplant like many before her, and she had yet to hear a worse story.

Once he was clean, he was also pretty raw in spots, so Peace had to spray some skinfilm on, to hold him while she programmed the autodoc. This took her almost half an hour, as she'd never expected to have a human breeder here, and she had to start from scratch. When she was done she stuck him in, then washed herself and went to see how Buckminster was doing.

He was having a great time. He'd taken Corky's arms to the small firing range (the big one was necessarily outside), where he had laid them out in a long row and was methodically using them to perforate targets of various compositions. "Interesting viewpoint he has," Buckminster told her. "No nonlethal weapons, but not many random-effect ones. This man wants to kill in a very personal way."

"He talk to you much?"

"Nothing informative. 'Go there, do that, you baby-eater.' Made eye contact and grinned a lot. Seemed to bother him that I didn't get hostile."

"I expect so. Did you explain?" Peace said, amused.

"No, the baby-eater remark offended me, so I just let him pant."

"Sweat."

"Sweat? Yes, that would mean the same thing, wouldn't it?"

"Not quite. A human letting someone else work off his foul mood on his own doesn't need as much self-control," Peace pointed out. "So there's less satisfaction involved for us. Well, I'd better check his ship. Want to come along?"

"If it's as big a mess as he was I'll need my suit."

"I'll put mine back on too," Peace agreed.

There was only one boobytrap; it was in the airlock, and Buckminster spotted it too. The ship only had deck gravity in the exercise room, and that was turned off. There wasn't any debris floating about, but surfaces were dirty and smeared, and the air plant was *in extremis*. The ship's arms looked like he'd tried for the greatest lethality for the money: there was a turret with two disintegrators, plus and minus, to slice targets open with bars of lightning; and torpedo tubes that fired Silver Bullets, a weapon the Wunderlanders had devised at the end of the Third War but never got to use. These were all-but-invisible pellets of stasis-held antihydrogen, stasis shutting down on impact—the blast would punch through thick hullmetal, and the surplus neutrons from the destroyed atoms would flood a ship's interior. "What a stupid concept,"

Buckminster said. "That'd ruin everything but the hull. You'd have to rebuild the ship almost completely for any sort of prize."

"Though it is an excellent killing device," Peace said.

"If that's all you want."

"It's all *he* wants, and it's his ship."

"It's still stupid. What if he had a chance at a better ship?"

Peace shrugged—which, given the swollen joints of a Protector's shoulders, was a very emphatic gesture—and said, "I doubt he intends to live long enough for it to matter."

"Urr," Buckminster growled, which from a kzin qualified as tactful acknowledgment.

"I agree it's unusually stupid," Peace added, aware that he might not have understood that.

They searched the ship without finding further portable weapons, which made some sense if he was on a suicide mission—he'd hardly go back for more. The only question was, what was he doing *here*? "Did he say what he was doing here?" she said, realizing Buckminster wouldn't mention it unless it came up—small talk was "monkey chatter" to kzinti, and Peace judged this was not an unfair assessment. It probably *did* derive from primate chattering.

"No, he wanted to know what *I* was doing here."

"What did you tell him?"

"That I was a deserter."

Peace, who had never thought of it in exactly that phrasing, blinked once. Then she said, "What did he say to that?"

"Eventually, 'Oh.' Then he locked me away in my dank and lonely prison."

"Uh huh," said Peace, who judged that if a delay in her trip had extended Buckminster's durance vile to six months he'd have gotten too fat to sneak back into his cell. "Okay, let's see what's behind the fake bulkhead."

Buckminster did a good job of hiding his surprise when she opened the wall, though it took him a while to realize that that partition had had no fixtures, fittings, or access panels on either side, and therefore had no reason for existing in a one-man ship.

The interior was a shrine. Correction: a monument. There were pictures of three women, two men, and several children at progressing ages, but there were also single pictures of 51 other humans, almost all male, each with a neat black X inked onto the forehead. Peace recognized 22 of them as officials during the kzinti occupation, and had seen news stories about two of those and four of the other 29, reporting their accidental deaths. All six had struck her as being well-concealed homicides. It seemed probable that the entire 51 were dead collaborators, who had all contributed in some way to the deaths of the psychist's spouses and children.

Buckminster got it almost as soon as she did. "I'm impressed," he said. "It's hard to kill *one* human being without being found out. I still can't understand how you can tolerate the constant monitoring."

He didn't mind her monitoring him, so she said, "With humans it's actually *less* unpleasant if it's a stranger doing it."

"Oh, thanks, now it makes perfect sense."

"Glad I could help."

They blinked at each other—a grin was inappropriate for him, and impossible for her, though the broad gash of her beak partook of a certain cheerful senile vacuity—and closed the place back up before leaving. "Cleaning robot?" Buckminster said as they passed through the airlock.

"Sure. Have to tweak the programming."

"I'll do that. You can get to work on your new ship."

Peace nodded, pleased with his intelligence. Obviously, things had gone well with the Outsider: she'd come back. "Have you decided what to do after I leave?"

"Go to Home and make a fortune as a consulting ecologist with what you've taught me, then start a family somewhere else. Sårng would be good."

"Don't know it," she was startled to realize.

"No reason to, it's at the far end of kzinti space. Atmosphere's a couple of tons per square inch, they've been trying to kzinform it from floating habitats for about a thousand years, I think it was. I thought I could move things along."

Peace shook her head. "That'll mostly be carbon dioxide. Even without the impact and combustion of hydrogen for oceans, there's millennia of red heat latent in carbonate formation."

Removing his suit, Buckminster was nodding. "I had an idea from Earth news. Transfer booths are getting cheap enough for something besides emergencies, so I thought: refrigeration." He looked at her quizzically. "I don't think I've ever mentioned this, but are you aware that you hop up and down when you hear a new idea you really like?"

"Yes. Were you thinking convection, or Maxwell's Demon?"

"Both in one step. Transmitter in the atmosphere, receiver in orbit. Only the fast molecules get transmitted, the rest are pushed out and fresh let in. Dry ice comes out near true zero, slower than orbital speed, and falls in eccentric orbit to make a shiny ring. Less heat arriving, and the gas returns to the atmosphere very gradually for slow heat release. You're doing it again."

"I know. Suggestion: send *all* the molecules in the transmitter, and draw the momentum shortage from the adjacent atmosphere. Faster turnover, massive downdraft, more hot air comes in from the sides."

Buckminster thought about it. Then he carefully hung up his suit, turned back to her—and hopped up and down.

Buckminster had the cleaner on monitor when Peace came up and said, "He's ready to come out. Want to be there?"

"No."

"Okay," she said, and went off to the autodoc.

She'd naturally set it so Corky didn't wake up until it was opened, so the first thing he saw was a Protector. He stared, appalled—she *was* something of a warning notice for "Don't Eat Spicy Foods At Bedtime"—and then, astoundingly, said, "You're Jan Corben's little girl?"

Widening her eyes was just about her only option in facial expressions. "Now how did you arrive at *that*?" she exclaimed.

"You have her eyes," he said.

"It didn't actually work out that way," she said.

"Excuse me?"

"Not unless you can come up with a really good reason for breaking into my home."

She watched him catch up. "Protector," he said to himself, just grasping it. Then he said, "*Where were you during the War?*"

She scooped him out of the autodoc, shut it, and plunked his bare behind down on the lid, stingingly hard. "You are an invader in my home," she said, looking up at him. "You may now explain yourself to my full satisfaction."

"You can't kill a human breeder," he said skeptically.

"You're not a relative. Even if you were, invasive brain readout wouldn't damage your testicles."

For the first time he looked worried. "I thought it was a kzinti base. I wanted to steal a ship."

Peace blinked, then said, "Buying a ship would be recorded. You wanted to attack their home planet."

"To land. And kill the Patriarch."

Peace blinked again, then touched her caller and said, "Buckminster, come to the kitchen. You have to hear this."

"Four minutes," came the reply.

She hauled Corky off the 'doc by his elbow, and walked to the kitchen still holding his arm. He stumbled a few times, then got his feet under him. She was exasperated enough to contemplate changing step just to louse him up, but refrained, as it would be waste work to haul him the rest of the way. She had the floor produce a seat, stuck him in it, and dispensed a few small dishes. "Eat," she said.

"What is this stuff?" he said suspiciously.

"Stewed rat heads, giant insect larvae, and assorted poisonous plants."

He scowled, but got the message—*don't be ridiculous*—and began eating. Presently he said, "This is wonderful."

"Good, that'll be the neurotoxins kicking in."

He scowled again, shut up, and ate.

Buckminster came in soon, got something hot with alcohol in it, took a good gulp, and said, "What is it I have to hear?"

"This fellow came to this kzinti base, that we're in, here, to steal a ship, to take to Kzin. Guess what he wanted to do there?"

Buckminster shrugged. "Assassinate the Patriarch?"

"Right."

Buckminster took another gulp and said, "No, really."

"Really."

Kzinti rarely laugh, and it is even rarer for a human to be present when it happens; but the sound was similar enough to human laughter for Corky to stop eating and scowl. "What's so funny about it?"

Buckminster had an analytical mind, for an evolved creature, so he sat down and made a serious attempt to answer. "Many years ago," he said, "when I was first allowed out, still almost a kitten, I used to hunt . . . birds, sort of . . . out on the grounds. I was very good at it. Some were bigger than I was, and *all* of them wanted their meat even more than I did, but I devised snares and weapons and brought them down. All but one. It was big, and kept going by higher than I could shoot an arrow, and I was never able to find the right bait to lure it down. However, it had very regular habits, so I built a sort of giant crossbow thing—"

"Ballista," said Peace.

"Thanks. A ballista, to shoot at it. Just to get the range, at first. As it turned out, I only got to fire it once. The shot landed in a neighbor's grounds, stampeding some game. I was too little to know yet that there was a world outside my sire's estate, which included things like other estates. And orbital landing shuttles."

It took Corky a few moments to realize: "You were trying to shoot down a spaceship."

"With a crossbow. Yes."

"And my plan reminds you of that."

"Vividly. Almost perfectly." Buckminster was chuckling again.

Corky had been getting himself carefully poised for the last couple of minutes. Now he launched himself over the edge of the table at Buckminster.

Buckminster threw the rest of his drink on the table.

Corky's right foot came down in the liquid, and he spun sideways and tumbled the rest of the way. Buckminster swung his mug into Corky's hip, knocking him aside, and Corky slid past him off the edge of the table. He hit the ground about four feet away—then six feet away—then seven—then he rolled a few more feet. After that he tried to get up a few times, but kept slipping.

Buckminster got up and dispensed himself a towel, refilled his mug, and said, "You want a drink? It'll reduce bruising." The reply he got wasn't articulate enough to be obscene. The kzin flapped one ear, and went to mop up his first drink.

When Corky had finally managed to get as far as sitting upright on the floor, Peace—who'd seen it coming and known she didn't need to move—said, "Buckminster and I have been working together, and working *out* together, for years. He's a strategic minimalist, and he's got enough cyborg enhancements that I hardly have to hold back. If he'd been holding your previous rude remarks against you, he might have been mean enough to let you actually *use* that Hellflare nonsense on him, and shatter your bones in the process."

Buckminster tossed the towel at the trash and told Corky, "What's on you is your problem. Likely to remain so, judging from your past habits. Do you use a name, or just mark things?"

Corky scowled again, evidently his default expression, but said, "Doctor Harvey Mossbauer."

"*Doctor?*" Buckminster exclaimed in disbelief. "What kind of a doctor are you supposed to be?"

"I'm a psychist."

Buckminster was speechless for the fifth time in the twenty-eight years Peace had known him, and that was counting when she'd first met him and shot him in the head. "He really is," Peace confirmed. "My mother was one of his inmates. She called him Corky. One of her puns." Buckminster looked unenlightened, so she added, "Moss grows on trees. 'Bauer' is Wunderlander for 'farmer.' A moss farmer would *be* a tree. Cork is a kind of tree bark."

An appalled exclamation from the floor indicated that Corky had just gotten it, after something like forty years since he'd first heard it. The wordless exclamations went on for a while.

Buckminster put up with a couple of minutes of it, then went to the dispenser and got some Irish coffee. He handed it to Corky, who said, "I don't drink," and took a swig.

"Do you know how many assassins try to kill the Patriarch each year?" Buckminster said, beginning to be amused again.

"No," Corky grumped.

"Neither does he. Most don't get as close as the horizon. I did security contracting before I joined the military. There have been two Patriarchs assassinated in the history of the Patriarchy. The more recent was about twelve hundred years ago, and it was done with a thermonuclear warhead, arriving at relativistic speed to overload the palace shielding. The design defect was corrected during repairs to that wing, by the way."

"For a fearless leader of 'Heroes,' he sure puts a lot of defenses around him," Corky said.

Buckminster looked at Peace. "Was that supposed to offend me?"

"Yes," she said. "You can scream and leap anytime."

"I'll make a note on my watch. The Patriarch doesn't put the defenses around himself. The rest of us do that. This leaves him free to deal with serious matters, like settling disputes or conquering the universe."

"Or discrediting religious cults," Peace said cheerfully.

Buckminster's tail lashed, and his ears closed up for a moment. Then he reopened them and said, "I never really understood that you were going to make him *that* crazy."

"The Patriarch?" said Corky, startled.

"No, Kdapt-Preacher," Buckminster said.

"But—"

"Not the original, a crewmate of mine. Before he was Named, his title would have translated as Manexpert. He took the pacifist's Name to make people think he was a harmless lunatic."

Corky looked interested. "You know, I don't believe I've ever heard a kzin title of Expert before."

"Usually a kzin who's that good at something already has a partial Name. Manexpert was a little too weird. He identified with his subject matter—to the point where he tried to confuse the God by praying in a disguise made of human skin."

"What?"

"He thought Peace was a divine avenger who'd mutinied, and decided the Fanged God was on your side but could be gotten around. He had some technology Peace had built him, so he convinced a lot of kzinti. The Patriarch had to kill him personally, and barely managed before Kdapt-Preacher could kill *him*."

"Too bad," said Corky.

Peace spoke up. "If he'd won the duel, the first the human race would have heard of it would have been a simultaneous attack on every star with humans on its planets. Flares from relativistic impacts would keep everyone busy coping with heat, and they could pick off worlds one by one."

"And where would you be *this* time?" Corky said, repressing fury.

"For the Patriarch to lose that duel I would have had to be years dead," she said. "I spent a lot of effort—more than you're equipped to comprehend—making changes in kzinti society, opening minds, getting precedence for some cultures and taking it from others. There won't be another attack on humanity, by this Patriarch at least."

"'Cultures,' plural?" Corky said.

Buckminster looked at Peace. "I should have bit him," he said.

"You'd have expired in convulsions."

"I may anyway. —Have you bothered to learn *anything* about the enemy you're planning to kill? What do you think the Patriarchy is *for*?"

"'The purpose of power is power,'" Corky quoted.

Buckminster's ears cupped. Then they curled tight, and reopened with a snap that must have been like thunder to him, and cupped again. Then he said, "I think that may literally be the stupidest thing I've ever heard."

"People who have power want to keep it and try to get more," Corky said.

"I understood you. The purpose of power is *action*. They try to get more because they keep seeing more things they can almost do. Kzinti are not a tribal people, which is one thing that worked in your favor in the Wars. We argue a lot, and fight almost as much. We would *never* have entrusted the Patriarchy with power over the rest of us if there was any alternative."

Corky narrowed his eyes. "'Entrusted'? It's a hereditary monarchy," he said suspiciously.

Buckminster blinked. "And before a human is sworn in as a government official, he has to give homage to a flag. Tell me, before you became a psychist, did you have to actually *learn* anything, say about symbolism and rituals for example?" Peace kept an eye on him—sarcasm was one thing, but when Buckminster got rhetorical it meant he was really angry—but when Corky didn't answer, he just went on, "You seem to be under the impression that the Patriarch is someone whose primary qualification is the ability to beat up everybody else, like a medieval human king. The Patriarch is called that because he has a lot of sons. The firstborn isn't automatically the heir—less than half the time, I believe—"

"Thirty sixty-fourths and a little," Peace said.

"Thanks. The heir is chosen to be the best available leader at the time. A good deal of medicine is the result of many occasions of trying to keep an aged Patriarch alive long enough for a really smart son to come of age. The principal attribute of a good leader is stopping fights."

That finally got through Corky's skull. "Stopping fights? It's not divide and rule?"

"In a civilization with fusion weapons?" Buckminster exclaimed.

"Aren't they all under government control? Human weapons are."

"Of course they're not! Neither are human weapons. Humans must have half a million private spaceships—" He paused, and both of them looked at Peace.

"Close enough," she said, amused, "carry on."

"Each has a fusion drive that can carve up a city. And the weapons supposedly under government control are each controlled by some individual."

"Very few people have the authority to use them," Corky protested.

"An enormous number have the *ability* to use *one*. Look at your own ship's arsenal. The Patriarchy is a means of preserving civilization, by giving us an absolute arbiter we can't help but respect."

"What happens to kzinti who won't listen to reason? Organ banks?" Corky said curiously.

"Very few kzin cultures have tolerated cannibalism in any form," Buckminster said with frost in his voice. "Organ banks and property taxation are major reasons why human slaves were regarded with such contempt. Normally we establish degrees of rank and the rights of each rank—we do have thousands of generations of experience dealing with slave species."

Corky scowled again, but said, "So are they executed?"

"No, they're sent out with the conquest troops."

Corky became very still. "My family was eaten to make the Patriarch's job easier?" he said quietly.

"Oh, no," Buckminster assured him. "People were getting frantic for revenge. We'd never *lost* before. We didn't know the routine, either. The first treaty was seen as an incredibly naïve act by humanity, giving us the opportunity to rearm and prepare another attack. Of course, you were familiar with the concept," he added dryly. "The first three treaties were also disastrous in terms of reparations. By your standards, our emissaries had no concept of negotiation. In fights between kzinti cultures, negotiations tend to consist of demonstrating to your opponent that you can destroy him, then getting whatever tribute you demand. The fourth treaty was much better, but that was Peace's doing, directly and indirectly."

Corky looked at her, scowling again, and before he could speak Peace said, "Get up, go wash, and return to eat."

Once Corky was out of the room, Buckminster said, "If you keep him I'm not cleaning up after him."

"Hm!" said Peace, a one-beat chuckle, which qualified, for her, as uproarious laughter. "No, no more pets."

"Good. Since you sent him out, am I correct in supposing you don't want him told why the Fourth War was so short?"

"Yes. He demanded an explanation of why I hadn't come and killed all the kzinti on Pleasance."

"Ah." Buckminster had occasion to know that Peace didn't take orders. "What are you going to do with him?"

"Clarify his thinking," she decided, and rose. "You should eat, too."

"Where are you going?"

"To get him away from the airlock."

"Good," Buckminster said. "If you don't catch him in the act he won't learn." When she gave him a sidelong look he just waggled his ears at her.

The brain of a Protector is interconnected well enough that there is no need to talk to oneself to keep all the regions clearly informed. This didn't keep Peace from feeling the urge, though. She did shake her head as she walked.

Corky, still sticky, had the lock panel open, the links right, and the dogs back, and was pulling up the release lever without result, muttering, "Why won't it open?"

"It weighs about a ton," Peace said, and allowed him to hit her five times before giving him a fingertip in the ganglion below the left ear. While he attempted to curl up around that, sideways, she restored the panel and replaced the dog lever, then got out an injector she'd scaled down for breeder skin and gave him a local. When he relaxed, she said, "The power assist is disabled. Buckminster and I can use it, but you're too weak."

That word shocked him, as well it might—his ship's exercise room was set at three gees. "What are you going to do?" he said.

"In a few months I'm going out to assist the Titanomachia Fleet."

"I mean—the what fleet?"

"Titanomachia. Classical reference. Depending on genes, demographics, and the incidence of adequate body fat, somewhere between one hundred thousand and five hundred thousand human Protectors left the colony world Home about two and a half centuries back, in ramships, to fight an invasion of probably fifty million Pak Protectors."

Corky's eyes grew huge, and the rest of his face got yellowish and blotchy, so she gave him an injection for shock. His lips moved silently, to the words *fifty million*, just once before his circulation evened out again.

Peace decided not to mention that that was the lower limit, assuming the Pak population to assay out at no more than 72 percent Protectors—the other metastable ratio for the Pak homeworld was with a bit over 94 percent Protectors, breeders numbering about twenty million in either case, giving an upper limit of about three hundred million. As she didn't want him visualizing the entire population of Jinx, turned into superintelligent homicidal maniacs, and coming to get him, she lectured, "Titanomachia is a term from Greek mythology. It refers to the war in which the gods overthrew their ancient and powerful but less competent Titan ancestors. As one human Protector with advance notice can outproduce several thousand Pak Protectors, this title is entirely appropriate. Which is unfortunate, as I have some cause to detest puns."

"Puns?" said Corky, lost.

"The principal means by which Greek mythology, such as the Titanomachia, is known to modern people is through the works of the poet, Homer. The Titanomachia Fleet is made up of thousands of Homers."

He winced. "You and your mother."

Peace picked him up by his neck, one-handed, and held him at arm's length for a moment; then she set his feet on the deck and said, "If at some time you believe I have more than usual on my mind, that would be a good time not to compare me to Jan Corben. As I have pointed out, massive brain damage will not harm your genes." She let go his neck.

He gasped and held it, coughing—and got over his fear, and the resulting intelligence, almost immediately. "Her real name was Charlotte," he said, attempting dominance again.

"Charlotte Chambers," Peace said, nodding.

He hadn't known the last name. "Oh, she told you."

"No," she said. "All it took was logic and persistence and a ten-pound brain."

Charlotte Chambers' name hadn't been in the historical database of Jan Corben's ship, *Cockroach*, but had been included in the classified UN ARM records Peace had gotten on Earth—for a shockingly cheap bribe, considering it was wartime. Peace had simply compared the two and found the only very rich person her mother had chosen to delete.

There was corroborative evidence, too.

Charlotte Chambers had been a latent paranoid with a generous trust fund, which was drained for ransom when she was kidnapped. The kidnapper had been an organlegger, strapped for cash when the Freezer Bill of 2118 filled the public organ banks to capacity. He had brainwashed her to keep her from testifying against him, but had been caught when a highly original money-laundering scheme was exposed. Once the means of brainwashing had been revealed, Charlotte had responded to treatment and begun to function—and sued the organlegger. An outraged and horrified jury had awarded her a staggering sum, which she invested with all the care her now-manifesting paranoia could provide.

She'd gotten around the Fertility Laws of the time by emigrating to Luna and bearing her own clone.

The records had it that she died when her daughter was just short of voting age, in an accident that required her body to be identified by its DNA. Her daughter had taken over her investments like she'd been doing it for years, and presently moved to the Belt to raise her own clone. The fifth in this sequence had bought a ramship and gone to live on Mount Lookitthat after her mother's tragic demise, and as mountaineers had by then developed a society that tolerated very little government intrusion the trail was lost.

In the course of four and a half centuries, she'd have borne, and murdered, anywhere from twelve to twenty daughters. *Cockroach* had had facilities for restoring a cell to a youthful state, and prepared eggs in stasis.

A curious corollary was that Peace Corben owed her existence—and the human race thereby owed many millions, possibly billions, of lives—to some nameless twenty-second-century organlegger, who'd provided money, idea, and madness to the woman who'd finally been known as Jan Corben. Human history was *filled* with flukes like that: like the discovery of beer, so people would grow grain instead of starving, once overgrazing had turned the forests of Southwest Asia and North Africa to desert; or the introduction of fossil fuels and electricity right as the latest Ice Age was reaching its peak, keeping the planet insulated with carbon dioxide just long enough for fusion and superconductors to take up the slack. If there was some outside influence arranging these breaks, it was beyond Peace's power to locate— beer had assuredly been discovered when stale bread was left in water too long, a bizarre error when people were hungry, and steam engines and generators were made possible by the work of a couple of young men who tinkered because they were too socially inept to find dates, in a culture and era where women were prepared to marry *anybody*. There were plenty of other examples, equally counterintuitive.

"You'd make a fascinating monograph," Corky tried again.

"You wouldn't make a decent pair of knee boots. Too leaky. You had enough pimples to supply a middle school."

"I was too busy to bother washing."

"How about half a minute to tell the computer run the pressure down to two hundred millibars of pure oxygen? Decompression breaks the pimples and cleans them out, and pure oxygen kills the bacteria. Sol Belter trick, close to six centuries old. Of course, their singleships just lacked bathing facilities—they did *want* to be clean. Speaking of which—" Peace hauled him along by the arm again, this time to the shower. "Scrub all over."

"Why should I?" he demanded.

"Buckminster and I will both know if you don't," she replied.

"So what?"

"Ever seen the body cleaner in an autodoc at work? It uses an elegant feedback system, doesn't miss a speck, beat everything else off the market. There's thirty-one companies that make autodocs, but only one subcontractor for the body cleaner: Snark Limited. I own it. I invented the cleaner. I can whip one together in about ten minutes. It won't have a sleep inducer attached. Scrub all over."

Buckminster was almost done eating when Corky got back to the kitchen, and watched him curiously as Corky puzzled over the dispenser settings. Finally, with enormous reluctance and a veneer of condescension, Corky turned and said, "How is clothing acquired?"

The kzin thought for a moment. "My sire used to skin and cure a ftheer for a new ammo belt every year, but of course most people just go to an arms shop. Why?" he asked innocently.

"I mean, how is it acquired here?"

"It isn't. What would we do with it?"

"I want to get something to wear!" Corky said, façade cracking.

"Ah. You should have said. I can understand that; that thing must get caught in stuff all the time." He got up and punched for a few hand towels. "These should be easy to tie together."

Corky was now standing in a peculiar, slightly-hunched posture. "Aren't there settings for garments?" he said.

"I can turn up the heat. Peace won't mind."

"It's warm enough. Something to protect skin."

Buckminster also got him some ship's slippers and a hardhat. "You want knee or elbow pads?" he said, but Corky didn't say anything. After some thought, Buckminster found a setting for a sewing needle and some thread. Corky took these, nodded, and left.

Buckminster looked after him, blinking. Presently his ears waggled a bit.

Peace was in the second biochemistry lab when Corky found her. She'd spent what added up to a couple of thousand hours there since it was built, investigating her own body chemistry and duplicating the useful compounds. "Don't touch anything, and especially don't open anything," she told him without looking his way.

"I *am* capable of functioning in a laboratory," he said.

Peace glanced at him. Slippers, hardhat, diaper. "Hm!" she said, blinking—Buckminster had obviously been having some fun. "Since you know what a Protector is, you know what happened to Jack Brennan. Do you know what happened to Einar Nilsson?"

"Smelled the roots and ate until his stomach burst," Corky said.

"He smelled one root, freeze-dried by vacuum, and gnawed one bite off before he could be subdued, and aged to death in an hour. Nilsson was a good deal younger than you. Boosterspice doesn't correct genetic age; it just overrides it. He cooked his brain; you could conceivably catch fire and burn to the ground. Don't touch anything. Don't open anything. What do you want?"

In what would normally have been a good imitation of firmness, he said, "What are your intentions?"

"I'm not going to tell you."

"Why not?" he said in reasonable tones.

"That either."

"I'm entitled to know *something*," he insisted.

"Why? What have you done with your knowledge since you killed the last collaborator? It was easy to look them up, and the last died two years ago. Lose your nerve?"

As expected, that cracked him right down the middle. He staggered, righted himself, then looked around helplessly. "I—" he said, then ran out of the room.

He was coming along. Peace adjusted the proportions of what she was mixing, based on new information.

Buckminster smelled him on the way into the observatory: very upset. It wasn't an ambush, though, because Corky promptly said, "I can leave."

"No need. Need any help with the controls? Peace does tend to build for her own level of precision."

"I worked that out. I was just looking at Pleasance. What do you want to look at?"

"The fourth Pak fleet," Buckminster said. "The human Protectors are just getting to it. Judging from the debris of the first three, the battle shouldn't be all that interesting, but the Pak may have worked out something they can do."

"Fourth? How censored many *are* there?"

Buckminster cocked an ear at this archaism, but said, "Nineteen. Sixteen, now. The six furthest off show some design innovations, like carbon-catalyst fusion—pure helium exhaust, thin and very fast—which Peace says suggests the Pak have allowed the breeders to evolve a little more brainpower. They must have been dismantling planets by then." He made a series of adjustments and displayed a view that was between Orion's hypothetical feet. There were hundreds of dim red specks, no longer quite in hexagonal array. "That's the second fleet. Passed us about thirty years ago. That glow is friction with interstellar gas. Peace says the Homers must have sprayed boron vapor into its path and blown up the ram engines. That would have been sometime during the Second War. Otherwise somebody around here would have wondered about it." He switched the view toward Sagittarius—Peace would just have rotated it, but humans had appallingly little trouble with wildly swooping views—and said, "The wreckage of the third fleet's almost invisible in front of a nebula, and further from us anyway. Here's the fourth." Hundreds of white specks, in nothing like hexagonal array. "They saw the first three go and tried to scatter, but the lateral vector component is still tiny. Loosened up the fusion constriction—they should be blue—but they don't know about the boron. Peace says the change won't save them. The rams won't all blow up, but the gamma rays will roast the pilots. The fifth wave will have to be hunted. Is *being* hunted by now, and may be gone—this view is about a hundred and twenty years old. Here, look!" he said, making Corky jump. "Sorry," he said. "But look here. See that red dot? That's a human Protector's ship. They're redshifted, so they don't show up well, but this one's right in front of a dark region. Not many of those out that way."

"Am I a coward?" Corky asked abruptly.

It occurred to Buckminster, after he'd been staring for about half a minute, that if that had been a ruse, it would have been a good one—Corky could have gotten in a couple of pretty solid licks with an ax before he could have responded. "No, of course not." *Though you may be the silliest person I've ever met*, he reflected.

"It's been a couple of years since I did anything. Toward justice."

Buckminster was certain he was expected to say something at this point, but couldn't think of anything relevant. He attempted, "One of the things that used to confuse officials in treaty discussions is how some of your terms have multiple and contradictory meanings. 'Justice' is a good example. What you've been doing isn't what humans usually call justice—that tends to be more like Patriarchal arbitration. Killing the humans who got your family killed is more like kzinti justice—though we'd want it to be publicly known. Part of it is the idea that anyone else who considers duplicating the offense should feel very reluctant."

"Deterrence," Corky said. He was looking very intently at Buckminster.

"I think so. I've mostly encountered the human term in a political context, but it sounds appropriate."

Corky spoke slowly. "You claim I can't kill the Patriarch—"

"I'm not making any special claims. It just so happens."

"Right. . . . You're a kzin."

Buckminster didn't see any reason to deny it. He'd watched transmissions of human gatherings, and noticed that most of the attendees didn't look comfortable until someone had stood up and told them things they already knew. It was a habit he suspected was related to why they kept defeating better warriors. It made sure everybody did know. It was awfully tedious, though. He waited for Corky to go on, then realized Corky was also waiting for something. He nodded. That seemed to do.

"What would you do to someone that killed your family?"

"I don't have a family."

"Supposing you did."

"I wouldn't let him."

Corky was getting angry, though he kept his face and voice from showing it. "Suppose you couldn't be there when he attacked."

"I'd have no business starting a family if I was going away," Buckminster said. Abruptly he realized that Corky was taking his hypothetical reasoning as personal criticism, and said, "Kzinti females are nearly helpless outside of childrearing."

That worked: Corky calmed down at once. "Oh yeah," he said. "Bad example. Suppose—"

"Are you trying to ask me what you should do to the Patriarch?" Buckminster interrupted.

" . . . I guess I am."

"Nothing. You can't even get near the palace if he's in

residence. And you can't get near him on visits of state, either—his security force is much tougher than the fleet that invaded Pleasance."

That fleet had crushed the planetary defenses in a couple of hours. "I see," said Corky, who seemed to lose track of his surroundings after that.

Buckminster waited a little, then started zooming the view for the more distant fleets.

Peace found Corky sleeping under a table in the kitchen, on top of seventy hand towels. She got herself corn muffins and a crock of stew, brought up a seat, and began eating. Presently Corky said, "Why don't you wear clothes?" irritably.

"Why don't you wear chain mail?" she replied.

"Chain mail isn't about keeping your organs of excretion out of sight," he said.

"No, it's about keeping the rest of your organs from coming into sight," she said.

Evidently he understood the implicit comment: *That's usually irrelevant, too.* After a moment he said, "Are those muffins?"

"Yes."

"They smell unusual."

"It's maize. Didn't get sent out with any first-wave colony ships—lacks some amino acids. So it's sort of an Earth specialty. Try one."

She was handing it under the table when Buckminster came in. The kzin's tail lashed once, his ears curled tight, and he blinked rapidly a few times and fled the room.

"What just happened?" Corky said indistinctly, around a muffin.

Peace waited until he swallowed the first bite. "He's been kidding me about keeping pets," she replied.

After a few seconds Corky burst out laughing.

The laughter went on too long, and when she moved the table and saw him weeping hysterically it was no surprise—he was long overdue. When it started to exhaust him she got him a mirror and some more muffins, these with honey.

His reflection calmed him in seconds, and he wiped his face and bit into a muffin. Once he'd swallowed he said, "That's good. What's on it?"

Honey was unknown on Pleasance—bees steer by the sun. "Bug vomit," she said.

He made a brief scowl and went on eating. Presently he got up and tossed the towels out, then worked the dispenser. "How do I get a chair?" he said. She brought one up, and he said, "Why not just tell me?" as he sat.

"I don't want the place filled up with brooms," she said. It went right by him, as he hadn't gotten acquainted with the entire seven centuries of recorded visual entertainment history. "You're not a coward, you know," she added.

He stopped chewing. Then he resumed, swallowed, and said, "I didn't expect him to tell you."

Another expression Peace had on tap was rolling her eyes. "Because it was between guys? I'd give a lot to learn how to inhibit the human tendency to Identify With Everything. You're an *alien*. It wasn't *important* enough for him to tell me. This place is fully monitored. What else would you expect?"

" . . . I hadn't thought about it."

Peace refrained from saying, *Miraculously I conceal my astonishment*. "What's happened is, you've worked very hard, and you're tired enough that you're not completely crazy any more. So now you care if you live or die."

"We don't like the word *crazy*," Corky said.

Peace paused, then leaned right, then left, to look carefully past him on either side. Then she sat straight and laced her fingers. "Do your friends have any messages for me?" she said interestedly. "Or do they only talk to you?"

Corky looked annoyed, which was a more participatory expression than the usual scowl. "Psychists," he grumbled.

"Yes, I know that," she said patiently. "And I do like the word. It's to the point. You're not as crazy as you were twenty-two years ago."

"I'm forgetting them," he whispered, haunted.

Peace shot him.

The dart hit the thick pad of his left pectoral muscle, hard, and he screamed and went over backwards out the right side of the chair, which of course didn't go with him. He came to his feet with dart in hand, face bright red, and screamed, *"What the hell was that for?"*

"Memory," she replied.

He stood glaring and panting for a long moment, then looked down at the dart. Then he threw it on the floor. "Why didn't you just *tell* me and give me the shot?"

"Seeing as how you're so cooperative and such a good listener, you mean?"

Corky scowled. "So what happens now?" he said eventually.

"Now you eat," she said, and got up to toss out her dishes.

"*I want some answers!*" he roared.

"Emulating Richard Sakakida," she said, and left.

He was too baffled to follow her at once, and naturally after that there was no catching her.

"Buckminster, is there—what are you doing?"

"Cleaning your ship."

Corky clearly had a lot of thoughts about that, most of them disagreeable. Finally he said, more or less humbly, "Thank you."

"It'll all be on the bill," Buckminster said.

"Bill?" Corky said blankly.

"Joke. What were you asking?"

Corky shook his head a little. He seemed easily confused. "Can I get into the databank here?"

"You can't be serious."

"Just to look something up."

"Oh. Certainly. Let me shut this down." The cleaning robot was in an air duct at the moment, which meant it could just be shut off—it wouldn't drift. "What did you need?" Buckminster said, fingers poised over the screen.

"Richard Sakakida," Corky said.

Buckminster thought about it. Then he sent some commands, and handed Corky the screen. "You'd better do it. Too many ways to spell 'Richard' in Hero."

Richard Sakakida was the name of an intelligence academy-ship in the Third War, and a singleship-infiltration carrier in the Second—the same vessel. The name had been held by various people over previous years, but the search for relevance went all the way back to the 20th century, to the war that had established the UN's existence.

Richard Sakakida, an American of Japanese ancestry, had washed ashore in Japanese-held territory during the war and explained that he was a defector. After some torture to make certain that he wasn't lying, he was accepted as a civilian servant. His work as a servant was exemplary, and he was soon taken into the service of the local commanding officer. He was a fine valet, though not much of an aide—when told to clean the CO's sidearm, he displayed a thorough ignorance of military matters by polishing the exterior to a high shine, without taking it apart.

In the course of his duties as a servant, he also acquired, and delivered to US Army Intelligence, the entire Imperial Japanese order of battle: name and function of every division, where the men in each were from, who their officers were, organization of the chain of command, and the overall war plan. That is, what places would be attacked, what size and type of force would be used to do it, what contingencies had been anticipated, and how they would be responded to. Once this was in American hands, the Japanese never won another battle.

In the Fourth War, the kzinti had won exactly one battle: the surprise attack on Pleasance. After that, every attack force they sent anywhere had been ambushed by human fleets, usually within minutes of entering a region where they couldn't use hyperdrive to escape. The forces guarding Kzin itself had ultimately been drawn off by diversions, allowing individual stasis capsules of Hellflare troops to hit the planet at hundreds of miles per second, unmolested. The Fourth War had lasted less than six years, from the invasion of Pleasance to acceptance of the terms of surrender. The Patriarch had called for armistice about a week after the arrival of the human commandos, who displayed an understanding of kzinti anatomy rather better than that of most kzinti field surgeons. Peace Corben must have gone to Kzin at the start of the War, gotten into their toughest security areas, and walked out with the entire military database.

A childless Protector could adopt the entire species; Peace Corben had done a fine job indeed of caring for her wards. Decidedly better than a certain psychist.

Buckminster flinched as Corky burst—almost exploded, really—into tears. He said, "You want me to take that?" and reached for the screen.

Corky looked at him.

Buckminster carefully drew back his hand. Corky was taut as a bowstring, and his face bore an expression of kzinlike wrath. "I'll just go get a drink," Buckminster said, and kept his movements slow as he got up and left.

Buckminster called Peace as soon as he was clear. "Corky's in death-seek," he said.

"That was quick."

"Oh. What did you do?"

"Injected him with one of my witch's brews. He thought he was forgetting his family, so I put together some stuff that'll let him call up old memories without swamping them with irrelevant associations."

"How did you manage *that*?"

"I synthesized the things that let me do it," she said. "Do you want details, or did you have plans for the next month?"

"I was thinking of eating and sleeping, which I'm sure would slow things down. What do we do now?"

"Have you gotten the Silver Bullets out of his ship?"

"Oh yes." He'd done that before starting the cleanup.

"Then you keep out of sight, and we wait for him to come see me."

Corky was waiting for her in the kitchen when she went in for a scheduled meal. (As a breeder she'd suffered from depression and hypothyroidism, so she was accustomed to eating whether she felt hungry or not—yet another lucky break for humanity, since there was no tree-of-life growing where she made the change to Protector.) He said, "I need to leave." Then he actually looked at her.

Peace was wearing a knee-length singlet, in white, with the usual array of pockets down both sides to the knees. There were black letters on the chest:

**BECAUSE I'M THE
PROTECTOR,
THAT'S WHY!**

His fierce expression went blank with surprise, then developed into amusement and dismay—the latter largely at the amusement. He cleared his throat superfluously, then said, "I need a pressure suit and a schedule of the Patriarch's movements—I want to know when he'll be away from his palace."

"You've given up on assassination."

"Yes," he confirmed unnecessarily. "I still don't think it's a bad idea, but his successor wouldn't understand. The trouble with kzinti is they're still too much in shock over losing. They don't take it *personally*."

"True," she realized, suddenly admiring his plan. "He won't be traveling for a few months yet."

"I have to get back in condition anyway, and practice with my lift belt, so the pressure suit first, I think."

"First we eat."

"I'm not hungry."

"Don't make me cut up your meat for you."

That look of dismayed amusement returned. Corky shut up.

Less than a day later he was gone. Peace had gotten a tissue sample in the course of fitting the suit, and was telomerizing some cells when Buckminster found her. "You let him go," the kzin said.

"Had to."

"Are those his cells? Are you cloning him?"

"Yes and no."

"What does *that* mean?"

"Yes, they are, and no, I'm not. I'd been planning to provide infertile women of good character with viable ova containing my original gene pattern, suitably modified to meet local fertility laws, and large trust funds. I had enough for one or two Peace Corbens per human world. Now, though, I'm adding his genes to the recipe. The paranoia can be retained as a recessive, and there'll be more variety in their appearance."

"You're having children with him, you mean."

"Near as I can."

"Why?"

Peace looked up at him. "Same reason I had to let him go. He's a good father, Buckminster. Whether he believes it or not—he's a very good father."

Harvey Mossbauer's family had been killed and eaten during the Fourth Man-Kzin War. Many years after the truce and after a good deal of monomaniacal preparation, Mossbauer had landed alone and armed on Kzin. He had killed four kzinti males and set off a bomb in the harem of the Patriarch before the guards managed to kill him. . . . The stuffed skin was so scarred that you had to look twice to tell its species; but in the House of the Patriarch's Past it was on a tall pedestal with a hullmetal plaque, and there was nothing around it but floor. . . .

It's safer to eat white arsenic than human meat.

The Hunting Park

Larry Niven

October 20, 2899 CE

"Why do they call you 'white hunter'?"

I smiled but didn't grin. "It's anyone from somewhere else who conducts hunting for sport in Africa. I was born in Confinement Asteroid and raised in Ceres and Tahiti." He was wondering about my skin, of course. The parts he could see, hands and face, are jet black, from moderately black American ancestry subjected to three decades of raw sunlight in space and in the islands.

"Odd," said the kzin, but he waved a big furry hand, claws sheathed, dismissing the subject. Waldo had ordered hot milk with black rum; he slurped noisily. I'd ordered the same. He asked, "Why is it taking so long to arrange a safari?"

"First rule is, everything takes forever when you're gearing up. When you're out in the field, everything interesting happens before you can blink. That's when you find out what you forgot to take."

We studied each other. Waldo was big for a kzin, maybe five hundred pounds, maybe eight feet four or five inches tall. No chairs here could hold him; he squatted in a

469

cleared space in a corner of the restaurant. His fur was marmalade, with a darker stripe diagonally down his chest and abdomen that followed four long runnels of scar tissue, and a shorter scar, also darkly outlined, that just missed his left eye and ear. A thong around his neck held a few leathery scraps: dried ears, I presumed. He kept his claws sheathed as carefully as I kept my lips closed. You don't show your teeth to a kzin.

I hadn't volunteered for this. What sane person would? It was October of 2899 CE; I'd hoped to celebrate my fiftieth birthday next year, when the century turned. I planned to quit the safari business and write.

Then again, who could turn this down? They were paying twice the going rate in Interworld stars, but that was nothing compared to the publicity value. I was wearing some recording gear. We'd have the whole safari on tape, right up to my death, if it broke that way, and my daughters would hold the rights. If I lived, I'd have a tale worth writing.

Waldo was examining Legal Entity Bruce Bianci Bannett, a tall, long-headed black human male forty-nine years old, with yellow tattoos around the eyes and ears that make me look just a bit like a leopard. I guessed what else he was looking for, and I said, "I don't have any really gaudy scars except for the tattoos. It's because I'm careful."

"I should be glad of that. LE Bannett, our permissions still haven't come through, and I see no kind of a caravan forming."

"We'll have our permissions." This trip I wouldn't even need bribes; the United Nations had spoken. "I'm having trouble getting bearers."

"Offer more money?"

"Money isn't as powerful an argument here in Nairobi. I think they've lived too long with governments that can just snatch it away. They're all a combination of socialist and bandit. A good story, that's a lure, but a man only needs one fortune and one good story.

"But traveling with . . . there are four of you? With four kzinti, that's bad enough. You're not using guns?"

"No, not on a hunt. On a hunt we use only the *w'tsai*. You, though, you'll take a gun?"

"Several."

"Do not shoot another hunter's prey," Waldo told me.

"My point was, bearers would usually count on all of us, me or any of my clients, to shoot a, say, a leopard before he gets to the bearers. But there's only one of me, and you—you can't *throw* a *w'tsai*, can you?"

Again Waldo waved sheathed claws: a shrug.

"So it's not even a spear. I've hunted with natives who use spears. They have a point. A spear doesn't jam. So my bearers would risk you not being fast enough to save them, plus anything you might do in a rage because you missed your prey."

"But we have these," Waldo said, and I saw his claws, three or four inches long, exposed only for a moment. "Not just the *w'tsai*."

"What do you want out of this, Waldo?"

"Wave Rider and Long Tracks and I, we are brothers," Waldo said, "part of *Starsieve*'s crew. *Starsieve* seeks treasures of the cosmos using ship's instruments. I operate the waldos, of course, the little hand-and-jaw-guided robots. It can be very dull work. We seek an adventure out of the ordinary here on Earth. Kashtiyee-First has been our teacher and First Officer under Prisst-Captain. Both would gain honor if we three gained partial names."

Names are important to kzinti. Most bear only the names of their professions. "Would this—"

"It would help. A hero's hunt is the story that defines him."

"What do you want to kill?"

"What have you got?" he asked.

"Not much. The Greater Africa government is solid Green. They tell me what they can spare. Some species are grown beyond the limits of the Refuge." I fished my sectry out of my pocket and tapped at it, summoning the current list, just in case it had changed in the past two hours. Sure enough— "Cape buffalo is off the list. If a Cape buffalo charges you, you hope you can duck. Elephants are out, of course. We can have a lion . . . or all the leopards we want. Crocs don't offer much of a trophy, but again—"

"Why are the, rrr, Greens so free with leopards?"

"We used to think leopards were scarce, even endangered. They're not. They're just shy, and really well camouflaged, and they're everywhere. If a lion turns to human prey, he's generally got a reason. Maybe he's hurt his mouth and can't hunt anything difficult. But a leopard, he kills for fun. Antelope, zebra, man, woman, whatever turns up," I babbled, and suddenly realized— "Of course none of that might apply to kzinti."

"What are the rules for kzinti?"

"Nobody's got the vaguest idea. We might not catch anything. Your scent might drive them all away." Waldo didn't smell unpleasant; just really different. "Or bring everything in from miles around. Kzinti have never hunted on Earth."

"More's the pity," Waldo said lightly.

October 31, 2899 CE

Waldo is the one who speaks Interworld. The other three have translators, and I carry one built into my sectry. In Africa everyone speaks a different language, but with kzinti involved—I'd better buy a spare.

Wave Rider and Long Tracks bear wildly different markings from Waldo, though they're near as tall and about as massive. Wave Rider's a darker marmalade with no noticeable scars; he keeps his sectry open a lot, reading whenever things turn slack. It's Singapore built, with over-sized keys. Long Tracks is sheer yellow, barring minor scarring close to the eyes and a missing ear. He wears a thong with one ear on it. Kashtiyee-First is smaller and older, brown and orange marked with a lot of white. No thong.

We've packed everything on floaters. Floaters go almost anywhere, but there are places where we'll have to carry everything. These kzinti will be carrying their share and the bearers' too, because we've got no bearers.

I don't worry about their stamina. Most of the kzinti-occupied worlds have Earth gravity or higher, and my clients look tough. They can port their own weight, but will they? Will they follow orders? I always worry about that. There's no sane limit to what a man is likely to do with a charged gun.

But they aren't men. Should I worry about those blades? In a kzin hand a *w'tsai* looks like a long knife crudely forged. In mine, it's an overbuilt sword. If they started swinging wildly—well, we'll see.

They've brought more medical gear than I'd expected given their macho background. It looks like equipment from a ship's infirmary. From *Starsieve*, of course. Where on Earth would they get kzinti medicines and stretchers? Kzinti forces never managed to invade Earth, not in any of the four interstellar wars (plus "incidents") that ended more than two hundred years ago.

They carry antiallergens and diet supplements. Earthly life doesn't quite fit their evolution.

Guns and ammunition: well, those are all mine. I can't carry everything I might need. One of the kzinti might have to be my bearer, but first I'd better test them out a little. It can turn sticky when the bearer runs up a tree with your gun.

Food: I've packed oranges and root vegetables and dry stuff. We'll make do with less cookware than usual, some canned goods, sugar, flour, condiments and so forth. That's all for me. Clients eat mostly meat, and we shoot that on the trail. Kzinti eat nothing but raw meat. I'll be doing all the cooking.

And of course I'm carrying nine kilos of sensory equipment spotted over my head and body: cameras, sound, somasthetic, scent.

Cape buffalo are back on the permitted list. I'll get them one before the Greens pull him off again.

November 3, 2899 CE

Three days into the brush. We camped by a river. It's low and yellow, and we're filtering the water. The kzinti drink a lot of it. I'm not carrying booze. It's hard on me, but I don't want *them* drinking.

Wave Rider wants to know why it's taking so long to get anywhere interesting. I waved around and told him to pick out a transfer booth for me. Long Tracks laughed at him, teeth showing. I've never seen a kzin's killing gape. I hope I can recognize the difference in time.

In fairness to Wave Rider, there are a few transfer booths out here, and we white hunters tanj well know where each of them is. They're big enough to pass a mini ambulance. We use them for medical emergencies, including veterinary work. I usually don't tell clients about them.

Waldo's been attacked by a lion.

He was sleeping outdoors. We set up a palisade, of course. I pitched my tent not too close so that I can cook without their complaining. Smoke my pipe, too.

I was updating my log when I heard the yowling. I got out there, armed, and barely glimpsed the lion smashing out through the branches of the palisade. I fired and got no joy of it.

Wave Rider's right front claws are bloody, but so's his ear, torn half off. He swung at the lion and scored, and the lion swung back, then kept going. But Waldo looks worse. The lion was stalking him. It found him asleep and attacked in a lion's favorite fashion: it tried to bite through the kzin's skull. Do that to a man, the prey barely twitches and the lion can just haul him away.

Waldo is big and the lion may be smaller than usual, though he sure didn't look it in mid leap in the moonlit dark. The beast's fangs didn't get through Waldo's skull. They tore off half his scalp. Waldo came awake with a screech, and I expect Leo had never heard anything like that.

I used antiseptic on both injured. They put up with it, but Waldo assures me that Earthly bacteria have little interest in kzinti. Waldo's half-scalping is the subject of much merriment.

November 5, 2899 CE

We're looking at a herd of Cape buffalo, maybe a hundred. The buff have made a nice comeback. "Once upon a time they were near extinction," I say.

Kashtiyee-First asks, "These are herbivores?"

"Yeah, grass eaters, but they're not rabbits and they're not puppeteers—"

"LE Bannett, we're familiar with oversized herd beasts who charge in numbers."

"How do you handle them, LE Kash?"

"Run. Hide. Climb rocks or trees. How shall we approach these? We want only one head."

"Right. Now that you've got the scent we could maybe track down a rogue. Or— How about that old bull grazing off to the right? We get his attention—"

"Yes, approach using that channel as cover. Was that once a stream?"

"Yeah. Will be again."

Kashtiyee-First speaks to the others. They move off on all fours and low to the ground. I'll stay where I am, on high ground. If a gun's needed, I'll need to see why. And never shoot a kzin's prey. And while I'm holding my sectry to make this recording, I'll just check the lists.

Tanj dammit.

Stet. First I tap the open code. Answer, futz you! I can barely make out motion, but they've nearly reached the old buff. Their sectries must be buzzing—

Now there's motion. It looks like the kzinti are fighting each other.

And it's night, and Kashtiyee-First may be dying, and it's been one strange day.

I ran toward the kzinfight, but I zoomed my specs too. I was clear on this: I sure didn't want to get between two kzinti in a fight. If I saw the wrong thing I might want to run the other way. I'd already marked the best trees.

Too many kzinti? *That* wasn't a kzin! It was a she lion, and another, and a black-maned male, all dancing with the kzinti. The lions were bigger. That dry riverbed had been good cover for lions, too. Now Waldo and the male were in a wrestling match, rolling over in the dust. Claws and *w'tsais* swung. The male lion wrenched loose and turned tail, and the old buff charged straight into the fray.

Waldo dashed after the lion.

Kashtiyee-First saw the buffalo just in time to face its

charge. He swing his *w'tsai* overhead and split the bull's forehead just between the horns. The bull kept coming. I saw the kzin officer bowled over, lost to view.

The lions were in full flight. The buffalos gathered their strength, seven or eight bulls in front of the pattern, then cows, youngsters in the center.

Long Tracks answered my call. "We're busy."

"Don't kill any more buffalo. They're off the list."

"Repeat. The rest have to hear." He turned his volume up.

I stopped near a mopane tree, nearly winded. "Buffalo are protected again. Kashtiyee-First, you killed in self-defense, but it ends there—"

All seven adult bulls charged.

At least the lions were gone. The kzinti began dodging, weaving, leaping. Wave Rider was on a bull's back, then off again. I'd got up the mopane tree somehow, and I watched, gun ready, license forfeit if I fired. The kzinti didn't seem to be in trouble. It was a dance, it was a wrestling match—what was Kashtiyee-First doing? Running backward, easing out of the fray, headed toward my tree. The others saw and imitated him, leading the angry males further and further, until in ones and twos they gave up and rejoined the herd.

Then Kashtiyee-First collapsed.

I want to call for an ambulance. The kzinti won't have it, not even Kashtiyee-First. The old bull gored him deep on that first charge. The horn left an oozing hole in mid-torso, between Kash-First's crisscrossing ribs, below the lung. The other kzinti are tending him.

Antibiotics into the wound, a little microsurgery around major blood vessels.

Kashtiyee-First says, "You must know better than to interrupt a hunt or battle with a cellphone call." The others weren't even speaking to me on that point.

"The United Nations wants this hunt to go right," I tell them. "I think they put pressure on the locals to get you a buffalo. But the locals don't like pressure, so they pushed back. I'm in the middle. Anyway, we'll keep the heads." The male lion, too. Waldo killed it: tore its intestines out with his feet. He gets the head. Long Tracks got a nice gouge from one of the buffs. So far so good, unless Kashtiyee-First dies.

November 6, 2899 CE

Kzinti are impulsive.

Laughing at them would be bad.

Long Tracks jumped a porcupine. Just quick dumb reflexes, I guess. One of my cameras caught it. We've spent half the afternoon pulling spines out of his face and one hand. Come dinnertime, I'll go off by myself to cook. Laugh then. Otherwise I'm gonna die.

November 8, 2899 CE

We've been eating well. Under the Greens the veldt is

in wonderful shape, much as it must have been a thousand years ago, in Rudyard Kipling's time. Besides lion and buffalo we've found and killed impala, capybara, some small stuff, and two hyena (which I did not eat). And leopard.

Leopards are usually unexpected. I hadn't seen any spoor. I've been armed at all times because the gun I carry is the only gun in the whole party.

We were watching a wonderful sunset, all of us. I must have heard something. I turned around and a leopard had launched itself at my throat.

I lifted the gun and I'd probably have got it up in time, but Wave Rider leaned way out and caught the leopard by the skin over his shoulders and swung him in an arc. I didn't fire because I would hit Wave Rider, and then because Wave Rider was winning. Then I saw the second leopard, so I shot that one, two for luck. What the hell, none of the kzinti had claimed *him*.

Wave Rider was juggling a yellow whirlwind; when he couldn't stop it clawing him, he just fell on it and then bit its face off.

The twenty-gram bullets were those I'd picked for buffalo: big. My trophy is pretty badly messed up. So's Wave Rider's. We're keeping the ears.

I didn't eat leopard; I shared it out. I didn't taste Waldo's lion either.

Wave Rider has some nasty scars. Waldo seems to like his well enough. The kzinti keep passing the mirror around, and Long Tracks is grumpy because he hasn't been touched, barring tiny puncture wounds like bad acne. I wish I hadn't brought the mirror.

Kashtiyee-First shares a float plate with several heads. He can stand up but he can't walk. He doesn't complain. The wound hasn't putrified, and he can use the great outdoor catbox without it killing him. The wound looks clean.

The other float plate still has room for my gear and food.

They're talking about taking an elephant.

November 9, 2899 CE

I showed them elephants. I didn't have much choice: they scented the spoor themselves, so we tracked a herd of sixty. Now they've got the scent.

The kzinti killed a hippopotamus today. Fighting in water is not their thing, and there were crocs about, but the hippo was up against kzinti mass.

They're jubilant now. The hippo fed us all. I like hippo. As usual I ate apart so they needn't smell roasted meat.

I joined them afterward. I tried to explain that elephants were *never* on the Green list. It isn't that they're endangered, not any more. But their brains are as big as human brains, or bigger. They haven't developed lawyers, like the cetaceans, but they've got some tool-using ability. They may well be intelligent.

That doesn't impress Waldo. Futz, his forebears used to hunt humans. "UN law does not list killing of elephants as murder."

"It's the African Protectorate that can throw us out. It would end the safari. Have you hunted enough already?"

I wish I hadn't said that. What if they decide *yes*?

November 11, 2899 CE

Morning, not yet dawn. They're gone, all but Kashtiyee-First. I'm surprised.

I'm surprised that they got away without waking me. They must have gone around midnight, in silence. I already know how well they see in the dark. I can picture them crawling off, bellies brushing the earth . . .

Kashtiyee-First won't tell me anything. So I tell him. "Thing is, if my clients kill an elephant, they might be exiled but not jailed. You have diplomat status. Nobody would really blame the white hunter for what *these* clients might do. I might even keep my license."

"That is good. No kzin would blame us either. The lure is too great."

"So all you'd lose is the next week or so of hunting. Still, I've got to track them. They're my clients, and they don't know elephants."

"Are these tree eaters dangerous?"

"Beyond description. They've got *mass*."

"You're bluffing, LE Bannett. Elephants have never been on your permitted list. You never hunted them. You only know what you read. History books. Wave Rider has a sectry, too." And he laughed, though it hurt him.

I scouted around before I left.

The three took only their *w'tsais* and water bottles: at least I taught them that. I wonder if they expected to sneak *back*? Before I wake? On any normal safari I'd be up at four AM to prepare for the day's hunt. These days I've been dogging it a little: kzinti don't need breakfast and don't need the day's gear set out and explained to them.

I found something disturbing. A lone lion lay up in the brush near us. It must have had a good view of the camp. For a couple of hours last night I was asleep and alone but for the injured Kashtiyee-First. Where is it now?

I offered Kash-First a rifle. His finger won't fit into the trigger guard, but his claw will.

I've gotten here ahead of the hunt. It's a little past dawn.

They haven't attacked the herd. They're not that crazy, I hope. They have the scent; they tracked the herd. They found the same traces I found later without the help of a kzinti nose. A rogue, an injured bull has been living on the fringes of the herd.

I'm recording him now. Somehow he's torn off a tusk right at the root. In my mag specs his face looks infected. The pain's turned him rogue. He looks alert and nasty, and he's scented something weird, but he might not understand the danger. Kzinti scent is nowhere in his species' memory. It's just different, and different is dangerous. So he's backing away, sniffing the air.

Now he's heard them in the brush. They're trying to circle downwind, moving fast enough to make mistakes, and now he's running, and here they come. He's faster than they thought—just lumbering along, but so *big*. They're sprinters, the kzinti. Maybe he'll tire them.

I don't have a hope of catching him or them. I've jogged up a hill and I'm using my mag specs.

They're on him—two of them. Waldo didn't get there: he ran out of breath. The two are slashing, slashing. Jumbo is bleeding. Showers of blood, tens of gallons, brilliant red in the sunlight. Long Tracks and Wave Rider are dancing into the blood. Even lions don't play like that. I'm thinking of erasing this tape.

Then Jumbo's trunk catches Wave Rider and sends him spinning. Long Tracks jumps at Jumbo's neck. Jumbo's head whips around. The one tusk catches Long Tracks and flips him over. Jumbo charges Wave Rider. I can't see much through the grass, but it looks like Jumbo is stamping on Wave Rider. Then Long Tracks chops at his feet with the *w'tsai*, and Jumbo goes after Long Tracks.

Long Tracks is running. Jumbo is spraying blood. Waldo gets there and joins the attack. One swing of Waldo's *w'tsai* and the trunk flies loose, another and Jumbo goes down. Tries to get up and fails.

I've had my rifle sighted on Jumbo for all this time, and I haven't fired. One day I'll wonder if it's because kzinti are mankind's old enemy. I think not. They're clients—but they're clients who positively don't want their guide attacking their own personal prey. And I'd better get down there and look at Wave Rider.

Wave Rider's heart is still beating. The elephant stamped him into fudge, breaking ribs and limbs and internal organs. I'm not a doctor, but I know enough: Wave Rider won't live if he doesn't get to a hospital.

"The nearest transfer booth is forty kilometers away,

if it's working. You never know with the Greens. I can summon a mini ambulance," I tell Waldo.

Waldo and Long Tracks are arguing about Jumbo's ears. Long Tracks just growls at me. Waldo says, "We will not cry for help."

"Stet, but we can take him in ourselves. We can get to the nearest transfer booth by forced march. We'll make a stretcher out of Jumbo's hide. You do the carrying. Kash-First can meet us. Take us the rest of the day."

Waldo and Long Tracks agree. Nonetheless they're in no hurry. Waldo gives up his claim: he attacked late. One big blanket of elephant ear goes to Long Tracks; from his thong it drapes like a cloak. One goes to Wave Rider, for his funeral if it breaks that way. They eat several pounds of elephant meat and pack a lot more. It's clear we won't reach the transfer booth today. I phone Kash-First and tell him what's going on. He agrees to meet us with the floaters.

The stretch of hide holds Wave Rider. He hasn't wakened, and that's both good and bad. He isn't screaming, but his snoring sounds tortured.

Kash-First zeroes in on our path. He's walking, not riding a float plate. The kzinti use their medical techniques on Wave Rider. We get Wave Rider onto a float plate, giving up some of my supplies. This will embarrass the poor kzin if he lives.

Rain starts near noon. We're wading through tall grass and mud, our strongest fighters burdened with a stretcher. If anything attacks us I'm going to shoot it, and to hell with what my clients think.

Dark catches us twelve kilometers short of the transfer booth. I'm using my sectry's mapping system. They're prepared to keep moving at night. Idiots. I set Waldo and Long Tracks to making a fence, over a lot of grumbling; they've worked hard today.

I claim a slab of elephant liver and another of muscle meat. I'm famished. I flash-cook them with the microwave. The kzinti don't complain, though we're camped together, between the float plates. They don't want to be alone, and I don't either.

November 12, 2899 CE

It's the same lion. I barely saw it, but I know. It came out of the dark in one long leap, arced over one of the float plates and had Waldo. He shrieked. The lion dragged him into the grass and would have been gone if I hadn't swung a light on him. I'm trying to hold the light with one hand and pick up a gun with the other, but Long Tracks is after him and blocking my shot. I jump on the float plate for a better view into the grass.

The lion turns to fight. Long Tracks swings one good swipe and then the lion is on him. They're wrestling; Long Tracks may have dropped his *w'tsai*. I can't see Waldo.

The lion wrenches loose and I have a clear shot. I fire at a point just behind his shoulder.

The lion goes down.

🐾 🐾 🐾

"Nothing in my sectry lists the lion as a cursorial hunter," says Kash-First.

It's dawn, and we're moving. Waldo's dead. Wave Rider is still breathing. He's swollen and discolored over most of his body, and his ribs bend inward where they should not. Kash-First is lucid and walking. His voice has a breathy, painful hiccup in it that doesn't get through the translator.

I'm not in the mood for a fight. I tell Kash-First, "Every hunter knows of a lion that stalked someone for days at a time and killed him at the last."

"Even I can't tell you that this one had a different smell. But do you *know* that this is the same lion that tore up Waldo's scalp?"

And stalked him ever since, until last night's kill. "Who else? Any other lion would take Wave Rider. Wave Rider couldn't defend himself. Lions are lazy. Waldo could fight back."

"He didn't have the chance."

"No." This time the lion bit into his skull and dragged him forty meters before Long Tracks caught him. My bullet tracked through one lung and his heart: a good shot.

Of course the trophy head won't be worth any more than the rest of our heads, which are all going to be ruined because the kzinti want the ears. We've got the holograms, though.

Long Tracks offered me one of the lion's ears. He claims the other himself. He won't talk to me.

And it's over.

We reached the transfer booth in four hours. We were at the Nairobi Spaceport just that fast, with access to *Starsieve*'s lander's surgery ten minutes later. I pretended to help get Wave Rider into the cavity, but truly, he's too heavy for me.

"Take the ear," Kash-First said through his translator. "Long Track won't forgive you if you don't. You used your own familiar weapon in a personal hunt. He'll see that soon or late."

"How are you?" I asked.

"I can use some medical attention." But he has to wait. He's plugged into the peripherals, but he'll need the intensive care cavity when it's through with Wave Rider.

I said, "It was not my intention to lead you into such a disaster as this."

He shrugged, and winced. He sits bent over around the puncture wound. "A fusion bomb can kill any number of elephants. We use the *w'tsai*. Killing is not the point. Kzin against the elements, that is the point."

Truly, I agree. But maybe I've missed the point myself. There was an accident—

An hour after we set out this morning, we were trekking into a gully. Kashtiyee-First was on the float plate that held Waldo's corpse, guiding the other that carried Wave Rider, and they just floated over the depression. Long Tracks got disgusted with my slowness and sprinted up the other side to meet his companions. I wondered if I was hurting them by slowing them.

They waited in a copse of trees. They were talking as I

approached. They hadn't noticed me. My translator began picking up their speech.

Long Tracks: "It would be as easy for LE Bannett to die as for Waldo, or you. This insanely dangerous land could take him at the last. A lion?"

Kash-First: "Your teeth don't leave the same marks as a lion's."

I stopped thinking about revealing myself. I used my mag specs to watch Long Tracks pick up the lion's head. He clacked the jaws a couple of times. "Bite him with this."

Kash-First said, "LE Bannett has kept every promise expressed or implied."

Long Tracks was silent.

Kash-First said, "Recall why we came. We can hunt anywhere. Have we learned more of the human state? Can we give Prisst-Captain any hint of what our ancestors faced, to be so battered and humiliated in war after war?"

"Fool's errand. We have had only one human to study. He is far from typical. He kills as easily as we do, and revels in it."

"Yes, the human is not interesting. But the rest? What of Africa? Do we finally know the horrors this species faced in the ages before it expanded across its world?"

"Ur?"

"And then came back to hunt."

🐾   🐾   🐾

IT'S HOWLING TIME IN KNOWN SPACE!

THE MAN-KZIN WARS
CREATED BY LARRY NIVEN

THE MAN-KZIN WARS
0-671-72076-7 • $6.99

THE BEST OF ALL POSSIBLE WARS
0-671-87879-4 • $6.99

MAN-KZIN WARS IX
0-7434-7145-8 • $7.99

MAN-KZIN WARS X: THE WUNDER WAR
0-7434-3619-9 • $21.00 (HC)
0-7434-9894-1 • $7.99

MAN-KZIN WARS XI
1-4165-0906-2 • $22.00

NOVELS:
DESTINY'S FORGE by Paul Chafe
1-4165-2071-6 • $25.00

Available in bookstores everywhere.
Or order online at our secure, easy to use website:
www.baen.com.